MW00655019

WATCH THE SKIES

WATCH THE SKIES

A TERRAN REPUBLIC NOVEL

CHARLES E. GANNON

&

KACEY EZELL, KEVIN IKENBERRY, AND WILLIAM ALAN WEBB

BEYOND TERRA PRESS
VIRGINIA BEACH, VA

Chris Kennedy/Beyond Terra Press
1097 Waterlily Rd.
Coinjock, NC 27923
http://chriskennedypublishing.com/

Cover Design by William W. Connors.

Ordering Information:
Quantity sales. Special discounts are available on quantity purchases by corporations, associations, and others. For details, contact the "Special Sales Department" at the address above.

Watch the Skies/Charles E. Gannon -- 1st ed.
ISBN: 978-1648552182

PART ONE

Chapter One

Curved plumes of dust erupted among the low buildings that were on the enemy's right flank. The best troops left in the town—the satrap's own guard and the liveried J'Stull elites—had made no secret that they were defending that zone with their superior firepower. As a result, the main thrust of the attack went to the left, leaving the most fearsome of the defenders unengaged. And, if their only opponents had been the indifferently trained and diversely equipped tribes or militias of the wastes, their ploy—to encourage the attackers to concentrate on the opposite flank, and so facilitate their escape—might very well have worked.

But they were facing professionals who had been trained for and blooded in the most ferocious wars of what was, at the best of times, a planet constantly beset by wars: Twentieth Century Earth.

The five vehicles that came roaring out from between the buildings on the right flank flung up grit and sand behind them. The two in the lead were turreted APCs: old but well-maintained, at least by local standards. The other three belonged to that class of vehicles that the Lost Soldiers' had dubbed 'technicals:' hand-me-downs that had as many salvaged or hand-tooled parts as rusted and battered originals. But all of them had automatic weapons that were stuttering and slewing from side to side in what their local opponents saw as fury but the cadre of Lost Soldiers recognized as a panicked imitation of suppressive fire.

After racing two hundred meters directly toward the positions of the troops ringing the town, the five vehicles cut sharply to the right. They maintained good formation as they turned, almost certainly cued by arriving at a waypoint feature or some unseen signal. Clearly, their aggressive run at the enemy lines had been a feint, one that got them beyond the rocky spur that sheltered the town on that side. Having cleared it, they could make a straight run for the open desert.

But it was one of the scenarios the Lost Soldiers had anticipated.

As the vehicles straightened out and began regaining speed, the scrub two hundred yards in front of them began sparking: muzzle flashes from M14-armed indigs. Although not many of the rounds hit, even the elite troops hesitated for a moment; this blocking force wouldn't be here at all if their escape attempt hadn't been anticipated. And what if the enemy now in front of them had heavier weapons?

The few moments they spent scanning for any sign of such weapons among the scrub-concealed indig riflemen was what their enemy had hoped to accomplish; even the elites were looking in the wrong place at precisely the wrong moment.

The Lost Soldiers had concealed two of their APCs and one medium AFV behind the opposite side of the rocky spur that hemmed in the town. Their larger weapons poured a ragged volley into the rear flank of the fleeing vehicles.

The first effect was instantaneous; a savage blast announced a hit to one of the enemy APC's ammo racks. The bright flash sent its small turret flying and a sudden gout of flame shot up from the main hull just before thick black smoke began gushing out of the track.

The largest of the fleeing technicals was riddled by heavy machine gun fire; a rear tire blew out, and the truck-become-troop carrier slewed to a stop. The other APC was hit by several twenty-millimeter rounds, pieces flying off even as it continued speeding away, now outpaced by a makeshift command car that had started existence as a four-wheel drive utility vehicle. They powered through the thin screen of riflemen who ducked as they passed, rather than trading shots at point blank range. It seemed that those two vehicles might make good their escape.

Until the howl of their engines was drowned out by the heavy beat of approaching rotors as two Hueys topped a low rise two kilometers in front of them.

The fleeing vehicles swerved wildly, the high-suspensioned command car tilting and then slowly toppling over from the sudden maneuver. The APC came around to its right rear flank, but the three well-armed combat vehicles that had ambushed them from the rear were bearing down on it from that direction. The APC swerved to the left but swerved back just as fast; that path would have taken it straight through the main body of the attackers. It steered erratically, seeking an avenue of escape…

Until the lead Huey, only ten meters off the deck, drew ahead, slowed, and then pivoted toward the APC as it sped past, leading it slightly.

Two 2.75-inch rockets streaked away from the pod-launcher mounted on the helicopter's left-hand outboard pylon. One flew long, hitting the ground almost fifty yards ahead of the APC. But the other hit it low in the rear chassis, and one of the disembarkation doors cartwheeled away. Smoke started brewing up as it lost power and began to coast. Survivors tumbled out of the drifting vehicle, sprinted for the rough ground over which the Hueys had risen, but about half the infantry screen was already running toward them. Given the range and flat trajectory of their M14s, those troops would either drive the fleeing survivors to ground or kill them as they fled. As the indig riflemen began taking their first shots, a fan of dust rose up from the AFV that had led the ambush, obscuring the grisly conclusion.

Colonel Rodger Young Murphy lowered the binoculars through which he'd observed Major Bo Moorefield's ambush of the five enemy vehicles. With the town's elite troops neutralized, any remaining defense would crumble. And, just as important, no trustworthy commanders would escape to make an equally trustworthy report to the oligarchs of the J'Stull Satrapy. Once again, the only news to reach the fear-huddling city of Stullhaan would come from those few stragglers desperate—or stupid—enough to not only risk that long journey, but to report yet another defeat.

Murphy felt the pressure in his temples begin to ease. The danger to his forces was essentially past. Now it was just a matter of mopping up, surveying the aftermath, and tallying the butcher's bill.

On the direct approaches to the town, seventeen immobile vehicles dotted the sand-and-scrub flatland, only two of which belonged to the Free Bands of the Hamain: the tribal indigs' name for themselves. A few of the local satrap wrecks were actual APCs, and there was even a much lighter turreted AFV: an armored car, really. But the others had started out as civilian cargo haulers, jeeps, or all-terrain vehicles. From over half of them, greasy black curlicues of smoke pushed up toward the blue-white sky that grew brighter every day: a sign of the creeping but inevitable approach of the other, F-class star in the binary system of 55 Tauri. In less than two years, that new sun would be so close that the wastes in which he stood would be almost completely lifeless, marking the start of seven hot, punishing years that the locals simply called The Searing.

Among the wrecks and abandoned vehicles were the irregular black shapes of fallen bodies. The great majority of them wore the clothes of townsmen: robes of finer weave, and little use of hides except as belts. But the weapons on the ground beside them ranged from muzzle loaders to much-repaired bolt action rifles, and even a few magazine-fed weapons of military origin.

The few inert casualties of the forces marshaled by the Lost Soldiers were distinctive in their rough desert cloaks and further marked by the prevalence of boots and gear fashioned from rough hide. But their weapons, the most common of which was the M14, were anachronistically both more advanced and uniform. The process of retrieving them had already begun, either to assist those too badly wounded to carry their own rifle off the field—a grave matter of honor and worthiness—or to be redistributed, pressed into the hands of even more of the long-oppressed Ashbanders who were finally paying back the towns and their satrap militias for centuries, if not millennia, of oppression.

The heaviest of the Lost Soldiers' wheeled AFVs—marked by an outsize turret that sprouted two long, seventy-millimeter smooth-bores—pulled up the slight rise from which Murphy had watched the battle unfold. As it slowed, Bo Moorefield popped higher up in the hatch and called an order down into the crew compartment. He climbed out of the turret and swung his legs to the deck as the AFV came to a full halt. As he scrambled down the bow glacis, he spun his fist where the driver could see it; as soon as he'd cleared the chassis, the engine revved and the vehicle rolled off to carry out whatever further orders he had imparted.

Approaching Murphy, Moorefield picked up one of the M14s that had been reclaimed from the dusty approaches to the town. "Gotta say," he said, checking it over, "these are pretty much the queen of every battlefield."

"Not bad for remans," Murphy muttered, using the Lost Soldier short-hand term that referred to both "remanufactured" original M14s and those that had been "replicated:" new builds, courtesy of the mass-production facilities of their off-world allies, the SpinDogs. Murphy crossed his arms, steeling himself to ask the question he always dreaded uttering. "How many people do you figure we lost here, Bo?"

Moorefield scanned the field, as if that would jog his memory of recent, scattered reports. "I'd say just under twenty indig KIAs." He sighed. "Mostly newbs." His tone added an unvoiced qualifier: *of course*. "About twice as many WIA. The tribal docs are already making the rounds."

Murphy nodded. No community in the wastes of the Ashbands was without a healer, and even the least skilled of them were able to produce medical outcomes with R'Bak's pharmaflora that seemed magical to the Lost Soldiers. "And is Cook okay?" Murphy asked. Although he tried not to discriminate between the lives of his own men and the indigs, he wasn't usually successful. In addition to the limited number of his fellow—and therefore, adequately trained—refugees from the wars of the Twentieth Century, it was impossible not to think of them as the closest thing to kin that he had left.

"Cook's just fine," answered Moorefield. "He just caught a splinter from one of the town-made hand grenades." The crude metal spheres looked comically similar to the smoking bombs favored by cartoon characters. "It was a through and through; it didn't hit the bone."

Murphy made sure not to blow out a great sigh of relief. He wasn't superstitious, but it had been over two months since they lost one of their own, or even had a casualty that the healers couldn't patch up well enough to return to duty. "And the opfor?"

Bo shrugged. "Well over a hundred casualties. Could be a lot more. Impossible to say until our guys enter the town."

"Vehicles?"

"Ours are fine. A couple have holes in them from some of the technicals' machine guns and a few more from large caliber local rifles. But other than that, no damage worth mentioning. Of the enemy platforms that can still move under their own power, I figure about six either belonged to the J'Stull troops or the local satrap's personal guard. The rest are junk."

"Or spare parts," said Harry Tapper, coming up from behind.

Murphy turned, cocked an eyebrow. "Didn't know you'd come back."

"Radio snafu on the Huey," the big SEAL explained with a shrug as he joined them on the crest of the rise.

"Enemy fire?" Bo asked.

Tapper shook his head. "Never got close enough for that." He and his rapid response force had been orbiting the area of operations at almost three klicks distance: a "free-safety," as the Lost Soldiers called it. If unexpected enemy reinforcements had shown up, or the ones in the town had effected a successful break-out, Harry and his hand-picked team had been on station to intercept them. "Probably just another mechanical glitch. The SpinDogs still haven't gotten it through their heads that the precision manufacturing that is so helpful in their spaceside tools isn't always a friend to us down here."

"Ain't that the truth," said Bo. "They over-engineer everything, but especially the electronics."

Murphy nodded. "But when all is said and done, the satraps are still on the run. It took a few months, but they've finally realized that counter-attacks are just a complicated form of suicide. They're retracting further north all the time—those that can."

"Yeah," added a new voice, "and that isn't going to make their Harvester-masters very happy." Horace Chalmers didn't add anything else until he'd finished trudging up from the CP/comms tent on the lee-side of the rise. "To hear the locals tell it, the Harvesters don't actually go out to find the cash crops themselves. For the most part, they rely on their local lackeys to gather it for them."

Murphy nodded, glanced at Chalmers. The chief warrant officer was scanning through summaries of what had been learned from defecting townsfolk and Sarmatchani tribesmen who'd traded with locals recently. Among the Lost Soldiers who boasted problematic service records, Chalmers had been particularly worrisome at first; however, he'd proven reliable and brave. And, despite his unrelenting alternation between gruffness and snark, he'd become not only a crucial member of Murphy's cadre, but the only one who had any real experience with the kinds of HUMINT ops that were standard on R'Bak: those involving informers, black-marketeers, and thugs who preferred the ostensibly legitimizing label of 'militia leaders.' He'd also proven adept at picking up the region's many dialects and was unquestionably the fastest at reading their written forms.

Tapper had come to stand beside Murphy, folded his bear-like arms and looked across the smoky battlefield as the indig-crewed lighter vehicles rolled slowly toward the town. Their commanders took up bullhorns in place of weapons and began calling for the residents not to resist and not to fear. "Amazing that we've been able to do all this," Tapper murmured, "and so quickly."

"Yeah," Murphy agreed with a sigh. "And it's even more amazing to think that it's just a matter of time before we give it all back."

"Give it all back, suh?" The voice was Corpsman Sonningen's, who'd been waiting near Murphy's CP for casualties that had yet to arrive. "But didn't you say we ahr making sure the indigs had tech that would allow them to hold on to places like this?"

"Not quite," Moorefield corrected amiably. "I think the phrasing was that the Bands and their tribes would be able to 'hold on in the Ashbands.' Big difference. When the Harvesters come, they'll take back the towns. No way to stop them. But in times past, it was also easy for them to control—or 'cull'—the tribes while they were at it." He shook his head, let slip a wolfish smile. "Not any more. There's already enough simple technology—from improved hand pumps and solar stills to crystal radio sets—coming out of the liberated towns. By the time the bastards from Kulsis show up, the tribesmen will have plenty of them."

"So they'll be able to coordinate and get enough water easier, suhs?"

Murphy nodded. "That's the idea. When the Searing comes this time, they can stay in the parts of the desert where the Harvesters are rarely willing to go. And if they do chase them there, the tribes can exchange info on sightings in decent code. They won't all elude the Kulsians, but this time, the tribes of the Hamain are going to be harder to find and harder to kill."

Chalmers leaned toward the corpsman. "And lots more indigs will survive to roll back into the towns and push out the satraps when the Searing is over." Chalmers' grin was vicious. "And then it will be another eighty years before their Kulsian pals come back. You gotta wonder how many of the satraps will be left by then—if any."

But Sonningen was frowning. "But suh, don't most of the tribes dive into their deep cavern hidey-holes when the Searing comes? You know, the ones Vat—er, Lieutenant Thomas found last year?"

Well, Murphy reflected philosophically, *that secret was* never *going to last.* "Unfortunately, only a third of the tribes have those refuges. But there's a silver lining to that. As long as the Free Bands of the Hamain remain above ground, communicating and coordinating with each other, they remain a force in being. And to make that possible, we had to furnish them with the means to reduce *all* the dangers their families face during the Searing: not just Harvester cull-squads, but exposure, starvation, and dehydration."

Tapper nodded. "That will not only get us more recruits, but more trust. And that means more contact with the tribes of the deep desert. If Vat is right—that they have access to a regional network of subterranean tunnels, caves, and aquifers—then we can move teams and supplies around the wastes without the satraps being aware of it."

"Suh," said Sonningen with a quizzical glance at Murphy, "soun's to me like you need to talk to the VC we've got in the group. Mr. Charles fought a whole war from tunnels."

Bo put a kind hand on the corpsman's shoulder, "I think the colonel is aware of that, Sonningen."

"Yes, suh. Sorry, suhs."

Murphy shook his head. "Nothing to be sorry about. It's a good reminder that I need to consult with the few Vietcong we have in our ranks. The odds are good that at least one or two of them can hold a master class for the rest of us."

Chalmers cracked a smile that presaged wise-assery. "Nah, the tribes aren't like the Cong, sir. The indigs are just seasonal fremen."

Murphy frowned. "They're just what? Or who?"

Chalmers looked askance. "Fremen, sir. A science fiction reference." He looked disappointed. "Didn't you ever read *Dune*?"

Moorefield snarled. "That movie was shit."

Tapper nodded solemnly. "*Twin Peaks* on steroids and 'shrooms." He glanced at Murphy. "Ever see it, sir?"

Murphy shrugged. "Flawed classic. Secretly directed by Timothy Leary and Carlos Casteñeda."

Chalmers chortled, but the corpsman frowned. "Who, suh?"

Chalmers shook his head. "You're too young and innocent for that reference, Sonningen." He folded the reports and pocketed them. "Besides, this place is more 'science fiction' than *I* ever hoped to see."

"More than enough," Murphy agreed with a deep nod. "Well, gentlemen, I've got a VTOL shuttle waiting for me over the shield ridge, so I'd better get moving."

"Back to the spins, sir?" Tapper asked.

Murphy nodded. "Straight out to the habitats ASAP."

"Why the rush?" Bo asked.

"A major operation. There's a lot of planning to do."

"What kind of major operation, suh?" Sonningen asked.

"Close assault?" Tapper wondered.

"Infiltration?" Chalmers guessed.

"Obstetrics," Murphy answered with a small grin. He started toward the spine of rocky ground behind them.

Chapter Two

Major Mara "Bruce" Lee was uncomfortable. She held herself still on the exam couch and willed the medtech to complete his scan faster. Mara had to hand it to the SpinDogs—their pregnancy monitoring procedures were *far* less invasive than the pelvic exams she'd endured with her first child. However, her bladder was about to reach max capacity, and the weight of her apparently enormous unborn child was starting to become a problem.

Though if that was the worst of her problems, she was probably doing pretty well. Mara took a deep breath and let it out slowly as she reminded herself of that fact. Life on a rotating space station, surrounded by alien humans and other soldiers who, like her, had been pulled from various conflicts during various eras on Earth, was certainly weird...but it was better than dying in Somalia or later when her helicopter crashed at sea.

"Thank you, Major," the SpinDog said in his harshly accented English. Mara pulled her attention back to the here and now to focus on the man's face as he spoke. "The healer will be in shortly."

"Thank you," Mara replied in the man's native Ktoran speech. "I will meet her here."

"Yes," the man said in Ktoran with a tiny, understanding smile. "The facility you require is just down the corridor. I believe you know."

"I do," Mara said. "Thank you."

After six months, even a habitat this size had no more secrets to hold. Mara had long since scouted out all the bathroom facilities. It was one of the first things she'd done after returning from her training mission pregnant with Ozendi's child.

The sudden pang of loss at the thought of her slain lover was as familiar as an old friend but nowhere near as welcome. "Better to have loved and lost," started the saying, but in terms of her emotions, it would have been a hard choice between the two options. She held her grief close as she levered herself out of the exam couch and focused on walking normally to the restroom. She was only halfway through the pregnancy; she would *not* waddle.

When she returned to the exam room, Nalyiriz hadn't yet arrived, which was a bit of a surprise. The doc who had become her friend and confidante—and sister in a way—was nothing if not punctual.

With a sigh, Mara climbed back up onto the exam table and wished she'd brought a book or a dataslate or something. She hated waiting with nothing to do.

"Mara," Nalyiriz said as the door slid open, and she entered the room. Her voice was warm and carried the sound of a smile, but her striking, dark-lashed eyes were serious.

"Doc," Mara said, with an actual smile of her own. "You sound mostly happy. Baby's doing well?"

"Very well," the doc said as she stepped toward the table, dataslate in hand. "All indications are that the child has inherited my brother's tendency toward robust skeletal and muscular growth."

"So, a big baby, then." Mara sighed. "Awesome."

"Yes…and also concerning. There are advantages in health to the infant, of course, but there is a problem when it comes to the act of giving birth. Several, in fact."

Mara inhaled slowly and straightened her spine. "Tell me," she said.

"While your bone and body structure is not as attenuated as most of our women, the child's growth rates are such that an unmedicated vaginal birth may prove difficult, if not impossible for you. We can mitigate this with a surgical birth, of course. I understand such procedures weren't uncommon in your culture?"

"Caesarean section. Yeah, I'm familiar."

"Well, that is one possibility, though I suspect our procedure differs from yours slightly. In any case, that does not address the more troublesome issue."

"More troublesome than getting my abdomen sliced open?"

"Yes. Your child carries the genelines of my people. One of the reasons we are so tightly tied to our Skydreamers and surface operators is that life in space still requires us to compensate with a variety of planet-sourced compounds. One of these compounds is required to normalize our births. Not only is our geneline distinct, but the spin gravity is only an equivalent, and it is also well less than a full gee. Without one of several crucial compounds, a pregnancy on the spins is likely to end in a spontaneous abortion at some point in the later stages of fetal development. The best source of these compounds is a plant that grows only on the surface; it is ineffective when grown hydroponically."

"You don't keep a stockpile of the compound?"

"Normally, yes, but we had to leave so suddenly that our stockpiling was interrupted. Fortunately, the plant is usually so readily available that it is easiest to just gather and refine the compound on demand."

"You said 'usually,'" Mara said, her eyes narrowing.

Nalyiriz let out a sigh and gave her a small smile. "Yes. You are perceptive. There has been a shortage for the past year. We are still investigating, but recently it has become harder and harder to acquire the necessary plant—it is called *tra*, by the way. However, do not fear; I have anticipated this need and identified a supplier on the surface. I need only go and make contact."

Mara waited.

Nalyiriz's smile grew before she went on. "Yes, of course there is more to the story. The supplier is…I believe you use the term 'shady?' He has done business with criminals in the past. I do not fear for my own safety, but I believe it would send a clear message if I were accompanied by some of your people when I make contact."

"And by using our people to get the stuff you need for all the babies, not just mine, we send another clear message to your leadership about how many ways we are helpful. Even necessary."

Nalyiriz inclined her head in acknowledgment.

Mara nodded. "We'll send El. I'll talk to Murphy and make the arrangements. When will you be ready to depart?"

"As soon as Sergeant Frasier is available." Nalyiriz stepped closer and reached out, placing her hand on Mara's rounded belly. "Thank you, my sister."

"No, sister," said Mara. "Thank *you.*" She smiled. "And safe travels."

Murphy was the last to exit the shuttle into the interior bay of *Spin One's* Docking Node Two. He'd claimed he'd lagged behind to secure some fragile and confidential samples and objects from R'Bak, but it had really just been to wait until he could control the tremors in his left hand. That kind of mind-over-matter determination was getting more difficult all the time, which meant his MS was progressing more rapidly.

So he made sure to stride down the tail-ramp with long-legged vigor and confidence…and almost ran headlong into Kevin Bowden: the senior, and damn near only, pilot among the Lost Soldiers.

"Whoa!" exclaimed the major, sidestepping off the ramp. "What's the hurry, Colonel?"

Murphy smiled sheepishly. "Sorry, Kevin; just eager to get to what is sure to be the most enjoyable meeting of my entire life."

"Ah," Bowden breathed sympathetically, "your tete-a-tete with Primus Anseker of family Otlethes."

"How did you hear?"

"I didn't. I just knew how to read that look on your face."

"And what look is that?"

"A man walking to his execution."

Murphy laughed. "Well, I guess I'll have to brush up on my acting skills before the meeting."

"Nah," Kevin waved casually, "you've got the right look. Every time the leaders of the Otlethes Family have shown up near our billets, they look like they're either going to or leaving a funeral."

"It's just their way," Murphy explained. "The meetings aren't bad so much as they're awkward. When you combine all the stuff that they're not willing to reveal with all the stuff that I can't share, it's like we're talking in code—and not the same one."

Kevin shrugged and smiled. "Better you than me. Sir. Besides, I've gotta have this beast ready for another run in half an hour."

"Why so quickly?"

"Priority personnel with priority mission on R'Bak."

As if on cue, the hulking form of Sergeant Frazier entered the bay from the entry in the inboard bulkhead. "Colonel, Major," he said, stopping to ready a salute.

Murphy waved it off. "Good luck planetside, Sergeant. I wasn't aware you were heading back, yet."

"New orders sir," he explained. "Major Lee needs meds. I'm gonna get 'em." He said it with the resolve of a man who'd taken an oath to complete a mission no matter the cost.

"Then I won't hold you up, Sergeant." Murphy nodded, turning back to Bowden as Frazier clumped up the ramp into the shuttle. "One question, Kevin: how are our new pilots coming along?"

"Well, but slowly." Bowden's eyes became distant. "The mission against the transmitter cost us the only ones with real experience. And they were good men, all of them."

Murphy made sure the following silence didn't drag on a moment longer than absolutely necessary. "Well, the current crop has a great teacher and example."

Bowden suppressed a chuckle. "Good thing you got marooned out here with the rest of us, Colonel."

"Why's that?"

"Because otherwise you would have gotten back to the States and become an insufferable politician."

Murphy laughed at the absurdity of the image of him shaking hands and kissing babies and taking other politicians—*any* politicians—seriously. "Come look me up when you get back on the *Spin*, Kevin."

"Oh? Why's that?"

"Mission to discuss."

Bowden rolled his eyes. "More shuttle work?"

Murphy tried to smile. "Something like that. Gotta go." With a carefully measured first step—those were the ones where the MS was most likely to ambush him—he started to the inboard door…

And stopped when he found himself looking—and then staring—into a pair of ethereally violet eyes: Nalyiriz.

It took him a moment to realize that she'd stopped in mid-step, too.

Murphy nodded. "Doctor."

She returned it. "Colonel."

He noticed she was carrying dirtside gear. "Going somewhere?"

"In fact, I am," she said. "I am going down to R'Bak to help Sergeant Frazier find the compounds needed for Mara's pregnancy." And then she did something he couldn't remember seeing her do before: her gaze wavered, and she looked away.

He stepped closer. "And what else?"

She stepped sideways out of the entry, toward the bays' stacked cargo pods. "I was not aware that I am under any obligation to report my actions to you."

Murphy followed her toward the cargo pods. "Obviously you're not. We—all of us Lost Soldiers—are just lucky to be your guests." The look she shot him was utterly perplexing: irritated, impatient, and…injured? "But," he continued more quietly, "I would be grateful if you'd share your other reasons for heading down to R'Bak."

"I did not confirm that I have any other reasons to share, Colonel."

"No, you didn't," Murphy answered. And he waited.

Her gaze wavered again. "While there, I plan to determine the availability of other needful medicinals."

Ah. "I just hope this isn't about my multiple sclerosis."

Her violet eyes were suddenly wide and intense. "And what if it is? That is my affair."

Murphy sighed. "Not if it means risking one of my men to do it."

Although Murphy wouldn't have believed it possible, her eyes widened even further. "Be unconcerned; as I stated earlier, these actions are my own. So, too, is the risk." Her neck was very straight, her head rigid atop it.

"No! I didn't mean…that's not what I…" Murphy sputtered before drawing her further away from the entry. "Look: I don't want you taking risks, either. But like you said, I only have authority over Sergeant Frazier's actions, not yours. And the bottom line is that with barely one hundred Lost Soldiers left, I can't detail people to run around looking for a cure that might not exist."

She crossed her arms, her head still erect. "You are wrong, Colonel. And it is not just your own men that you are jeopardizing. Now it is my Family's survival, too. Probably almost every one of us SpinDogs."

"What? Look: disease or no disease, it just doesn't make sense to—"

"Colonel, you are essential."

Murphy shook his head. "Now that's just not—"

"To argue against such an ineluctable conclusion is indicative of foolishness, denial, or false modesty. Perhaps all three. I can not tell; your culture is still puzzling to me. But inasmuch as I am charged with the welfare of my Family and my people, I must ask: whose computer was it that contained the various blueprints and information that gives us any chance of prevailing in the coming conflict with Kulsis? Who was the only individual authorized to learn the location of the Arat Kur translator—and decoder—that your superiors left behind in deep space? And who has the codes, or retina, or genetic pattern that the computer will once again require before it shares any further classified data or instructions that it may be programmed to release?"

Murphy was not accustomed to losing an argument so thoroughly that he couldn't find a single valid refutation or rebuttal. Now it was his gaze that wavered. "Damn stupid 'superiors,'" he muttered, "relying on a guy with MS."

Nalyiriz shook her head sharply. "Quite the contrary. Your leaders determined that if you and your Lost Soldiers were enslaved or tortured by those of the Spindogs that distrust you, you would divulge whatever information you had. So the first and crucial condition your computer was seeking to confirm was your long-term safety. Which is why it was only *after* the Hardliners' failed coup that it released the truly sensitive information upon which so many of our joint plans now depend. And at that point, your multiple sclerosis arguably became as much a benefit to their plans as a detriment."

Murphy blinked. "What?"

"Colonel, tell me: where is the safest place to keep a person—leader or otherwise—who is also the sole possessor of secret means of access to extremely sensitive information?"

Murphy swallowed. "Here. Spaceside."

"Precisely. They rightly determined that you would not wish your condition to endanger your men by joining them in planetside operations. So you would remain on the habitats, although it is not your natural inclination to do so."

She uncrossed her arms and leaned forward. "Clearly, therefore, they considered you *absolutely* essential." Her declaration finished on a tone that made it also sound like an appeal.

Murphy nodded, understanding. "Sure, because if I die too soon, that might cause undecided SpinDogs to believe that our plans are too unlikely to succeed, and so they'd join what's left of the Hardliners to come after—or betray—your Family."

Nalyiriz did not blink or react in any other way. All she said was, "You are essential."

Her tone had changed again, but Murphy couldn't suss it out and didn't have the time to try.

"I don't want to hold you up. And I'm overdue for a meeting."

"Yes, with my Family's Primus and Guild-mother." Her face softened slightly. "Shumrir is far more patient than Anseker. He will take it as an affront if you are late."

"Well, then he just might have to be affronted. I've got to get a few sitreps before the meeting. Travel safely, Nalyiriz." He started to leave, stopped, turned back. "Look, I don't want anything to happen to you just because I'm…well, just promise me you'll be careful. Mara, your niece, your Family: they all need you. I'll be okay for a while, yet—long enough to get the job done. And that's what really matters."

"Yes," she said slowly, watching him go. "That's what matters."

Pistol Pete Makarov raised a hand to attract Murphy's attention. "I have the majors on-line now, sir. The Dornaani microsats only give us a ten minute window on both their positions. We could slightly extend that window if I recalibrate for audio only, but—"

Murphy shook his head. "Leave it as is, Pete. I don't have ten minutes, anyway. Let's start the party."

"Very good, sir." Makarov opened the comm link.

Bo Moorefield and Harry Tapper appeared on the split screen. Bo was already wearing a wide grin. "So," he prompted, "how's that 'major' operation coming along, Colonel?"

"As expected," Murphy replied with a smile. Which was technically true. As Nalyiriz had warned, Mara's pregnancy required the same precautions as other mixed-parentage pregnancies: no flying or other activity that could trigger a miscarriage or, later, premature labor. Infants whose genes were an amalgam of planetside and spaceside genetics were less likely to be carried to term, and their mothers faced ten times the risk of placenta previa.

But right now, that was a comparatively distant concern. Murphy checked his watch. "In seven minutes, I'll be in a mini-summit with our SpinDog hosts, so, if you've got any updates, I'm all ears."

Tapper shrugged. "My detachment didn't reach the north range of the Greens until two days ago, sir, so I don't have a lot to report, but…well, it is unusually *diverse* up here."

"Explain."

Tapper lifted a palm with an expression that all but said, *where do I start*? "One of the first things you notice about the Ashbands is that the terrain and the biota is pretty consistent. Not a lot of variation.

"I knew it would be different in the Greens. The variation in biomes made it inevitable, just like back on Earth. But on this planet…" He shook his head. "Sir, from one forest to the next—or even within the *same* forest—the trees, the undergrowth, the animals, they're all…" He stopped, apparently trying to both find words and collect his thoughts. "Sir, imagine combining patches of the Amazon rainforest, stands of Nordic pine, temperate deciduous woodlands, and then mix in baobob trees and some of the stranger varieties found on Socotra. Then let them mingle for a few decades. The forests of the Greens are like *that*, sir—except some of the trees look more like upright zucchini. Or giant ferns. Or mushrooms." He sighed. "Sir…it's just not right."

Makarov shrugged. "Major, it *is* an alien planet."

Murphy shook his head. "I don't think that's what Harry's getting at, Pete. It's not that the flora is extremely different from Earth's. It's that a lot of it doesn't seem to be related to the rest." Makarov's frown prompted him to clarify. "On Earth, in any given biome, you see variations on a theme. Plants can be grouped together into families and species because they're all just the offshoots of an earlier, common type."

Tapper was nodding. "And it's not just the flora that's so unrelated, sir. It's the fauna, too, and in *every* biome. As a result, farmers or loggers or shepherds have radically different skills, lifestyles, and needs from one region to the next. The only thing they seem to have in common is language—more or less—and an awareness that there are more raiders in their regions over the past year and that the numbers are growing."

"But not enough for the indigs to make common cause with us, from the sound of it."

Tapper nodded. "So far, the satrap's proxies have mostly taken goods, not lives. And up here, the Searing just doesn't bring the same lethal increase in heat or raiding that it does down in the Ashbands."

"Have you encountered any of those raiders, yet?"

"A few, sir. Some literally peed in their pants when we rolled up on them. The few that we had the opportunity to debrief bore out our conjecture that there wouldn't be any consistent dirtside explanation as to who destroyed the first batch of reavers from Kulsis and their transmitter. But the news spread pretty quickly, as did word of the tribal uprisings in the Hamain.

"Most of them also heard that off-worlders were involved, but the farther north you go, the fewer people believe that. Those who do presume it's some kind of war being fought between different Kulsian factions." He smiled. "You can tell our SpinDog hosts that no one in the Greens suspects they exist."

"And the satraps there?"

"The further north you go, the fewer there are. But they're just like the ones near the Hamain: they're scared by the unrest and changes and are realizing that this Searing won't be like any other. So they're sending out more groups to do their own preemptive Harvesting to be in a better position to bargain with whoever shows up. The groups are mostly freelancers, though."

Murphy smiled tightly. "Because when rent-a-thugs run into each other, it's just a nasty Wild West shoot-out, not a formal declaration of war between satraps."

"Exactly."

Murphy nodded, turned his eyes toward Moorefield's side of the screen. "What about you, Bo?"

The cavalryman shrugged. "Nothing new in the Hamain except that, as our operational tempo tapers, the tribes and towns are relaxing enough to come up with their own preferred versions of what's going on and what to do about it." He shook his head. "Watching rumors become 'fact' is kind of amusing, but also kind of depressing; everything starts out loose and sloppy, but before you know it, hearsay starts hardening into stone-cold 'truth.'"

"The only thing that people hate more than bad news is uncertainty. And it sounds like two different narratives are forming."

Bo shrugged. "I wouldn't call them narratives, exactly. None of the locals are really wondering about why everything is suddenly going off the rails. Their focus is on how to stay alive or grab power while it does. The tribes are a little drunk with success, amping up a sentiment that basically boils down to 'we're finally showing the satraps and townies who's really the boss out here! So you want to be a part of this, because we're changing the world and winning every battle. With few casualties.'"

Murphy smiled. "Sounds like recruitment should go up."

"Colonel, you don't know the half of it. I've had young bucks walk in out of the wastes with nothing more than their robes, their boots, their knives, their desire for one of the mystical M14s, and their impatience to attack the enemy." He smiled. "At first, lot of them balk at the discipline and training prerequisites, but not many leave; the ones who've already gone through the process are all ready to declare that they're too weak-willed to do what it takes to become *real* warriors."

"Sign up those hazers as DI's, Bo," Trapper suggested with a grin.

"Working on it. Now, town-dwellers don't have many details about what's been happening elsewhere, except that Ashbanders have been grabbing other communities. Most of them have come to accept the ubiquitous reports that there's almost no looting, and that killing and rape is punished by either a noose or bullet."

"If these towns are isolated, how is the word spreading?"

Bo shrugged. "Merchants. Unless we can see that they're moving military supplies, we've left them alone. So their arrival in a town is de facto proof that we've been allowing trade to continue. And their ability to lower prices to be more competitive is proof that the taxes in occupied towns have been lowered." He smiled slightly. "The overall mood of the townies seems to be that if push came to shove, it might be a lot better—and safer—to throw in with the tribal barbarians and off-worlders."

Murphy nodded. "Well then, I'd say we've reached that moment when we should pause offensive operations." He saw the quizzical looks on both faces in the computer screen and explained. "Once a narrative is moving in the direction you want, you don't mess with it. You don't keep throwing new events and wrinkles into the mix. You let it set...like cement." He smiled at Bo. "Besides, the Hamain only has two remaining destinations for Persons of Interest."

Moorefield crossed his arms. "Imsurmik and Heshdehar. So that's why you kept them out of the mix. They were our Hiroshima and Nagasaki."

Makarov started. "You cannot mean to use nuclear weapons on them!"

Tapper smiled. "That's not what they're talking about."

Murphy turned toward his adjutant. "I was certain that they would have taught you about this in the Soviet Union."

Makarov sniffed. "I was taught that those cities were the targets of the only atomic weapons ever used and that they demonstrated that the United States had no reservations about using them."

"Well," Murphy smiled, "we won't complicate the debate with the little matter of both the military and civilian casualties projected for an actual invasion of Japan. What we're all referring to is that those two cities were intentionally excluded from the conventional bombing lists. That way, the effects of the atomic bombs could be accurately assessed."

"You are saying that…that they were lab rats? Whole cities?" Makarov's eyes and mouth remained wide open.

"They were," Murphy confirmed. "And we could have a very lively debate about the long- and short-term ethics of that decision, but that's not the issue right now. Major Moorefield is correct that I made a similar decision to leave Imsurmik and Heshdehar unmolested. But in this case, it was to narrow down the number of places to which PoIs would flee."

Tapper nodded. "Sure, because you wanted to create a funnel that would herd PoIs to the towns they would probably have wanted to go to anyway: the biggest in the Hamain and the closest to the Greens and Stullhaan."

"Okay," Bo said with a nod, "so now we've hopefully created two 'target rich environments' for finding PoIs. But colonel, when you said 'pause' operations,' was that code for *terminating* them?" His smile became brittle.

"For the most part, yes. At this point, we want PoIs to be able to travel to those towns, but once there, be unable to leave easily. That's why we've been letting people enter them but actively interdicting any satraps' caravans or large forces that try to leave."

"And smaller forces?"

"You're the one on the ground, so it's your call, Bo. At this point, your job is to keep a close eye on the two towns and decide which one has the better chance of attracting a reasonable number of PoIs. And once you have, you're going to have to sneak into striking range without the use of airlift."

"Still, that's all easy duty compared to what we've been doing."

Murphy smiled. "Are you saying you *want* me to make the job harder?"

Bo smiled back. "Now, I didn't say that, exactly. But I don't want my people to lose their edge."

Murphy nodded. "I get that. But you've also complained—rightly—that there hasn't been enough down time to keep up with repairs, or maintenance, or—"

"Or rest," Bo finished as he folded his arms meditatively. "Yeah. I'll finally be able to rotate all the battalions—uh, Bands—through an R&R rota. Our own people, too."

Tapper grinned tightly. "The classic problem of a successful insurgency: the bigger it grows, the less nimble it becomes."

Murphy smiled. "Even success has its drawbacks. But all things being equal, I'd rather have the scales tilting in our direction rather than the enemy's."

His two field commanders nodded solemnly. "*Nolo contendere*, sir," Tapper intoned, then glanced at his watch. "Just one other thing, Colonel."

"Which is?"

"I believe you're going to be late for your meeting."

Chapter Three

The one thing that Murphy *did* like about meetings with the SpinDogs was that, despite the formality, they were utterly devoid of pomp or laudatory mutual appreciation statements and other ass-kissery. Once everybody was introduced and relative levels of authority established, it was down to business.

On the other hand, he reflected as he took his seat opposite Anseker, Primus of the Otlethes Family, a meeting with SpinDogs—even allied SpinDogs—might be cooperative in intent, but that didn't keep it from being a competitive, elbows-out exchange. There was always jostling and jousting for preeminence, which really didn't help build a sense of fellow-feeling or common purpose. Murphy remembered all the times when—like every officer and enlisted in the US Army of his epoch—he had inwardly groaned whenever the term "team-building" came out of the mouth of whoever was running a meeting. It was the Army's semi-ruggedized version of holding hands and singing Kumbaya, and it was roundly considered to be the closest administrative analog to Being In The Suck. But right now, Murphy had to admit that a little team-building would not be amiss in dealing with the SpinDogs.

As soon as his rump hit his chair, Primus and the rest of his small party—Guild-mother Shumrir and a nondescript assistant they did not bother to introduce—nodded at the colonel without acknowledging Makarov's entry a moment later. "Let us begin," Anseker said. "We are eager to hear what you have achieved on R'Bak."

Murphy frowned, glanced sideways at Makarov. "Primus Anseker, have you not received the weekly updates relayed by my staff officer, Captain Makarov?"

Shumrir shrugged. "We have seen and heard many reports of various activities and events on the surface, but there has been no complete overview of the operations and their outcomes. Not such as can be provided by a commander with full oversight of all the details and objectives."

Makarov frowned, opened his mouth to object—just as Murphy nudged his foot under the table. *Read between the lines, Pete: the big-wigs want to hear from* me. As Murphy had already experienced, SpinDogs deemed it a snub if one leader communicated to another through an underling. It was the equivalent of saying, *you're not important enough to have face-time with me*. But he'd thought that with allies, the meetings might be more casual. Apparently, he had been very wrong.

Murphy simply nodded. "Of course," he agreed, and decided if they wanted a brief, then a brief they would get. "Operations, first. Since destroying the intersystem transmitter just before the start of summer in the Hamain, our CONOPS has been simple: we exploit the enemy's surprise and uncertainty by snapping up his towns, isolate any that are too big to take outright, and use our success to attract more recruits."

"And your results?" Anseker was barely suppressing a smile; he'd obviously read the reports Makarov had forwarded and knew that the news would be good.

"As of today, sixty percent of the satrap towns in the northwest Hamain and the adjoining Ashbands have fallen. The indig forces under our direct control have increased steadily. We have almost twelve thousand partially-trained irregulars in 'war-bands,' all bolstered by improved technology. Their primary role has been to exploit breaching attacks mounted by our fourteen hundred trained regulars. Special operations are carried out by two hundred elites, usually led by Lost Soldier officers and NCOs. Given current training cycles, we project the number of regulars and elites to roughly double over the next seventy days. Major operations are supported by your replicat—er, 'autofabbed' Hueys and a growing number of captured ground vehicles. Better vehicles are coming on-line all the time."

"On-line?" Anseker echoed with a frown. "You mean you have only started to use the best vehicles recently?"

Murphy nodded. "That was a matter of necessity, not choice. Most of the technicals—predominantly small trucks and all-wheel drive vehicles—are maintained by the indigs that use them; they're not part of our 'motor pool.' However, most of the advanced or 'factory-spec' Kulsian vehicles we took from the satraps needed maintenance and increased operating reserves before we could put them into the field. They also needed trained crews."

Shumrir folded her hands. "Colonel, I have not studied the specifics of your battles, so I remain puzzled how it is that so many of the best vehicles have been taken intact."

Murphy nodded. "The J'Stull and their closest allies sent nearly all of their most modern and electric vehicles to help power the transmitter. So when they lost that battle, they didn't just lose the ability to warn Kulsis, but their best combat platforms. That's why, instead of sending out roving recon or strike groups, the satraps are now hunkering inside their walled cities on the northern edge of the Ashbands and the near margins of the Greens."

"And what are your next objectives?" Anseker asked.

"For now, Primus, we are pausing our offensive in the Hamain in order to consolidate our gains and train more regulars."

Anseker shook his head. "Despite your many successes, I still think the greatest achievement is the control you maintain over these barbarians, that you can keep them from running wild."

What's next, Anseker? Asserting that they're all lesser beings, just as Kormak did right before you reduced him to water and protein? But Murphy simply shrugged and said, "Maintaining unit cohesion is our single largest investment, both in terms of time and personnel. Almost half the Lost Soldiers are assigned as officers or senior NCOs among the indig formations."

Shumrir's gaze was calm but penetrating. "Leaders never enjoy such success without also identifying and rectifying problems among their own forces." She was silent for a moment. "What problems do you have, *Sko'Belm* Murphy?"

Murphy shrugged. "Not enough specialists."

"Are you referring to your elite troops?"

Murphy shook his head. "No. We have plenty of people willing to fight, and enough of them will ultimately become elites. What we *don't* have are enough people—soldiers or not—who have the skills to maintain our equipment. If we can't recruit more of them, we cannot preserve our technological edge."

Shumrir frowned. "That is a challenging problem. Do you have a plan for remedying it?"

Murphy shrugged. "Towns in the Greens have more persons with technical skills, and their literacy rates are much higher. But until the satraps make their lives miserable, I doubt many of them would join our ranks. So we've been exploring the possibility of recruiting people from areas that the Kulsians routinely use as their planetary bases of operations. Rumors suggest that many technical skills become family trades, passed down from one Searing to the next."

Shumrir nodded. "That is true. Groups of families organize into craft guilds that serve the needs of the Kulsians. Unfortunately, their contracts are actually held by the satraps who, in the years between the Searings, use them to maintain the devices they inherit from the Harvesters or which they find as salvage. So the technicians you seek are already well-paid thralls of your enemies."

Murphy's smile was small. "Yes, well, I never said I thought recruiting them would be easy."

Anseker frowned in response. "I suspect you will find it impossible. Indeed, any present changes in the habits and actions of the R'Baku are unlikely to persist a minute beyond the arrival of the Harvesters. Or even the surveyors, who we must presume shall arrive in greater numbers than usual."

Murphy nodded. "And sooner, as well."

Shumrir frowned. "Your affirmation almost sounds eager, colonel. Do you actually consider an early arrival by the surveyors to be desirable?"

Murphy shook his head. "No. We can use every second to prepare. But that doesn't change the fact that if they don't come, we can't defeat the Harvesters."

The young assistant looked up, clearly puzzled. The plans that underlaid Murphy's comments had been approved by the two senior members of the Otlethes Family, but were otherwise closely held secrets. And they would remain so until the Lost Soldiers secured a sufficiently well-informed person of interest: the primary objective of Bo Moorefield's pending attack upon either Heshdehar or Imsurmik.

The assistant glanced at his superiors, obviously seeking clarification. Shumrir noticed; she turned and stared at him, her eyes like stone. The assistant quickly looked back down at his notes.

Anseker was nodding over steepled fingers. "If indeed the Harvesters can be prevented from landing on R'Bak during this Searing, that will undoubtedly sway many of the R'Baku to join us."

Shumrir shrugged. "Joining us would be helpful, but the best outcome will be if ten dirtsiders stand aside for every one who becomes our ally."

Murphy nodded. "From what we can tell, only the satraps and their chosen lackeys actually like the present order. The rest of the locals just play along, careful not to complain."

Anseker smiled. "Much like you, then."

Murphy managed not to blink, flinch, or allow his hand to quake in response to Anseker's mysterious—and not very reassuring—remark. "I'm afraid I don't know what you are referring to."

"Do you not?" One of Anseker's eyebrows rose as he examined Murphy's face. "Well, perhaps it is not foremost in your mind, but surely you must still chafe at the silence we imposed upon you during Primus Kormak's execution."

Those words sparked the memory of what the SpinDog was referring to, caused Murphy's mind to reflexively replay the moment. He had been sitting in a pressurized observation gallery/jury-box when Kormak had uttered the word that

Anseker was obviously referring to now and which Shumrir had forbidden him to inquire about.

Glancing at Murphy, she had said, "About that word you heard: Reification. You are not to ask us about it." He discovered all the witnesses in the gallery were watching him. "It would put our alliance in great jeopardy," Shumrir concluded.

He had shrugged and replied, "I can live with that." But had silently added, *For now.*

As Murphy emerged from the memory, Anseker was nodding. "It is admirable that you have scrupulously held to a promise that you clearly did not wish to make."

Murphy frowned. "Should allies do any less?"

Anseker smiled. "You must believe us poor allies then, since we often press you for information you clearly do not wish to share."

Murphy shrugged. "I did not explicitly ask you to refrain from doing so."

Anseker's smile acquired a wolfish cast. "You also have little choice in the matter."

Ah. So there it was: the inevitable jockeying for control, for "dominion." If Murphy agreed that the Lost Soldiers had no practical autonomy, he would seem weak. However, if he challenged Anseker's assertion, that could lead to a dangerous rift.

Or was this a test? And if so, Murphy wondered, was it a test of his resolve or of his ability to manage an apparently lose-lose situation? Murphy decided to assume the latter. "One always has a choice," he said.

Anseker sat straighter. "I do not see the logic of that statement. Your daily survival is dependent upon us. If we were to issue an ultimatum, you could not refuse to comply. You do not have any meaningful leverage."

Murphy smiled. "Don't we?"

Until now, Anseker's expression had been subtly amused, as if he were playing a game. Now, it became a rigid, serious mask. "Are you saying you would reveal our existence to the Kulsians?"

In fact, that was not what Murphy had intended to say at all; his vague reply had been a means of sidestepping without acquiescing. But Anseker had instantly assigned an identity to that undefined threat, had presumed it was a reference to the biggest monster lurking in the SpinDog closet of nightmares: discovery by the overlords of Kulsis. Speaking slowly, carefully, Murphy answered, "I did not say that."

"But nor have you denied it, even now. You realize, of course, that you and your men would be the first ones to be killed. After being tortured to divulge whatever useful information you might have."

Murphy knew that whatever response he might make, it could not suggest a lack of resolve or courage. So, another sidestep: "Actually, since we have no analogous leverage over the Kulsians, I am not sure they would execute us."

"I wasn't speaking of the Kulsians."

Shumrir did not manage to suppress a start at the Primus' words or cool tone.

Murphy suppressed a sigh: *so, if we're really playing hardball...*"Primus Otlethes, if you actually feel that we pose such a profound threat and are so profoundly untrustworthy, I cannot understand why you haven't already sent us out your many airlocks."

Anseker stared, seemed to be grasping for a swift retort that did not materialize.

Murphy thought: *gotcha. And now, to finish:* "I do understand your position, though. After all, you can't hope to fight Kulsian spacecraft with your present equipment. Nor could your people continue the ongoing dirtside operations, since only a few of you can remain active in that gravity for more than a few hours. And you can't simply go back to hiding any more than you can walk away from R'Bak, because if the Harvesters land there, they will have the time and resources to investigate what happened to their coursers and discover a trail of breadcrumbs that leads off-world. And ultimately to this very habitat. So I suppose you probably *can't* safely space us, after all."

Anseker frowned, but there was something like new respect in his eyes. "Perhaps Kormak was right; you *will* be the death of us."

"Why do you say so, Primus?"

"Did you not just threaten us?"

"Primus, actually I *haven't* threatened you. But *you* threatened *us* when you intimated that you would preemptively space us if we gave you reason to distrust, or merely doubt, our resolve to maintain the secret of your existence." He smiled. "Of course, I think it's far more likely that you staged this debate to see if, when pushed, I would push back." Murphy shrugged. "And now you have your answer."

Anseker let a small grin creep into existence at one corner of his mouth. "Your ways are strange—unaggressive, would be the most charitable description—but you have a spine. That counts for much amongst us. So, in regard to the other matter on which you have not pressed us—our maximum autofab capacity—you shall have your answer soon. But as for what we call Reification—"

Murphy waved dismissively. "I hope we shall earn enough of your trust that you will elect to share it at a later date."

Anseker smiled and rose. "I enjoy our discussions, *Sko'Belm* Murphy. We shall have another one soon."

Murphy smiled back, nodded, but thought, *Not if* I *can help it.*

Chapter Four

Elroy Frazier looked up through the surreal "trees" of R'Bak and reflected, *I've been away so long, being gone feels like being home.*

He remembered the first time he'd heard that sentiment. He'd been in the 'Nam for all of two weeks, and the man speaking had barely looked human to his then-cherry eyes. Between the dead, unblinking stare and the gaunt, animal lines of the dude's face, he'd exuded an air of danger and madness that had stuck with young PFC Frazier throughout his five tours and several promotions.

Eventually, the thought that had once seemed so alien, so inhuman to a homesick kid from Georgia, had made perfect sense to whatever it was he'd become by the end of his first tour. It was why he'd kept coming back for more. Some folks called it a "war addiction." But it was simpler than that.

On his first trip back to "The World," he'd looked around and realized that the world wasn't his anymore. He didn't fit, and the knowledge that he didn't fit was like a constant itch just under the surface of his skin.

So, he'd turned around, volunteered for special ops training, and gone back to war. MACV-SOG wasn't the big army he'd known as a Huey crew chief, but it was a hell of a lot more home than the World had become. And before long, it was the only home he wanted.

It was his deepest secret: he hadn't missed the World one bit. He never wanted to return.

Still didn't, as a matter of fact.

Which had worked out well, all things considered.

He took a deep breath and closed his eyes as the afternoon sunlight slanted over his face. He'd always liked dusk, whether back in the 'Nam or here on R'Bak. When the sun sank toward the horizon, he felt his body and mind waking up, alive to the possibilities of what could be done under cover of darkness. That was one reason he liked being planetside much more than hanging out on the spin habitat. They varied the light and dark cycles there, but no matter how much they tried to ergonomically design it, he could always sense the artificiality. There was no true dawn or dusk. No transition time for easing into and out of the different states of things.

Kinda like waking up out of cryo. No transition. Just a new reality.

He'd gotten used to most of the vagaries of living in space—MACV-SOG had taught him to be flexible, after all—but he'd never gotten used to the lack of dusk.

"Welcome back to the world." The voice that accompanied the hand on his shoulder was known and friendly, so El didn't react badly as Jackson dropped down to a seat beside him on the fallen log that had wedged itself between trees at the top of this particular hill. Instead, he shifted over a bit in welcome.

"This ain't the World, brother," El said softly. "But it's closer than space; that's for damn sure."

Jackson leaned back a bit and turned to study El's face. "Yeah, that's what I meant. I forgot you Vietnam Era guys used that term."

"So did you guys from the Mog."

"It wasn't as widespread. By the time we came around, technology was good enough that we could call home and stuff. I don't think we felt quite the same sense of disconnection you old guys experienced."

"Fuck you, Jackson; you're older than me!" El said with a grin. Jackson grinned right back, his teeth flashing against the deep mahogany of his skin.

"Bullshit. I was born in 1965. When were you born? Like 1940 or something?"

"'47, but I'm only twenty-five now. You're what, forty?"

"Huh. Really? I mean, minus the hundred-plus years in between, is that so? I thought you were older."

"Ain't the years, brother; it's the mileage. Five tours in the 'Nam will age a body."

"Ain't that the truth. And look at us now, still in the shit."

"Well, you know what they say: old soldiers never die…they just get kidnapped by fucking aliens."

Jackson snorted, chuckled, then let out a deep, throaty laugh. El grinned at the man who'd become something of a friend and joined in, letting the good feeling of a shared joke wash over him with the last rays of the sun. 'Nam had taught him that, too. Enjoy the funny moments when you can.

Down the hill from their vantage point, a door to one of the shelters opened, and a woman stepped out. El sat up and leaned forward, his eyes tracking her movements as she started up the slope toward them.

Jackson nudged him gently in the side. "Is it like that? You got eyes for Doc Nalyiriz?"

"Nah, man. We've just got nieces in common," El said. "She's a good doc and a good friend, but that's it." He didn't mention the flutter deep in his belly that hit every time her amber-flecked violet eyes lit up in a smile at something he said.

"Uh huh. Sure."

Elroy tore his gaze away from the approaching woman and stood up, brushing his trousers clear of debris as he looked down at his friend. "Hey, man, we're not all creepers like that horndog partner of yours."

"'Creepers?' That's not sixties slang," Jackson said. His tone was mild but El could hear the subtle warning. For some reason no one could figure out, Jackson was protective of Chalmers, no matter how many people the man rubbed the wrong way. El respected Jackson, so he respected the boundary. But he didn't like Chalmers.

"Learned it from my pilot," El said with a grin that didn't quite meet his eyes. Jackson snorted, then stood up himself as Nalyiriz came within earshot.

"Gentlemen," Doc Nalyiriz said in perfect English. Her slight accent gave her words a lilt that El found beautifully musical. He let himself give her a tiny smile.

"Doc," Jackson said, reaching out a hand. Nalyiriz squeezed his fingers with a smile of her own.

"Mister Jackson. It is nice to see you. I did not know that you and Sergeant Frazier were friends."

"Brothers gotta stick together," Jackson said, and Nalyiriz wrinkled her smooth forehead in a frown.

"Brothers? I was not aware of a familial connection."

"It's an expression from home," El said, stepping toward them. "It's slang for black men. Where we came from, we weren't always treated well because of our skin color. So, we black men—brothers—had to stick together to survive."

Nalyiriz tilted her head to the side as she considered this. "Your skin color—it was known as black? How odd, I would have expected 'brown' as a descriptor for your melanistic phenotypes. Interesting. And this was seen as a liability? But I understood that you had both served in areas of concentrated exposure to ultraviolet light. Why would having a highly melanistic complexion not be an asset?" Her puzzled frown showed that she, clearly, had never considered such things, even though her own skin tone was almost as dark as Jackson's. If El had had to place her on Earth, he would have said she looked Hawaiian or Filipina…maybe even Indian. But those eyes told anyone who looked into them that she was something else entirely.

El snorted. "It's a long story," he said. "And not really important. Anyway, was there something you needed, Doc?"

"Yes," she said, squaring her shoulders and lifting her chin to meet his eyes. "I came to tell you I have finally made contact with my main supplier of the rarer local herbs. We have a meeting tonight."

"Tonight?" El asked, raising his eyebrows in surprise. "That's sudden. What's the rush?"

Nalyiriz took a deep breath before she spoke. "I had hoped that it would be otherwise, but…Mara's child is likely to be born early. This is a common occurrence with female Skydreamers, and so we have methods to ensure the safe delivery and recovery of both mother and child, but we need certain compounds that can only be found in the local flora.

This herb I spoke of is the best source, but it is hard to find, and harder this year than most."

El held himself perfectly still, letting the news roll through him while he held himself locked in iron control. He felt Jackson reach out and grip his shoulder tightly in support.

"Is that why I came down planetside again so soon?" he asked softly, once he was sure that he could maintain his bearing.

"In part," Nalyiriz said. "Mara wanted you on the ground to see to the procurement, and she was afraid you wouldn't leave if you thought she was in any danger."

"Is she?"

"Not if we can get the herb." The doc reached out and touched her fingertips to his forearm. "Which we will do tonight if all goes well. An hour after sunset, I will meet you outside the healer's tent."

Elroy watched Nalyiriz walk away, waiting until she was out of earshot to jerk his shoulder out of Jackson's hand and spin to face the other man. He could feel the heat of anger burning along the sides of his face, and a quiet, dispassionate corner of his mind noted that he really must look terrifying, because Jackson actually took a small step backward before he caught himself.

"Did you fucking know about this?" Elroy said, keeping his voice low, even as it spiked with anger.

Jackson shook his head and lifted both hands, palms out. "No, man, I swear to you. The briefing I got said you were supposed to help Chalmers and me look into some of the black market movements going on. That's it! I had no idea Mara was sick."

"She's not *sick*," Elroy said, rage curling his hands into fists. Rage was good. It kept the fear and helplessness away. "She's fucking pregnant, and if she loses the kid, I'm not sure she's gonna come back from that!"

"El, Mara's tough. She'll be fine."

"I *know* she's fucking tough. That's the problem! She'll push and push until her body gives out, and then she won't rest properly and let herself recover! *This* is why we shouldn't let women fight. Not because they can't—hell no! It's because they go so damn hard they break!" El sucked in a ragged breath, his chest heaving and head pounding in the wake of his explosion.

Jackson stared at him and said nothing.

El stared right back, letting his rage cool as the sun sank toward the western horizon, and the shadows began to rise around them. Eventually, the inferno within him sputtered and faltered, then faded away, leaving only worry in its wake.

"Fuck," he said softly, looking down and kicking at the dirt. "Sorry man, didn't mean to unload on you."

"I know she's your pilot, but this is personal for you, isn't it?"

"Yeah, but not like people think. We ain't fucking. She's…she's like my sister. She helped me out when I woke up, when I didn't know what in hell had happened. She's so damn strong, but she's just a woman, and she's fragile, too. Hell, we all are, I guess. But we're a crew, and we keep each other alive and…" He trailed off as the myriad threads of connection tangled together in his mind. Truth was, he couldn't articulate exactly what Mara had become to him, but she *was* important. More important than his own breath in a lot of ways.

He inhaled slowly and tried to focus on the scent of the dirt and the unusual biting, acidic scent of the trees: sharper than pine, but also rich, with a metallic tang that hinted at the makeup of the soil beneath. Further south, the air smelled scorched, like burned metal with an odd overlay of millions of spices. Even the water smelled different here: less fishy, more like a high mountain lake. But only kind of. R'Bak wasn't short on distinct smells, but, in all the myriad of aromas, El often had a hard time finding something familiar. None of the almost-sweet scent of decay that the jungle had carried. None of the comforting warm scents of home.

But focusing on his senses helped still his mind. *Fix what you can, boy. Let God handle the rest.*

Growing up, El's mother had seen to it that he and his three brothers went to church every Sunday morning. He'd gone because his mother wouldn't have had it otherwise, though he'd never managed to find the deep faith she had. But that sentiment stuck with him: fix what you can, and let God—or fate, or whatever—handle the rest. He opened his eyes and exhaled, then met Jackson's worried gaze.

"You good?" Jackson asked.

Elroy nodded. "I'm gonna help the doc get her herbs tonight. And then I'm gonna take them back spaceside. If that's all Mara needs, I'll come back down here to help you out. But I'm gonna see to her first." He spoke softly, but his tone was clear: despite the disparity in their ranks, Elroy wasn't asking permission. Like the smart NCO that he was, Jackson recognized that, and nodded his assent.

"I'll let Chalmers know," he said.

"Wait until after doc gets the stuff," El said. "I got a feeling."

"About the meeting?" Jackson's eyebrows shot up. "You think it's dangerous? We shouldn't risk the doc. She's too valuable, both to her people and to ours."

"Not exactly," El said. "It's more like a 'mamasan's got a friend who has a friend who talks to Charlie' feeling. Not a 'we're walking into a fucking trap' feeling."

"That's not exactly reassuring," Jackson muttered.

Elroy shrugged. "We work with what we've got, brother. I never claimed to be psychic."

"Fair enough. Still, you want company for this meeting?"

Elroy shook his head. "Nah. I can keep the doc safe, and if we show up with a bunch of grunts, we might spook her contact and prevent her from getting the stuff she needs."

"Your call," Jackson said. "But I think I'll have a squad standing by with a handheld, just in case you need us."

"I'll take it. Thanks." He reached out a hand, and Jackson took it.

"Don't mention it," Jackson said. "It's what we do, right? Look out for each other?"

"Somebody has to," Elroy said, surprising himself with a tiny smile. One of the things he'd loved about the MACV-SOG world was the brotherhood. This wasn't the same…but in a lot of ways it was similar. He and Jackson—and hell, Chalmers and Mara and Murphy himself—were going through some crazy shit. No one who hadn't also experienced it would ever understand. That created a powerful bond, and El knew that a bond like that could sometimes be the only thing keeping you going.

Not what he'd been used to, growing up...but in the roughly six months since he'd woken, El had realized that, as motivations went, he could do worse. If his teammates were what motivated him to keep fighting for the next breath, the next objective...Well, like he'd told Jackson, he would definitely take it.

After all, he thought as he turned to watch the last rays of the sun drift through the tangled trees, *it sure as hell beats the alternative.*

Chapter Five

Night came quickly on R'Bak. Once the sun finally set, the darkness rose up from under trees and hills, bringing with it a new cacophony as the nocturnal wildlife began to go about its deadly business. Something in the trees sounded similar to the screaming cicadas El had known as a child. He pulled in a breath of the rapidly cooling night air and walked toward Nalyiriz.

He hadn't intended to sneak up on her, but four tours in the bush had changed the way he moved. El would never be a man who stepped heavily, without consideration to what sound he might make. Like it or not, hard experience had made him a ghost among trees. Still, Nalyiriz turned to face him as he approached, her lips curving in a welcoming smile.

"How did you know it was me?" he asked, his voice slightly gruff due to the way her smile caused a momentary tightness in his chest. But he wasn't going to think about that. Not ever, preferably.

"I was expecting you," she said, as if that answered his question. El drew his eyebrows together and was about to question further when she turned away and gestured for him to follow her down the main path leading away from their base. "Come; I do not want to be late. We must not miss this meeting."

"Who, exactly, are we meeting?" he asked. He fell into step just behind her, his hand resting lightly on the SpinDog assault rifle slung across his chest.

"A local man. He is an expert in herbs. I often buy from him when I come planetside." Elroy tried to take comfort from the light, easy tone in her voice. *He* might have a bad feeling about this, but Nalyiriz sounded as unconcerned and serene as ever.

The night was clear overhead, and starlight filtered down through the trees. El had taken the precaution of letting his eyes adjust earlier, so he could see well enough as the lights of the base fell away behind them.

Several questions floated to the front of his mind. Foremost among them: why had she specifically requested—nearly demanded!—him as escort for this transaction? He'd never known her to take protection with her before. Was it just because this was for Mara? Nalyiriz and his pilot were close for several reasons, so that might be it. He wouldn't put it past either woman to be subtle enough to understand and sympathize with his unease regarding Mara's condition. But that didn't feel exactly right. El couldn't have said why, but something else bothered him about this situation. It was like an itch under the skin that he just couldn't scratch.

They headed quickly down the path: a dirt road wide enough for the rickety native ground vehicles he called "trucks." After a few minutes, the road ended at a wide clearing, and Nalyiriz turned off onto a much smaller, wilder looking track heading off beneath the trees. El closed the distance between them and walked just behind her shoulder as they headed deeper into the darkness.

As they went, El listened hard, peered into the gloom, inhaled deeply—anything he could do to perceive what was out there. He focused on extending his senses to their absolute limit. So, when Nalyiriz spoke in a soft undertone, it knifed through his nerves, and only the severest exercise of his will kept him from flinching in surprise.

"You are nervous?" she asked. He thought he could hear a gentle undercurrent of humor in her tone.

"Wary," he corrected. "Ready."

"Ready for what?" she asked. "We are unlikely to be attacked. This area is well known to my people."

"You never asked for protection before. Something feels off. I'm just ready. Just in case."

She fell silent for the next few yards—meters—and El got the feeling she was mulling over his response.

"You are a warrior," she said after a while. "All of your people are."

"Yes," he said, turning his head so as to try and listen with the ear farther from her. "We are."

"Do you think this makes you more…?" she trailed off, as if she were unsure of the correct word.

"More what?"

"More scared?" He heard a soft puff of annoyance. "Not 'scared' exactly. But—"

"I know what you mean," he said. "And maybe. It's like walking quietly. I had to learn to stay alive, and so I can't be loud even if I want to. Being ready, listening, paying attention—it's all the same. I stay ready, because Charlie is out there, and he's for damn sure ready."

"Who is Charlie?" she asked. "Another of your soldiers I have not yet met?"

He let out a short huff of laughter.

"No," he said. "Charlie is—Charlie was the enemy in my old war. That was just what we called them. It comes from Viet Cong. They called themselves something else, but our ARVN allies called them Viet Cong, which we abbreviated to the letters VC, or Victor Charlie. Then it got shortened to Charlie, even when they weren't just VC anymore."

"But this is also a name in your language, yes? Why give your enemy a name? Would that not foster sympathetic feelings for them?"

A barrage of memories flashed behind El's eyes all at once: the face of his buddy Dan lying scorched and bleeding while the rotor wash from a Huey blasted the tall grass flat around them as it landed; the sudden, acrid tang of piss and blood as El slid his knife into the lung of an NVA scout; the cordite-scented smoke filtering through the wet jungle leaves as they pulled back from an untenable position—

"El?"

He blinked, gave his head a little shake, and refocused on her shadowed face. They'd stopped, and she was very close.

"You gotta call 'em something," he said flatly.

Nalyiriz stepped back slowly, then nodded and continued back down the narrow trail in silence.

El followed close behind her.

Ready as always.

Their meeting spot was another small clearing where the game trail stopped at a shallow stream. Breaks in the vegetation and ground cover indicated another trail ran alongside the stream. By the look of it, El could tell that it carried human traffic as much as native wildlife.

"There's a small village down there," Nalyiriz said, pointing downstream along the track. It was the first thing she'd said since their earlier conversation under the trees. "My contact lives there."

"Hostile?" El asked.

"Not at all," Nalyiriz said. "Quite friendly, as a matter of fact."

"So why the secrecy?" El asked. "Why not go down to them?"

She gave him a level look and sat on a boulder on the edge of the stream.

"You know why," she said. "We have explained to you that my people are very careful when we interact with the R'Baku."

"Are you, though?" Maybe it was her probing questions earlier, but he felt suddenly irritated with her, and the urge to crack that serene calm kicked through him. "You guys seem to be talking to the natives all the time, and if you're so *careful*, how do you know they're friendly at all?"

Her eyes narrowed slightly, but not like she was mad, more like she was studying him because he'd done something interesting. His irritation ratcheted up another notch, and he inhaled slowly. His eyes locked on to hers, and he stared her down, willing her to speak, or question him, or do *something* that hinted at the woman behind the mask of serene control.

But she just smiled and shook her head lightly, as if that answered anything. Then she turned away from him and looked downstream, clearly indicating that, as far as she was concerned, the conversation had ended.

El swallowed a curse and turned away as well. He pulled in another breath and forced his mind away from her and back to their situation. She seemed content to sit and wait there for a while, so he decided to walk the perimeter of this little clearing and see what was what.

Maybe she was right, he thought as he walked quickly and quietly to the nearby tree line; maybe he was a little paranoid. This wasn't the 'Nam.

But hell, he was still breathing, wasn't he? That was worth a little paranoia in his book.

El faded back into the trees. He kept Nalyiriz in sight, though he knew she couldn't see him. He saw her look around, as if searching for him, but she didn't call out and she didn't move from her rock, so he stayed hidden. If she was comfortable with this situation, let her stay comfortable. He'd be ready, and he could reach her in less than five steps if he had to.

His hands moved over the angular, big-gripped assault rifle, checking configuration and readiness. It was almost as light as plastic and fired what the SpinDogs called a self-consuming cartridge. All El cared about was that he knew how to use, strip, and reassemble the weapon by touch alone, that it was handy, and that it dropped what it hit. Next, he took a moment to feel the weight of his backup pistol against his leg and the long knife on the other thigh. He had other, shorter knives, too, stashed here and there on his body. Those had come in handy a time or two in the past, and he never left his bunk without them.

Hell, he never stayed in his bunk without them, for that matter.

El worked his way back and forth around the semi-circular clearing a few times. He identified several vantage points, but the best one was almost directly behind Nalyiriz. One tree had fallen against two of its fellows, and he climbed up the slanted trunk to find a spot that allowed him a full view of the clearing but kept him hidden in the shadow of the branching leaves.

He settled into place and used the scope on his rifle to peer downstream at the path that paralleled the water. He inhaled slowly and exhaled at the same pace, letting his irritation fade away, settling his mind into the open, quiet place where he waited for whatever was going to happen next.

Sometime later—he couldn't have said how long—Nalyiriz stirred and stood up. She turned toward him, her eyes going unerringly to the spot where he was waiting. He knew she couldn't see him, but as before, that didn't seem to matter. She knew where he was anyway.

"Elroy," she said, her quiet voice carrying a strange note. Something he hadn't heard before from her. Worry?

"Here, Doc," he said.

"Something is wrong. My contact should have been here before now."

He let himself down from his perch and stepped out of the tree line. By now, he didn't expect her to react the way anyone else would when he suddenly materialized out of the shadows, but a tiny corner of his mind hoped—and was disappointed. She simply looked up at him with a smile that didn't reach her eyes.

"What do you want to do?"

"It is imperative we obtain these herbs. I would say that we can go back and try to arrange another meeting, but I fear that Mara will need the medicinals as soon as possible. We must go down to the village and attempt to learn more."

"Let's *didi mau*, then."

Nalyiriz drew her eyebrows together in a frown at the unfamiliar expression.

"Sorry. Let's go. Quickly."

"Ah." She nodded sharply and began walking down the stream-side trail. Elroy suddenly noticed that she moved every bit as silently and carefully as he did.

The trail sloped downhill, which made sense, since it followed the stream's flow. Though wider than the game track they'd used earlier, it was still narrow and treacherously slippery in places where bare rock showed through the thin layer of dirt. El stayed close, stretching his senses as before. More so, if anything, because the contact hadn't showed. Something was wrong. They were off the plan and improvising. That always made things exciting.

They spent most of the next hour easing their way down the stream trail. Eventually, Nalyiriz came to a stop and held up a fist for him to do the same. It took El a moment to realize that she'd used his own hand signal and to wonder where she'd learned those gestures.

She turned her face to him and went up on tiptoe to breathe her words directly into his ear. "The village is just through there. I don't want to announce our presence. My contact's home is on the far side. We will stay in the trees."

El nodded to show he understood. She moved off the trail and followed the tree line to skirt around what appeared to be a relatively small mountain village. Like the other villages he'd seen on R'Bak, there appeared to be a central area ringed by various sized buildings constructed of local materials—in this case, most of the small houses were built from the wood of the surrounding forest. The stream itself cut through the heart of the village, and El could see some buildings nearby had been built up on solid stone pillars. In case it flooded, he supposed.

The village was quiet as they moved around it. There wasn't any foot traffic visible out near the edges, and when they passed close to the buildings on the fringe, he could hear the normal nighttime sounds of people used to living and working during the day. An infant sent up a thin wail and was quickly muffled. Not far away, one of the local draft animals let out a low, sonorous moan. A light breeze ruffled the trees at the edge of the clearing, bringing with it the scent of herbivore manure.

Nalyiriz guided him to the far side, then stopped and pointed at one particular hut set close to the tree line. Once again, he nodded to show his understanding and readiness, and pointed at his chest then touched her back lightly to show that he would be right behind her. She nodded and then crept toward the hut.

This time, he couldn't help but notice her skill.

The approaching primary star remained below the horizon, and Nalyiriz moved like a professional through the true darkness that resulted. She stepped from shadow to shadow, angling her body away from the starlight above and the faint glow of fires that leaked through nearby windows. Any sounds she made were easily lost in and masked by the natural rhythms of the night. She moved with purpose as she ducked around to the front of the target dwelling and reached for the door.

It wasn't quite closed. El noticed just as Nalyiriz did, because he saw her hand freeze before she touched the latch. He brought his rifle up to the ready as she inhaled slowly and pushed the door open the rest of the way.

It was dark inside the hut, impenetrably so. As the door swung wide, the clear starlight fell in an elongated rectangle, illuminating a dirt floor and the corner of a patterned rug. It was probably brightly colored during the daytime, but darkness leached the color from the threads, leaving only the vaguely geometric pattern for the eye to fix upon.

El pushed past Nalyiriz and stepped to the edge of the rug. He held his rifle at the ready with his stronger right hand. With his left, he reached into his pocket for the Zippo lighter he always carried. He hadn't been able to get any kind of lighter fluid on the spin habitat—fire was the ultimate fear in space, apparently—but once he and Mara had established the helicopter training operations, he'd been able to work a deal with the guys replicating their fuel supply. So, he had a working lighter again. He, of course, had neglected to mention that every time he'd gone back to the habitat. If the SpinDogs noticed when they scanned him in, they hadn't said anything.

He held his lighter high and flicked it open, then spun the wheel with his thumb. A small, steady flame appeared, and he could see more of the interior of the little hut.

"Don't burn the roof; it's only wood," Nalyiriz said softly. Belatedly, El looked up and realized that his lighter was, indeed, within a foot of the polished tongue-and-groove ceiling. He lowered the flame to eye level, since it didn't seem like anyone was home.

Anyone alive, that is.

As he lowered the light, Nalyiriz made a soft sound of discovery, maybe tinged by distress. A body lay sprawled on the far side of the rug, near the opposite wall. At its feet was a low brazier set into the floor. While Nalyiriz knelt next to the body and began examining it, El lit the brazier so they could see better. He held the Zippo's flame to the kindling readied there until it caught. A soft, steady light began to fill the room.

The house itself was small, maybe four hundred square feet, tops, and roughly rectangular in shape. El looked around, noting the major features of the one-room space. Besides the area immediately next to the brazier, where shelves held a myriad of pots, pans, and other kitchen implements, almost every wall held racks and racks of containers: bottles, boxes, vials, a couple of bags that looked like sewn-together animal bladders; baskets of every shape, size, and type, some of which were piled onto the shelves, while others formed precarious stacks on the floor. A small, narrow cot ran along the wall to the left of the door, and even that had baskets and boxes stacked around it. Aside from the cot and the rug, the only other piece of furniture was a low, wide table that held a variety of items that might or might not be related to cooking. El recognized a stone bowl and a roughly cylindrical grinder of the kind he used to see in pharmacies when he was a kid. He couldn't remember what they were called.

"El, please help me, I must roll him over," Nalyiriz said.

El turned back to her and bent to roll the corpse over onto its back. Though he hadn't been a large man in life—easily as thin as Nalyiriz and half a head shorter—the body was all dead weight and awkward. Still, it wasn't the first time El had moved a dead body, and he quickly got the man flipped over.

"Is this your contact?" he asked.

"Yes," Nalyiriz said. She sounded distracted as she pulled at the man's collar, then bent to sniff near his mouth. El kept his face straight and blank, even though vomit crusted the man's chin, neck, and chest.

"I'm sorry, Doc."

"For what?" She straightened, her brows furrowing together, like they did when she didn't understand something.

"Uh, I'm expressing sympathy."

"Oh," she said briskly, "thank you, but it is not necessary. The supplier did not have meaning to me; he was merely useful."

El felt his eyebrows shoot up at the coldness of her statement. He pressed his lips together to keep from asking the question that came immediately to mind: namely, did *he* and his people have "meaning" to her? Instead of speaking, El looked around at the contents of the hut again.

"Who was this guy? Some kind of local healer?"

"An…apothecary, I suppose, is the closest word in your language," she said as she continued her examination. She patted the dead man's pockets, looked inside the various leather pouches tied to his belt, then reached down and lifted one of his wrists, pulling back the long sleeve to look at the cooled flesh there. "He would harvest herbs and medicinals for the village and surrounding area. That is why I used him; he knew where to find even the rarest herbs." As she lowered his arm something dropped from his sleeve and rolled onto the dirt floor.

El bent to pick it up; a vial, half-filled with a dark, viscous liquid.

"Ah!" Nalyiriz said. "That is what I suspected. May I have that?"

El held it out to her. With quick, eager hands, she took it and drew out the stopper then raised it to her nose and inhaled. She wrinkled her nose, and, even from where he crouched, El could tell that whatever was in the vial had a strong, pungent scent. Like pine, but…sharper.

"What is that?" he asked.

Nalyiriz stoppered the vial and sat back on her heels. "It contains a distilled elixir of *Tustaib*. It is an…antidote of sorts. In its diluted form it can be used to prevent animals or children from dying if they've ingested something poisonous."

"And in the concentrated form?"

"It could be fatal."

"So, is that what killed him?"

"It would seem so. His vomit shows signs of internal hemorrhaging, which would be consistent with an overdose of *Tustaib*, but I cannot imagine why he would have done such a thing. As an apothecary, he knew very well what dosage would be safe."

"Maybe he didn't want to be safe? You think this could be suicide?"

"Again, I do not think so. There are thousands of poisons on these shelves. I can immediately point out ten that will cause a gentle, painless death. If he wanted to die, he would have chosen one of those. None of this makes sense."

El looked at Nalyiriz's downturned lips and furrowed brows as she worked her way through this puzzle.

"All right, so if he didn't take this stuff on purpose, and he didn't accidentally OD—"

"OD?"

"Overdose."

"Ah. Yes. I do not think it was accidental, at least not on his part."

"Then could someone have forced him to take too much?"

"It is possible. Look at his wrist. There is abrasion there, as if it was chafed by a tight binding."

El pivoted on his toes and picked up the wrist she'd looked at earlier. Sure enough, there in the warm, golden glow of the brazier, he could see an angry red abrasion running along the top of the wrist. A rope burn.

"Let me look at his head," El said. Nalyiriz waved a hand in invitation. He rose, and bending at the waist, peered down at the dead man's face. El wasn't a cop, and certainly not a homicide detective or anything like that, but he'd held a pistol against a head or two in his time. If this had gone down like he thought…

"Yeah," he said, finding the telltale bruising just above and behind the dead man's ear. "Look here; see this shape? That's from the muzzle of a firearm. You're right, Doc, someone forced him to drink that stuff."

"But that still does not make sense!" she said, and he could hear the rising frustration in her voice. For the first time since they'd met, her serene facade cracked enough to let her anger show. She'd been calm enough when they found her contact murdered, but the fact that she couldn't figure it out? That pissed her off.

He didn't know whether to be fascinated or appalled. In truth, he was both, but he was appalled at himself for *being* fascinated. "Why doesn't it make sense?" he asked. Focusing on the puzzle at hand was infinitely preferable to following his initial line of thought. "Talk it through."

"Again, if someone was forcing him to take poison, they would have used something more effective. Why, here on the table alone…" She looked at the low table he'd noticed nearby, and then froze.

"Oh," she said. "Oh, I see."

"What? What do you see, Doc?"

She turned back to him, her serene mask securely back in place. "It seems I was not his only illicit customer." She rolled gracefully to her feet and picked up a small woven-reed box off the table. From this, she lifted out several small, pale pebble-shaped objects and let them fall through her fingers back into the box.

"This is a local seed. It has many names, and it is very deadly if eaten. I suspect that our friend here ingested some in order to avoid speaking with whomever held the gun on him. They tried to force him to take some of his emergency *Tustaib* to prevent his death, but he outwitted them and swallowed a fatal dose."

"But why? And who? And does it concern us? Other than he's your source for this herb you need for Mara?"

Nalyiriz shrugged, searched, and picked up a woven lid from the table. She fitted it over the sides of the box and placed it on a shelf. She expanded her survey to the other shelves, opening lids and peering behind boxes in search of something.

"I suspect it was a simple deal gone bad. Our friend probably cheated his other customers in some way and declined to admit it or make good his debt. I cannot be certain, but I suspect they were smugglers, especially if, as you say, they held a gun on him. Firearms are not universal on R'Bak, as you know. It was likely a member of one of the smuggling cartels, or perhaps an agent of one of the satraps. It seems they are ranging further north in search of the same resources we seek. As many resources as they can get, if I had to guess. When the Kulsians come, they are known to collect…well…everything. I suspect some enterprising satrap has decided to try and have a stockpile ready for them, especially since they haven't yet reappeared." She paused and shrugged again. "But the reason for the shortage is a secondary matter. Our focus must remain entirely upon finding the herbs my contact collected for me."

"What if we can't?"

Her expression remained, but somehow her demeanor changed from her normal serenity to something a great deal more serious. "We must. Mara's life depends upon it."

Chapter Six

It took them a few hours to comb through the dead man's inventory, and El could tell that Nalyiriz was growing gradually more and more impressed with the collection, even as they failed to find the motherlode they sought. But the night wore on, and as sunrise threatened, they finally had to call a halt before they were discovered.

"How much do we have?" El asked Nalyiriz as she placed another small packet of herbs into the bag she'd appropriated from the dead apothecary's stash.

"Enough to synthesize the first few doses," she said, and, though her tone was calm as ever, he heard the fatigue and worry in her voice. If nothing else, at least the night's activities had shown him a glimpse behind her mask. "But I will need more before the child is born."

"All right," he said. "Let's get back to the base, and we can come up with a plan. Maybe…hell, I don't know, maybe we can find out where he got his stuff and…" he trailed off, then met Nalyiriz's eyes with worried eyes of his own.

She gave him a tiny smile and reached and patted him gently on the arm. "We will make a plan," she said. "I will think on it. Let us…what did you call it?"

"Didi mau?" he asked, cracking his own tiny smile.

"Yes, exactly. Let us *didi mau.*"

Before they left, El noticed that Nalyiriz added a few more of the late apothecary's stash to her bag. She apparently didn't feel the need to explain herself to him, and he didn't ask; he just followed her back into the last vestiges of night.

By the time they reached the meeting spot where the game trail intersected the creek, false dawn had spread its gray light across the eastern horizon. Once the adrenaline of their discovery had faded away and the chance of being seen leaving the dead man's house was past, El felt fatigue fraying his focus. Nalyiriz, too, struggled, stumbling a time or two as they worked their way back toward their base.

When they reached the main dirt road, he took the bag from her and slung it over his shoulders. She smiled at him in tired gratitude before resuming their hike.

The morning sun had fully risen by the time they walked back into base. Nalyiriz took the bag and headed straight for the unassuming hut that housed her infirmary, while El veered off to find Jackson or Chalmers.

He found them both huddled over steaming mugs of the local coffee analog, sitting in front of one of the camp's fires. Without a word, he walked up, grabbed one of the communal mugs from the table next to the fire, and filled it from the kettle sitting on the grate in front of Jackson. He felt, rather than saw, the two former CID men watching him with a bit of incredulity as he took his first, desperate gulp of the beverage.

It was hot enough to scorch his mouth and sear the taste buds on his tongue, but he didn't care. He felt the kick of caffeine and the sweetener that someone had added to the brew, and it was like someone had given him a shot of feel-good. He swallowed the drink, lowered his mug, and let out a full, weighty sigh of tired relief.

They'd made it.

"El, what the fuck? Don't tell me you just got back?" Jackson said, his pitch rising in disbelief.

Without looking in his direction, El took another sip of the drink and nodded.

"What. The. Fuck? You left at sundown! What the hell happened?"

"Long story," El muttered between sips. "Tell you in a sec."

"Did you get the shit?" Chalmers asked, leaning forward to look at his partner.

"Yup," El said. "Mostly."

"Mostly? The hell does that mean?"

Elroy lowered his mug and turned to look at Chalmers.

"Look, *sir*, it's been a long fucking night, and I'm tired as hell. I got the doc back safely, and she's already at work in the infirmary. I'm gonna tell you the whole story, but I am only gonna tell it once, and only once she's ready for us. So, if you don't mind, I'm going to finish my drink, wake the fuck up, and organize my thoughts, and then we'll all go in, and I'll answer all of your questions. Okay, *Mister Chalmers*?"

"El," Jackson said lowly, a note of warning in his tone.

El just looked at Jackson over the rim of his mug as he took another drink. On Jackson's far side, Chalmers snorted a laugh.

"Whatever, asshole," Chalmers said. "No sweat off my sack if you and the doc were out making a little bang-bang in the woods all night. Good for you, I guess!"

Jackson turned to his partner with a disgusted look, but El smiled tightly and turned his attention back to his mug. Chalmers could think what he wanted, and it was kinda funny to contemplate what Nalyiriz would say if she heard his crude language.

Though, honestly, it might not bother her at all. The SpinDogs' attitude towards sex was quite different than what he'd grown up with. But, regardless, she could certainly handle her own against a dick like Chalmers.

And the brew in the mug really was delicious. It deserved his full attention, which he gladly paid until he drained the last drop. He was thinking about pouring more, just to get Chalmers' goat, but Nalyiriz stepped out of the infirmary hut and walked over to the three of them. She moved crisply, as if she hadn't just been up for a full eighteen-hour day, which El thought was odd, considering how tired she'd obviously been on the trek back.

"Oh, good," she said as she approached. Her eyes met El's, as if not registering the presence of the other two men. "I was going to offer you a stimulant, but I see you have had some *ihey*. That will work just as well. I need the three of you to follow me, please."

With that, she walked back the way she'd come, her spine straight, her air one of perfect confidence that she would be obeyed.

And she was. El stood up and looked at Jackson, who threw up his hands as if to say he was at a loss and stood as well.

Chalmers, too, came to his feet. He smirked at El and winked, jerking his head in Nalyiriz's direction. El snorted and paid him no other mind as he followed the doc.

El, Jackson, and Chalmers followed the doc through the outer hut, with all of its shamanistic accoutrements, along a back hallway that appeared to be dug into the side of the hill. Once past the first clacking bone-bead curtain, the floors evened out and the whole place looked entirely modern—if temporary. Like any good field hospital, everything El saw looked like it could be broken down, packed up, and shipped out within a matter of hours. And knowing the way the SpinDog surface liaisons operated, that was probably the case.

Nalyiriz led them past several open treatment rooms and at least one office before she turned right and opened a more rugged-looking door than the ones they'd seen so far.

"This is my field laboratory," Nalyiriz said. "Please do not touch anything inside."

El followed her in, carefully keeping his hands and arms close to his body. The lab was also a prefabricated modular structure, but, unlike the treatment rooms, it looked like it would take at least a day to pack up, in part because of the wealth of delicate glassware spread over the two long tables. He had a sudden mental image of himself with bull's horns galloping through the place and tried to make himself as small and compact as possible as the other two men joined him.

With three of them, it was a tight squeeze, and a fair amount of shuffling commenced as they tried to arrange themselves into as small a footprint as possible.

Nalyiriz didn't seem to notice or care, however. She closed the door behind Chalmers and walked to the other side of the table. She had several instruments set up there. El recognized a simple microscope, but everything else might have been magician's props, for all he knew.

"The situation is not dire," Nalyiriz began, and El snapped his eyes to her face. She gestured at the bundles of herbs lined up in a neat row in front of her. "But it is not ideal. This is what we recovered from the apothecary's home last night. With this,

I can synthesize enough medicine to give Major Lee the initial doses she will need to ensure her health and that of her child."

"Initial doses?" Chalmers said. El may not have liked him, but he couldn't deny that the former CID investigator had a sharp mind and an ear for detail. "How much more will she need?"

"Over the course of her pregnancy? Perhaps five times this much, and therein lies the problem. I don't know what Sergeant Frazier has already told you—" She broke off and looked over at Elroy.

"Nothing," he said, shaking his head. "Figured I'd wait for you."

"Thank you." She gave him a tiny smile, and El tamped down hard on the sudden warmth he felt deep in his gut. "That is good," she went on, "it will make this a more coherent tale.

"Last night, when Sergeant Frazier and I went to meet my local source for these herbs, he failed to arrive. Because of the urgency of our need, we elected to follow the trail to his village to see if we could learn why. There we found my contact dead in his home and evidence of homicide."

"What evidence?" Chalmers leaned forward and put his hands on the table, his face sharp as he asked.

"Muzzle-shaped bruising behind the ear, ligature marks around the wrist," El said quietly. "Not exactly a homicide, though. More like a suicide under duress. Doc thinks the guy took poison in order to avoid the consequences of a bad deal, and when those other customers tried to force him to take an antidote, he OD'ed on that instead."

"What the fuck do you know about homicide investigations?" Chalmers turned his head to look past Jackson. He nearly spat the words. "You wouldn't know a 'ligature mark' if it bit you on the ass."

"Try again, asshole. I don't know shit about homicide investigations, true, but I've done a few interrogations in my time. People tend to twist if you tie the ropes too tight." Elroy kept his voice empty and level as he turned to stare, unblinking, at Chalmers. For just a moment, he let his mask drop and let his eyes show the true nature of what he'd become out in the bush. Chalmers blinked.

El smiled.

"Yes, that is more correct," Nalyiriz said, drawing the men's attention back to her. "Either way, it leaves us with a problem. I must have more of these herbs, and I do not have the wherewithal or the knowledge to get them."

"So, what are our options?" Jackson asked as he stepped forward to put his body between Chalmers and El, blocking their line of sight to each other. El folded his arms, still smiling. Jackson was a better partner than Chalmers deserved.

"I can see only one viable course," Nalyiriz said. "I must synthesize this compound and return to Mara as soon as possible. I will depart during tonight's launch window. In the meantime, one of you must acquire more herbs."

"And how do you suggest we do that?" Chalmers asked.

Nalyiriz turned her eyes from him to Elroy. "I believe Sergeant Frazier knows a way."

El felt, more than saw, Jackson and Chalmers swivel to look at him. He kept his eyes on Nalyiriz's face.

"The customers?"

She nodded. "They were not expecting his death. They have taken nothing from his house. I suspect they will return tonight to rectify that error. If they are, as I suspect, procurers for one of the planetary satraps, nearly everything in that house will have value to them and their masters further up the line in the network. If you follow that network, there is a good chance you will find more of this herb. The satrap forces collect *everything*."

"Why?" Chalmers asked.

"Does it matter?" Nalyiriz said, looking at him. Her face and voice remained calm, but El thought he could see the tiniest bit of temper showing in her eyes. Was he beginning to see behind that mask she wore? "I cannot think of another way to get what Major Lee's child—and indeed, all of our children—will need. If any of you have another option, I am listening."

"No," El said, uncrossing his arms. "You're right, Doc. This is the best option, and I'm the guy to do it."

"You'll be totally isolated," Jackson said quietly. "The best we have are short range, line-of-sight comms. I don't even know if they'll be able to passively track you from the habitat."

"They will, but not from the spins," Nalyiriz put in. "I have spoken with Colonel Murphy. Mara is en route to Outpost, the covert station that precedes R'Bak in its orbit around Shex. She will provide mission following and command and control from there. She may not be able to communicate with Sergeant Frazier directly, but she will certainly be in touch with you two here at the base."

"And we can stay in touch with Frazier," Jackson said.

"If so, then great," El said. "If not, then it won't be my first trip into Indian Country. Anybody got anything else?"

He looked from Jackson to Chalmers, who shook his head. Then he turned back to Nalyiriz, who smiled at him again.

"I think we have a plan," she said.

"Sounds good." El eased past the other two men and opened the door. "It's been a long night. You guys figure out the command and control with Mara. I'm going to rack out for a few hours so I'll be ready to go whenever you say, Doc."

"As soon as the sun sets, I would imagine."

"Sundown," El said. "Transition time. Perfect."

The nice thing about *ihey* was that when you wanted to sleep, you could sleep. After the conversation in the lab, El headed back to his quarters, grabbed a quick shower to wash off the film of night ops, then headed for his bunk. He closed his eyes.

He opened them about six hours later, according to his watch. It was annoying as hell converting from his watch's twenty-four-hour day to the local eighteen-hour one, but he'd eventually figured it out.

After a meal, a workout, and another shower, he went to find Nalyiriz, who was still working in her lab.

"You haven't slept?" he asked as he walked in the door.

"I have been busy," she said, not looking up from her microscope.

"Humans need sleep. Don't make a mistake because you are tired."

She looked up then and gave him a small smile. "I am fine," she said. "I am well supplied with stimulants and this work is well known to me. Did you need something? It is too early for you to leave yet."

"Not for a few more hours," El agreed, coming closer. "And I didn't mean to disturb you. I can come back if you want, but I wanted to talk to you about what it is I'm supposed to be looking for. What is this herb?"

"The locals call it *tra.* At least, the ones here in the polar region do; it has other names. It used to be more commonly available, but it has recently become difficult to find." She pointed to the table in front of her. Earlier, she'd had more than twenty hand-sized bundles arrayed in front of her workstation. Now, it seemed she was down to four. He glanced at her for permission and picked one up.

The plant itself was nothing spectacular. It had a short red stem and between three and seven wide, oblong dark green leaves. It honestly looked a little bit like a weed he used to have to dig out of his mama's yard when he was a boy. The big difference was the root, which was bright red and quite long and thick; one plant was nearly the length of his forearm. It didn't have a lot of offshoots, but it looked like it would be a bitch to dig up.

Hopefully, the apothecary's customers would lead him to some that had already been collected. He wasn't sure what he'd do if he suddenly had to dig up some local's weed garden. Well, that wasn't entirely true. He knew what he'd do. For Mara, he'd get down on his goddamn hands and knees and start digging. But he wouldn't like it.

"So, this is it, huh?" he said, turning the bundle over and setting it back on the table. "Doesn't look like much. How many more bundles like that do you need?"

"If you are getting bundles that size, perhaps a hundred, though more would be welcome. But I had an idea while you were sleeping," she said, stepping back from the table. She waved for him to follow her and went to a cabinet on the far side of the room. She unlocked it with a key and removed a tiny vial that held a bright, ultramarine blue powder.

"This," she said handing him the vial, "is the compound that I have synthesized so far. The color comes from several of the reagents we use. *Tra* really only has this one use, so I think there is a good chance you may encounter it in this refined form. If you can, then that is preferable to the raw herbs. A single, eh, kilogram of this powder will meet our needs for a year."

"I can't take this with me, can I?" El asked. He squinted at the vial and held it up to the light, angling it so he could study the distinctive color.

"No, I must take that to Mara. But very few other medicinals have this vibrant blue color. It should be easy to recognize."

"So, you say," he muttered. He handed the vial back to her and nodded. "All right. Either a kilo of the blue powder, or boo-coo plant bundles. Got it. Anything else?"

"Yes, actually. I mentioned before that it would be helpful to know if my hypothesis regarding the collection of these herbs was correct. I understood from our previous conversations that you have some experience in gathering intelligence. Please find out all you can about what, exactly, is being collected and by whom. This intel may prove vital to future operations as we draw nearer to the Searing."

El nodded. "I'll find out what I can."

"Thank you. Please take care of yourself, Sergeant. Mara needs you to return successfully, and she needs you to return whole."

"You're being awful formal, Doc. You called me El, before." He wasn't sure why he said that, but the words tumbled out before he could stop them.

She smiled again, and this one actually reached her eyes.

Fuck, she's pretty.

"El, then," she said. "Be careful and be smart. I shall see you when you return."

"Count on it, Doc," he said. He sketched a quick salute in her direction and turned for the door before his mouth could get him into any more trouble. As he stepped across the threshold, he heard her voice one last time.

"I *am* counting on it. We all are."

Chapter Seven

From the corner of her eye, Mara Lee watched Murphy as he, in turn, watched Nalyiriz's report on his computer monitor. He was studying the recording closely, but his focus wasn't that of a scrutinizing analyst or a stooping hawk. Rather than his typical incisive attention, he was wholly absorbed in what was emerging on the screen and from the speakers. He was all at once more engaged than usual, but also more relaxed, more like—

More like someone who listens to a voicemail or a video from back home while they're stationed in The Suck.

She looked from Nalyiriz's face to Murphy's and almost started. Really? *Them?* She refrained from biting her lip: *damn, if those two ever—*

She shifted her eyes back to the screen just before Murphy turned back toward her; another instant and he would have noticed her steady gaze.

Fortunately, she didn't need to pretend that she was staring at the pixelated version of Nalyiriz's face; whatever tension or carefully constructed expressions she saw there were probably the best way to determine just how risky the situation on R'Bak had become. Mara stabbed a finger at the display to replay the recording, determined to once again absorb all the data contained in the burst packet from the surface. The message was already several hours old, having taken that long to transit to their current location. Mara felt frustration grinding along the edges of her bones. She was too far away! They'd already wasted so much time.

"According to what she reported and when, the SpinDog flight controllers project she'll be back tonight," Murphy said when the recording finished. His face remained as stoic as ever, with no hint as to his thought process.

"Unless we send a burst right now to stop her."

"Why would we do that?" Murphy asked, raising his eyebrows slightly as he turned to look at Mara. She had pulled a chair around to his side of the desk in order that they might view the encrypted data message together.

"Sir," Mara said in a low tone. "You heard what she said; El's going to go on this mission to track down these smuggler/procurer guys to get the stuff that we need—that the Spin babies *all* need. He's going to be completely isolated. We have to give him something. Some kind of top cover. Some command and control at the very least. If nothing else, it will continue to demonstrate our commitment to our allies."

"As it happens, I think you're right, Bruce," Murphy said. "The clandestine nature of the mission means we can't send a full package after him, but we can certainly provide comms and smooth the way, as it were."

"Great," she said, sitting back in her chair, her smile wide with relief. "I was afraid you'd fight me on this. I'll send that burst to tell doc to stay put, and I'll be on the next shuttle—"

"Hold on," Murphy said. "Mara, you can't go to the surface."

"What?" she asked, sitting up straight again. She felt her smile vanish and her eyebrows furrow. "Why the fuck not? You just said—"

"That we need to support Sergeant Frazier's op. And I meant it. But *you* can't go to the surface, and you know very well why."

Mara stared at him, feeling the muscles in her jaw clench. She inhaled slowly through her nose and willed her raging emotions to calm before she spoke again.

"My baby," she said.

"Yes," Murphy said. "Your baby. Ozendi's family has made it clear that they consider the baby—and by extension, you—a part of their family. To send you to the surface would mean removing you from their control."

"They don't control—!" she spat, but cut herself off when he threw up a hand.

"It would signal, to them, that we were removing you and the child from their control," Murphy went on, the softness of his tone belying the hard edge of his stare. "Which is not a signal we can afford to send right now. You are the bridge between us, Mara. You *have* to be the bridge."

She inhaled again slowly, forcing herself to fill her lungs and slow down her racing mind. "So what do you propose?" she asked.

"Chalmers and Jackson are in place. They have multiple resources that can provide flexible support to Sergeant Frazier. And I do think you're the best asset to provide command and control, just not from the surface."

"Then where—?" Mara broke off as Murphy's plan suddenly became clear in her head. "The Outpost."

Murphy nodded. "As a covert observation and staging site, it has enough passive monitoring capabilities to track El over the whole planet. And, since it's concealed among the other rocks near the leading trojan point of R'Bak's orbit, Outpost has constant line of sight to the facing half of the surface—and Dornaani microsats that can show, or relay to, the other half. The comm protocols are extremely strict, but you should be fine."

"All right," she said. And then, because she had gotten to know Murphy well enough to realize he never did anything for one reason alone. "What else?"

Murphy smiled. "And you being there sends a rather different message to the new matriarch of your adoptive family."

"That we trust them to take care of me on Outpost?"

"Hmm…yes. That, too. Think on it. I'm sure you'll figure the rest out as you go. For now, go pack."

"I'm already packed," Mara said. She let herself smile a little and pushed to her feet. "But I recognize a dismissal when I hear one. Time to go to work."

"Indeed. Good luck, Major."

"Thank you, sir."

Murphy heard low voices in the corridor outside as he turned off the monitor. He had heard two sets of muted footfalls—Mara's receding, another approaching—converge and stop just as the whispering began. Then Mara's lighter footsteps continued away from the CP…just before knuckles rapped on the coaming of its entry.

Murphy smiled to himself. "C'mon in, Lieutenant."

Vat—who never went by his actual name, Victor Allen Thomas—turned the corner. He glanced suspiciously into the corners of the small compartment. "You have a snoop scope out here? Or just really good ears?"

"Neither, but I figured you might arrive early."

The weapons merchant turned liaison/conman took the chair Murphy indicated. "And what led you to that conclusion. Sir?"

Murphy allowed himself another small smile. "Because I knew you'd want to 'bump into' Major Lee as she left, see what the temperature in this room would be like."

"You mean whether the CO's mood was as cold as ice or hot as hell?"

"Pretty much." Murphy leaned back and considered Vat for a moment. "You really do like her, don't you?"

"Who? Mar—uh, Major Lee? Yeah." Suspicion crept into Vat's voice and eyes. "Why?"

"Because she and her child are going to need your help."

"I'm not much of a hand around a nursery."

"No, but you've got extraordinary talents when it comes to getting accepted by the locals and learning essential information."

"Oh. So this is about finding the medicinals she needs for her pregnancy."

"You heard about that?" Murphy smirked at his own question. "Wait: why did I even ask? It would be freakish if you *didn't* hear about everything that goes on in this tin can. But most immediately, yes, it's about gathering information that might help us get those compounds. And then later, key pieces of intel we need in order to deal with the Harvesters."

Vat looked sideways at Murphy. "That's new. Not sure how I feel about that. Sounds risky."

Murphy sighed. "Vat, you still seem to think that you can negotiate your duty and orders. Wake up and smell the coffee: circumstances don't permit it, and, even if they did, I wouldn't permit it. Yes, you have special skills, but you're still a soldier just like everyone else. And if anyone thought that you were getting special treatment, they'd be right to call for me to step down—voluntarily or not."

"Not like there aren't plenty who'd like to see that already. Sir."

"Not like I can afford to care…although we *will* be coming back to that topic. But for now, my job is to help get you situated on R'Bak Island and as close as possible to what the locals call 'Downport.'"

"Me and who else?

Murphy shook his head. "Just you."

Vat rubbed his chin. "Okay, so you already anticipated and answered my first question: 'why me?' But now I've gotta ask, 'Why *only* me?'"

"Because you excel at travelling, working, and *living* under the radar. We can't afford to send in operatives who might give away their real identities because that could reveal our existence to the Kulsians and their flunkies."

Vat mulled it over. "I'll have to stay in the shadows, at least at first. Until I can get my bearings, learn the local dialects, figure out what sort of habits or behaviors would mark me as a total outsider, not just a traveler."

Murphy nodded. "That's why we're going to try to slip you into Downport City on the sly. According to all reports, it's large enough that you can remain faceless while you learn the culture there. It's also the planet's main destination: lots of merchants and salvagers arriving from every corner of R'Bak."

Vat nodded slowly, then smiled. "You're not fooling me, Colonel. Oh, I know you've got a practical, bloodless reason for everything you do and every order you give. But this assignment seems to be a little more personal than that."

Murphy managed not to show any surprise. "I don't know what you mean."

"Yes, you do. Because this isn't the first time you've tried to make life easier for me. Like when you learned that one of the local ladies had become infatuated with me. You got me out of there with a reassignment within the week."

"You were needed elsewhere."

"Actually, I wasn't. I figured you were just being a creep, moving me away from the guys in my team. But then I spoke to Mara. Seems as though despite your Tin Man act, you actually do have a heart."

"Vat, I—"

"Look, no more dancing, Colonel Murphy. The facts are pretty straight-forward: as a gay man in a company of other men, most of whom disappeared from Earth no later than 1972, I've had to walk a pretty careful line. More than half of the guys would shun me if they knew; more than a few would probably gut me like a fish. The only ones who are half-way human about it are the others who were on that helicopter that went into the drink just outside of Mogadishu." He sat back. "And here you are, just happening to send me on an urgent mission to a place where I'm going to have to work in the shadows. Where I'm going to be in contact with all the elements of R'Bakuun society that, just like on Earth, all run together because they're doing something illegal or taboo."

He smirked. "And don't give me the innocent and ignorant look. You know damn well why gays always knew more about drug dealers, junkies, bookies, loan sharks, and black marketeers; it's because we were all shadow dwellers. By necessity." He smiled. "So that's the other reason you're sending me to the one place that maybe, just maybe, I can find some like-minded people. Where I might find a group in which I *don't* have to play at being someone I'm not for every hour of every fucking day." He smiled crookedly. "Even though I have to pretend I'm a local while I'm doing it."

Murphy waved off Vat's disconcertingly accurate insight. "Getting you into Downport isn't for your personal gratification. It simply gives you a convincing cover story, a personal reason for why you would travel a long way to get there."

Vat frowned. "What do you mean?"

"Well, it's just like you said. Even though homosexuals are not actively persecuted on R'Bak, and just because most of the locals don't have the crazy puritanical notions we inherited on Earth, being gay is still considered taboo, something to be hidden. It's like the Army you first served in: 'don't ask; don't tell.' So, actually, your sexual orientation works as part of your cover, explains why you drifted into a career as a black market broker: you were already living in the shadows, anyhow."

But Vat was smiling again. "Sorry, Colonel, but you're not fooling me with that 'plausible deniability' bullshit. Sure, it's logical, but I know a con job when I hear one—and you're not really that good at selling it. So I guess Lee was right; you actually *are* an okay guy."

Murphy almost smiled. "You spread that around the unit, and you'll find I've still got plenty of airlocks from which to eject your sorry ass."

"But you can't," Vat smiled, preening. "Because you need me to get information about—?"

Murphy smiled back. "About where and how the Kulsians operate on R'Bak. Particularly around Downport. Details that only locals would know."

Vat's face became serious. "Don't the SpinDogs have any useful intel on that?"

Murphy shook his head. "Not much. For them, survival has always meant avoiding any place where Kulsians might show up. Besides, we can't really trust the SpinDogs yet."

"Not even Mara's new family, the, uh, the Otlethes?"

Murphy shrugged. "It's still difficult to know which ones we can trust and how far. Besides, with the Hardliners gone and a post-purge power vacuum to fill, the SpinDogs have a lot of their own crap going on." Murphy was pretty sure his smile was rueful. "Just like we do."

"And what crap would that be, sir?"

"Don't play coy, Vat; it's not one of your better skills. You know exactly what crap I'm talking about: that the only thing a hundred problematic soldiers from the latter half of the Twentieth Century can agree on is that they hate my guts."

Vat smiled. "Sir, it wouldn't be the military if everyone *didn't* hate the CO."

"Again, stop being coy. I know that. And you know I do. I'm talking about the resentment that's burning a hole in their bellies: that they had no say in being here, no say in continuing to serve and fight, and no real information about when—or even if—they're ever going to get back home. Which isn't really home anymore."

Vat rolled his eyes theatrically. "Oh, *that* crap. Sir, let me put you straight. The situation isn't as straightforward as you're assuming. Hell, the bitching here is…well, it's not like any bitching I've ever heard before. Probably because this isn't like any situation any of us have ever been in. I mean, yeah, rank and file is never clued in on the Big Picture. But here, none of us can see much further than what's right in front of our noses. Sure, there's that little song and dance about how Earth has changed and who it's fighting, but we don't really know why, except that aliens invaded and that they're really, really bad people."

Murphy shrugged. "One of the Terrans who briefed me—'Nephew,' I think—referred to the Ktor as 'A cross between Nietzsche and Caligula. On steroids.'"

Vat shook his head. "But that's just more vague BS. What we want to know is this: what happens when we're done on R'Bak—if we ever are? Which raises a further problem: what if this is the only home for us, now? I mean, if Earth's changed as much as they told you, and some big shots there want us dead, then maybe we won't be safe anyplace else. And that would really suck."

Murphy nodded. "All perfectly good reasons to hate me."

Vat shook his head. "Not that simple, sir. Yeah, at first, a lot of us were sure you were just a shill for the two guys who dumped us here. But when the Hardliners almost offed you, people started realizing that maybe you were in the same situation we were. Except that you were the one left in charge of this hot mess.

"But you know how it is; if something hurts a soldier, he wants—he's *trained*—to hurt it back. Or at least hate it. So the guys were always gonna find someone or something *real* to blame. Not a pair of Terrans who ghosted us, or aliens we've never seen: it was going to be *you*."

Murphy tried not to sound exasperated. "So no one is stopping to think through who's really to blame."

Vat smiled indulgently. "Colonel, you're not too bad an officer, but you'd have made a lousy salesman."

"Or con-artist."

Vat's smiled broadened. "True. But I'm both, so here's the bottom line. For most people, most of the time, their reactions don't come from what they think, but what they *feel*. And although every Lost Soldier's brain is telling him that you're in the same Suck that he is, his guts want—*need*—someone to blame.

"A commanding officer is *always* going to be the default target for bitch-fest. But in this case, that's not entirely satisfying either, because who's the actual CO? Nuncle and Nephew? Guys who *also* got the short end of a stick because they dared to keep us from getting swept under the rug—or into a star?" Vat shook his head. "When the question of who to blame gets that complicated, most people—soldiers and civilians alike—just figure, '*ah, fuck it*,' and hate whoever's closest." He frowned. "Nasty situation. I don't really see a way out of it."

Murphy shrugged. "I didn't expect you would. I just wanted to take the temperature of the company. At least it's no worse than I thought."

Vat's smile was rueful. "Trying to prevent a palace revolt?"

"Actually, I'm just trying to figure out the best way forward."

"For victory?"

"For survival. And to do that, it's necessary to identify what we need as a group so that we don't tear ourselves apart."

Vat shook his head. "Yeah, well, good luck with that."

"Thanks," Murphy replied. "Now, since I don't want you to get bored, there's one other intel item you need to be watching for when you get to Downport."

"Just one?" Vat asked sardonically.

Murphy did not smile. "Yes, just one. But it's a big one."

"How big?"

"As big as R'Bak itself. We've got to learn about other regions, other continents, other climates, and if the Harvesters handle those areas differently or not. Because the revolt we've started in the Hamain has two possible endgames; it stays regional and dies, or it becomes global and thrives."

"Ooo," breathed Vat as he rose. "Poetic."

Murphy waved him out. "In case you want to look at what little data we have on the other regions, just let Pete know. You have full access."

Vat nodded, stopped halfway out the door. "And about my new assignment in Downport…thanks, Colonel."

"Thank me if you survive," Murphy grumbled irritably. But, once Vat's footsteps were sufficiently distant, he added silently, *You're welcome. I just wish I could have done more.*

Chapter Eight

As R'Bak's K-class star sank down lower through the forest canopy, El situated himself comfortably at the edge of the tree line that ran alongside the apothecary's village.

After his conversation with the doc, he'd found Jackson talking to a sunspotted native he didn't recognize. El waited until they finished, then told Jackson he was leaving. Jackson made sure he had one of the line-of-sight short-range handheld comm sets in his pack, along with his usual food, water, and ammo.

"I don't know that I'll be in range to use this," El said.

"Me neither," Jackson said. "But better to have it and not need it, right?" El couldn't argue with that, so into the pack it had gone. He departed just as the sun was leaning toward the western sky.

And now here he was.

El's objective in arriving early had been to find a solid hiding spot with a good view of the house, preferably somewhere he wouldn't be sitting awkwardly for hours. He ended up finding a seat in the spreading branches of a tree. If he let his feet dangle, they would be five feet above the ground, but he could see the front door of the house, as well as a pathway from the center of the village.

Shortly after he was in place, he watched one of the village women approach the apothecary's door. She called out and scratched on the doorframe, in the local way to announce her presence. When she got no answer from the dead man inside, she pushed the door open and stepped tentatively across the threshold.

The scream came approximately thirty seconds later.

After that, a lot of activity ensued, and El was glad he'd elected to arrive early.

The woman ran from the apothecary's hut into the center of the village, wailing out her discovery as she went. El had studied the local dialect, but his command wasn't good enough to fully understand her words. Not that it mattered. Her meaning was clear enough. She'd discovered the apothecary's dead body.

She returned a few minutes later, leading a gaggle of people that swelled as it went. At its head, the weeping woman held onto the arm of an older man wearing a necklace that looked like a badge of rank. The village headman, perhaps? Someone of authority, anyway. El watched as he spoke calming words to the woman and turned to give orders to the group of people who followed them.

Eventually, six men entered the house and soon emerged carrying the apothecary's corpse. An older woman with large decorative beads braided into her iron-gray hair accompanied them as they walked toward the center of the town. Most of the crowd drifted after them. The headman pulled the weeping woman into an embrace and spoke over her dark head as she pressed it into his chest. Another figure—he couldn't see clearly enough to identify either sex or distinctive dress—stepped behind the headman and pulled the door of the hut closed.

The headman bent and murmured something to the weeping woman—his daughter, maybe? They moved slowly toward the center of town. A few minutes later, the apothecary's home was deserted once again. As the sun slipped below the horizon and the dark of night rose from the forest floor, El noticed that firelight blazed all around and through the windows of one of the large buildings in the center of town. Was the older woman there, washing and preparing the apothecary's body? El remembered his mama doing the same for a deceased auntie or two. Was caring for the dead still considered woman's work, even here across the stars, billions of miles from home?

A low rumble interrupted his musings. El looked through his rifle scope. There was just enough light for him to see a dust cloud rising from the trees at the far end of the village. As he lowered the rifle, El noticed that one of the apothecary's neighbors had stepped out of her hut and was looking in that direction. He couldn't see her face, but she turned and called out sharply with what sounded like fear in her voice. Two children, not quite teenagers, he thought, responded at a run. The woman hustled them inside with quick words and hurried gestures and shut the door firmly in their wake. El imagined her turning a deadbolt, or, more likely, dropping a crossbar into place.

Like his mother had done when the neighborhood gangs started acting the fool.

Interesting. If that dust cloud was caused by the apothecary's customers, did the village know about his business arrangements? And if they did, did they know about Nalyiriz? Could she be in danger?

"Not your problem, El," he breathed to himself as he raised the rifle again to peer through the scope. "Focus on the mission." He thought maybe he could get a look at whatever vehicle the customers were using…but no, they were still obscured by the rising darkness under the trees and the shape of the village itself as it followed the little stream.

Another glance at the parts of the village he could see showed quite a few people were abandoning their outdoor tasks in favor of more pressing matters inside their homes. So, the apothecary's neighbor wasn't the only one wary of their visitors. Just who *were* these guys, anyway?

Whoever they were, he didn't have much longer to wait to find out. Within minutes two vehicles swung around the corner, stark white lights mounted atop their cabs, the bright beams illuminating the central lane through the village.

The lights from the second one allowed El to get a good look at the first. The vehicle looked a lot like the "trucks" he'd used at the training base with Mara. That made sense, since those trucks had been, as far as he knew, designs copied from machines in use by the native R'Baku. Or, at least, in use by the native R'Baku who could afford things like motorized vehicles. Which, as it turned out, really only meant those working for one of the satraps. Another point in favor of Nalyiriz's theory. It looked like the late apothecary had sold to everyone. What an enterprising guy.

The trucks didn't seem to be in any particular hurry. They took their time, engines growling as they crawled through the town. At one point, they forded the little stream, their tires leaving big, muddy gouges in the bank as they crossed to the side path leading up to the apothecary's house. El stayed put, peering out through the trees, watching the scenario unfold.

Waiting for his moment.

The trucks rumbled to a stop, one a few seconds behind the other. A hatch clanged open near the top of the first one. The lights stayed on, focused on the apothecary's hut and throwing the area around it—including El's hiding spot—into a deep, knife-edged shadow. He lifted his scope again as a tall, lanky fellow climbed out. He wasn't dressed like the villagers, instead wearing something that looked like dark-colored fatigues cut off at the knee and shoulders. He carried some kind of rifle slung across his back, muzzle down.

El watched as the man walked to the other truck and banged on it with his fist. The second truck's hatch opened in response, and El could just see the head and shoulders of the occupant. They talked for a moment, then the second truck's driver ducked back into his vehicle. A moment later, the engine cut off, and a sudden silence filled the space, broken only by the sound of the second driver getting out of his truck and joining the first before walking up to the apothecary's house.

El had been in place long enough that he'd been hearing the sounds of small wildlife all evening, but now? Nothing.

He smiled at the thought that he wasn't the only one hiding and watching to see how this would work out.

Warm, yellow light flared within the house, shining through the single window in the back of the hut. It wasn't strong enough to make much difference against the truck headlights at the front of the hut, but El could still see that the apothecary's customers had left the door partially open—again. For just a second, he wondered why that was such a trend with them. His mother would have said they were raised in a barn.

He was contemplating slipping down from his perch when movement from the village caught his eye. He lifted his rifle and looked through the scope.

It was the village headman. He stepped out of the large, well-lit building in the center of town and walked toward the apothecary's hut. El caught a glimpse of his face before he stepped out of the light. The man looked determined, angry.

He looked like he was gunning for a fight.

A man fell into step behind the headman. Then another. Eventually, El counted eighteen men and four women walking up to the apothecary's hut and standing between the trucks and the door.

The headman called out, and El thought he recognized the word for trespass. As El lowered his rifle, the first customer reappeared, stepping slowly through the open door. He took up a wide, aggressive stance: feet apart, arms crossed over his chest. He said something too quietly for El to hear, but a ripple of angry muttering went through the village men in response. The headman spoke again, his voice cracking sharply through the night. He stabbed one finger at the hut, then whipped his hand to the side to include the whole village in his gesture.

The customer responded and uncrossed his arms, letting his hands drift down to his belt.

This was El's moment. Now, while they were distracted by the confrontation. He slung his rifle across his chest so that it would make as little noise as possible and carefully placed his hands and feet to climb slowly out of the tree. He dropped the last few feet to the ground and began creeping through the shadowy tree line toward the side of the hut where the trucks were parked. As he moved, El kept one eye on the growing confrontation, even as he maneuvered to avoid the spill of light through the back window.

Voices rose in volume and pitch, their anger palpable. El rounded the far corner of the hut and took a moment to look toward the open doorway. The headman and the customer stood nearly nose to nose, anger clear on both of their faces. He was finally close enough to hear their words, even if he didn't understand all of them.

"Ertro was ours!" the headman said, his words hissing through clenched teeth. "He has family here, *dainost!* My niece carries his child! Ertro's home and *rurshekht* belong to her!"

"Your *vithor* niece does not concern me," the customer said, his words cold and iron-hard. "Ertro owed the *busaphren.* That debt must be paid."

"We can pay—"

The customer cut him off with a slash of his hand. "With what? Furs? Worthless chits written on leaf-paper? You have nothing. Nothing except what is in this hut." He turned, as if to go back into the apothecary's house.

"But without the *rurshekht*, how will we—?"

"Enough!" the customer snarled. He turned, and before El or anyone else could do anything, he drew a knife from his belt and drove it deep into the headman's neck, just where it met the shoulder.

Blood fountained, pulsing forth from the wound. The customer spat out a short, ugly word that was probably some local equivalent to *fuck* and sidestepped. But he was too late to avoid the dark, iron-heavy spray of blood. The headman himself looked shocked, surprise widening his eyes and mouth for a moment as he staggered toward his murderer, before slumping forward to his knees, then his face.

Silence reigned for a single heartbeat.

Then, for the second time that night, a woman's wordless scream split the air.

"Hold!" It was the second customer. He held a weapon to his shoulder as he stepped out of the dead apothecary's home. The weapon wasn't a rifle; that El could tell. It looked something like a shotgun, but it had a large, bulbous tank where the stock should have been. *A flamethrower?*

Whatever it was, the sight of it sent a murmur of fear rippling through the shocked, angry crowd. None of the villagers moved, neither toward their dead headman nor toward the first customer, who was busily engaged in cursing and rubbing his hands over his face to try to clean off the blood.

"Go back to your homes, now," the second customer said, his voice so low El could barely pick out the words. "Or this hut will not be the only one I *desfirab.*"

No one moved.

The second customer lowered his face to the tank, as if sighting along the barrel of the strange weapon.

Someone whimpered near the back of the group, and the crowd broke. To a man, they turned and ran, reaching out to help each other along, pushing the women and younger men ahead and looking fearfully back at the two interlopers who had brought so much death with them.

As they ran, the second customer activated his weapon. A powerful spray, violently orange in the harsh light from the trucks, shot forth, arcing toward the fleeing villagers. It landed on the calves of one of the older men. He screamed and crashed to the ground. El could smell a sickly-sweet smell as the strange liquid began to dissolve the unfortunate villager's tissues. The man writhed in agony, and the first customer let out a laugh.

"Your aim is true," he said, clapping the second man on the back. The two of them walked unhurriedly toward the victim as the other villagers continued to run amid cries of terror and grief. They stopped next to the thrashing man and stared down at him, unbothered by his soul-rending screams as his entire leg deliquesced, and his flesh began to melt away from his pelvis and hips.

El inhaled slowly and stepped out from the shadowy corner where he was waiting. While the customers stood over their victim, El slipped across the hut's front yard to the open door of one of the trucks. He held his rifle close and pulled himself through the cramped entry into the cab, careful to make as little noise as possible.

Inside, he found a pair of seats, several papers and documents, and an instrument panel that showed the usual data for a ground vehicle. What he didn't expect to find was that the truck apparently had an intercom setup between the drivers, because he could hear the customers' conversation issuing through speakers high on the dash.

"Want to do more?" the first customer asked as soon as the man's screams died off. "That *morraw* really scared 'em, hey?" Even through the speakers, El could hear laughter in the man's tone.

"Don't want to waste it," the second man said. "Shame, though. It was fun to see them run."

"Next time. Let's get the *vith's* stuff loaded up and get out of here. With last night's delay, our time is limited."

"Of course."

El risked a glance out the windshield and saw the backs of the two men disappearing once more inside the hut. He let out a breath and took the moment to look around inside the truck. Like the one he'd driven in the past, the driver's compartment opened to the cargo bay via a narrow hatch in the back wall. It was a strain, but his familiarity with the basic design helped him maneuver his way past the vehicle's controls and squeeze through the opening, ducking his head to keep from hitting the roof.

It was dark in the cargo bay, and El didn't dare risk a light. He reached out behind him until he found the wall separating cargo from driver and followed the uneven metal surface until he found the sidewall. He tried to step in that direction, but he immediately kicked something large, heavy, and unevenly shaped. Further blind exploration with his hands and feet revealed it to be something like a large sack filled with multiple small, hard objects. In his mind, he imagined an oversized gunny sack filled three-quarters full with potatoes, so there was enough slack in the bag to let it slump rather than stand up straight.

He continued to feel his way around the compartment, listening to the customers' conversation as they hauled baskets and boxes out of the apothecary's home and loaded the other truck. El spared a moment of thanks to God or luck or whatever made them decide to start with the other vehicle—though it might just have been because it was closer to the front door. Or the fact that this truck was already half-full of crates and more of the oversized bags.

Whatever the reason, El didn't delude himself that he had much time. He worked back to the front of the compartment and pushed and shoved at that first "potato sack" until he was able to create a space large enough for him to crouch beside the driver's compartment wall. He settled himself inside, hoping against hope that he wouldn't need to keep his body folded in this uncomfortably small space for too long. He wasn't as bad about small spaces as some guys he'd known, but it was never fun to lose feeling in your legs.

He waited, crouched in the dark, listening as the two men talked about something that sounded like a game of some kind. Occasionally, their conversation was interrupted by the sounds of shattering glass, or the static pops and hisses of a weakening transmission. Eventually, though, he heard an exchange that sent a jolt through his system.

"Ugh, we're full." It was the voice of the first customer, and a series of grunts followed. "See," he said a few minutes later. "I can't get the hatch closed. I don't want to leave this, though. It's worth a fair bit, and the *busaphren* can use all of it."

"Let's check my vehicle," the second man said. "I probably have some room if we rearrange those crates. Then we should get moving. The moon's coming up."

El drew in a deep breath and let it out slowly, then focused on being as small and still as possible, on making himself invisible, incorporeal, one with the darkness.

He heard the heavy *ka-thunk* of the back cargo doors being unlatched. Metal squealed on metal as they opened, and a tendril of fresh air whispered by his cheek.

There was another loud *thunk* as they dropped something heavy onto the floor of the cargo compartment. El felt the vehicle's suspension flex beneath him, then held his breath when the doors didn't immediately close.

Slowly, so slowly, he began to ease his rifle around…

"Last one," the first customer said, his voice tinny as it came out of the speakers—which let out a squeal of feedback in protest. There was another loud sound, another bounce from the suspension, and they slammed the cargo doors closed.

El let his breath ease out between his lips. He missed what else the two men said to each other; he was busy trying to calm the pounding rush of blood in his ears. A moment later, the second customer climbed in through the hatch to the driver's seat, pulled the levers to fire up the engine, and they slowly rolled out of the village, leaving nothing but cooling bodies and the apothecary's violated home in their wake.

El didn't want to let them get too far down the road, but his options were limited. On the one hand, he was in a terrific position to see where these two had planned to take the apothecary's goods. If Nalyiriz hadn't taken the *tra* first, El figured it would have been loaded up as well. He also figured his chances of finding more down the line were not too bad.

On the other hand, he was hidden in a truck with a proven killer and another one in the convoy. Not the most secure position he'd ever been in. And it would only get worse the longer he waited to act. He didn't have much time.

Still, dying due to a crash in the mountains would nonetheless mean mission failure. So, he waited until they had wound down the narrow switchback trails and the road evened out, widening as it crossed a level valley. The sun was just starting to stream between the peaks to the east, glinting through the viewport and painting a thin rectangle on the floor of the cargo compartment as it shone through the hatch.

Time to earn the pay I don't get anymore, El thought as he drew his combat knife slowly, silently, from its sheath.

Chapter Nine

El was in the act of positioning himself near the hatch into the cab when the driver announced, "Beautiful sunrise."

El froze, knife raised.

"Yes," the other driver said, his voice crackling through the speakers. "How are you feeling?"

"I am well. Not tired yet."

"Want some *ihey*?"

"Perhaps another hour or so. When the sun rises fully we can stop for a short break then." El's driver shifted in his seat, rolling his shoulders around.

"If you like. We've got perhaps…oh…three more hours after that—"

El never heard the rest of what the other driver was saying. Instead, he whipped himself through the small opening and plunged his combat knife deep into the joint between his driver's neck and shoulder. The man let out a gurgled cry and hunched, jerking the control levers and causing the truck to veer abruptly to the right. El let go of the knife and smashed the man in the face with his elbow once, twice, while the vehicle continued to careen wildly. El was thrown to the side, and his next elbow strike went wide, hitting the hilt of his knife and knocking it askew. A bright, hot fountain of blood pulsed forth, spraying the inside of the compartment and blinding El as it shot into his eyes. He reached out, desperate to grab onto anything in reach. His fingers closed around a cylindrical shape and he pulled, trying to get his center of gravity back.

The truck shuddered and slammed to a stop. El and everything in it was thrown forward, crashing against the front dash panel before the vehicle tipped inexorably to the left.

The world cartwheeled end-over-end. El let go of the lever and hunched, trying to protect his neck and head as he tumbled. Something heavy slammed into his back, the top of his head, his shoulder, his hip.

Then, suddenly, it was over, save for a high, incessant ringing like a distant scream in his ears.

El pulled in a ragged breath and forced his eyelids to open, despite the blood sticking to his lashes. Was he hurt? His feet moved, and then his hands as his eyes focused on the vacant stare of the driver's corpse inches from his face. The hilt of his knife still stuck out of the dead man's shoulder. El grunted and shifted, suddenly realizing that the truck was upside down. The roof had collapsed, and the viewport had crumpled and shattered. There was glass everywhere. As he thought about it, a thousand tiny cuts started shouting at him…

No. No, that was actual shouting, coming through the speaker next to his face.

"Tewken! Tewken, are you all right—?" The speaker crackled and spat forth more garbled words El didn't recognize. Then: "Just hang on. I'm turning around. I'm coming back! Just…"

The transmission dissolved into static which pounded into El's head, but he ignored it. He had no time to waste. He grabbed his knife, yanking it free of the dead man's collar bone. More blood welled from the torn wound, but no more arterial spray. The driver's heart had stopped.

El couldn't keep from groaning in pain as he shifted his body, pulling himself closer to the driver's seat. The driver hadn't been wearing a restraint, so his body had tumbled about the cab of the vehicle just as El's had. Every surface carried a layer of the man's blood, and it smeared as El pulled the body up and over himself. His weapon remained slung, but he didn't have enough room to bring it around to the front, so he reached for the backup 1911 he carried inside his jacket. He positioned the dead man's arm over his own and waited for the other driver.

Here's hoping, he thought as he looked around. He wasn't fully hidden, not by a long shot, but maybe the blood and carnage would be enough to distract the other driver long enough for El to get the drop on him. It wasn't exactly how he'd planned for this to go down…but hell, adapt and overcome, right?

Soon, he heard the other truck's engine growling as it approached. No, not a growl…it was higher, almost a whine.

The other guy must be damn near to the redline—or whatever the natives called it here—to cause the engine to make that sound. El took another deep breath, ignoring the iron tang of blood and the sewer smell of death as he tried to steady his nerves. He peered over the corpse's bloody shoulder and waited.

"Tewken! Tewken, talk to me!"

The signal got stronger and clearer as the engine noise stopped with the sound of skidding gravel. El heard a slam, then the sound of running feet, and then the deep *ker-thunk* as the driver's hatch opened from the outside and the morning sun poured in.

"Tewken!"

The other driver's head appeared, silhouetted in the light. El couldn't see his face, but he recognized the horror in the man's voice just before he squeezed the trigger twice, firing the rounds point blank into the man's face. The *pop-pop* echoed inside the confined space, and the almost-faded ringing in his ears came roaring back, blocking out all sound as the driver's silhouette fell away from the blindingly bright rectangle of the open hatch.

El laid his head back and closed his eyes, waiting.

Nothing.

Eventually, the ringing faded again, and El realized that he'd done it. He'd killed them both, and he was still alive. Somehow, he'd even managed to make it without any major injuries.

But make it where? What was he supposed to do now?

"Whatever it is," he heard himself say out loud into the diminishing ring of tinnitus, "it's time to get moving."

Maybe he'd avoided major injury, but he felt every bruise, cut, and contusion as he fought to pull himself from under the first driver's corpse and climb out of the mauled truck. The other driver lay crumpled on the ground beside the wreck, the back of his head blown out by El's bullets. The sun had risen above the line of peaks to the east and light spilled into the valley, illuminating the lingering wisps of ground fog from the night before.

El walked to the other truck and looked inside. Another map sat on the seat. This one was folded to show a line that meandered through the mountains and across the plains to the coast. He thought for a minute, then walked back to the wreckage to find his pack.

Time to see if the radio Jackson gave him was worth a shit. "Any Lawless, this is Huey Seven."

"Huey Seven, this is Maneater. Ass in a sling already, Huey Seven?"

Fuck. It was Chalmers. El let out a sigh and keyed the mic again.

"The opposite, Maneater. I've got a sitrep for you."

"Ready to copy."

"Am in possession of two native vehicles filled with black market cargo. One usable, one disabled. Request you recover disabled vehicle and return goods inside to place of origin. Doc November will have more details on that."

"Roger, standing by for coordinates."

"I don't have coordinates, exactly. I'm using a native map, but I'm…" He looked around and identified two major peaks that they used for aerial navigation. "In a valley between Hills 246 and 1820. On an east-west road headed out of the mountains."

"Confirm road? Not a fucking goat track?"

"Road," El said. "Aerial recon should pick up the wrecked vehicle. Or ping my radio."

"Can't fucking make it easy, can you?"

El rolled his eyes at the other man's lack of radio discipline. "Standing by to transmit."

The radio crackled, as if someone was sighing on the other end. Then, "Go ahead."

El pressed the tone button, waited, then released it.

"Got it," Chalmers said. "We'll see you in a bit."

"Negative," El said. "I'm taking the working vehicle and following the trail. I'll be traveling out of radio range."

"Estimated time of return?"

"Don't know. When I'm back. Out." El switched the radio off. He permitted himself a small smile as he imagined Chalmers' face, then he pulled the batteries out of the radio and stowed them separately in his pack before walking back to the working truck. He did a quick search of the cargo area and driver's cab before finding what he'd been looking for: a bag holding the dead driver's roadtrip stash. There were two canteens of water, as well as several strips of what looked like dried meat and a collection of dried fruit. *Good enough.*

He dug further into the bag and found another coverall garment. Since his own uniform was growing stiff with drying blood, El ignored how stupid he thought the thing looked and shucked off his clothes. He used a bit of water on the cleanest part of his pants and wiped his head, face, and hands down, then put on the alien coveralls. They were uncomfortably snug, particularly in the crotch, but he eventually found a workable arrangement. He stepped back into his boots, put the food back in the stash, dumped his bag in the passenger seat, and climbed into the driver's position.

El wanted to be well down the road before anyone from base showed up and tried to stop him, so he fired up the truck and pushed the lever forward to accelerate. He took out a piece of the meat and bit down. As he expected, it tasted a lot like beef jerky, but with a hint of *ihey*. It wasn't bad, just surprising. He tore off a hunk with his teeth and focused his attention down the road.

Barduz, an auxiliary of the Memshoon Satrapy, looked out the mud-spattered windshield of the lead cargo ATV and cursed. He hated driving through the forests far in the north of the Greens. First of all, they didn't really look like forests, at least not all of them did. In some places, there were normal trees. But here, for mile upon mile, it was more like towering columns of fungus vying for space against tall, narrow tubers with spatulate flowers sprouting all the way up their sides. At the top, they joined and sent out a florid effusion of sky-pointing leaves and shoots.

The only thing Barduz liked about driving through such areas was that most of these growths tended to have shallower and softer root structures than the trees from which wood was harvested. That made it comparatively easy to keep roads through these forests passable. Once a year, a single good pass with a well-loaded tracked vehicle could smash aside and pulp any growth which had encroached over the course of a season or two. Which meant that, although Barduz found the tall, strange growths inexplicably unnerving, it was easy work traversing them.

Except today, because one of the fungus-towers had fallen across the road.

It was almost five feet thick and, while soft and pulpy, was still a considerable impediment. In some ways, it would have been easier to remove a wood-tree. While much heavier, the tree would at least hang together. This swollen column with the texture of a half-cooked gourd was more like moving a decaying body that might fall to pieces if handled or twisted in the wrong way.

"Ganf! Jakut!" Barduz shouted into the intervehicle microphone, "Dust cakes and crotch crabs, what the scorch are you two waiting for? We'll need winches and cables to get that out of the road. You'd probably better bring axes, too."

The second and the third ATVs in the formation slowed. It had been annoying enough to be pulled off their tribute-gathering rounds to intercept some rogue indig who'd grabbed a cargo van in the far northern woods. And it was more annoying still that the satrap's vizier had ordered them to do so at maximum speed.

Now, with this massive tuber blocking their way, they would be forced to split into two groups. The ATVs would have to clear enough of the vegetable matter so that the small scout vehicles could race on ahead. Meanwhile, Barduz and the heavier vehicles would need to continue widening the gap until it was large enough for them to pass and follow the first group.

As the scout vehicles took up flanking positions, watching for enemies that almost never appeared, the crews of the three ATVs popped their hatches and clambered out.

Barduz stood on the bow deck of his lead track, barking annoyed orders at the uncertain crews. "That spool is tangled. You're going to have to reel it out, and then reel it back in before we can use it. No, no! You can't just slip it around the middle of that thing! You'll pull it apart. We've got to cut it into sections and move each one separately, or it will make the job that much longer. And messier. Listen, you idiots: we don't have the time to—"

Thunder erupted from the upslope tree line. Armor-piercing rounds screamed and sleeted between the vehicles, playing across their surfaces and hunting after the figures that sprang and sprawled away from the murderous fire.

Barduz let himself fall backwards into the cab of the ATV. He hit the tow-line release, gunned the engine, and brought the steering wheel over to take the big tracked vehicle downslope.

But before he could, three twenty-five millimeter high-velocity shells disintegrated the passenger side window, made a ruin of the control panel, blasted the steering wheel thirty yards down the hill, and vaporized most of Barduz's torso.

Harry Tapper surveyed the carnage, hands on his hips and a grim, if satisfied, smile on his face. "Report," he asked his indig lieutenant, Hax Uruns.

"It doesn't look like anyone got away," Uruns answered. "The first and second ATVs took too many hits to be salvaged."

"Not a worry," said Harry. "Destroy in place. What about the scout vehicles?"

"One took a penetrator through the engine block. But the other simply has holes and a great deal of blood and organs to clean off."

Tapper checked his watch. "We have thirty minutes. Collect what you can. Inflict any ritual defacements on the bodies typically used by bandits or tribes in this area. And set charges in the vehicles we can't drive from the site."

Uruns frowned at him. "You wish us to mutilate the bodies? Only the most savage tribes do that!" he exclaimed.

"I'd tell you to eat them raw if that would encourage the satraps to think that it wasn't off-worlders or rebels who did this. Now get about it. We have another convoy to intercept. Radioman, the window to Glass Palace will be opening in five minutes. Tell Captain Makarov I have a report for Colonel Murphy."

"I have to tell you, sir," said Tapper, "I'd be happy to have this duty every day of the week. The forces of the northern satraps walk into these ambushes fat, dumb, and happy."

Murphy nodded. "As much as I'd like to, Harry, I can't indulge your appetite for the hunt."

Trapper shrugged. "Understood, sir. If we do this once, twice, maybe three times, the satraps would still presume that it's just some local bravos encouraged by a few early successes. But after that, they might start putting two and two together. As the saying has it, every deception has a shelf life. I imagine we've just about exhausted this one, sir."

Murphy nodded. "Yep, just about."

Tapper glanced at one of the big-wheeled armored vehicles behind him. "These high-end APCs and AFVs sure have made this job easy, and the indigs are starting to get the hang of them. You're going to have a decent mechanized cavalry force before long, Colonel."

Murphy smiled. "Seems like I might have one already."

Tapper shook his head. "Excuse my bluntness, sir, but don't get too optimistic. There's still a lot they don't understand. But with time, training, and a few who've learned how to read the manuals, yes, you'll have a decent unit here."

"Well, then," Murphy said, "you'll be happy to learn that you can keep every one of your shiny toys for the foreseeable future."

Tapper felt his eyebrows rise, even though he kept other signs of surprise off his face. "Really? I expected you'd be wanting at least a few of them shifted back down south to Bo's force, once it was decided where he was going to bring the hammer down in the Ashbands. At least long enough to spearhead that attack."

Murphy shook his head. "Bo and I discussed it, but in the final analysis, he's right on the money when he pointed out that we actually have too many vehicles as it is. Between the civilians converging upon both Heshdehar and Imsurmik, and the limited cover in which to set up a forward base from which to launch the attack, he won't be able to conceal all the vehicles he'd hoped to use. And, all the civilian influx makes him worried about the chances of accidental discovery. So he wants to keep his force driving around in only the ragtag technicals and grab-bag AFVs we took in the very first battle against the J'Stull. As he said, if someone stumbles across his base, he wants them to see nothing but Mad Max rejects held together with baling wire, duct tape, and a lot of hopes and prayers. He's going to keep one or two heavier assault vehicles concealed further off until he starts the countdown clock."

"So you're saying that my nice clean APCs would stick out like cherry Lamborghinis at a demolition derby?"

"At least."

Tapper checked his G-Shock. "Well, it's time for us to get moving to the next intercept point."

"Belay that. This was the last ambush, Harry. The other groups we've got on satellite surveillance will never catch Sergeant Frazier, even if he slowed by half. And if satraps further to the south have sent units to intercept, they're not showing up on the Dornaani microsats' scanners. Time to call it a day, Major, and fade back to your highland laager. Lie low, get the salvaged vehicles ready for transfer, make repairs to your own, get food and sleep."

"You can bet on it, sir, because I know you'll be calling us again soon enough."

Tapper saw a hint of apology in Murphy's smile. "You know me too well. Glass Palace out."

Chapter Ten

The sun was riding high in the sky, arcing overhead and slanting toward the western horizon before El stopped again. He'd ignored everything but driving. The radio had crackled with requests for status reports. He couldn't fake the local dialect well enough to pass and didn't know the right lies to tell so he just left the calls unanswered until they stopped.

He'd also ignored what might have been thunder or a landslide or even distant gunfire far to the east. He was only vaguely aware of the bizarre mix of flora that covered the slopes which had started stepping downward like ocean swells shrinking and lengthening as they neared land. He had no recollection of finally leaving the mountains behind and beginning to follow a ruler-straight track across a vast grassland that stretched to all horizons. To the naked eye, it looked perfectly flat, but as he drove he could feel the slight undulations of the ground beneath him.

What he didn't feel was tired.

Still, his bladder was clamoring for his attention, so he worked the levers and steered the truck gently to the side of the road, mindful of how the other vehicle had reacted to sudden changes of direction. El coasted to a stop then stepped out, reaching his hands up above his head and feeling the stretch all along his back and legs.

A little stiff, but not tired. Interesting. According to his watch, he'd been awake and active for about twenty hours: more than a full R'Bak day. He'd pushed on for long periods of time before, but he'd always felt it. Especially in the way fatigue frayed his attention and made him jumpy and jittery.

But he didn't feel any of that. He felt...fine. Like he'd just had a cup of *ihey*.

He took care of his bladder's pressing need then walked a lap around his vehicle, checking the tires for problems. He even got underneath it and looked at the engine with his flashlight. Sure enough, it was similar in configuration to the compressed gas engine he'd become familiar with back at the helo base. That was good news; it meant he was likely not to have to stop for fuel too often. According to the map, he was headed to a port on the coast with a name and a symbol that could represent a city or town. If luck continued to smile on him, he'd be able to get fuel there, find out where the goods were going, and, hopefully, locate more *tra.*

A corner of his mind wondered if Nalyiriz had kept one of the bundles to plant, or had harvested some seeds, or something. If it was so hard to get, and so necessary, he figured they'd probably want their own source of the stuff, so they didn't have to keep buying it from shady apothecaries year after year. Especially if she was right and the satraps were buying up everything they could get their hands on as the Searing got closer.

But that fell squarely under the heading of "not his problem," as did the memory of Nalyiriz's face lighting up when she smiled. He pushed both thoughts away and wormed his way out from under the truck, stretched again, and swung back into the driver's seat. As long as he felt good, he'd keep going. One of the dead men had mentioned a tight timeline, after all.

He didn't want to be late.

"Doc, can't we make this quicker?" Mara asked, uncomfortably aware that she sounded petulant and impatient.

"My sister, I have inserted the catheter directly into your antecubital. I am pumping the *tra* concentrate into you as quickly as physiologically possible," Nalyiriz responded, her tone laced with tart affection as she straightened Mara's arm and taped down the tube going into the bend inside her elbow.

"Sorry," Mara sighed. "It's just…El cut comms with the ground team, and I want to get back to the monitoring station.

He's still moving, and I have no idea how. I mean, the man can go over a day without sleep, sure, but..."

"It is likely he is drinking *ihey*," Nalyiriz said. "You know this substance; it is perfectly safe."

"Even in large amounts? Without sleep?"

"Mara, you have enough to worry about. Do not...what is your phrase? 'Borrow trouble.' *Ihey* is powerful, but it is so diluted by the water used for brewing that it's impossible to drink enough to cause damage. His body will literally flush it out before it can cause a problem. He will sleep in a day or two."

"It's already been—"

"Mara," Nalyiriz said, leaning forward and putting her hands on either side of Mara's face. "Look at me. El is a grown man, an experienced field operative. As I understand it, he was surviving in hostile environments long before you were born. You must trust him. He will keep himself safe and bring us the *tra* you need. Your job is to grow a healthy child and make it worth his effort."

"And to clear his way," Mara said with a sigh. She smiled and gave Nalyiriz a tiny nod to show she understood and accepted the doc's gentle correction.

Nalyiriz returned the nod and straightened, letting her hands drop away from Mara's face. She turned to check the mechanism pumping *tra* into Mara's vein. "What does this mean, 'clear his way?'"

"He's driving southwest, toward the coast, as far as we can tell. It's mostly uninhabited, and turns into wasteland toward the end, but there are a few settlements where he'll need to stop for fuel and supplies. We're sending teams in by helicopter to make contact and ensure he can get what he needs...and to keep any scavengers or other procurer teams off his back."

"Will not this highlight our interest in the mission?" Nalyiriz asked. "That seems risky for El."

"We're being covert about it. Tapper's already carried out two interdictions on forces trying to intercept El. One on a mixed convoy of heavy tracks and light scout cars and a second on a half-dozen vehicles similar to El's. We don't know if they're all from the same group of bully boys or not, but we'll find out once the evidence is analyzed. What evidence Tapper brought back in, that is. He does very thorough work."

"It may be the same group, or it may not. There is no large organization in the Greens of the northern hemisphere. There, even the satraps are fragmented and as likely to be working against each other as with each other."

"Yes, and isn't *that* an interesting situation we might be able to use to our advantage?" Mara asked, settling back in her couch. As Nalyiriz's machine pumped the *tra* into her body, she began to feel an edge of euphoria around the borders of her mind.

"How so?" Nalyiriz asked.

"I don't know," Mara said. "I'm not sure yet. Maybe El will learn more."

"As long as he returns, preferably with more *tra*, I do not care what else he learns," Nalyiriz muttered.

Mara glanced up at her, but the doc was looking away. "You care about him, too," Mara said. "I'm sorry. I tend to forget that I'm not the only one who has connections with people."

"Of course, I do," Nalyiriz said. "He is a good man with an impressive aptitude for violence. His loyalty to you runs deep, Mara, and he is equally devoted to Dio. He may not be a leader among your people, but he was born for the role of senior subordinate and protector. His performance as my backup only confirmed this."

"You're not telling me anything I don't already know, sis," Mara said with a sigh. "That's part of the reason I'm so anxious to get back to monitoring his progress. Dio's already lost one father figure. She was just starting to bond with El. If she loses him, too…"

"Diozera is a child of my people, Mara. She honors her parents, and she knows that their deaths were not in vain. Do not take yourself down this mental path, my sister. No good can come of it. And El truly can take care of himself."

"So he can," Mara said, pushing back the nausea that followed in the wake of *tra's* euphoria. She closed her eyes and focused on breathing in through her nose, out through her mouth.

"Speaking of my niece, would you like me to bring her in?" Nalyiriz asked quietly. "I think she would enjoy sitting with you for a while. Before too long she will be so busy with schooling that she will not have much time, or permission, to cuddle."

"Yes, please," Mara said. Her voice sounded small and sick, but she didn't care. Just like with El, she couldn't do anything about it, so she let it be. Sometimes, the only way out was through.

"I will go and fetch her," Nalyiriz said. "It will be good for you both."

"You're late."

The man who spoke was short, maybe just a hair over five feet tall, and wore a mean, pinched expression. That, in addition to his impatient, demanding words, screamed "little man syndrome" to El. He sighed and cut the truck's engine, then opened the hatch and stepped outside.

"And there's only one of you! I was told to expect two!"

"Tewken had an accident," El said, trying to mimic the accent of the men he'd killed as best as he could remember it. "Lost control, rolled it over. The whole thing burned like unprotected skin. I couldn't get him out."

"Huh, serves him right. Shoulda been more careful," the little man said, stepping back slightly and looking up at El. "Who are you? Don't remember seeing you before."

"New hire," El said. "Where do you want this stuff? In there?"

The man raised his eyebrows and turned to glance behind him, where two large doors yawned wide, leading into a huge warehouse that appeared well on its way to being stuffed to the rafters.

"What are you, an idiot? That's for long-term storage. This stuff's all going to the island starting tonight. Drive around to the back and follow the alley to the docks. Find Umaren. He'll tell you what to do with it."

El nodded and got back into the vehicle, grateful that the little man's curiosity seemed as stunted as his physique. He'd been on the road for two sunrises and three sunsets. Or ten sunrises and eleven sunsets…or maybe it was the other way round. It was hard to say. Every time he thought about it, he felt as if he was still driving, the sunset blasting through his back viewscreen, glaring off of his engine instruments. Eleven…or maybe twelve? It might have been a thousand. A thousand sunsets. A thousand transitions. A thousand changes.

Or maybe just one big change. Hell, who was he to say? He did know he'd stopped at two good-sized towns to refuel the truck and buy more of the local food. Or maybe he'd commandeered it. People had taken one look at his coveralls and just handed him whatever he asked for. No arguments, no payments. No fear. Another change.

El didn't know if it was lack of sleep or whatever stimulant was in the food he'd been eating, but his perception of time wavered and rippled, and the numbers on his watch didn't really make sense to him anymore.

And he still hadn't slept.

And he felt just fine.

The route marked on the map had taken him across the grasslands, through a scrubby half-desert, down to the coast. Then he'd turned due west and followed a short peninsula to this town whose name he still couldn't make out on the map. It was a bigger place, though: certainly more than a village, with its fair share of permanent buildings, particularly along the waterfront.

Where he was now.

He followed the little man's instructions and found himself driving along a quay. The place looked deserted except for a lone man standing next to a strangely-shaped boat—

No, El realized. *Not a boat.* Not with those wings…it was a seaplane!

He cut the engine to idle and coasted up to the man. He cracked the hatch and leaned out.

"I'm looking for Umaren," he said.

"He's below," the man replied with a smile that was so unexpected it almost startled El. He appeared young, with tanned skin and long black hair tied behind his head. "I'm Vizzel, his brother. Can I help?"

"I'm El. Little man out front sent me. I've got his cargo…for the island?"

Vizzel laughed. "Don't let Furo hear you call him 'little,'" he warned. "But you're in the right place. I'll get Umaren. Can you help us load it up?" Vizzel's body language said he clearly expected to be told no.

"And unload," El said quickly, his mind racing. "I'm supposed to see these goods all the way to their destination."

"Oh, excellent!" Vizzel said, his face lighting up with a smile. "That will make things so much easier! I'll be right back!" He turned and started toward the odd-looking seaplane, while El cut the engine and got out of the truck. By the time he walked to the back of the truck and opened up the cargo hatch, Vizzel had returned, leading a man who looked to be a few years older, with skin darker than El's own. There were flecks of gray starting to show in his black beard, and he was completely bald. Truth be told, they didn't look much like brothers, and he could swear they'd been holding hands as they came out of the cargo hold of the plane. But El figured it wasn't his business and stepped forward to meet them both with a nod.

"Greetings," the new man said. "I am Umaren. Vizzel tells me you have a cargo for me."

"For the island," El said. "Furo said to see you about it. It has to leave tonight."

"And you're coming with it?" Umaren asked.

"That's the deal," El said. "I'm to see it all the way to its destination."

"That's a long trip. Between fuel stops, almost two days in the air." Umaren rubbed his chin. "Must be something special."

El just stared at him. Somewhere, a horn blew, and water splashed up against the quay.

Finally, Umaren nodded. "Fine," he said. "Vizzel and I will be glad of your help with the heavy lifting."

"Happy to help," El said. "Just show me where to go."

"You got a manifest or anything?"

El turned back to the truck and grabbed the packet of papers that had accompanied the map. He couldn't read all of the words, but he'd been able to make out enough to realize that at least one of the sheets held an accounting of the contents of the truck. He handed this to Umaren, who looked it over and whistled, his eyes going wide.

"Something special indeed," he said. "The boss has been trying to get his hands on some of this stuff for a while."

Vizzel stepped up close behind Umaren—uncomfortably close, El would have said—and looked over Umaren's shoulder with a frown.

"Why?"

Umaren straightened up and tucked the manifest away. "Never mind that now. We'll talk more in the air. Let's just get this stuff loaded."

El took that as his cue to reach in and grab one of the crates from the back. He pulled it out and waited while the two brothers did the same before leading the way to the cargo hold of the seaplane.

They worked in silence for a few moments, until Umaren spoke up as they were securing tie-down straps around the cargo. "Interesting that you've been assigned to escort this shipment. Normally, there's too much collection work to spare *busaphren* men."

"Like you said," El grunted as he hauled on a strap to tighten it, "the boss has been trying to get his hands on this stuff."

"Yeah," Umaren said, his hands going still as he turned to look closely at El. "But he's been trying to get his hands on *all* the stuff—tying up the local markets, you know, in preparation for the Searing. And this isn't even close to the most valuable cargo I've carried recently. So, how about you tell me what's going on, El? Or maybe I'll have my brother run out to tell Furo that something's not right with this cargo?"

"Your brother?" El asked softly. "Or your lover?" It was, he admitted to himself, a bit of a stab in the dark. All of his interactions with the local populations had indicated that homosexual relationships were not the norm. They were, in fact, almost as taboo as they'd been in the world El grew up in—sort of. Here, they seemed to focus more on who was dominant in the relationship. However, the less dominant half of the relationship—the younger and often weaker partner—was treated worse than a genuine pariah. Sometimes they became general targets for assault, particularly if the relationship with their protector had ended. Or if the protector wasn't around.

The whole concept made El uncomfortable, but even to his eyes, the abuse heaped on the unfortunate "lesser partners" was excessive. And then there was Vat, who was homosexual, had become close friends with Mara, and was therefore something of an ally when it came to keeping her safe. Same-sex attraction still struck him as weird and unnatural, but El had recently decided that it fell into the category of "not his business" and let it go.

Judging by Umaren's reaction, however, he was in the minority here on R'Bak. Or at least in this community.

The bald man started backward, his hands shaking. "I-I don't—! What do you—? How dare—?"

"Relax," El said, turning back to his strap. "I don't care. I'm certainly not going to mention it to Furo or anyone else. Not my business. Just like my business is not yours, right?"

"But I'm not—"

"I said it's okay," El said, turning back to face the man. "We both have things we want kept quiet, right? This is an easy situation. You just take me to the island with the cargo, let me go drop it off, then fly me back with you. Everyone is happy."

"What are you going to do on the island?" Umaren asked.

"Nothing that will come back to haunt you, I promise."

"Good," Umaren said, his voice steadying and taking on a hard edge. He leaned forward, so the light coming from the cargo hatch fell over his face, illuminating his fierce, intense expression. "Because I promise you this, El; I don't know who you are or where you're from, but if anything happens to Vizzel because of you, I will find you, and I *will* kill you. Not even the boss himself will stand in my way."

El stared back, letting his own eyes empty out, letting Umaren glimpse the animal he could become. To the other man's credit, he didn't flinch. He just looked into the abyss inside of El and let his own intensity burn forth.

El couldn't help it, he smiled. "You love him," he surprised himself by saying.

"With everything that I am," Umaren said.

"Does he love you?"

"Enough to shoot you dead before you can move," Vizzel said, his youthful voice hard. El turned his head to see the young man silhouetted in the cargo door holding one of the local projectile weapons pointed at El's back.

El nodded slowly. "Fair enough," he said. "I can respect that. I propose a deal, then. You two help me get onto the island and back out again, and I'll put you in touch with some people who can get him—and maybe you—to a safe place, where you can be together openly, as yourselves. Because if I can see it, anyone can see it. You can't hide your relationship forever, and then what happens to him?" He turned back to look at Umaren. "What do you say?"

Umaren blinked rapidly and swallowed. El saw the other man's eyes flit to Vizzel and back.

"Maren?" Vizzel asked, his voice going soft, vulnerable.

Umaren closed his eyes and then nodded. Then he opened his eyes and held out his hand to Elroy. "I accept your deal," he said.

"I won't leave you, Maren!" Vizzel cried out. Umaren held out a hand imperiously, and the younger man fell quiet.

El clasped the older man's forearm in the manner of the villagers he'd met. Then he let go and fought not to wipe his hands on his coveralls.

"Good," he said. "Let's finish getting this loaded up, then?"

"Yes," Umaren said. "Otherwise, we'll never be airborne by sundown."

Chapter Eleven

By the time they got the cargo loaded, the wind had picked up. Gusts blew spray up over the quay and tugged at any loose clothing or fabrics. The lines securing the seaplane to the dock snapped and creaked as the swells started to build.

"Are we still good to take off in this weather?" El asked.

"Just fine," Umaren said confidently. "The winds always pick up around midday. They'll die down again in the afternoon once the temperature starts to cool off. But you need to get strapped in. Both of you." He looked at Vizzel, who stood with arms crossed over his chest, clearly still livid about the arrangement El and Umaren had made concerning him. In a way, El could understand; he'd be pissed as hell if someone acted so high-handed about his life. But he also realized that Umaren was desperate to see his lover safe, even if it meant losing him.

What would it be like, El wondered, *to love someone that much?* For just a moment, Nalyiriz's face rose up in his mind's eye, but he shoved the thought away and turned his attention to getting strapped in.

To his surprise, Vizzel sat down beside him in one of the seats lining the cargo bay.

"You're not sitting up front?" El asked.

"Not if he doesn't want me up there," Vizzel said, his tone brittle and angry. "Which he obviously doesn't if he's going to send me away with you. I'm not a slave, you know. I won't fuck you willingly!"

"I don't—that's not what is happening here," El said. "I'm not a f…I'm not interested in men…that way. Umaren's just trying to keep you safe. You have to know how people will react once they find out."

"They don't have to find out!" Vizzel snapped, his hands flying over the latches as he strapped himself into his seat. "Nobody knew until you showed up! And anyway, I can take care of myself."

"Against one man, sure," El said. "Against three or four? Son, I've killed more than a handful of men, and those odds would worry me. And like I said, if I can see it, others can too. Can you honestly say that no one in the city has looked at you guys a little too closely? Furo or anyone?"

Vizzel opened his mouth to reply, but then paused, as if a thought occurred to him. Up front, Umaren started the seaplane's two big engines, and all conversation ceased as the deafening, chest-thrumming drone permeated the cargo bay. El closed his eyes and put his head back against the metal frame of the bulkhead, letting the engines' vibration soak through him.

He still hadn't slept. He still wasn't tired.

Just as when he'd been driving, El lost all sense of time passing. He was vaguely aware of the engines' whine changing pitch as Umaren applied more power. He felt the world tilt to the side and his safety straps bite into his skin as they rotated for take-off. He smelled the sweet burnt scent of the engine exhaust. It wasn't quite the same as the JP-4 exhaust he knew so well...but it wasn't totally different, either. The deck of the aircraft dropped out from under them and then bumped back up as the surface gusts became turbulence as they gained altitude. He felt Vizzel moving on the webbed fabric of the seat next to him, but El kept himself still. He sank into the memory of turbulence on other flights, countless miles and hundreds of years away, while the world shuddered and shook around him.

At some point, Umaren and Vizzel switched places because El opened his eyes and saw Umaren snoring on the webbed seats opposite him. He closed his eyes again and let more time wash over him in that strange, dreamlike state.

"Viz!" Umaren's voice crackled through a speaker El hadn't noticed mounted high on the bulkhead above their seats. The urgency in the pilot's voice cut through the grinding drone of the engines, and he felt Vizzel move on the seat next to him in response. The pilots must have traded places again. "Viz, something's wrong with the right engine. I need you to go check it out. But be careful moving around; the turbulence isn't easing off."

El opened his eyes in time to see Viz reach out and grab a necklace with a small round cylinder hanging from it. He slung it around his neck and lifted the cylinder to his mouth. He said something into it, because El could see his lips moving, but he couldn't make out the words.

"The rate of flow is too high. Check the fuel control panel and see what's going on," Umaren's voice said, as if in reply to a question. The necklace thing had to be an intercom microphone, similar to what the drivers of the trucks had used back in the village. El watched as Vizzel nodded and stood up, bracing himself against the turbulence with one hand on the bulkhead.

Something, some instinct he couldn't name but never ignored, told El he needed to go along, so he unbuckled and stood beside the younger man. Viz looked at him quizzically but didn't say anything. He just turned and led the way across the cargo hold to the access hatch for the seaplane's wing. El hadn't gotten a good look earlier, so he took the opportunity now.

Unlike the ground trucks, the seaplanes seemed to run on liquid fuel, much like the internal combustion and turbine engines he knew back home. As Viz opened up the hatch to reveal a terrifyingly narrow catwalk structure inside a metal tube, El realized that the seaplane's fuel was stored in its wing—another similarity to Earth airplanes. But unlike the C-141s and other cargo planes he'd flown in, this seaplane had a long extension under the wing that allowed a crewmember to access the engine directly during flight. For a moment he wondered what could possibly be so important that they wouldn't wait to land to fix it—and then decided he didn't want to know.

Regardless, it seemed he was about to find out.

El took a deep breath and concentrated on "thinking thin" as he squeezed sideways and crouched down into the hatch behind Viz. They walked along the catwalk, feeling the structure of the wing buck and sway with the turbulence. El swallowed hard and willed his stomach to not rebel. He could handle this! He'd done worse in his lifetime.

Though honestly, right now, he couldn't remember when.

Doesn't matter, he told himself, and forced himself to focus on Vizzel. The younger man had gone most of the way down the catwalk, and El abruptly realized the strangely curved shape of the bulkhead at the far end was the engine case itself. Probably the equivalent of a combustion section if the radiant heat was any indication.

To his great relief, Vizzel didn't reach for anything on the engine. Instead, he reached out and opened the fastener securing a small cabinet-like hatch in the bulkhead on the trailing edge of the catwalk.

The hatch flew open and a deluge of liquid sprayed forth, hitting Vizzel squarely in the face and chest and knocking him backward against the side of the catwalk. El felt a deep bong reverberate through his feet as the young man's skull connected with one of the metal support uprights. The spray impacted the upright, as well, and then diverted and started to spatter the engine case.

The *hot* engine case.

"Shut it down!" El heard himself screaming as he lunged forward. He ducked under the spray to grab Vizzel's slumped form and awkwardly throw his bodyweight backward so that the two of them fell to the surface of the catwalk. With one hand, he scrabbled for the microphone hanging around the unconscious young man's neck. With the other, he hauled Vizzel onto his chest and crawled backward as fast as he could. "Umaren! Shut it down! Fuel leak in the engine compartment!"

He had no idea if Umaren heard him. He just kept pushing himself and Vizzel backward along the catwalk. If the hot engine ignited the fuel spraying through the air, the resulting fireball would kill them faster than he could get them to safety.

Still, he had to try. So he pushed, and screamed, and someone somewhere must have smiled on him because the spray abruptly slackened, then slowed to a trickle just as he reached the access hatch back to the cargo hold. He let go of the microphone to reach up and push the door open, and then let himself and Vizzel tumble out, drawing in big gulps of air not tainted with the stink of fuel.

"Viz?" Umaren's voice stabbed through the cabin speaker, spiked with fear. "Viz, what happened? Are you all right?"

El pushed Vizzel's limp body to the side and pushed himself to a seated position. He looked up at the access hatch but decided to leave it open. He figured keeping the spilled fuel ventilated could only be a good thing. He scrubbed one hand across his face and reached again for Vizzel's neck mic.

"Umaren, Vizzel hit his head when the fuel spray impacted him. He's breathing, but he's unconscious. Is there help for him on the island?"

"Yes," Umaren said, "but we're still an hour out. We'll never make it all the way to Downport on only one engine! And if they're expecting this delivery via air, they'll sink us on the water before I can identify—No. We'll have to go to Landfall. It's farther away, but I can land on the water and coast in. It's the primary seaplane landing port anyway. I can signal them with an emergency. They'll understand...have a doctor waiting for him."

"Can you request someone to come from, uh, Downport to pick up the cargo?"

"Viz is hurt! I don't care about your cargo!"

"I know, Umaren," El said, trying to sound conciliatory over the intercom. "But this stuff is special, and I can't risk not getting it where it needs to be. You're calling ahead anyway, right?"

"I'll flash the emergency light signals at them; it is all I can do! Just...take care of Viz!"

"I'll do my best," El said tightly. He understood Umaren's fear, but he felt his own frustration sitting like a lead lump in the back of his throat.

The vibration in the aircraft's floor changed, and El experienced a slight tilting sensation as they began a slow descent toward the water below. He let out a breath and forced his mind to focus on Vizzel.

The younger man was breathing, just as he'd said, but when El touched the back of his head, his fingers came away bloody. It also felt like a sizable bump was forming, too.

"Let's hope you just split your scalp, kid, not your skull," El muttered as he bent to slide his arms under Vizzel's in order to drag him over to the webbed seats. "Either way, you're going to have a hell of a headache."

With a fair amount of effort, he eventually got the young man strapped into a webbed seat. He spent the rest of the interminable flight checking the kid's pulse and breathing, and hoping he'd come to. He didn't, but eventually Umaren announced through the speaker that they were about to land. El felt the seaplane pitch up, and then bump harder than he would have expected once, twice, before settling to a neutral position and rolling slowly forward through the waves. The turbulence disappeared, replaced by the rocking motion of the ocean swells.

The speaker crackled overhead. "How is he?" El could hear tears in Umaren's voice.

"Still with us," El said into the mic. "Just get us to the port. That's all you can do for him right now."

Umaren didn't answer, but El felt the remaining engine rev, and he swayed aft as they started motoring for the shore.

As soon as El felt the seaplane bump softly against the dock, he jumped up and opened the side cabin door. Waiting to board the plane was a group of individuals all dressed alike in dark green coveralls. One of them was an older woman with salt-and-pepper hair and a long scar dominating her right cheek. She held a large bag.

"Healer?" El asked, hoping his regional dialect would translate.

"I am," the woman said. "Someone is hurt?"

"One of our crew," he said. "Hit his head on one of the metal support struts. He's unconscious, with at least a scalp wound. He may also have gotten fuel in his eyes, mouth, and nose."

"Let me see him," she said, and held out a hand. El took it and helped her cross the narrow gap between the dock and the passenger door. He stepped back and gestured to the seats where he'd positioned Vizzel, just as Umaren stepped back from the cockpit.

He looked terrible; his face ravaged with worry.

"Healer—" he said, his voice broken. El stepped in and took his arm gently, turning him away. Umaren didn't resist but twisted so he could keep his eyes on his lover's pale, unconscious face.

"The injured man is the pilot's younger brother," El said over his shoulder to the healer. "He's obviously very concerned."

"I will do what I can," the healer said, her voice serene. She reminded him a little of Nalyiriz in that. A tiny corner of El's mind wondered if they learned that intense calm in healer school, or whatever they called it here. She called out to one of the men still waiting on the dock, and El nodded and turned his attention back to Umaren.

"You have to get it together," he said quietly in the other man's ear. "She's going to know you're more than brothers if you're not careful. Vizzel is going to be fine. She obviously knows what she's doing, so take a deep breath and…Get. It. Together!"

Umaren's eyes, wide and frantic, flicked from Vizzel to El, then narrowed. He stared at El for a long moment. Then he closed his eyes, inhaled deeply, and, finally, opened them again with a nod.

"You are right, my friend," he said. "Thank you. And thank you for—" He broke off.

"Don't thank me yet," El said.

"No. If not for you, we would all have died. I would not have known about the fuel leak, and Viz…well. You are right. This healer is known to me. She is very skilled. He will be fine. I must focus on what I can control."

"Good," El said, letting go of the man's shoulder now that he seemed to have regained control of himself. "That's good. That's exactly right. Can you fix the leak?"

"I must take a look but most likely, yes. I will work on that while the healer tends to Viz. And you—I will speak with one of the harbor men. They will get in touch with the main port and tell them what happened. Someone will come for your goods. Will you go with them?"

"I have to," El said. "I'll come back, but I may be in a hurry to leave when I do."

"Then I will get to work on the fuel leak as soon as I speak to the harbor man." He reached out and squeezed El's shoulder hard, pressing his lips together as he did so. El met his eyes and nodded, acknowledging the deep emotion there. Umaren nodded then stepped away. He didn't look at the healer or her assistant bent over Vizzel's prone body; he just went to the passenger door and called to one of the men outside.

A while later—again, El had no idea how long—Umaren returned to speak with him.

"The main port sent a team to pick up your cargo. They have arrived. I am about to open the cargo door."

"Do they know I'm going with them?" El asked.

"They have been informed," Umaren said with a tiny smile and a glint of hard humor. El was glad to see something besides worry in the other man's expression, and he responded with a tiny smile of his own.

"Good," El said. "I'm ready."

Neither spoke as they lowered the combination door and ramp and loaded the cargo into a larger version of one of the native trucks. The healer and her assistant continued to work on Vizzel, and Umaren appeared to be focused entirely on fixing the seaplane's fuel leak. He waved a hand in response when El told him he was leaving but otherwise didn't look up from what looked like a maintenance manual of some kind.

El took his cue and followed the cargo team out to their truck. They didn't seem to be talkative types either, sitting silently as the vehicle pulled away from the small port and headed up a bumpy, rutted trail through the island's back country. Eventually, they topped a rise, and El got his first glimpse at the sprawling settlement that ringed the large, long bay that led to the massive harbor. It was deep, too, judging by the intense indigo blue of the water. It looked like something that belonged on a postcard, but it wasn't the picturesque beauty that drew his eye.

It was the spaceport.

Or whatever it was. He didn't know what else to call it because it looked like nothing so much as the newspaper photographs he'd seen of the Kennedy Space Center in Florida. Only this was much bigger, and with far more facilities. No fewer than ten large pads and twice the number of smaller ones, all of which were connected to short, wide landing strips, although there were none of KSC's tall, tower-like gantries jutting up into the sky. The complex stretched out over the water on the far side of the harbor. Some of the pads were obviously still in various stages of construction, but it was clear that even if the R'Baku weren't capable of spaceflight they understood—or were following the instructions of people—who knew what was required to move large amounts of material to orbit—before the Harvesters even showed up.

Murphy and the SpinDogs were going to be *very* interested to know that.

The vehicle bumped again, then it settled onto a much smoother road. They continued toward the spaceport, and El did not want to appear to be gawking, but it was really hard not to stare as he tried to memorize every detail. Rows and rows of boats, VTOLs, and seaplanes dominated the water and shore around the site. Every space not dedicated to the pad construction looked like a military staging area for one hell of an amphibious operation. He wished he'd brought a camera, though he could hardly have gotten away with snapping a Polaroid. Still, it would have been nice to capture that first view, especially as the buildings of the city began to block the spaceport from his sight.

They continued winding through the city, heading for the harbor, until they stopped next to a loading dock that led to one of hundreds of warehouses. As El looked at them stretching away in both directions, he was reminded of something Umaren had said back on the mainland: The "boss" was collecting "all the stuff."

Nalyiriz was right. And El was certain she'd find it very interesting that all of these collected goods had been brought here, to this island and its sea of warehouses next to so many launch pads. He couldn't help but wonder what else was being staged here.

The slamming of the driver's hatch jolted El out of his hypothesizing, and he pushed to bring his mind back to focus on the objective at hand. He waited for the driver to open the cargo door, and then stepped out and began to help with the unloading, following the driver's instructions as to where to put the items among the almost endless racks and shelves in the warehouse.

He wanted to be subtle about it, so it took a few minutes, but eventually he was able to separate himself from the other two workers as they hauled crates back and forth. Once he found himself alone at the drop off point, he stacked the crate he was carrying and stepped quickly around the other side of the shelf. There wasn't a lot of light in the place, but there was enough for him to see that goods were organized like by like—and he was in the raw materials section.

He picked a direction and followed the shelves deeper into the warehouse, blessing his luck when the crates and baskets and barrels turned to jars and bottles: refined goods. More time passed—and he still had no sense of how long he had searched—but he eventually came upon a box holding twelve large jars of the unmistakable ultramarine blue powder.

Jackpot.

Only one problem remained: how was he going to smuggle out an entire box of this stuff?

"Where are you, you dark skinned *vith*?"

The senior of the two cargo handlers rounded the corner of the nearest stack of shelves and spotted El standing in front of the *tra*. The man's face hardened with suspicion, and he approached, flexing his hands and bowing up as if preparing for a fight.

"What are you doing over here? This is not where I told you to go."

"I got turned around in the shelves," El said, smiling slightly and spreading his hands to appear harmless and incompetent. "I was trying to find my way back. Thank goodness you've found me so quickly!"

"Quickly? You've been gone for hours." The man frowned, his voice dropping into a low, aggressive register. "Don't give me that shit. I think maybe you're a thieving *vith* and you need to be taught a lesson!"

The man whipped a knife out of his sleeve and lunged at El, who jumped backward, feeling the swish of air against his belly as the man's strike missed. Without thinking about the action, his hand shot out and captured the man's knife hand, then turned and twisted hard. The man yelped and dropped the knife as he collapsed to his knees. El continued his movement, feeling the snaps as the man's wrist, and then elbow, dislocated. Then he bent, picked up the knife, and drove it into the man's neck, just as he'd done to Tewken however many days before.

"Beors? Did you find him?" It was the second cargo handler.

"Help us," El called out. "The crates collapsed and Beors is hurt!"

"Where are you?"

"I'm here, over by the bottles!"

"What are you doing over there?"

The second man rounded the corner at a run, caught sight of his comrade's bloody body, and tried to stop short. But he had too much momentum, and Beors' blood made the floor slick. He slipped and went down hard. Before he could recover his balance and wind enough to sit up, El was on him. A quick twist and a slice, and a second body was bleeding out on the floor of the warehouse.

Not the cleanest operation, but it would do.

El inhaled deeply and focused his mind on calming his breathing and heart rate while he figured out what to do next. He had to get back to the seaplane, obviously, but if he just left the bodies, it would be evident that something happened here, and he wanted a head start getting off the island.

Then he remembered the barrels he'd passed. A quick trip back through the shelves showed him that, indeed, several empty barrels sat stacked near the loading dock.

He removed two and rolled them one by one back to the bodies. Then he stuffed each man inside a barrel, sealed the lid as best he could without tools, and rolled the two barrels to join the ones fitted into the lowest level of shelves. Then he found a bucket of sand and a broom—presumably some kind of spill kit—and cleaned up the blood as best he could. He dumped the bloody sand into another empty barrel and loaded that one into the truck. He figured he could dump it off the wharf just before Umaren took off. Then he went back to the precious *tra* and took two full boxes containing twelve jars each. Each jar was easily the size of his head.

That ought to be enough for a while. He jumped into the driver's seat, started the truck, and slowly rolled back the way he had come.

More time passed. Somehow, he found his way back to the little port. He still wasn't tired, but he noticed that his attention was starting to fray. He tried to review the timeline of events since he'd killed the drivers of the first two trucks, but there were an increasing number of blank spots the closer he got to the present. He had no memory of leaving the city, but here he was, pulling up to the wharf where Umaren's seaplane rocked in the water next to the dock.

He cut the engine of the truck and got out, carrying the boxes of *tra* with him.

Now he was on board the seaplane, and Vizzel was looking at him with concern. He was lying down, his head wrapped in a bandage, and he had the beginnings of two black eyes. The seaplane's engines thrummed through El's body.

"Where's the *tra*?" he asked. His voice sounded weird in his own ears. He let out a short laugh, then couldn't remember why he was laughing.

"You loaded it," Vizzel said, reaching out and almost touching his face. El flinched, and Vizzel froze. He dropped his hand, but kept speaking in that same kind, concerned tone. "You loaded it. And also a barrel from the truck. Then you parked the truck by the others and came aboard. Then you passed out."

"Where are we?"

"Out over the ocean."

"There may be…pursuit…"

Vizzel smiled and shook his head. "No. And even if there were, Maren would lose them in the dusk growing ahead of us. You're safe, El."

El reached back to push himself up, but his head started to spin, and he paused, trying to keep it steady. "We have to dump that barrel."

Vizzel reached out again and pushed him down.

"I'll take care of it. You just rest, El. Let us take you home."

Chapter Twelve

"So, Sergeant Frazier's mission was a success then?" Murphy asked, though his tone made it clear that he wasn't really asking anything. Mara hated the way he could do that and wished she could figure out the trick for herself. She pressed her lips together and let that tiny irritation become just one more log on the bonfire of rage burning in her mind.

"Nominally so, sir," Mara said, her voice clipped. She knew Murphy could tell something was wrong, but she found she didn't mind. Let him see how pissed she was. "El recovered enough *tra* to see the SpinDogs and our people through the Searing. Nalyiriz says that birth rates tend to decline around now anyway. She's equally enthusiastic about the intel he brought back: that the satraps appear to be seizing as many of R'Bak's pharmacological resources as possible while they wait for their Kulsian masters to reappear. That, plus the data El gained about the island and the facilities, and his contacts with the seaplane captain, have made her very happy."

"So, what, then, is the problem, Major?"

"The problem, *sir*, is that my NCO and crew chief may never fully recover! He's still under round-the-clock care, and Doc Nalyiriz says his adrenal system is nearly completely burned out, as is his ability to perceive the passage of time. He's like a dementia patient, sir! And all for what? If I could have just been there—"

"What, Mara?" Murphy asked, his voice low and dangerous. "What would you have done? He still would have had to collect the *tra*."

"Not by himself! We could have sent a full mission package to get it! Fuck! It's not worth—"

"One man's life? I think you forget yourself, Major. You're not thinking like a leader."

"Fuck you! I absolutely *am* thinking like a leader! *I'm* putting the welfare of my people ahead of some bullshit diplomatic 'necessity' that may not even exist!" Mara surged to her feet and slammed her hand down on Murphy's desk. "You know as well as I do that if the SpinDogs needed this *tra* so badly, they would have done anything to get it—including a full-scale operation—instead of sacrificing *my crew chief*! All for a little secrecy and recon that we could have done *just as well* from our orbital scans and overflights!"

"Lee: sit down." Murphy's voice cracked through the room and brought her up short.

Damn that stupid military indoctrination! She stared at him, her teeth bared in fury, her chest heaving with emotion as the echoes of her rant faded away. Murphy met the firestorm of her temper with his own controlled, immovable ice. Maybe she was an inferno, but the man across from her was a fucking glacier, and he never let her forget it.

She let out a growl and sank slowly back into the chair across from him, daring him to speak.

"For someone so damned smart, Mara, you're being incredibly stupid right now. I've told you before that your unique position—"

"Don't start that 'you're the bridge' bullshit again—"

"You. Will be. Quiet," Murphy snapped. "You had your rant and told me to go fuck myself. Now you will shut your mouth and listen. Mara, open your goddamn eyes and see. *What do you think we're doing here?*"

"What? We…we're building an alliance—"

"We're building a *community*," Murphy said. "We're building a *culture*, an entire fucking *civilization*. I get that you're mad that your friend got hurt. I regret the necessity for it, too, but make no mistake—it *was* absolutely necessary! I can't risk you on the surface right now because who else is going to take over when I die?"

Mara froze, her rage sputtering and fading like embers in a downpour. "When you…what?"

"Do you know why I was on your helicopter in the first place? I was being sent home because I have multiple sclerosis. No one knows that, and you're not going to tell anyone. And that is an order.

"Nalyiriz knows, and she is working on it, but I don't have a lot of hope…nor do I have any idea how long I have. But in that time, however long it is, I must do two things. I must ensure the survival of our people and create a new home for us, because you and I both know there's no going back, and, *if* we're to survive, we need allies, and, *if* we're to work with the SpinDogs as we've decided to do, then we *must* adapt to their culture and environment. You know that even the most receptive among them are still suspicious of us, our culture, our motives. The most conservative factions range from being unhappy with our presence to being willing to shove us out airlocks given the chance. So, it is vital—*vital*—that you maintain the relationship with your child's family and allow them the semblance of some control over the child. Otherwise, their enemies will have everything they need to cast us adrift, and we won't have a prayer of surviving.

"You *have* to understand these things, Mara, because there isn't anyone else. I'm dying, and when my sun sets, yours *must* rise. Whether you're technically in charge will be beside the point. You are the conduit to the SpinDogs, and that makes yours the highest hand on our side of the table. Because when I'm gone, it has to be *you* who makes these tough decisions. So, while I appreciate your concern for your NCO, you can't afford to let that distract you from the bigger picture. El is a combat veteran. He knew the risks he took. Don't make his sacrifice worthless by destroying our only hope of long-term survival."

"Sir, I…" Mara said. Murphy waved a hand and she fell silent.

"I didn't tell you this to gain your pity. I don't want it. What I want is for you to show me that you can be the leader I need you to be. That *all* of the Lawless need you to be. You are the only one who can do it, Mara. Not just because of your rank, but because of who you are, of how the SpinDogs see you. I'm just a commander. You? You'll be our first matriarch…and that's something they understand. So, don't fuck this up, Mara. Got it?"

Mara pressed her lips together and nodded, her head spinning.

"Good," he said. "Now go."

Mara stood and walked to the door, then she paused and turned back to him. "Murph," she said softly. "For what it's worth, I'm sorry I said all that."

He looked up at her from the slate he'd started studying.

"I-I was mad; you're right. It's no excuse, though."

"You're right. And don't ever make the mistake that I'm choosing to make right now."

She frowned. "Wh—what mistake?"

"Not throwing you in hack for talking shit at me. And no, I'm not worried about following some asinine regulation. I'm talking about observing and maintaining the basis, the *foundation*, of respect. Even if you don't care about that, and the Lost Soldiers don't care about it, you can be sure the *SpinDogs* will care about it. If they see you accept the slap of having a subordinate tell you to fuck off, why, they'll be next in line to do it louder—and harder. It's who they are and how they're built; they will fuck you over but good, and what happens to you will happen to every last one of us." He turned his eyes away as if she wasn't even standing there. "Thus endeth the lesson. Dismissed."

She tried to place the movie from which he'd stolen the line, gave up, started to leave—but turned back again. "I'm—I'll figure it out. The leadership thing."

He looked at her and stared for a long moment before nodding slowly. "See that you do. And start by demonstrating what all leaders must: that they can follow orders just as well as give them." He kept watching her. "Follow my order, Major."

"What order?"

"The one I already gave." He smiled slightly. "You are *dismissed*...Mara."

Remaining well within the margins of the room's darkest shadows, Mara let the door open, let the familiar silhouette get half way to the wall panel that controlled lighting, temperature, security, pressurization command overrides. She was about to speak when the shadow halted sharply, then relaxed.

"Hello, Mara," said Nalyiriz.

How the hell *does she do that?* "Hello, sister."

"Why are you here waiting—?"

"I needed to see you. But I have to be quick. Before anyone notices I'm here."

In the near dark, Nalyiriz's teeth shone in a ghostly smile. "Surely you are aware that we have security protocols that record all comings and going from our quarters."

"And surely you have sufficient rank and skill to get access to those records and erase—or loop—them before anyone reviews the countless dull hours of traffic in your very quiet section of the spin."

The shadow sat across from her. "Astute." A long pause. "Murphy told you."

Don't I get to drop any *surprises?* "He did. And now you've told me."

"Told you what?"

"That Murphy told *you*."

"Actually, he did not. I saw the signs of his condition. Actually, Kelrevis saw them first and took steps to see if legends of a cure deserved any credence."

Mara frowned. *Took* what *steps? Wait*—"Is that why Kelrevis was on R'Bak? Looking for a cure?"

Nalyiriz's shadow nodded. "It was necessary. And your presence here tells me you, too, understood that the moment Murphy told you."

"Well, it took about a minute. But I was only a dozen steps from his office when it hit me. If he dies of a wasting disease, that's just the first domino to fall."

"I am still not sure what a 'domino' is, but if by that you mean it would be a misfortune that would spawn many more, you are correct. And that is why I knew you had come here secretly. There is nothing else that would make it necessary for you to seek to have a conversation with me that no one else would witness, and of which there would be no record. Because you realize the risk it presents. To all of us."

Mara nodded. "Your people would see his disease as indicating his weakness as our leader, our *Sko'Belm*. Our allies will stand back. Our enemies will become more bold."

"And the Otlethes Family will be deemed flawed and untrustworthy for having championed an alliance with such an inferior leader possessing such an inferior force. It will support the arguments with which Primus Kormak sought to extirpate us, will suggest to those who are undecided that they were right after all."

"Well…did Kelrevis find anything?" As the words left Mara's mouth, she realized why Nalyiriz had insisted on searching for the *tra* herself. "Or did *you*?"

The shadow's narrow shoulders rose and fell: a shrug. "Before she was killed, Kelrevis confirmed that it was not merely myth. All I learned was that the answer is not to be found in the Greens. If such a cure exists, all evidence is that it is to be found in the Ashbands, possibly beyond them."

"You mean, closer to the equator? Can anything even live there?"

"Possibly the equator, possibly the southern hemisphere. All I know is that the mixture of folklore and possible fact pertaining to this rumored cure come from outside the Greens, not within them."

"So what do we do to—?"

"Sister. *We* can do nothing. I must do this. Alone. As the Healer of the Otlethes Family, I am the only one with the knowledge and role that allows me to search without raising any suspicions." The shadow stood. "And now, if you mean to keep your visit secret, we must bring it to a close."

Mara rose, made for the door.

"No," Nalyiriz murmured, "there is another way, a passage within the bulkheads themselves. Very few know of it. Follow me."

PART TWO

Chapter Thirteen

"Desperado Actual is on the line, Colonel."

Murphy nodded his thanks at Makarov and leaned closer to the microphone. "Bo? How do you read me?"

"Five by five, sir. To what to I owe this unexpected pleasure?"

Murphy smiled at Bo's butter-wouldn't-melt-in-my-mouth irony. "I know it's late—well, early—but I have an update that couldn't wait."

"I'm all ears, sir. But according to my watch, we don't have a lot of satcom window."

"Pete tells me we've got just over five minutes. I just received some crucial intel about potential PoIs."

This time, Bo's response was crisp and eager. "Ready to copy, sir."

"This intel is from the locals who helped, and were helped by, Sergeant Frazier during his recent mission. In addition to having direct contacts on R'Bak Island, they have routine contact with commercial agents of many of the Ashbands' satraps. That gives them insight into their current changes in behavior.

"Specifically, with so many lesser satraps getting pushed out of the Hamain, and, with all of them unnerved by the lack of Kulsian response to the elimination of the reavers, they're slipping into an 'every bastard for himself' mentality. That's why they're ranging into the north Greens to get medicinals; they figure that having those cash crops already in hand is the best way to ensure the continued favor of the Harvesters, no matter the conditions when they arrive—*if* they arrive. The satraps have never had to deal with this before. They're panicked and getting desperate."

Bo paused before responding. "Well, sir, that's good news for us, but I'm not sure how it helps me find PoIs here in the Ashbands."

"Here's how: in explaining why the satraps are all starting to go a little mad, Sergeant Frazier's friends explained that it's making things particularly dicey for the Kulsians who were planetside when we took out their spaceside elements. And any of them who weren't near the Downport are now trying to return there—quickly. Because the crazier the satraps get, the more likely it is that the Kulsians could go from being respected guests to potential hostages…or liabilities to be eliminated."

"Hmmm," mused Bo, "one of those wayward Kulsians could prove to be a *really* useful person of interest."

"Exactly. Any of them who was more than a thug with a gun is likely to have some crucial insights on Kulsian operations and protocols on R'Bak Island and at Downport. After all, some of them had to be competent enough to oversee dirtside activities and the reavers on task."

"Yeah," said Bo, "and I'll bet the guys who got that job had no great love for it. I mean, they've got the skills, but they haven't been assigned to the Harvesters, or even the surveyors. They've been sent out to mind and herd the crazies. To get a shit job like that, they must have drawn the short straw in a bad luck lottery back on Kulsis."

"And if you're right, it means they might already be somewhat disaffected."

"Logical," Bo agreed, "because the odds are good that anyone who was in that lottery came from the bottom of the barrel. Possibly because they just come from the wrong part of town or the wrong side of the tracks, whichever they have on Kulsis."

Murphy thought for a moment. "If you're right, we might get lucky and find somebody who was sent to R'Bak with the reavers, not because they were incompetent or untrustworthy or insubordinate, but simply because of bigotry."

Murphy heard the disgusted shrug in Bo's voice. "I've seen *that* in enough places, including inside our own army. Worse among the warlords in the Mog, though. So much worse that there aren't even words."

"I remember," Murphy affirmed grimly. "Now, how do we maximize our chances of getting our hands on one of these Kulsian PoIs?"

Bo's answer was swift and decisive. "I recommend putting more of our focus on Imsurmik, sir. The traffic is heavier, and there's a tower nearby for docking airships. For my money, that makes it the most likely travel hub for PoIs, particularly ones who are trying to get back to Downport from inland regions. But I still don't want to concentrate my forces there, not until we've got better intel. If we go too early, we increase the chance of being spotted."

"It's a tough balancing act, Bo, because you might get actionable intelligence without a lot of lead time. A PoI could be spotted before you've got all your people on site, let alone ready to cross the line of departure. And the PoIs could change location in just a few hours."

"Could be less time than that," Bo amended sourly. "But if that's the case, then we'll have to go with what we've got ready. Because we need a window—or better yet, a pipeline—into the Kulsian port and shipside operations. Without it, well…as you've said, that could be 'game over' for all of us." He paused. "But fair warning, Colonel: without enough lead time, an attack on any town can get messy—and costly. Particularly since our 'plan' may not be much more developed than the CONOPS we've all agreed on: breach the walls, send in a snoop-and-poop team, and as soon as PoIs are confirmed for extraction, tell the team their new mission is now grab-and-go."

"I agree, Bo; it's a lousy way to run an op. So I've been considering some steps we can take to reduce the amount of force you have to preposition in one location."

"I'm all ears, sir."

"There's a village less than two days march from Imsurmik that your reports categorize as 'highly amenable to recruitment.'"

"Yes, sir. That's Nuthhurfipiko. I've been wondering why you haven't moved on that intel."

"Because we can get troops from all over the Ashbands, Bo, but any that come out of Nuthhurfipiko are going to have a good deal of knowledge regarding Imsurmik. Some may have even been there. And they can remain in their own village until a day before you attack. So I'm going to send someone down to recruit a special team from Nuthhurfipiko and train it nearby, just in case Imsurmik becomes our target."

"Well, that *will* make my job easier. Breaking into a satrap stronghold will be tough enough. But finding and extracting a PoI? That really requires special troops, trained for the job."

"Yes," Murphy agreed, "and that's why I'm going to have a chat with their possible commander right after I sign off."

Bo broke a long silence by asking, "Are you thinking of using Cutter, sir?"

"You know his story?"

"A bit, sir. Are you sure he can, well, handle it?"

"*Can* he? Yes. *Will* he? That's what I'm going to find out. Glass Palace out."

Lieutenant Tyree Cutter figured it wasn't a coincidence when Colonel Murphy entered the mess hall scant seconds after he finished breakfast. Unlike their previous meetings, where Murphy appeared more friendly than serious, Murphy was all business. The colonel's reflective scowl meant the moment Cutter dreaded had arrived.

After waking up in a world he barely comprehended, he'd assumed the moment would come when he found out *why* somebody had gone to so much trouble to save his life. Cutter didn't kid himself that they wanted him for anything other than his combat experience, so he suspected he knew why Murphy was there, and that the colonel wouldn't like Cutter's answer.

"Good morning, Lieutenant," Murphy said, sitting across from him.

"Is it, sir?"

Not only didn't Murphy fall for the bait, the downturned corners of his mouth made it clear he didn't appreciate subordinates laying verbal traps for him. In 1944, Cutter would have cared about a superior officer's response. Now he didn't.

"Yes, Lieutenant Cutter, it is both good and morning. And you have just wasted ten seconds of my time. Don't do it again, is that clear?"

"Yes, sir. Sorry, sir."

"I doubt very much that you're sorry, Lieutenant. You certainly don't sound like it. Nor should you think I'm unaware of what your answer will be when I give you your first mission orders. You plan to say no and that response is unacceptable, so be advised."

Cutter used his thumb to scrape at his front tooth, a nervous habit he'd picked up early in the fighting after coming over Omaha Beach on D-Day plus five. The hedgerows of the Normandy bocage country made for claustrophobic warfare that only grew worse at night, when a man could only grab sleep in brief snatches.

"May I speak freely, Colonel?"

"Yes, but be quick."

"If you've come to give me a combat assignment, I'll take it and do my best. But if it's a combat *command* assignment, I'm not the man for the job."

Murphy's scowl softened into something more akin to an empathetic frown. He clenched and unclenched his left hand several times before he glanced down and realized what he was doing. "That answer is no more acceptable than it was ten seconds ago. You're willing to fight and perhaps die, but not to order others to do the same thing?"

"That's the size of it."

"Do the circumstances matter?"

"No, sir, not really."

"In France, you fought an enemy that was among the toughest on Earth: well trained, well led, well armed, and, for the most part, highly motivated. The losses your platoon suffered were not your fault, Lieutenant Cutter. Other American units suffered worse than yours."

"No offense, sir, but it's hard to suffer worse than 'wiped out.'"

"And now you have survivor's guilt, is that it?"

"Something like that, Colonel. I was entrusted with the lives of thirty-seven men who followed me into France on June 11, and, two months later, they were all gone. I assume you want me to repeat that failure with a new bunch of guys, because, otherwise, why are you here?"

"What were you doing when you were rescued?"

"We've already discussed this, sir."

"Discuss it again."

Cutter shrugged. *Why not?* "Pre-dawn on August 7, we were dug into a little hill east of the French town of Mortain, right in the path of a German counterattack. My platoon was down to twelve men at that point, one squad, and we were supposed to pull back later that day to absorb replacements.

"The morning was warm, and there was the usual mist hanging low over the countryside. We heard German tanks coming, lots of 'em, down this lane that ran straight below our position. I radioed company HQ, and they told us to hold as long as we could and then pull back.

"We didn't have a bazooka or any heavy weapons, but we'd captured a German *panzerschreck* with some ammo, so I ordered two men to get it and cover the road. The first tank that came into view was a Panther. The man with the *panzerschreck* asked permission to open fire at forty yards, but I told him to wait until the range was down to twenty yards. The lane was narrow, and if we knocked out the lead tank, we'd gum up the works for the whole Kraut attack. That's what got my men killed, that extra twenty yards of waiting."

"Could the weapon have penetrated at forty yards?"

"Maybe. Panthers had pretty thick front armor, so it's hard to say. But once you fired a *panzerschreck,* everybody knew where you were because of all the smoke. We'd killed plenty of Germans because of it, so I knew we'd only get one shot and wanted to be sure of a kill."

"That's a good tactical decision, Tyree."

Cutter shifted in his seat at hearing his first name. "Thanks for saying it, sir, even if neither one of us believes it."

"When we're alone, please call me Rodger, or even Rog."

"Uh, sure, sir…I mean, Rodger. And most people called me TD, but not because I played football; my middle name's Denning."

"TD it is."

"So, anyway, on that morning, while the boys were waiting on the Panther to get close enough, *panzergrenadiers* slipped across the field on our left and got behind us. By the time we took out the Panther, we were cut off. I ordered the men to make a break for our lines and stayed behind to cover them, but I waited too long. I heard MG 42s and watched my men get chopped to pieces, and then the world went black."

"And you woke up here." Murphy's left hand twitched. He lifted it and rubbed his wrist. "Would it change your mood to know that seven of your men survived?"

Cutter's eyes narrowed. "How could you know that?"

Without turning his head, Murphy's eyes roamed over the interior of the rotating space habitat that was home to their hosts, a branch of humanity (mostly) that referred to itself as the SpinDogs. "In light of your present environment, does it really seem so far-fetched? Eleven of the thirty-seven men you led into France wound up killed in action, three were taken prisoner, and sixteen more were wounded. That's thirty casualties out of thirty-seven men: by no means an unusual casualty percentage in the ETO. It wasn't even the worst in your regiment. By the time the war ended, the 30th Infantry Division, *your* division, suffered 18,446 casualties, more than three thousand of whom died. That's close to one hundred percent casualties, TD—worse than your platoon—but the division CO, Major General Leland Hobbs, is considered one of America's finest division commanders who served during World War Two."

Cutter digested the information for a few seconds before responding. "Thank you, Rodger, I guess that's something."

Something changed in Murphy's expression and tone, something that tipped Cutter off that the hard sell was coming. "Tell me, if it was 1942, but you had your memories, if you knew what was going to happen to your men, would you do it all over again? Fight against America's enemies, I mean."

"Sure I would."

"Why?"

Blood flushed Cutter's face, and he tensed. "I'm sorry, Colonel," he said, dropping the first name familiarity, "but that's kind of an offensive question."

"Answer it anyway."

"Because the Japanese and the Nazis were evil."

"And all it takes for evil to triumph is for good men to do nothing, eh?"

"Something like that," Cutter said. Sensing he was being set up, Cutter tried to outmaneuver Murphy. "But fighting and leading aren't the same thing…sir."

Murphy matched Cutter's indignation, although Cutter couldn't tell if it was an act or not. "You must really have been a terrible platoon leader, Lieutenant Cutter, so maybe it *is* better that you just carry a rifle and do what you're told. That way, even if your replacement is incompetent and gets everybody killed, you can die with a clear conscience. The platoon will be just as dead, but it won't be your fault."

Damn! "That's…not what I'm saying, Colonel."

"That's exactly what you're saying, Lieutenant. It's not death you fear; it's obvious that you're no physical coward. What scares you is making decisions that lead to the deaths of others. Correct?"

Cutter stared at him without responding. Murphy took that as a tacit "yes" and kept going.

"What you don't understand is that by declining to accept a command, you are still making a decision that will lead to men dying. Somebody has to take them into battle, and what you're saying is that you'd rather let someone less qualified do it, even if more men die, because that way their deaths won't be on your conscience. That makes you a *moral* coward."

"If you think insulting me will change my mind, Colonel—"

"I don't have the time or energy for insults; that's just the plain truth. And here's another truth for you: if men die because you didn't have the balls to lead them, then their blood is on your hands far more than if you did."

Cutter opened his mouth to speak, but Murphy held up a hand.

"Lastly," the colonel said, "I can't just hand you a weapon and point you at the enemy. My officers aren't expendable, and having them taking orders from non-coms doesn't work, so if you're only willing to carry a rifle, I'll need those bars."

Reaching up, Cutter's long fingers, which his grammar school music teacher said were perfect for playing the piano, traced the surface of the cool, silver metal on his left shoulder. Now that it came to it, he couldn't imagine giving them up.

"What about me being their training officer?" he said, trying one final gambit.

"Lieutenant Cutter…TD…" Murphy glanced around, maybe a little too theatrically for Cutter's taste, but he understood. Even if the SpinDogs were their allies, that didn't make all—or even most of them—friends. And it certainly wouldn't stop any of them from bugging the room. "I don't have the luxury of putting you in a training slot. The people down on R'Bak are fighting the same war the French fought during World War Two. Evil men are sucking the life out of locals for their own benefit, and we're trying to help those indigs survive. That you were trying to liberate Paris and we're trying to liberate a planet called R'Bak is merely a distinction of time, place, and name: the fight is the same.

"If I combined every Lost Soldier into one command, we couldn't field more than two platoons, plus a few replacements. We've already suffered casualties, we're gonna suffer more, and time's running out. So, I need your answer: can the indigs count on you to help them like you helped the French?"

"I'm Catholic, sir," Cutter said, stating the non-sequitur with a straight face.

"What does that mean?"

"The way you lay on the guilt, sir…you remind me of my mother."

For the first time since they'd met, Murphy cracked a smile that didn't seem false. "I'll take that as a compliment. You'll accept the command?"

"One question first."

"What?"

"So if the aliens who brought us here—the Dornaani?—came all this way, why didn't they just do the dirty work themselves?"

"That's a long, complicated answer, TD. And I'm not sure I've been given all of it, myself."

"Old aliens never die, they just kidnap old soldiers to do it for them?"

Murphy managed a grunt. "Something like that. Start getting ready, TD."

"What did you have in mind, sir?"

"We've got some people here who can give you a primer in the local language. And you'll want to brush up on any skills you're going to teach. Not that *Spin One* has a lot of great spaces for that."

"Not an issue, sir. I just need a private compartment."

"That's all?"

Cutter thought. "And guns, Colonel. One of every type the indigs will be using."

Murphy rose. "You'll have them within the hour."

Chapter Fourteen

Over the following weeks, Cutter underwent intense training with the newer weapons systems, like field stripping, cleaning, and assembling the M14 until he could do it blindfolded and could therefore teach his troops how to do it as well. He didn't have to; Murphy didn't require it. But Cutter's command style was to know his men's jobs better than they did. He also received intensive and more in-depth language training, sessions on the history of R'Bak, the political situation, and the climate. It all came to him in what he remembered as a long blur of endless lessons.

When Murphy finally sent word he was ready to lay out the mission, Cutter knew it was his last chance to back out. If he did so, the men selected for his dirtside command wouldn't be looking to him to lead them; they'd be relying on someone else, someone less worried about screwing up and more worried about completing their assigned mission.

When Murphy arrived, Cutter had an M1A1 Thompson submachine gun on the table in front of him. The gun had been replicated by the SpinDogs in every detail except the maker and manufacture marks. Those had been eliminated in the attempt to conceal the actual origins of the weapons, if any of them got into what the colonel cryptically referred to as "knowledgeable hands."

Cutter had tied the sleeve of a spare shirt around his eyes as a blindfold, and, with the ambient noise in the SpinDogs' habitat, he hadn't heard Murphy's approach. As he'd done during the black nights in Normandy, he practiced field stripping his weapon without being able to see it; he'd learned first-hand you couldn't rely on having enough light any more than you could rely upon a dirty weapon.

By feel alone, he pushed up on the catch located above the trigger and released the magazine. Pulling back the bolt, he checked the chamber using his left pinkie finger, then pushed the bolt back into place. A small button on the rear of the frame, near the stock, released the top of the gun, but it wouldn't come fully loose until he pulled the trigger. Once the Thompson was in two halves, he felt for the button on the back of the top half, pushed it, and applied pressure to the recoil spring guide rod to remove the buffer. Next, he removed the spring and guide rod, careful not to let them shoot across the room. After pulling back the bolt, he took out the cocking knob that held it in place. With that done, he removed the bolt itself and made ready to clean the weapon.

"Impressive." It was the voice of Colonel Murphy.

"I'm outta practice," Cutter said, slipping off the blindfold. "It still took me twice as long as it used to."

"It *has* been a few years."

"Just a few." Tyree decided not to point out that in terms of consciousness, it hadn't even been one. "What can I do for you, Colonel?"

Murphy sat opposite Cutter, careful not to disturb any of the gun parts on the tabletop. He didn't revert to the first names they'd briefly used, which told Cutter the status of their relationship better than words.

"You're needed dirtside, Lieutenant. We've got a target. The one we've been expecting: Imsurmik."

"So I gathered from your message."

"Then you'll appreciate that I mean to keep this briefing short. You'll be leaving in six hours."

"Technically, I never said I'd accept the command, Colonel."

"Doesn't matter; you're going down there either way. The only question is whether you turn indigs into soldiers or waste your talents lugging a rifle and cleaning latrines. Which is it?"

Cutter propped his elbows on the table, clasped his hands, and placed the middle knuckle of his forefinger against his lips. Using his thumbnail, he traced the gap between his front teeth. "May I ask the mission first, sir?"

"Normally I would deny that request, Lieutenant. I'm only making an exception out of respect for your bravery in action. Your psych evals say you don't have PTSD, but I'm not so sure about that."

"PTSD?"

"Combat psychosis, in 1944 terminology."

"You think I'm nuts."

"I think you may have lingering psychological effects from enduring intense and extended combat, yes, which is why I'm cutting you some slack. It's also why I gave you as much lead time as I could. Not so much to teach yourself how to be an instructor, but to prepare yourself—your mind—for the job ahead. But whether you choose to lead or not, I need you down there now." He pointed at the floor to indicate R'Bak. "Would you like to hear the mission? You'll be going one way or the other."

"Yes, sir."

"Our intelligence indicates that we won't just be facing the enforcers, raiders, and local militias of a powerful local satrap, but a contingent of J'Stull, as well. The J'Stull are collectively the suzerain of the other satrapies in the region, and they have a professional military of sorts. So this operation requires more than simply recruiting more men from among the rest of the indigs. We have to turn some of them into first-class soldiers. Which is where you come in. You've studied R'Bak's topography and what we know of the people?"

"Studied is a pretty generous word for it, but yes, sir, I think I've got the big picture."

"The target is Imsurmik, a small city that lies at the northern fringes of the Ashbands: a kind of transition zone between the vegetated belt called the Greens and the scrub desert known as the Hamain. Under normal circumstances, Imsurmik's population is about twenty thousand. Most of the people live in rude stone and adobe hovels separated by narrow alleys and crowded streets. That's the Outer City. Think of it as...I can't think of a frame of reference you might understand. The Outer City is a slum. Higher up, on a slight ridge, is a walled area where we assume wealthier citizens live, and above *that* is another compound dug into the side of a ninety-foot-high rock plateau. The F'ahdn—the satrap's local governor—rules Imsurmik through fear and intimidation.

"We have intelligence reports that Imsurmik is a refuge during the Sear caused by the approach of the primary star. It is also said to be a gathering spot for those moving north to escape the worst effects of the increasing heat. Major Moorefield plans to insert a human asset into the city—"

"Human asset? Is that like a spy?"

"It *is* a spy. As the Sear approaches, bringing with it the Harvesters, who come to rob the people of their medicinal plants, we have been told there will be a cache of those plants waiting to be handed over. Hundreds of outlying militia will pour into the city at that time, bringing with them their harvests and causing further overcrowding.

"All this is complicated by another factor: the rock formations in the region are honeycombed with natural caverns cut by millions of years of water erosion. Throughout the wastes, the indigs have expanded those. Imsurmik went further: in addition to housing dug into the plateau, there is likely an extensive tunnel network under the city. A river bypasses its outskirts, and it has both artesian wells and a spring."

"No wonder people are heading there."

"When the world becomes an oven, water and shelter mean life."

"How many men are you giving me?"

"I'm not *giving* you any. Approximately fifty men from a village west of Imsurmik have volunteered to oppose this F'ahdn, but it's up to you to convince them to stick around through the training and then to actually risk their lives for the freedom of their people. He has been preying on them for a long time, so there's a lot of built-up resentment."

"You can't want me to seize the city with such a small force."

"No. As things stand now, Major Moorefield's job is to seize the ways in and seal off the exits. After he declares it secure enough for you to enter, you'll lead your elite platoon to round up persons of interest who might have information we can use against the J'Stull and their out-system overlords, the Kulsians."

"My men are elite?"

"I trust you'll make them so."

"And I'm supposed to do that with a platoon? Hell, Colonel, you'd need a battalion for this mission, maybe a regiment."

Murphy shook his head. "First, the J'Stull presence in the city isn't extensive, so there aren't many regulars for you to deal with. Second, don't confuse militia with trained soldiers, and third, I just said I don't expect you to assault Imsurmik."

"In my experience sir, any headquarters above company didn't know shit from shinola about what was going on up front. You say one thing, but when it comes down to it—"

"This is the mission, Cutter. I'm already short of officers, so trust me when I say that Major Moorefield will kick open the doors. It will be your job to find the HVTs inside."

"Colonel, I know you think I understand that jargon, but I don't. What's an HVT?"

"High Value Target, one of the persons of interest I mentioned."

"In other words, a big shot?"

"Possibly, but not necessarily. We believe they have information about enemy security procedures and protocols, as well as potential codes, call signs, and protocols that relate to orbital operations. They may also have knowledge or access to ship designs, weaponry, operating systems, and similar functions. Imsurmik is the mostly likely place for one or more of them to be gathering, so it offers a unique opportunity for an intelligence windfall."

"How many of these…uh, HVTs…are there?"

"We don't exactly know how many there are, but not that many. Major Moorefield will be better able to inform you once the operation is underway."

"Do they wear different uniforms than the others? Maybe have rank badges or something?"

"No, nobody's in uniform except maybe the F'ahdn's immediate bodyguards."

"Is there *some* way to distinguish them from everybody else?"

"I would imagine their clothing is better-made, cleaner, and their shoes are probably of better quality. They'll be well fed. If anyone has access to bathing facilities, it will be them. Look for jewelry, necklaces, chains—that sort of thing. Oh, and their paint. I'm given to understand the people of Imsurmik use paint to protect their skin from the sunlight, rather than layers of cloth like those in the rural areas. They've also come to use it to distinguish their place in society."

"They paint their faces? Like war paint?"

"Like that, yes, except their whole face. The ancient Celts did that, too, sometimes."

"So how do I read this paint stuff?"

"That's unknown. It's one of the things we're hoping you can discover."

"That's not much to go on, sir."

The colonel paused and thought for a moment. "What was the largest city you visited, back on Earth?"

"New York City."

"Good. When you strolled down the sidewalk and looked at all the other people, could you tell by looking at them who had money and who didn't?"

"Now that you mention it, sir, yeah, I guess so."

Murphy nodded. "And the women's makeup—could you tell just by looking at them who might be a working girl?"

"Sure, yeah."

"It's the same thing here, Lieutenant."

Leaning back, Cutter studied Murphy for clues as to the actual difficulty of what he was being asked to do. It *sounded* impossible, yet that was exactly what convinced him to do it. Murphy's logic finally made him realize that if he, a combat veteran, couldn't lead men safely through such a FUBAR mission, what chance did an untrained man have?

"Just so I'm straight on the mission, Colonel Murphy, I'm being asked to chase shadows while trying to remain a shadow myself. In a free fire zone."

"That's about the size of it, Lieutenant Cutter."

"I must have a screw loose…all right, Colonel, I'll do it."

"Of course, you will." Murphy smiled. "I never figured you for cleaning out shitholes. I can't give you a timeline on the mission yet. Some of it depends on how fast we can train up the rest of the indig force we'll need in order to have a chance of success with the main attack. You won't have that many men, but that means each one will need to be trained to a higher standard: an elite standard, if you can manage it. You'll want to concentrate on small unit tactics; that's where your experiences in France should help.

"One more thing, Lieutenant…I've already said we can't do this alone, but that includes officers, too. There simply aren't enough of us, and not every Lost Soldier is officer material, nor should they be. We've got some of the best non-coms you could ask for. If you run into Rodriguez, you'll see what I mean, but there aren't enough of them, either. That means we need to identify, recruit, and train indigs up to our standards in those roles, as well. The sooner you can identify such men, the sooner you'll be combat ready."

"What's the process, sir? Do *I* appoint them as lieutenant or sergeant?"

"Provisionally, yes. You're now an O-2, you can appoint an O-1, a warrant officer if you need one or two, and non-coms. Unless I see a potential problem with your choices, I'll back up the decisions of the man on the spot: you."

"That doesn't sound like the rank structure I'm used to, Colonel."

"Then it's lucky you've got a few hours to learn it."

Chapter Fifteen

If waking up in the SpinDogs' orbiting habitat, or the weeks that followed, hadn't been disorienting enough, the trip to the surface of the planet left Lieutenant Tyree Denning Cutter doubting his sanity. Sure, he'd read pulp stories about spacemen and rocket ships while on the transport over to England in 1943—the same ragged magazines that circulated through every man's hands in the 30th Infantry Division—but reading about them out of boredom didn't prepare Cutter for the real thing.

Once on R'Bak, however, things became more familiar. According to Colonel Murphy's brief, his first step was simply a matter of passing through Major Moorefield's command on the way to a village with a name he couldn't pronounce. There, all he had to do was turn men with whom he had nothing in common and who had no familiarity with Earth weapons, discipline, or command structures, into combat-ready soldiers so they could participate in joint operations with Moorefield's command.

He'd trained men from the ground up before and knew how to do it well. What he didn't know was how to keep them alive once they entered combat. And that would be his biggest fight: the mental one with himself. Everyone he spoke to insisted that losing his entire platoon in France wasn't his fault, but he couldn't manage to believe it. He couldn't force himself to believe that some of his men survived and other units had suffered worse casualties than his. But it was too late to worry about the past. Now, he could only immerse himself in training the indigs to the exclusion of all else.

Wagons pulled by R'Bak's ubiquitous whinaalanis delivered the weapons, ammunition, and other supplies necessary to train and outfit his platoon, escorted by a single armored personnel carrier occupied by Cutter and five guards. Rounding a low hill, Cutter glimpsed a wide river valley on his left as their destination came into sight straight ahead. Built on the crest of a bluff parallel to the river, the stone and wood homes lay in the shape of a long, narrow rectangle. Compared to other parts of the region they'd traversed, the vegetation was thick and reminded Cutter of pictures he'd seen of the Great Plains.

People working in a nearby field spotted them rounding the hill and alerted the village, so that, by the time the convoy stopped in the center of the main road, children were running alongside the wagons, laughing and shouting. Adults lined the path, and a well-muscled man in his late twenties or early thirties waved them to a stop in front of the largest home. Beside him stood a woman of similar age with black hair that shimmered in the harsh sunlight. Both had lowered the facial coverings necessary to block R'Bak's deadly UV radiation so he could see their faces, which Major Moorefield had told him was a show of greeting and friendship.

"I am Tanavuna," the man said after Cutter stepped out of the APC, stiff and hot. "I am the son of our hetman, Nokina, and this is my wife, Kesteluni, our *shevfashli.*"

"Shevfashli" was what this village called their healer, a title of great respect. Cutter bowed his head in the appropriate response. "I am Lieutenant Cutter. It is my great honor to train and assist you in your struggle against the satrap."

"We have heard impressive things about your victories over the J'Stull," Kesteluni said. There was a languid tone to her voice that Cutter found quite soothing.

Cutter thought about mentioning he'd only just landed on R'Bak, but thought better of it. "I've often regretted how much my people know about war, but as long as evil men seek to dominate others, men like me will be necessary."

"I only ask one thing of you, Lieutenant," she said, smiling the friendliest smile he'd ever seen. "Bring my husband home alive, if possible, but if he is fated to die, help him to do it well."

Tanavuna lifted an eyebrow. Before he could speak, she turned the smile on him, and the words died on his lips.

"Let me introduce my father," Tanavuna said. As they entered the home, the drivers and guards began unloading the wagons.

Drenched in sweat, Cutter immediately noticed how much cooler it was inside the house. Instead of windows to allow breezes to pass through, a gray compound that resembled concrete sealed all the joints and seams. Tanavuna introduced his father, a mirror image of his son, only older. After an exchange of courtesies and refreshments, Cutter asked how the heat could be so much less inside the house when it hurt to breathe the hot air outside.

"Do you see the pipes coming out of the ground?" Nokina asked. "The air in the ground is cooler than above and is brought to our homes through those pipes. We seal our homes to retain it, only coming and going when we must so the cooler air does not escape."

"That—this is ingenious."

"Our knowledge of such things comes to us from those who came before," the hetman said.

"As does our knowledge of the healing arts," Kesteluni added. Cutter sipped the water she'd given him. It had a faintly sweet flavor unlike anything he'd tasted on Earth. "I sensed that you felt worry at being among us, so your water contains a mixture of *urot*, *palankea*, and *fel-franzh*. The recipe has been handed down from healer to healer for many generations. I hope you take no offense."

"Not at all. I am grateful you think me worthy of your gifts."

"Are you sure you're a man of war, Lieutenant Cutter? Your courteous words do you credit."

Tanavuna sat beside his wife, beaming as she held court. It surprised Cutter that neither Nokina nor his son objected to her dominating the conversation.

"How do you remember everything about all those plants?" he asked. "I can't remember my father's phone number." Having no R'Bak equivalent, he used the English word phone.

She wrinkled one eyebrow. "Your father's foes were so numerous?"

"No, a phone number is…well, never mind that. I was just saying I have a poor memory."

"Part of being a healer is not forgetting the lore entrusted to you. That is very important."

Preparations for a feast in his honor began in the early afternoon and lasted until the lighting of a bonfire after sunset. Once the sun went down, everyone could relax and remove their robes and face coverings, which, in itself, gave the occasion a festive air. Cutter ate the unfamiliar food with trepidation, but growing up in rural Mississippi during the Great Depression meant he had learned how to enjoy a variety of dishes city folk wouldn't have eaten if they were starving. After a few bites of various meats, he discovered the flavors had a gaminess he liked. Among the vegetables, or what he thought of as vegetables, the stir-fried bulb of a purple flower reminded him of okra.

As the night wore on, the men of his soon-to-be-activated platoon drifted over to say hello and introduce their families. Fatigue from the long day made it impossible to keep all the names and faces straight, except for one older woman who knelt in the dirt and took Cutter's hands in hers. Beside her stood a lean boy—Cutter had trouble thinking of him as a man—with the embarrassed pout of a teenager.

"I am Issikoffa, and this is my only son, Suukamanu. I give him into your care, Lieutenant Cutter. He is a good boy, but impetuous: brave but unwary. Please bring him back to me."

Cutter wasn't sure what to say. On top of the latent guilt he carried from World War Two, how could he assure this mother that her son would come home alive? Combat just didn't work that way.

"Perhaps he should wait a year or two, to gain maturity?" was all he could think to say.

Issikoffa leaned back as if slapped.

"He is grown now, and he will defend his people as a grown man does," she said, obviously offended. He tried to apologize, but she hurried off. Her son spread his arms in a helpless gesture and went the other way, leaving Cutter to gape and wonder what had just happened.

"Take no heed of Issikoffa," said Kesteluni. Sitting on Cutter's right, she'd heard the whole exchange. "She lives to be offended. Her son looks younger than he is and will make a fine soldier."

"I knew people like that back on Earth," he said. But his thoughts were on how the air around her felt alive, like an aura of static electricity surrounded her. It was all he could do to get the words out.

"Earth is your home?"

"It was."

"And it is up there, among the stars?"

"So they tell me."

"Can we see it?"

"I don't think so."

"Did you leave family on Earth, Lieutenant Cutter?"

"My parents, a brother, and two sisters."

"Do you hope to see them again?"

He smiled sadly. "Not in this life."

Kesteluni lifted his chin and locked eyes. It felt like she was hugging him. He wanted to cry. "But in the next?"

"I hope so."

"If living well matters, then you will."

He grunted. "The friends and families of those I've killed would argue differently. They likely felt the same way about their loved ones."

Kesteluni paused to consider his comments. There was a slight upturn to her nose that made her resemble Disney's Snow White. "There is no contradiction in the idea of two warring peoples both living good and fulfilling lives."

Cutter leaned back, struck with the simple but profound truth in her words. "Doesn't that make killing my enemy worse?"

Kesteluni tilted her head the way a proud mother does when her child learns a valuable lesson. "It makes killing your enemy more difficult, and that is the way to peace, but only if your opponent believes as you do."

A small child ran up and whispered in Kesteluni's ear. She nodded and whispered something in return, then got to her feet. "I must go now, Lieutenant Cutter, but I know my people are in good hands."

Once she'd gone, Cutter spoke to Tanavuna with admiration in his voice. "You are one lucky man, Tanavuna."

"Yes, I am very lucky," he said, watching his wife disappear into the darkness, "as Kesteluni reminds me every day."

"She doesn't seem like the type to do that."

"She speaks no such words. She does not need to."

It was not light seeping into the hetman's home that woke Cutter, nor the muffled noises heard through the thick stone walls. Sweat soaked his uniform, but it wasn't because the natural cooling system failed. He wasn't overheated, he had chills. What forced his eyelids open was the throbbing pain of the worst hangover he'd ever experienced. The room's ambient light was dim, but it proved too bright to bear. When did he drink alcohol? Cutter couldn't remember and thinking hurt too much. He closed his eyes and tried to sleep, not even bothering to react when the door opened and closed again. As he drowsed his nostrils picked up a citrus smell, like fresh squeezed limes, and then he drifted off.

Soft words woke him sometime later. He had no way of knowing how long he'd been asleep, but he felt the surface of a woven blanket against his bare skin. Somebody had stripped him and...bathed him? After once going three weeks without the chance to wash, he again felt the joy of being clean. Best of all, the headache was gone.

"Are you awake, Captain Cutter?" whispered a soft female voice.

Pushing up to his elbows, Cutter waited a few seconds until he could make out the slim figure in the dark room. "Either that or I'm dead and gone to Heaven."

"Heaven is the next world you spoke of last night?"

"One of them. How long has the sun been up, Kesteluni?"

"Not long. A mist still hangs over the river. It burns off quickly."

Cutter started to get up before remembering he was nude. "Uh, what happened to my clothes?"

A single candle outlined her face and hands. From where he lay, Cutter could not make out details of what she was doing. Kesteluni appeared to be pushing down and twisting something inside a large vessel. It sounded like rocks grinding together, and after a few seconds he recognized the sound as coming from a mortar and pestle. When the *scritch* of stone-on-stone ended, Kesteluni walked toward him holding out a cup of beaten metal. Cutter admired the effortless flow of her stride, the way her hips moved and, being nude under the blanket, he felt a reflexive reaction that might prove not only embarrassing but dangerous. Twisting to one side he tried to picture the old mule he'd ridden as a boy, anything to dampen his arousal.

If Kesteluni noticed, she didn't mention it. "Drink this," she said, in a gentle tone that nonetheless carried authority.

Careful to drain every drop, Cutter handed her back the cup. "Hair of the dog?"

"What is a dog, and why would you drink its hair?" she said. "Does it heal the body?"

"Some say so. It's another old expression that doesn't translate into R'Baki. It means that drinking alcohol will relieve the headache you got from drinking too much alcohol the night before."

"I see. Did your village healers use this method?"

That sparked an explosive laugh, which devolved into coughing. "Some did," Cutter said after clearing his throat. "Some did way too much."

Kesteluni reacted as if he was describing an actual medicinal treatment. "I do not understand this method. Do you not eventually have to deal with the after-effects of too much alcohol?"

"Not if you keep drinking."

"Forever?"

He could think of nothing to do except shrug and change the subject. "Umm…about my uniform."

"Yes?"

"Well you see, I can't get up without clothes on, and I slept all night and kind of have to…use the latrine."

"Why do you need clothes to do that? Do they not get in the way?"

"It's hard to explain," he said. "I guess you'd say it's cultural."

Rising, she crossed the room and returned with a robe. Cutter managed to slip it on without getting out from under the blanket. Thankfully, his earlier reaction had receded. It was hard to tell in the shadows, but he thought he saw her smile.

A closet-sized room in one corner served as the bathroom. Once finished, Cutter came out to discover that he felt wonderful—better than he could remember feeling in years, in fact. Elation filled him with energy, yet he also felt at peace.

"What did you give me earlier?" he said.

The candle's illumination didn't reach far across the room, so Kesteluni lit a small lamp. The sudden glow was so bright that it was as if one of R'Bak's suns had materialized inside the dark space. Cutter blinked and turned away until his eyes adjusted. Being the home of a healer, he expected what he saw at the far end of the room. Shelves lined with jars, cups, bottles and beakers brought memories of the Rexall drug store in downtown Holly Springs where he'd worked as a kid. A chair made from heavy wooden slats stood to one side, and Cutter recognized the simple movable arms that allowed it to lay flat if desired. It could only have been for Kesteluni to examine afflicted villagers and apply treatments.

Answering his question, her laugh was that of a young woman given gravity by the concern and compassion of a much older country doctor. "It was a mixture my people have used for many lifetimes, to help with sleep. It also has the benefit of easing body and head pains." He could tell that wasn't all she wanted to say, but after opening her mouth, she turned away.

"What were you going to say?" he blurted, before softening his tone. "I'm sorry, it's been a long time since I've been around women for any length of time."

Kesteluni cocked her head. "I am a woman, but what does that mean to you?"

Now his face flushed with embarrassment. "I meant no offense. Where I come from…and *when* I come from, most women had no job other than housework, cooking, and raising the children. The husband worked away from home."

"Hunting?"

"Uh, yeah, in a manner of speaking. Anyway, we—that is, us men—well, we kind of looked on our women as being special. It's hard to explain."

"But the men 'worked?'" Now he saw that the slim, graceful young woman also had a stern side. Crossing her arms, there was no mistaking the disapproval in the set of her jaw. "You speak as if keeping the home is a simple thing. Let me tell you, Captain Cutter; it is not."

"Forgive me, Kesteluni, here I am a guest in your home, and I've given offense. My mother worked harder than anyone I've ever met, taking care of our family and running a farm. I don't know why I said that. I'm sorry, I'll leave now."

As fast as disapproval had transformed her out of the caring healer he'd known until then, now she reverted back to smiling.

"You will *not.* The morning meal will be ready soon, and then we will both eat. But first…would you allow me to examine you?"

Cutter instinctively took half a step back. In pre-World War Two America, doctors were men and good women didn't touch any male except their boyfriend, husband, or father. Girls could be nurses, sure, and many were, but he'd never been treated by one. Plus, what would happen if Tanavuna's father walked in?

"I don't have to take off my robe, do I?"

That brought a full laugh and a sympathetic smile. "I am bonded, Captain, and have attended to many men, so the sight of a disrobed man is nothing new to me. The customs of your land are not those of R'Bak, but if it puts you at ease, for what I intend I do not need you to disrobe. Let me adjust the chair so you may lie down."

The regimentation of the wartime US Army conditioned Cutter to obey orders whether he liked them or not. Ultimately that overrode his reluctance to let a woman touch him. Many men from his platoon had come from big cities with looser morals than small-town Mississippi in the 1920s, but none of that had rubbed off on him. As a child he'd listened to his grandfather spin stories of the days when he'd ridden with Forrest against the Yankee devils, and Cutter had absorbed the old man's ingrained reverence for women.

Kesteluni knelt and held a small burner close enough so Cutter could inhale fumes from its smoldering contents. Immediately, his racing pulse slowed, and his anxiety dimmed. When her fingertips traced the wrinkles in his forehead, Cutter closed his eyes.

"That feels—"

"Ssshhh…"

Kesteluni applied varying amounts of pressure to Cutter's cheeks, lips, mouth, neck, behind his ears, the top of his head, along his shoulder blades, under his armpits and along his cheek, particularly the muscles leading to his shoulders. Nor did she only use her fingertips, but sometimes the side of a finger, or even its top. Under her touch he lost track of time, like falling asleep yet being conscious the whole time. Cutter had never experienced anything like it. By the time he realized she was no longer touching him, Kesteluni had returned to the beaker-laden table along the far wall.

"It is war that keeps you awake at night, is it not?"

"How do you figure?" he said. Confiding to Murphy was one thing—he was a soldier too—but how could he expect a woman to understand? Yet, as soon as the thought came to him, he knew it was wrong; Kesteluni was the local equivalent of a doctor, so she must have seen a lot of death despite her comparative youth.

"In the time and place I come from, talking about such things isn't something men do, but with you…for some reason I don't mind talking about it." Collecting his thoughts, Cutter continued. "It isn't war itself that disturbs my sleep, though. I've studied history, the history of my people that is, and I know that sometimes you have to fight. And when war comes, people die. What haunts me are the faces of the men who died under my leadership, and whether a mistake I made led to their deaths."

Kesteluni leaned close, no more than six inches from his face, so that his nostrils flared as he inhaled her scent. Cutter couldn't say what he expected her to smell like, but tart orange would not have been on the list. All he could think was that it came from the residual oils of some plant she'd ground into his drink, even though it had no orange flavor.

"I do not think that is correct, Captain."

"Beg pardon? I mean, why do you say that?"

"Because you are a smart man, and you know that while your mistakes *might* have resulted in their deaths, it is equally possible that your skill and judgment kept them alive longer than if someone else had been their battle-leader."

"Uh…"

"I think what troubles you is the futility of their deaths. From what you told me last night, this war you fought in…France?"

"Yes, that's right, France."

"The war you fought in France did not have to occur. It was the result of one man, whose greed and hatred caused the deaths of many. That is what I believe troubles you, Captain Cutter, and the similarity of conditions on R'Bak have brought those feelings back to the front of your mind."

"I had not thought of it in that way."

Kesteluni's smile stretched across her entire face, resulting in widened eyes and deep dimples. Her teeth seemed impossibly bright to Cutter.

"Then I am glad to have helped you. Now, you can help me by training my husband to be as great a leader as you are."

Chapter Sixteen

The last dragging hours of daylight felt to Cutter like being back in the landing craft approaching Normandy on June 11, 1944; anxious but not scared. Omaha Beach had been secured four days earlier, and the disembarkation of troops and supplies went off with highly choreographed precision. Mostly. Danger would only come once Cutter's Cutters came into direct contact with the enemy, just as it would now.

Not yet acclimated to the unrelenting heat, Cutter took frequent breaks from organizing the supplies they would need during the coming months of training. Once he'd done all he could do in daylight, he stepped inside the village's communal dining hall and found Kesteluni lecturing four younger healers on the benefits and dangers of various plants. During a break, she introduced her students, two young men among them. Before he could ask why they hadn't joined his platoon, Kesteluni answered his unspoken question.

"Healers protect our people as much as warriors," she said. "It is my responsibility to teach others what I know, because death comes for us all. I cannot leave my people unprotected."

"God will never allow you to die," he said, blurting the words without meaning to. Something about Kesteluni loosened his tongue, kind of like being drunk.

She giggled. "Maybe not your gods," she said, turning his singular into a plural, "but ours are more capricious."

Cutter became so enrapt in Kesteluni's teaching that he lost track of time, and Tanavuna had to fetch him just before the unit had to pack up and leave.

Nightfall came swiftly on R'bak. The line of carts and wagons stretched beyond the last house at the village's western end. Anyone traveling on the river, or perhaps in one of the satrap's blimps flying toward Imsurmik, would have found such a large gathering curious if not suspicious. To avoid spying eyes, Cutter waited until full darkness to start the process of loading.

Keeping Tanavuna close, Cutter began teaching the new officer the basics of 'combat loading' a convoy. In a reverse from Earth, R'Bak's two small moons, Mnul and Psah, appeared as distant points in the night sky, barely more distinguishable than the stars. Even when full, their light provided little illumination. However, with eons of adaptation—possibly some of which was evolutionary—to operating at night, the spray of stars alone gave enough light for the R'Baku to move about freely, aided only by a few lanterns. Cutter could see the general shapes of the gear and supplies being loaded on the wagons, but few details. It meant that Cutter had to rely on Tanavuna to correctly load their convoy, according to the off-worlder's instructions. The process of building unit cohesion had begun.

The place Colonel Murphy suggested as a training camp dovetailed perfectly with the one Tanavuna suggested. Finding their destination in the dark proved to be no problem for the indigs. They led him to a black slash in the starlit ground, where draws angled downward through scrub vegetation and a few large trees. Rocks made footing iffy, but Cutter was prepared to put his trust in Tanavuna and chance a fall when the lieutenant stopped him.

"It is too dangerous in the dark, Captain," Tanavuna said. "Morning is near; let us wait."

"Very well," Cutter said, managing to inject a hint of disappointment into his voice.

Once morning broke, Cutter could inspect their new home from the vantage point of the ridge, roughly one hundred feet above the floor of the draw. Over uncounted years, a now dried-up wash of the river had cut a deep channel between two high ridges. The valley it had left behind measured nearly three hundred feet across. Scattered boulders must have once caused whitewater rapids, and Cutter imagined that fishing there must have been quite good. If R'Bak had a version of trout, that's where they probably would have been found.

From a practical standpoint, the ridges blocked direct sunlight for half the day. That allowed the men to wear lighter robes than had they been on the ground above. In turn, that extended the time they could spend in intensive training, since their bodies didn't have to fight the effects of the brutal sunlight. Even men adapted to such conditions had their limits, as Cutter quickly discovered.

They pitched camp in a grove of trees near the western wall, where a small spring bubbled up through the stone and watered the flora. The overflow evaporated long before reaching the river channel. It wasn't a lot of water, but by assigning a man to fill jugs and canteens around the clock, it would be enough for Cutter's platoon.

When it came to physical labor, Cutter outworked every man. The unrelenting heat sapped his strength faster than it did theirs, but he refused to let it slow him down. The essence of leadership was to inspire the men to follow him, not to force them into doing so because of the military rank structure. That's how he'd been taught, and that's how he would now teach it to his new command. To that end, he stood with the first watch, and only when relieved did he get some sleep.

Dawn came with a swift sunrise on day two. Cutter felt like he'd pulled every muscle in his body during the previous day, but when the first shaft of light brightened upon his eyelid, he woke and climbed to his feet at once. Thinking about it only made it worse, as he knew from experience, and only warming his muscles through use would lessen the aching. After a fast breakfast, he called the men together to lay out his training plan.

"We are going to build a street like you would find in Imsurmik," he said. "Then we are going to build our own quarters, and we are going to finish that work within a week."

Grumblings led to a few cries of "I'm not a draft animal" and "you sound like the satrap!" Cutter turned to Tanavuna, whose frown indicated his own disapproval of Cutter's plan. Rather than take him aside, Cutter purposely had the discussion so the men could hear it, hoping he could persuade them without embarrassing the man whose support he needed most, Tanavuna.

"It is the executive officer's duty to keep the platoon in good order," Cutter said.

"The men are correct, Captain. What you ask cannot be done."

"Are those the words of a hetman? Do you lead by popular vote?"

"I—"

"If an enemy attacks your home, do you ask your warriors to fight, or do you order them to?"

Tanavuna's frown deepened. He took a step back and folded his arms. "You are not hetman," he said.

"No, I'm not. I'm your commanding officer. I don't make decisions about what crops to plant, or decide who is right when a squabble erupts over ownership of a wagon or ceramic jar. My decisions only involve war, killing and being killed, life and death. I want to keep as many of your men, and now *my* men too, alive. As many as possible. I know how to do that." He paused. "Do you? If you have experience in street fighting, then tell me now, and I will step aside.

"Men," Cutter continued turning to face the whole group, "before making a decision I may ask advice based on your knowledge of Imsurmik, but once I have given an order you must obey it immediately and without question. Once we are in contact with the enemy, failure to do so may not only get you killed but the rest of us, too. We will be heavily outnumbered, but as I've learned through hard combat experience, training and teamwork can overcome even the worst odds. So the choice is yours, and you have to decide right now. Do you want to throw off the shackles of the satrap badly enough to obey my orders immediately, or do I look for other men who will?"

Cutter had addressed his remarks to the platoon as a whole, but he knew that only one opinion really mattered, so when all eyes glanced toward Tanavuna, his did too. The hetman couldn't keep his inner conflict from tensing the muscles of his face. After fully half a minute, he turned to Cutter and gave the best salute he could.

"How long do you want this street to be, Captain?"

Chapter Seventeen

Bo Moorefield slipped into the dedicated shack that had replaced Camp Stark's comms tent. "How's the signal?"

"Five by five, sir. Glass Palace Actual is standing by."

"Glass Palace, this is Desperado Actual. Go ahead."

"Bo, the microsats are showing unusual traffic converging on Imsurmik. Makarov will send fast-burst packets detailing it, but the short version is this looks like what we've been watching for."

"Airship, sir?"

"And more conventional traffic from the north. All the right kind of activity." Bo heard Murphy take a deep breath. "All arrows are pointing toward Imsurmik. You called it, Bo."

Moorefield couldn't keep a smile off his face. "Guess it's about time to move my attack force to Hotel California."

"And to sharpen those steely knives. Glass Palace out."

"The air is calm today, Silci," said the airship's captain. There was no hiding the nervousness of his grin. "It is surely a good omen."

Seated in the captain's own chair, Yukannak, the satrap's *silci*—an archaic word best translated as "representative with authority"—praised his own good fortune. The captain's evident worry hid Yukannak's own. At any moment, a radio call could order his arrest if the next wave of his fellow Kulsians found out what he'd done, and floating two thousand feet above the hills below left him no path for escape. He thought about leaping to his death if that happened, but while Yukannak was many things, suicidal wasn't one of them. He'd spent his life talking his way out of one difficulty after another, and, while his most recent transgression was unforgivable, habit and ego nevertheless gave him hope. It was also likely they would never learn what he had done. Still, the time might come when, under Kulsian torture, he regretted passing up the chance to die quickly.

"A good omen it is, Captain," he said in a well-practiced tone of friendly tolerance. An airship captain wasn't the social equal of a silci, but he wasn't a peasant, either, and needed to be shown the proper respect. Especially since men with guns obeyed the captain's orders. "It bodes well for my mission to Imsurmik. Rest assured the satrap will hear of your competence and that of your crew."

"My lord is too kind."

Heavy double shutters blocked sunlight on all sides, save for slitted view ports. The sunlight from the planet's parent star, Shex, always punished R'Bak's middle latitudes, but the approach of 55 Tauri's primary meant a deadly increase that thoroughly baked it. The resulting Sear had already turned the once-green plant life on the rolling hills underneath the airship to a crusty brown. Peering through the slats only gave Yukannak a general impression of the terrain, but what he saw gave no comfort. Should he need to flee Imsurmik, there was nowhere to go except into the wild, and, while his survival skills in the cutthroat world of Kulsian politics had kept him alive long after he should have been dead, his skills in the open country were non-existent.

The gravity of Kulsis wasn't much different from R'Bak, but the heat was another matter. Temperatures on Kulsis ran to the higher end of what the human body could endure, and Kulsians had long since adapted. Under the grueling Sear on R'Bak, though, his lungs ached from breathing air heated to the point of pain. Yukannak knew it was an illusion, that his lungs really weren't baking, but it felt that way.

Cooler air filtered through the vents in the gondola floor as hot air seeped out of identical vents in the roof. The temperature variance wasn't great, but, inside the airbag's stifling control cabin, it felt like a cool breeze. The heavy clothing and face paint necessary to combat sun damage itched and chafed. His skin was particularly sensitive to it since he had spent the past few years mostly living in space, so he noticed even the small improvement of the airflow.

Remaining rigid, he tried not to show his discomfort. Several hours after takeoff, the ground began to creep toward the airship, and, in his peripheral vision, Yukannak saw the captain watching him. The level of water in the glass provided for him showed a definite downward cant, but again he resisted showing a reaction.

"Docking towers in sight, Captain," called the helmsman, staring ahead through a system of telescopes designed to cut down on glare.

The captain pulled down a flexible tube that extended upward into the airship's framework. "Grappling crew to your stations."

Yukannak had always disliked heights, and the irony wasn't lost on him. For a man who'd traveled from Kulsis, to be uneasy at flying a few thousand feet above the ground made no sense. But it was the unfathomable nature of distances in space, and the fact that concepts of up and down were only relative there, that kept it from bothering him. Once they were on the ground again, he'd be fine.

Time crept by as the airship lined up with the docking towers, and the crew attached the clips. Heavy ropes ran up the poles to raise and lower the ship using several large beasts to turn winches. It was a slow process, with lots of jerks and stops, but eventually Yukannak stepped out of the gondola onto the powdery soil of the plateau north of Imsurmik.

"Greetings, Silci Yukannak," said a man with the white-painted face of a J'Stull. A red smudge on each temple marked him as a commander, which immediately pumped cortisol and adrenaline into Yukannak's veins. The fight or flight impulse nearly overwhelmed his self-control, but the only outward sign of his inward struggle was a twitch of the left eye. "I am Subitorni. Welcome to Imsurmik." Using one finger, the J'Stull motioned for the four guards with him, each with various designs on their white paint, to retrieve the silci's luggage.

"Your courtesy is appreciated, Subitorni," Yukannak said. "I look forward to working together, as I'm sure we both wish for the Harvesting to go well."

"We do, Silci."

"How goes the early collection?"

"I am told it exceeds estimates, but, as you may imagine, my duties lie elsewhere. In the meantime, there are worse places to prepare for the Sear than Imsurmik."

"It has its charms, then?"

"It does indeed. And this man knows them all." With that, Subitorni motioned for another man to step forward. He was shorter and heavier, with a green-painted face marked by yellow stripes on each cheek. Once close enough, Subitorni lowered his voice so the guards couldn't hear. "This is Zeesar, an important local militia leader and a man who knows more about the ways of the city than even the F'ahdn. He is the yuzbazzi of Imsurmik, a man who the F'ahdn relies on to enforce his will. Because time is short and the harvesters are flooding the city in larger numbers every day, I asked him to act as your guide."

Zeesar turned his right hand so the forefinger touched his lips and the pinkie finger pointed at Yukannak in the local gesture of respect. Having read up on Imsurmik's peculiar customs, Yukannak knew that if the middle finger touched the bottom of the nose it was an insult. His didn't.

"I am honored to be of service to our beloved satrap," Zeesar said, his eyes cast down but his mouth tilted up at the corners, "through his trusted and most respected silci. I pray that my humble efforts will prove worthy."

Yukannak smiled in turn. While nothing about Zeesar relaxed him, he knew the man's type well; his loyalty lay with whoever could do him the most good, and, at the moment, that was Yukannak. That intuition, well-honed in the crucible of Kulsian politics, is what had allowed him to survive so long in what often proved a short-lived and sometimes fatal profession. Particularly for one of his background. Familiarity with Zeesar's type was not a substitute for trust, though.

"I suspect your efforts are rarely humble, Zeesar," he said, "but thank you. I'm sure you will prove a great help to me."

With all his luggage unloaded, and the airship's crew preparing to return home, Yukannak walked with Subitorni and Zeesar toward the edge of the plateau more than half a mile south, the guards trailing behind. They'd gone fifty paces before he asked if they had to walk the entire way. Instead of answering, Subitorni smiled and led them ten paces more, stopping at a waist-high dirt mound, where Yukannak spotted tracks in the ground that abruptly ended with no further sign.

Subitorni made an upward motion with his hand. Ahead, a man hidden in a clump of scrub trees stepped forward and, using the heel of his boot, kicked the ground. It made a hollow sound, as from wood. Then the creak of hinges needing oil preceded a large square rising from the dirt, leaving an opening into a dark space underneath. A small vehicle rumbled up a ramp and out onto the plateau floor.

With instincts honed over decades of dangerous in-fighting to read the slightest facial clues in possible enemies, Yukannak focused his peripheral vision on Zeesar and was rewarded by the militia leader's brief, nearly imperceptible squint in the direction of the J'Stull commander. It wasn't much, but it was enough. Although nobody else would have given the expression a second thought, it told Yukannak two important things: Zeesar had been surprised by the trap door, and that surprise meant that Zeesar didn't expect Subitorni to be keeping secrets about events regarding the city. By Subitorni's own words, that should have been Zeesar's responsibility.

"Please forgive the need to walk so far, my lord," Subitorni said, "especially with the sun high overhead, but the Offworlders are rumored to be in the area. They have aircraft of an unusual design that are small and very fast."

"And you do not wish anyone to know of this entrance?"

"We do not."

Strictly out of habit, Yukannak took the chance to drive a wedge between two of the power brokers of Imsurmik, as doing so might reveal ambitions he could exploit. "So only the

F'ahdn's most trusted advisors know of its existence?" he asked.

"Yes," Subitorni said without thinking. Then, rethinking his answer as Zeesar's nostrils flared, he said, "but not *all* of the F'ahdn's advisors, because it was only recently finished and some have only just returned to the city. There hasn't been time to inform them of everything. Mostly, though, we are worried about the Offworlders."

"The growing presence of the Offworlders is part of the reason for my visit," Yukannak lied. "I am to judge your preparedness in case they move toward Imsurmik."

This time it was Subitorni whose eyes shifted to Zeesar for half a second. Yukannak was right, there *was* something between them they didn't want him to know about. Under other circumstances, his suspicions might have led him to run, except, on the baked surface of R'Bak, there was no escape. So he climbed into the vehicle and maintained a serene expression, all the while remembering the pistol strapped to his thigh.

The trap door measured fifteen feet wide and twenty feet long. Just below the surface, a road was cut into the plateau's bedrock, angling downward in a gentle slope. Two thick metal rods, one on each side, raised and lowered the door through a series of pulleys and winches. Sitting beside Zeesar in the dim lighting during the downward drive, Yukannak could watch the militia leader's feigned nonchalance. All of it was new to Zeesar, who no doubt realized that digging out such an entrance involved engineering on a massive scale. There was nothing recent about it, despite what Subitorni said, and Zeesar was trying hard to hide his irritation.

Good. Yukannak needed eyes and ears inside the F'ahdn's circle to warn him of danger, and a disaffected yuzbazzi was perfect. As his mind whipsawed back and forth about his own predicament, he decided that, whatever happened, he would not return to Kulsis alive unless those he'd betrayed lost power.

At the bottom of the ramp lay a large chamber with tunnels leading off in different directions. The vehicle stopped near four others parked along the south wall as the driver spoke to a mechanic who was bent over an engine compartment. Pulling off again, they continued until they came to a large central tunnel with daylight at the far end, half a mile distant. Stopping about one hundred yards from the exit, Subitorni explained that Yukannak's quarters were in the wealthy section that was cut into the plateau itself. The tunnel, however, terminated in the Inner City where the merchants lived. Surrounding the Inner City was a high, thick wall made from mud brick and stone.

"The F'ahdn sends his apologies, but he is unwell today. Your evening meal will be brought to your quarters or, if you would like to mingle with the people, there are celebrations each night after sundown. Tell the food vendors you are a guest of the F'ahdn, and he will pay for your meal and drink."

"Are these celebrations for the better folk or for everyone?"

"Everyone."

Large, loud crowds often hid assassins. Back home he could spot someone who seemed out of place, but *everyone* on R'Bak looked suspicious to Yukannak. "Then I will eat alone and rest."

Subitorni left after Yukannak settled into his quarters, and the guards went with him. At Yukannak's request, Zeesar stayed behind. A servant provided by the F'ahdn brought them cool water from the artesian well that supplied the city, pumped directly into the small kitchen. Heavily padded chairs and rugs of densely woven cloth softened the feel of the rooms, cut as they were from living rock. As a matter of course, Yukannak assumed that even if the F'ahdn didn't have electronic listening devices, he had some way of monitoring the conversations of his guests.

"Being on the edge of the Ashbands, Imsurmik can be a dangerous city," Zeesar said. "Especially with so many outlying militias coming here. The local citizens are generally a quiet enough lot, but things are becoming crowded now, and they are wary of the newcomers. Many are only passing through, which leads to thievery and even kidnappings. You may not always be shown the respect you deserve. Should you need a guide, I again offer my services."

"And I accept them. It is good to get varying viewpoints about who the satrap may and may not rely on in coming days."

"And the Kulsians as well?"

Yukannak paused. Few people mentioned the Kulsians in such a direct manner. Was he wrong about the listening devices, or was it a trap? "Yes. It is even more crucial for my people to know whom they may trust."

"Wise. One can never have enough friends."

"No, one cannot."

Zeesar rose to leave and let Yukannak remove his paint and rest from his long trip. But first he bent close and lowered his voice.

"Trust no one," he said.

"Including you?"

That brought a grin. "Especially me."

Chapter Eighteen

Captain Tyree Cutter stood atop the highest hill before the river valley to watch his platoon's third training exercise of the day. The men were tired and hungry and sick of month-after-month intensive learning. Everything from advanced small unit tactics and hand-to-hand combat training, to field stripping and cleaning all the platoon's weapons blindfolded. They'd shot so many rounds on the firing range that the M14s had left their shoulders sore and bruised. Supply convoys had twice brought more ammo, which, due to their proximity to Imsurmik, had to be hand carried the final seven miles so as not to attract unwanted attention. Griping was epidemic, and Cutter smiled at every second of it; he worried much more about silence than bitching.

His executive officer, Lieutenant Tanavuna, had run the training now for more than two weeks with no input from Cutter. That way, if Cutter took a bullet in the first minute of action, the platoon could still carry out the mission. Being the son of their hetman and married to their healer, Tanavuna was the natural choice. Fortunately, he also happened to be a damned fine officer.

The men in his platoon had been away from their families for months now, with only a few leaves to visit them. Being separated, they had fewer distractions to interrupt their concentration, and they had rapidly bonded as soldiers. It was Cutter's version of Army boot camp.

Everyone hated the arrangement, but as Tanavuna's father was hetman, his word carried the force of law. Once convinced of the necessity for the young men of his village to learn the Offworlders' way of war, he had agreed to Cutter's suggestion that they move the training camp a few miles to the west. After two months of standard weapons' training and drills, Cutter had named Tanavuna as platoon executive officer, and three men named Riidono, Brakkel, and Scussian as sergeants, each commanding one of the platoon's three squads. His platoon was nicknamed Cutter's Cutters after the unit he'd led back on Earth, although the name thrust faces into his mind, shadows of the men he'd led to their deaths.

Months earlier, his men had laid out the representation of a town on the mostly barren expanse, and they had used it to practice urban combat techniques. Clumps of brush or trees, hillocks, and boulders all had designations as buildings or other structures. Gullies became sewers, and Cutter tried every way he could to simulate moving through foul sludge to acclimate his men. He didn't want to play that card any more than they did, but it was a lot better to stink than die, and the enemy would never expect anyone to immerse themselves in raw sewage.

Four hours remained before twilight when the latest exercise ended. With enough time to run another assault, Tanavuna walked to the foot of the hill where Cutter stood, and, with obvious reluctance, asked if the captain wanted them to do it again. Just because he'd lived his entire life under R'Bak's brutal sun didn't mean he liked being out in it all day, every day, particularly as the approach of the Sear began turning the surface into an oven.

"No, no more training," Cutter said to Tanavuna's relief. "The men are ready. Bring them in."

Cutter came down from the hill and motioned for his men to gather around. Forgetting their fatigue, it only took minutes for the forty-seven members of his platoon to circle him. "Pack up, boys," he called out. Within their culture, calling them boys could be considered an insult, but Cutter had explained that where he came from it was a term of endearment, and they accepted it. "Major Moorefield is moving on Imsurmik the day after tomorrow. We'll march east tonight, hole up during the hottest part of the day, and then get you home. We'll camp outside the village, but I can give you three hours to see your families and make some babies."

They laughed, both at the accuracy of Cutter's words and with pleasure that the training was over. He'd seen it in 1944 and now again two hundred years later: the relief of finally moving toward engaging the enemy.

If only they knew what awaited them.

Life on R'Bak had more than its share of violence, but tribal warfare and blood feuds were a far cry from combat against an organized enemy who wanted you dead. And, despite Murphy's assurances otherwise, Cutter assumed that was exactly what the militias in Imsurmik wanted, to kill them all. If they turned out to be the disorganized amateurs that Murphy and Moorefield said they were, fine, but as a combat commander, he had to plan as though they were R'Bak's version of the Waffen-SS.

The men always moved fast at night, being the preferred time of travel during the hottest season. Now, after six months of intense physical training, they maintained a pace double that of before, while Cutter rode a whinaalani at the head of the group. Some of the men flanked the column at a distance of three hundred yards as a tripwire-skirmish line. The rest either marched in column or led the other whinnies being used as pack animals.

They moved fast and arrived at their camp west of the village just as night fell. Cutter made them delay rushing home to their families until everything was staged so they could pull out at dawn. He ordered them to be back in camp three hours later, and, except for one man, they were. Fifteen minutes later, they were in their sleeping rolls, dozing. Or trying to.

The locals called their village of six hundred people *Nuthhurfipiko*, which, in their dialect, meant "near the dry brown hill." Cutter wasn't sure how it got that name, since the hill had dots of trees and scrub greenery over most of its slopes. As he lay staring at the unfamiliar stars, he could hear the river nearby, and the illogic of the name kept his mind racing. The hill was neither brown nor particularly dry, but as he'd learned in France, place names didn't always make sense. He mentally dubbed it *Nuther*.

Even with the sun down, he felt sweat trickle down his neck and sides, so maybe Nuther got its name during the last Sear, or the one before that, or the one before *that*. As hard as it might be to imagine, supposedly it got much hotter when the two suns blasted the planet's surface like a flame-thrower, so he could see the hill turning brown under all that heat. Too bad it didn't kill off the stinging insects, too.

Snoring nearby was a reassuring memory of the men he'd led in France, every one of whom he'd trusted with his life. Cutter felt the same way about the R'Baku of Nuther. The new platoon had been training for six months, but as much as he wanted to believe that his new men would react in battle like the old ones, that could only be verified when the shooting started.

He should have been exhausted, and physically he was, but his mind wouldn't shut off. Instead, it kept repeating the same scenes over and over again, until he thought it would drive him mad. Eventually he dozed off.

Dawn was still an hour away when distant gunfire interrupted the already brief R'Bak night and woke him. Momentarily disoriented, he sat up shouting, "Take cover, Krauts!" in English. A lean indig man ran over to him, squatting close enough for Cutter to see his face. It wasn't his second-in-command, Lieutenant Tanavuna, but Sergeant Riidono.

"Lieutenant Cutter," the non-com said. "Come! We must hurry. Our village is being attacked!"

"By who?" Cutter asked, pushing to his feet. He'd slept fully clothed and needed only to pull on his boots and grab the Thompson before following Riidono across the hill at a run. They'd camped two miles from the western terminus of the ridge, close to the village but out of sight behind its crest. Nuther lay on a lower slope, closer to the river but far enough upland to avoid the occasional floods. Driven by fear for their friends and loved ones, his men sped over the ridge toward their homes, with Cutter stumbling after them as he shook off the effects of sleep. Normally he came instantly awake at the first sign of danger, but fatigue and the illusion of security had allowed him to slip into a deeper sleep than usual. Now, as they neared the top, Cutter knew the red glow ahead meant that his men's homes were on fire. Despite the risk of tripping in the semidarkness, he ran faster.

From the ridge top, he saw flames licking out the windows and doorways of every home. Although built mostly of stone, the doors and roofs tended to be animal hides stretched over wood frames, both of which burned fast and hot. Cutter got there after his men had saved the ones they could. Smoking bodies lay strewn about, with people dousing them in water retrieved from the river.

Mothers wailed for their dead children, children for their dead mothers, and Cutter's men went berserk at seeing their families cut down. Calls for the healers exceeded their numbers, so he pitched in wherever he could. Within minutes, Cutter's hands were bloody after applying pressure to a gut-shot girl, but the wound proved fatal. As death settled over her, Cutter watched her young face relax to something approaching peace.

Most of those still alive had been hiding in the huts when the raiders set them ablaze, and there was little Cutter could do for them. Battlefield first aid only went so far in treating burns, and with no medics, morphine, or first aid kits, he could only do what he'd learned back on Earth. Mainly that consisted of ripping cloth strips from robes and shirts, wetting them from a jug of water he found near a hut, and keeping their wounds moist. Tanavuna's wife, the village's most revered healer, was nowhere in sight.

Over the screams of the injured and crackling of flames, Cutter heard angry yells coming from the western end of the village where a cluster of his soldiers had surrounded a man lying on the ground. Cutter flashed back to a day in late June, 1944, when his platoon moved into an open field surrounded by bocage and a German MG 42 cut one of them nearly in half. The machine gun's loader took a BAR round in the forehead, but his men captured the gunner and kicked him to death. They hated the MG 42—"Hitler's Buzzsaw"—and, by extension, the men who operated it.

Cutter could have stopped them back then. The German's terrified face still haunted his dreams; his *soldbuch* gave his age as sixteen. He'd been a scared boy, drafted and stuck in the front lines. Just a kid who'd fought for his country. Worse, once the immediate hatred wore off, guilt at what they'd done tormented some of his men.

Cutter wouldn't let that happen again. He sprinted over to the group, pushed them away, and confronted his XO, Lieutenant Tanavuna, who was standing over the man pointing an M14 at his head. In the flickering firelight, he could see the white paint on his face.

"Stand down, Lieutenant!"

Tanavuna's glare made clearer than words that Cutter was an outsider. "Do you not see what they have done?" he asked, the rifle shaking as his hand trembled with rage. Cutter feared he'd squeeze off a round without meaning to, and, with all of the stones littering the area, a ricochet was entirely possible. "They took my wife, Cutter; they stole her and slaughtered my people! They killed my father, and now I am hetman. I decide on justice against those who injure my people! Do you understand that? It has nothing to do with you or your mission; this is about the people of Nuthhurfipiko. Leave us be!"

"Listen to me—"

Tanavuna swung the gun to point at Cutter's nose, the barrel less than two feet from his face. No sanity softened the indig's face, and the trembling of his body increased. The other men stepped back, while the ones behind him moved to either side.

"Klooannii caught him assaulting Dristtaluppu with a knife at her throat. She was a young mother, and they killed her child! When Klooannii found them, this man thrust his blade into Dristtaluppu's neck. And now you wish me to spare such filth?"

Even in the semidarkness of the new dawn, Cutter saw terror in the raider's eyes, a silent plea for mercy and hope that the newcomer with the strange accent might save his life.

"Killing me won't bring the mother back, Lieutenant Tanavuna, nor her child."

"You would spare him?"

"I would question him. You say they took your wife?"

That refocused the distraught indig leader and began the process of restoring logical thought, even analysis. "Yes,

Kesteluni is gone. We must go after her." His men cheered and waved their rifles.

"We will—"

"Each moment takes them further away; we must go now! If we do not, they—"

"Do not interrupt me again, Lieutenant!" Cutter roared, intentionally yelling louder than necessary to stop the rising mob reaction. It could have caused Tanavuna to pull the trigger, but that didn't bother him. He'd stopped fearing death the moment he'd awakened on the SpinDog habitat. What *did* bother him also surprised him: retaining control of his platoon. Because now they *were* his platoon, every bit as much as his men in Normandy had been. Staring into the muzzle, he grabbed it and pulled it against his forehead. "Shoot me now or obey my orders, Lieutenant. The choice is yours. So are the consequences."

The captured raider held his hands in front of his face, his terror obvious.

"I *must* go after them, Captain Cutter. Don't you understand that? I must!"

"Of course you must, but not alone, and not without a plan. And your people are suffering while we stand here yelling at each other. Let's question this man and tend to your people, then we can pursue them with a real chance of getting Kesteluni back. She showed me hospitality and kindness, and I will help you save her if I can. As it is, you don't even know who the attackers were."

"We know, sir," said Sergeant Riidono. Using the tip of his rifle, he jabbed the prisoner in his right cheek. "Only those who serve the F'ahdn of Imsurmik may wear white face paint as part of the J'Stull guard. These purple stripes on his cheeks mark him as coming from a tribe loyal to the satrap, and through the satrap, the F'ahdn. Others wear blue, red, or green paint, or combinations of those colors. He would wear his tribe's purple, unless aiding the J'Stull. Then he could wear nothing but white."

Cutter nodded. The whole paint issue had befuddled him from the start. He understood its protection against UV, but the intricacies of the patterns and symbols were beyond him. Thank God his men used clothing for the same purpose.

Without meaning to, Riidono gave him the distraction he'd needed. Ignoring the steel touching his head, Cutter knelt, grabbed the prisoner's throat with his left hand, and pushed the barrel of the Thompson under his chin with the right.

"What's your name?"

"Hisnatandu, my lord."

"I'm not your lord; I'm your enemy. I'm also the only reason you're still alive. Tell me why you attacked this place."

The man stammered and couldn't get the words out. Closing his eyes, he took several deep breaths and then spoke. "Please don't kill me. Please! I have a family."

"So did the woman you murdered. Now answer my question."

"The F'ahdn's yuzbazzi, Zeesar, gave the order."

Cutter glanced up at Riidono. "What does yuzbazzi mean?"

"It means someone you trust to carry out your orders," answered Tanavuna, once again engaged in the present. "Someone who will do bad things if you ask them. But I have met Zeesar, and this attack does not seem like something he would do, even if he could."

Good, he's back to using the logical part of his brain.

"A hatchet-man," Cutter said. "That's what we called such a one. Why don't you think it was this Zeesar?"

"Zeesar is a militia leader. He is the yuzbazzi; yes, that is true. But Subitorni commands the J'Stull guards of Imsurmik. I do not believe Subitorni would allow Zeesar to give orders to his J'Stull."

"What about that?" Cutter said, poking the terrified man lying in the dirt.

"I know nothing of such things, my lord; please do not hurt me. I am from the village of Murri. The J'Stull commander, Subitorni, ordered us to come here with his men to punish those who are disloyal to the F'ahdn. I heard some of them whispering about a healer, Kestel-something; I could not hear the rest—"

"Kesteluni!" Tanavuna said.

"Ssshhh," Cutter said, hoping the sound translated to the same thing on R'Bak as it did on Earth. To the prisoner, he said, "Continue. Imsurmik isn't far away; why would he order this done now?"

"I know not!" the man squeaked.

But Cutter had interrogated enough Germans to know when a prisoner was lying. "You get one last chance to tell me the truth, before I let them have you."

"No! I only know the rumors."

Cutter nudged his throat with the sub-machine gun. "I'm listening."

"It is said the F'ahdn suffers from the Bleeding Black on his face. I know a woman who attends his household, a masker; she told me that the F'ahdn blamed her for his affliction, accusing her of not painting his face correctly. If it cannot be cured, she will pay with her life."

Once again, Cutter gave Tanavuna a questioning look. "Bleeding Black?"

Tanavuna answered, "I have told you of this, Captain. It is the reason we wrap our faces and others apply paint. The sun burns and darkens us all. But sometimes, it turns smaller spots black and they often bleed. Cutting off a limb may stop the spread, but often does not. There are treatments using plants that sometimes work, and Kesteluni is known to have succeeded many times in curing the Bleeding Black. People come long distances to be healed by her. If the F'ahdn has it, he will die unless she can save him."

"It sounds like something we called skin cancer," Cutter said. "But I don't understand why he sent a raiding party instead of just asking her for help."

"It is not his way," Tanavuna said. "He does not ask for help; he requires it from those under his so-called protection—the ones who share their harvests so he does not destroy them. We have resisted those demands."

"He asked—demanded—your wife treat him?"

"No, she would not have turned him down, whether he asked or demanded. She would have attended him. He must not have been willing to take the chance. The F'ahdn is a prideful man. And vain."

"Will he release her once she treats him?"

Tanavuna shook his head.

"So he's just another bully. I know all about those."

Cutter stood, his knees aching, and stepped back. As his platoon watched, he brought up the Thompson and squeezed the trigger when the muzzle came level with the prisoner's forehead. The man jerked a few seconds as neurons fired after brain death and then went limp.

"The vengeance was mine!" Tanavuna cried out.

"Killing a defenseless man is not something you ever forget. The faces of the men I've killed already keep me awake at night. I spared you those nightmares. For me, one more won't make any difference."

Cutter turned back toward their camp, only to find a knot of people kneeling beside someone dead in the dirt. Once he was close enough for the growing light to reveal details, Cutter saw it was his missing soldier. They hadn't even gotten into combat and he'd already lost a man.

Chapter Nineteen

Tucked against a low, tilted plateau rising from west to east, the town of Imsurmik sparkled with life in the early evening twilight. The days approaching the Sear grew ever warmer. Working outside, even to feverishly harvest the last of the seasonal crops, grew more difficult to endure, and its citizens slowly transitioned toward nocturnal schedules and events. Typical human behavior was one of the first casualties of the rising temperatures and radiation. Across the city, its inhabitants worked tirelessly to secure their own survival. Some settlements planned to migrate north in search of cooler climates. Others expanded their underground refuges and fortifications. For all of them, the plan was the same: endure the Sear.

Her eyes on the glowing city, Aliza Turan made her way up the curving road from the farmlands toward the central fortifications. Around her, farmers returned from the fields after gathering their crops. Miners carried tools and dust-covered implements from the long hours of digging before the nightly feasts. As she passed through the gate, groups of women and children carried water from the central spring to fill artificial reservoirs. She paused there and washed the thick, protective paint from her exposed skin. Without it, skin cancers were common on R'Bak. The cool water felt heavenly. Excited voices chattered around her in a myriad of dialects. The buzz of general activity wound deeper into the city where the bazaar, nearing the end of its needfulness as a trading center, transformed nightly for what could only be called a party. The town's collective excitement grew as the crops approached harvest, but something special was in the air. Tonight, and every night for the next two weeks, would be the Festival of the Kr'it.

Aliza stepped into the mud and rock home she shared with a group of friendly migrants to change her garments for the evening's festivities. All the women greeted her with smiles and barely contained excitement as they too prepared for the night. Everyone's spirits were higher than she'd seen before. She'd known and lived among the migrants for months. They'd agreed to smuggle her into the town so she could gather information as long as she played her role and worked the fields alongside them. Moving into town had been easy, even if daily life was difficult. Now, there was a different energy in her surroundings with the approaching festival. With full darkness settling across the countryside, there would be no need for the thick, preventive face paint to cover their exposed skin. Nor would the locals need the traditional robed and hooded garments. While she appreciated the cover they provided, she was more than happy to let her dark hair blow free in the relatively cool evening breeze.

Like the others, Aliza prepared a basket with large, flexible handles that could double as shoulder straps. Before she tied it shut, she checked inside and carefully laid the few tools they would need for the harvest atop a concealed parcel. She glanced at her olive drab Timex watch, tucked underneath the long sleeves of her garment, and saw the time was much later than she'd expected. While the harvest was a significant and time-consuming event, the Festival of the Kr'it was casual by comparison. After nightfall, the lack of urgency in Imsurmik's citizens surprised her. The hours in total darkness on the planet were limited, yet everyone around her appeared content to wait until the night air was as cool as it could get before moving to the thermal pool.

One woman, the one the others called Momani, looked at her sternly. "Patience, young one," she said. A thin smile grew across the woman's leathered face.

Over the last several months, and with considerable time and practice, Aliza had become fluent in several dialects. *You're a regular chameleon,* Bo had said proudly. *Prisoner, survivor, teacher, and now officer. Is there anything you can't do?*

The military lifestyle of their band, the Lost Soldiers, hadn't come easily to her. Yet she'd been assimilated and become one of them as much through shared experience as through actual leadership. Colonel Murphy's desire for her to identify medicinals and teach soldiers how to ride the whinaalani, the lizard-like mammals who served as beasts of burden and skilled combat mounts, had led her to a life she'd never imagined. All of it felt strangely perfect, even if there were some finer nuances she hadn't quite nailed down.

"I will be late, again."

The woman shrugged as if to say things would happen in their own time. For a people so concerned with their survival through the Sear, their almost laconic response to the pressure of time surprised Aliza, but there wasn't anything she could do about it. Maintaining her cover meant keeping such emotions in check. Following the crowd had always been difficult for her, and being late reporting to Bo, and subsequently to Colonel Murphy, wasn't her only concern.

She doubted Bo would be too upset with her. While she held the rank of first lieutenant, Bo had been promoted to major and was technically her commander. Yet they were a couple. They'd shared the same bunk since the operation they now called the J'Stull Job. Fraternization, once frowned upon by leaders in modern militaries, wasn't a concern. For the lot of them, despite the differences in their lifetimes, experiences, and even countries, they were the only friends they had. Moreover, they'd become family. Each of them carried the weight of their previous lives. For some, it was easier to start over than others. Aliza was resilient and independent, yet she'd come to learn she not only needed those around her—she loved them. They filled a void and salved each other's pain to whatever extent they could. Even in their bunk, Aliza and Bo Moorefield felt the sum of each other's fears and the uncertainty of the past they had left behind.

Aliza often laid awake at night wondering if she could've saved Ben Mazza during Operation Markolet in Palestine;

they'd been young, careless, and brave. What she wouldn't give to go back and stop them and tame their foolish bravado. Ben had died a few meters from her, and she couldn't save him. And then, as if to underscore the finality of her powerlessness, the Ktor had taken her almost two hundred years into the future.

Bo's path had been no easier. She knew Bo laid awake at night wondering if he could have saved his marriage. Neither one of them had had the chance to resolve their relationships before fate took the opportunity out of their hands. It weighed heavily on them both, yet Aliza framed the experience differently after her time in Dachau. During the height of the Holocaust, she believed even the worst possible life beyond those walls would be easier than surviving within them. Human relationships were simple things, comparatively. There was no need to complicate the ideas of love and hate with what Bo called baggage. As long as they both looked ahead, instead of into the past, the rest should have been easy. Yet, both of them struggled.

Things weren't easy, and she knew better than to assume they would be. The mission was inherently dangerous, and they leaned on one another as best they could. Bo could be quiet, almost sullen at times. She knew he took criticism personally and dealt with lingering doubts about himself and the marriage he'd lost. When those times came, all she could do was weather it and hold fast to the truth of the pattern: Bo would forgive himself, and his smile would return. It was dumb luck he was in the unsmiling phase when she'd had to leave. The order from Colonel Murphy had come in the middle of the night almost a month ago. Aliza quietly gathered her things and set off for the perimeter to join up with Momani and her band, ostensibly just another worker going to the city to take part in the harvest.

Bo had met her at the gate astride his whinaalani, Scout. The whinnie cooed a greeting. Bo's hand touched the brim of his boonie cap.

"On patrol for the night?" Aliza stepped up next to the whinnie and patted its muscular neck.

Bo nodded. "George Patton said to never ask your troops to do something you wouldn't do yourself."

"I'll try to remember that."

Bo smiled at her. "I wish you wouldn't be mad at me."

Aliza took a deep breath. "I'm not mad at you."

"Sometimes I feel like I can't say anything right."

"And you think that's better than saying nothing at all?" Aliza kicked the dirt and tried to rein in her rising frustration. "Let me love you the way I can."

Bo glanced up at the distant horizon for a long moment. The way he did when trying to formulate his words. Aliza kept quiet, making him reply. He started slowly. "Maybe I could say the same about loving you. I do my best, but I stay quiet so my words don't get in the way. Past experience tells me I screw things up when I talk. I clam up so I don't sound like an idiot and upset someone I care about. There's so much I want to say, but…." He ended with a shrug.

Aliza stared up at him. She knew he cared for her, but it was so damn hard to get him to say anything. "You're not an idiot, Bo. You know that, and you know I love you, yes?"

His eyes bored through her, and his face was still as stone. Standing at the gate, she waited for him to climb down from Scout and wrap her in his embrace. When it was apparent he would not, she tried not to frown and dammed the tears trying to leak from her eyes. "One of these days you'll have to tell me what's on your mind. Be safe, and I'll see you soon."

He touched his cap again. "I will. I love you, too."

Aliza realized she'd frozen halfway through dressing herself. She drew in a quick, sharp breath as the humble and familiar walls of the house seemed to suddenly reappear around her. If any of the others noticed, no one said anything. Aliza quickly finished her preparations as to not have them waiting for her. Dressed and carrying their woven packs, the women exited into the small thoroughfare near the artificial canal running west to east through the Inner City. The group emerged into a festive atmosphere. There was music from an otherworldly instrument. Its screechy chords and earsplitting crescendos intermixed with a constant warbling sound, but it sounded joyous rather than morose. They joined several women along with more than a few young boys decorating their hair with blossoms of the extravagant indigo *donmaar* flowers that grew near the river. The Festival of the Kr'it seemed quite the affair.

Along the primary thoroughfare, everyone danced. It was celebration and camaraderie Aliza hadn't seen on the planet since her arrival, and, frankly, it gave her more than a measure of hope for what they were doing. These people had survived for hundreds of years in this hellish environment. The entire town of Imsurmik had once been built entirely into the rock face of the plateau. Over time, its promise drew thousands of others to the mid-latitude city, and it grew outward. Walls were built and defenses prepared. Farmlands were laid, plowed, and irrigated. As Imsurmik expanded, though, so did their social order.

Carved into the side of the plateau, in a cavity etched into the rock over millions of years, lay the dwellings. Beneath the cover of the overhang, elevated ten meters above the city, were at least two rows of richly appointed homes, with the wealthiest citizens occupying those furthest under the cavern's lip for protection.

Below the dwellings, atop a hill overlooking the farmlands, lay the Inner City. Protected by a rough stone and wood glacis around ten meters high, the Inner City comprised the trade and commerce center of the city. The Inner City itself was further delineated. Around the bazaar and thoroughfares were houses and small businesses built around the seasonal trades. It differed from anything Aliza could remember seeing on Earth, but, having spent most of her childhood inside Dachau, she'd barely known the outside world at all.

Outside the walls and down the slope from the Inner City was the Outer City. She'd been there a few times, visiting the farmers' market where they sold the fresh produce from the lush, irrigated fields south of Imsurmik. The Outer City was an entirely different sort of place. Agriculturally focused, the city itself in those outer areas was, in some places, in little more than squalor. Every day, migrant parties collapsed their shanties, gathered their belongings, and resumed moving north. Aliza wondered why they would bother coming back.

The surrounding festival was the first time she'd seen happiness on R'Bak. No one wore the traditional face paint to cover themselves from the intense light of day. Fire-lit faces shone in the darkness far beyond their smiles.

As they reached the bazaar, the women turned north, pushing toward the cavern and the central bazaar. On the north edge of the squared market, an underground aquifer sprang from the precincts of the cavern dwellings into a man-made canal roughly three meters wide and a meter deep. The water was crystal clear and delightfully cool. The artificial canal directed the water from the center of the Inner City along the cavern wall to the far eastern edge, where it dropped through a spillway in the glacis, creating a fifteen-meter waterfall. Below, the reservoir was easily an acre in size. She did not know how deep it was. The locals said there was no bottom to the pond itself because it was a natural hot spring. The unused water from the city's aquifer drained there via the artificial canal and mixed with water coming up from the geothermal spring. Without the aquifer's water, the pool would have been frightfully hot. The engineering feat of joining the water supplies enabled the growth of certain organisms and food sources for the town and contributed mineral-laden water to the fields. With the approach of the Sear, the kr'it rose nightly from the depths to feed upon an abundance of smaller organisms near the surface and along the bank. Kr'it were a delicacy, and the harvest was undeniably special to Imsurmik's citizens.

The unexpected joy of the entire town overwhelmed her. More than once on the path toward the waterfall, Aliza found herself swept up in the dancing. The movement, the music, and the atmosphere did more to raise her spirits than she realized. Bo would have enjoyed it, too, and Aliza regretted he couldn't be there with her. While she doubted he was the party type, he might have enjoyed seeing her as happy as she was.

As time dragged on, and their prearranged time for radio communications slid past, Aliza knew Bo would be sitting out there in the darkness on the bluff across the narrow valley, trying not to worry. It couldn't be helped. No one else in the procession seemed all that intent on getting out to the pond itself. Apparently, there would be ample opportunities to harvest the kr'it.

From what she understood, the organisms were something between a shrimp and an iguana. They possessed four tiny legs, which allowed them to crawl around the edge of the warm pit, and a long, thick tail for swimming. Each was pale and sensitive to light. She hadn't seen one yet, and when she did, she wasn't certain whether she would be revolted or intrigued. But all that mattered, at least to the citizens of the town, was that they were apparently good eating.

After dark, when the heat waned, the typical activities of the day returned, culminating with the feast of the harvest. The procession of women and children would go outside the walls, wade in the waters around the edge of the pond, and collect the kr'it. As they filled their woven baskets to the brim with the precious creatures, Aliza would use the PRC-77 radio hidden in her basket to report on the day's activities to Bo.

Colonel Murphy had given her several key requirements on which to gain intelligence. Given the approaching Sear, outlying stations and militias were banding together in towns and gathering forces under individual satraps. Such was the case in Imsurmik. A growing militia was forming in the town itself, and she was determined to discover its strengths and weaknesses. She also needed to fully understand where the militia leaders were placing their weapons and how they intended to use them.

Murphy had also given her the task of locating credible intelligence relating to the efforts to lift items to orbit. The Harvesters were coming, there was no secret about that, and part of the farming and local mining seemed to be geared toward providing them a host of things to remove from the planet during the Sear. Aliza had observed several caravans arriving in the Outer City with large pallets heaped high with bushels of medicinal plants. Some of them she identified easily, and others were mysteries to her. She'd learned as much of the regional flora as she could, and the specimens she did not recognize indicated more distant origins. What else was she missing? That lack of knowledge gave her more than enough impetus to visit the Outer City as often as possible to learn exactly what was being harvested and why.

Finally, Murphy believed there were individuals gathering in the towns who knew the security procedures of the orbital operations. They would prepare the landing sites and storage facilities. He believed they might possess the tools and knowledge necessary for other Lost Soldiers to accomplish "an important operation in orbit"—and that was all he was willing to say about it. Identifying those persons of interest—what Bo called high-value targets—was the last piece of Aliza's job.

The procession conducted itself to the eastern wall and through the opening where the aquifer and canal exited the glacis. Aliza and the other women emerged into the relative darkness beyond. There were several boys carrying torches to help them descend the steep, slick path by the waterfall. Negotiating the narrow path was difficult with the heavy pack on her back. More than once she had to grab an offered arm, but the young men apparently didn't mind; they were there for that purpose.

When they had descended to the level of the pond itself, the women and children spread out to the left and right. There was no rushing, no competition. The procession was a concerted effort to ring the pond and begin their collection. No sooner had Aliza started along the edge of the pond, trying to move to an area as far to the southeast as possible, than she saw her first kr'it.

Despite everything she'd been told, it was actually much uglier. It was a robust creature and undoubtedly would provide what the locals needed nutritionally to survive the Sear. There appeared to be millions of them. Most of them hovered just below the surface, swimming back and forth, feeding on organisms she could not see with her naked eye.

Aliza and the women found their designated place on the southeast corner of the pond. After a few minutes of adjusting the baskets and their garments, they waded into the shallows and began the work of harvesting the kr'it. Women and children used quick hands to secure their prizes and toss them to others on the shore for processing.

Playing her designated role as just another worker, Aliza went through the motions, mainly, and grabbed one of the squirming creatures. They reminded her of snakes—their skin was soft but had a sheen to it. Each of the kr'it also possessed small, sharp claws. The triangular head and rows of tiny teeth were not sharp enough to do any damage to her skin, but it was just ferocious enough in her grasp that she was glad to be done with it. She bashed it over the head with a heavy rock and then passed it to another woman who used a sharp knife to decapitate the creature. Its squirming body was then tossed into one of the woven baskets. Each woman could expect to gather sixty to seventy of the kr'it in one iteration. They would fill their baskets three or four times during the nightly harvest.

As the women worked, they sang softly, an older song with an archaic dialect which Aliza could not fully understand, but that wasn't its intent. The song was to cover Aliza sitting with her basket and bashing kr'it over the head with a rock while speaking on the radio. Carefully, Aliza brought up the handset and put the earpiece to her ear. She glanced at her watch, trying to see the luminous hands.

She was over thirty-eight minutes beyond her appointed contact time. Standard operating procedure dictated she try every fifteen minutes for one hour until they made contact. The lifespan of the irreplaceable lithium batteries for the radios was limited, and nobody wanted them to run out.

Aliza continued to work on the kr'it, staying occupied until the next call time. There was a peaceful routine to the work and the unfamiliar, yet beautiful song of the surrounding women. She tried to lose herself in both for a few moments. At forty-five minutes past the hour, she reached into her basket, turned on the radio by feel, and placed her thumb on the push-to-talk button.

"Desperado Six, this is Queen of Hearts. Over."

Chapter Twenty

Across the narrow valley from Imsurmik, Major Bo Moorefield sat cross-legged atop an exposed outcropping overlooking the terrain below. The city itself reminded him of Mesa Verde, a place he'd visited in Colorado on several occasions. Built into the rock of a plateau, the city concerned him, but his worries were on other things at the moment. With the radio at his side, he turned it on to monitor the set frequency precisely at the top of the midnight hour. Once again, Aliza was late. Whatever the reason, she was not able to transmit on time for the fifth day in a row. While he tried to tell himself she was busy, that she was ensuring her own security, he was worried. She was fiercely independent and could hold her own, but she wasn't a soldier, no matter the rank bestowed on her.

Why did Murphy promote her?

Bo chastised himself at the thought. During their first battle on R'Bak, Aliza had taken command of a defensive position when Sergeant First Class Whittaker was killed. Even before the skirmish, she was a natural leader and teacher. In more ways than one, she was a better officer than most of the people Bo knew during his life in the 1980s and '90s back on Earth. She deserved the rank and, frankly, had earned it in combat.

Bo leaned back on his hands and stared up into the unfamiliar heavens. He knew where to look for Earth, but there was nothing there for him anymore. Everything he needed, and everything he wanted, was right there. The problem was he couldn't articulate it well enough for Aliza. Either the time wasn't right, or the words wouldn't come out. While he knew he shouldn't be thinking about it, he couldn't help it as he waited for her. If all went well, he'd see her soon.

For the last seven days, he'd deployed his cavalry force to scout Imsurmik from a distance. He could have moved them closer but decided against it. From his current position, he had a commanding view of the area around the town of twenty thousand. There were two major roads which intersected about five kilometers to the southeast of the town. The crossroads sat almost exactly a kilometer to the west of a junction between a wide, shallow river flowing from the northwest to the southeast and an intermittent creek from the north. The river, known as the Sallus, flowed all the way to the R'Bak Sea. Eventually, the bulk of the Lost Soldiers would follow the river as the operation progressed, and he would provide security for them. For the moment, though, his attention was on the town and the roads leading into it. Traffic had burgeoned over the last several days, and, if Colonel Murphy's intelligence was correct, it would continue to do so.

What troubled Bo more than Aliza's tardiness was the number of armed militants he'd seen moving into the city itself. From a distance, it was hard to determine if the weapons systems he saw being moved by vehicles were staying in the Outer City or if they were being pushed into the Inner City itself. Until the enemy emplaced their weapons along the top of the glacis, there was no way of telling. Therefore, he had to assume the worst, which was that the enemy was merging their forces. So, with every passing day, they grew stronger, which would be a problem for the Lawless.

"Once you get the intelligence we need from the inside," Colonel Murphy had said, "you'll move on the town and secure it. After your initial attack, a strike team led by Captain Cutter will go in and grab our high-value targets."

Bo had known it couldn't be that simple. "So, my only job is to attack the town and open a breach for the strike team to get in and grab the PoIs?"

Murphy smiled. "Actually, Bo, if worse comes to worst, and we can't get off the planet, this could be a site where we could hole up for the Sear, if necessary."

Bo shook his head. "The CONOPS has always been to get off the planet and back to the spins before the Sear sets in. What changed?"

"Nothing has changed, Bo. That's still the plan. But you of all people know that, particularly in combat, things don't always go as expected. If the microsats discovered the surveyors inbound now, I'm not sure we could get our jobs done and get spaceside before they came into sensor range. So we have to prepare for the unexpected, no matter how successful we are."

Bo knew that all too well. His experience in Somalia with the United Nations coalition had been a less than stellar effort. Far too often, they had gone on convoys and minor operations without the proper intelligence. Granted, in an urban area like Mogadishu, credible and actionable intelligence had been almost impossible. The state of the enemy was always in flux, and they held the advantage and the initiative on the ground they knew like the backs of their hands. Frequently, Bo's forces were engaged by irregular troops and armed civilians they had not expected. Staring across the valley at the low houses of the Outer City, Bo couldn't help but think how familiar Imsurmik looked. He could have mistaken the Outer City for areas of Mogadishu, and the similarity did not sit well with him.

He leaned forward and checked his watch again. It was almost fifteen minutes after the hour. Bo turned on the radio, as procedure dictated, and listened. Nothing. With a sigh, he turned the radio off and kept looking up at the unfamiliar sky. After a few moments, he saw the streak of a falling star, and it brought a smile to his face. As a teenager, he'd enjoyed taking the family's pontoon boat out on the southern spur of Pickwick Lake. One night, just before his sixteenth birthday, he'd been out on the boat alone, lying on one of the long, padded seats, watching the sky. He'd caught the peak of the annual Leonid meteor shower; over one hundred shooting stars per hour lit up the night. For a moment, he could have almost been back home, and Bo let himself enjoy the wait. To his surprise, at precisely forty-five minutes after the hour, he heard Aliza's voice.

"Desperado Six, this is Queen of Hearts. Over."

Bo's heart leapt at the sound of her voice. He could tell she was whispering, and he didn't want to yelp or excitedly ask how she was doing. They didn't have much time. "I'm here. How are things? Over."

"The same as yesterday. More forces coming in. I'd say we're at a couple of hundred now. Heavier weapons have arrived, too. Mainly rockets from what I could tell. Over."

Bo's gut tightened. Rockets meant standoff distance. Standoff distance meant it would be harder for his vehicles to get close enough to breach the walls for Cutter's strike team.

"I understand. What about the other priorities? Over."

"Nothing. My contacts have not identified anybody, yet. I was able to get eyes on Foxtrot today, but none of his entourage. There are at least two new 'players' of interest who arrived today. No names on the new players yet. Over."

She'd at least been able to identify the F'ahdn, the town's mayor, for lack of a better term. That was good news.

"Let me know when you know something about them. Over."

"I will. Hopefully tomorrow. How are you? Over," Aliza whispered.

Bo chewed his lower lip for a moment. *I miss you. I love you. I'm sorry. I really need to do better at everything.*

With all the thoughts in his head, Bo's sense of caution swelled. "Everything's fine here. We'll talk tomorrow. Over."

"Okay. Good night, cowboy." Her voice was hesitant and shaky. Maybe, just maybe, she felt something similar and couldn't articulate it. But he didn't wait to find out.

"Desperado Six, out."

Bo leaned forward and turned the radio off. He sat forward and rested his face in his hands, his elbows on his knees. A soft noise came from behind him. No matter how many times he heard it, he couldn't help but think it sounded like a cross between a neighing horse and a purring cat.

Bo lifted his head. "It's okay, Scout. Everything's okay."

The gentle whinaalani call came again, and Bo realized Scout knew him almost better than he knew himself. Over the last several months, he and the other Lost Soldiers had gotten to know quite a bit about the whinnies. The animals were far more intelligent than they'd assumed, and while they had had little luck in developing true communications between the two species, there was no doubt the whinnies understood them and often anticipated the humans. Bo looked over his right shoulder and saw Scout peering intently at him in the near darkness.

"You don't have any expert advice about dealing with women, do you?"

Bo saw the alien blink slowly, but there was no other display of understanding or emotion.

"Of course, you don't, buddy. I'm all alone in this kind of shit again, huh?"

Scout didn't respond.

"I know I have to tell her." Bo sighed.

There had been plenty of opportunities for him to have similar conversations with his ex-wife while he was deployed. He'd chosen not to. While he had forgiven Sharron for her decision to leave him, and he regretted not having the opportunity to reconcile with her, there were some things that made him feel helpless. Articulating his feelings—communicating what was on his mind without filtering it—was still something that needed a tremendous amount of work. He believed Aliza would be patient. They loved each other. At one time, he'd believed love would be enough for anything, but losing Sharron proved otherwise.

Let's just get through this operation, and I'll do it. The fact that there will be another mission can't stop me again. There's always gonna be another mission. I might not get another chance to let her know.

You ain't getting no younger, Bo.

Scout made his restless noise again and came forward to sit next to Bo and looked across the valley. Bo followed his gaze and realized the time had come for him to put together the plan. He'd been thinking about the possibility of a raid across the valley since their deployment, but it was clear they were going to have a target soon. It was only a matter of time until Aliza got the intelligence they needed, and, rather than sit in the dark and wonder about the rest of his life, Bo needed to decide on a course of action. He would ensure it took care of the people, and Aliza, as best as possible.

At the top of the next hour, Bo and Scout were still sitting on top of the rock, looking across the valley at the town. This time Bo reached for the PFM, the sardonic acronym they'd adopted for the space-capable radio. The joke of alien technology referred to as "pure fucking magic" never failed to bring a smile to his face. While it didn't have the same power requirements or perishable power supply as the Vietnam-era PRC-77s, it was still something he didn't want to turn on until necessary. From everything they knew about the inhabitants of the town, his own communications capabilities did not appear to be at any risk of enemy jamming or compromise. But Bo also knew Murphy would've been happier if they'd been able to just use UHF; the PFM operated somewhere north of the S band. Either way, Bo didn't really know that much about the electromagnetic spectrum. All he knew was that when he turned on the radio, it worked, even though Murphy was hundreds of miles away.

"Home Plate, this is Fenway Park. Over."

Surprisingly, Colonel Murphy himself responded. "Fenway, Home Plate Umpire. What are the balls and strikes?"

Callsigns and radio procedures were always designed to confuse the enemy, but in this case, Bo had taken an extra step. He'd set up his unit with a second set of references that would totally bewilder anyone who might be listening. He doubted anyone outside of his forces knew who the Eagles were. They'd have no idea about baseball, either. And if by some chance a local had learned about either from one of the Lost Soldiers, it was beyond plausibility that they would have learned about both.

Bo grinned at the layers of subterfuge. He'd never pegged Murphy as a baseball fan, and the likelihood was that his commanding officer was not. Bo's knowledge of the sport was mostly limited to the games played by his beloved Atlanta Braves. At the time of his disappearance, things had been looking up for them and their competitiveness would surely have taken them on to more World Series. He wondered what had happened to those teams, but it wasn't pressing enough for him to actually look it up. Still, the J'Stull and the others on the planet did not understand what baseball was, and that was what mattered.

In their communications procedures, balls were the number of Priority Information Requirements they'd been able to gather. Strikes were the persons of interest and other Commander's Critical Information Requirements.

"One ball, one strike," Bo reported. "Confirmed on Foxtrot."

"How's the pace of play?"

Bo chuckled. "Speeding up. Seeing more players in the dugout."

"How's your pitcher?"

"Got a pretty decent pitch count today. Still looking good," Bo replied.

Truth be told, he wasn't exactly sure what Aliza was doing, but doubt was the least of the things he could give her the benefit of.

"Understood. Got your relievers ready?"

"Always ready, Home Plate."

"Glad to hear it. Keep me informed. What's our inning?"

Bo gave it some thought. According to the procedures, bottom of the ninth with the bases loaded would be the time for the attack. "Bottom of the third, Home Plate. No runners on base."

"Bottom of the third, understood. All green?"

"All green," Bo replied.

"And what about you?"

"We're fine, Home Plate. Bottom of the third, no runners on base. All green."

"Understood. Maintain procedures. Home Plate, out."

Bo shut down the PFM and stood up, dusting off his pants. Scout rose to a standing position but kept staring across the valley. Bo followed his mount's eyes. In the gloomy darkness, Imsurmik's lights glowed against the exposed façade of the plateau, illuminating the upper part of the escarpment.

What's up there?

Bo put his hands in his pockets, preparing to walk back to his makeshift bunk. Instead, he stared at the plateau and wondered if he'd been looking at the mission, and the terrain, wrong. All the principles he'd learned about key terrain pointed to the valley and the riverbeds as their fastest avenues of approach. Yet the wide, flat top of the plateau could prove valuable for his forces.

At the very least, it merited some reconnaissance. Bo smiled to himself. Aerial reconnaissance was out of the question. The Hueys had their own mission to prepare for, and, until the attack, stealth would be the name of the game. Any reconnaissance of the plateau would have to be a mounted excursion.

That's exactly what we'll do.

And it's what we do best.

Chapter Twenty-One

Bo woke after only four hours of sleep. It was still the total darkness before R'Bak's unusually swift sunrise. He finally rolled himself upright from his comfortable-enough sleeping position on the top of his command vehicle, realizing that some part of his mind had been thinking about the Troop Leading Procedures all night long. They were the cornerstone of small unit leadership. Everything he learned from ROTC forward always came back to them, yet he'd forgotten to incorporate some of them, and apparently his brain wouldn't let him sleep until he figured out what needed to be done. In the end, everything pointed at the need to conduct a leader's reconnaissance.

After staring across the narrow valley at the plateau, Bo realized his knowledge of the objective, even with Aliza embedded in the town, remained tentative at best. He needed to see the ground to better understand it.

The plateau sloped gently from west to east where it ended in an escarpment of exposed rock some thirty to forty meters tall in places, and the whole thing was about fifteen kilometers long. Its western end butted up against the low hills that meandered over a hundred kilometers to the east until they ultimately rose into the massif upon which they'd established Camp Stark many months before. It was from there that they had courted the land to make an undetected approach to what was now their forward operating base. Called "Fences," it lay fifteen kilometers behind Bo on one of the best sections of key terrain they'd found. There they had high ground with excellent fields of fire, clearly marked avenues of approach coverable by that fire, and almost complete concealment in the tall scrub atop a similar plateau they called Masada. Yet the base itself was nearly vacant. Colonel Murphy's intent to move the Lost Soldiers off the planet as the Sear approached was already well underway. Everything remaining on the surface had one mission: get everything to orbit and be ready for the next phase of the operation.

Bo knew conducting a leader's reconnaissance with the bulk of his vehicular forces was not a good idea. They had considered disguising the different platforms to allow them to pass as one of the armed caravans moving along the roads between Imsurmik, the J'Stull capitol of Stullhaan, and the smaller satrapies arrayed in a rough arc along the border of the Hamain Ashband and the Greens. His larger platforms, the major weapons systems, couldn't be camouflaged. If news traveled fast between the settlements, everyone would know they had captured those vehicles from the J'Stull: a far larger and more determined adversary which would likely sortie immediately against them. So once he rolled his big platforms out of their concealed locations, they needed to be ready to attack.

However, Bo wasn't quite ready to show his hand. Removing the vehicles from the reconnaissance meant his whinnies needed to be the maneuver element. There were fourteen of them with trained riders. Given their herding nature, there were usually twice that many whinnies around who consented to being beasts of burden and would help move equipment and supplies as necessary.

Bo watched them graze for a long time and considered whether a wild herd of whinnies would migrate naturally through this area at this time. Since his forces had repositioned from the high country near Camp Stark, he hadn't seen many whinnies, but that didn't mean the occasional herd might not cross the valley, especially with a good-sized river flowing through it. Bo carefully weighed the pros and cons before deciding the whinnies would be his best effort. By the time the others were awake, he'd settled on his plan.

Sleep didn't come for Aliza. After four hours of harvesting and another two spent dancing and eating kr'it and a variety of things she'd never imagined were edible, much less good, she finally laid down to sleep on the tiny grass-filled mattress.

Except her brain refused to cooperate. It spun and explored variables, playing them out to logical conclusions until the only thing she could be sure of was that there were far, far too many of them. For five days, she'd moved through Imsurmik, her eyes darting quickly from potential subject to potential subject. On more than one occasion, she had felt eyes on her, as well. Her features were not typical for the region, and Aliza suspected that many of the locals assumed she was from the Greens or further north, near the Pole. But she disarmed them with a smile and her mastery of the local dialect. Children loved her, and the old women took her under their wing. Integrating into the routines of Imsurmik had come easily.

Still, the atmosphere of the town changed daily. As caravans arrived, and the farmers and other migrants departed, there were more and more fighters. Some were bright-eyed and nervous, like the recruits she'd seen coming to Dachau as prison guards. Others, the ones who worried her, had the steely-eyed stare she'd seen in so many of the Lost Soldiers. Among the arriving soldiers, there weren't many of such hardened types, but they had clearly seen conflict and had a more thorough understanding of warfare. Given the chance, they might put up more of a fight than the Lost Soldiers would be capable of handling.

And so, her mind continued to wander.

"When things overwhelm you, Aliza," Colonel Murphy had said over the PFM before her mission started, "focus on the priorities you've been given. Identify who is in the town. What are they doing? Most importantly, what information will Bo need to prepare his attack? Because, rest assured, he'll be coming 'round the mountain, so to speak."

What information will Bo need?

Without the training of a military officer, Aliza relied on her brief experience in Palestine working with the Haganah. Ben Mazza, her oldest friend, had taught her to ask the questions. On the ground, what can you see? What do your enemies see? Is there some place that has an advantage over every other place? Could an enemy cover it and its approaches with supporting fire? What would stop someone from getting there?

Lying in the darkness, Aliza closed her eyes and envisioned the town of Imsurmik as if she were flying over it like an eagle. She'd focused on the layout of the town with the diligence of a cartographer. Now she visualized the town, starting at the Outer City and the irrigated farmland, moving toward the hill where the Inner City lay. With the detail she'd collected, making a scale model of the town would have been easy. Developing a way to attack and seize the town, though, would have been difficult.

I need to look at this like a soldier, not like a tourist.

Aliza fumed silently, staring at the mud and thatch roof above her for a long time. She focused on her breathing and tried to relax, but that allowed her mind to wander, too. The visual of the town faded. In its place came memories from Palestine. After the dreary winter of 1944, trapped inside Dachau, the chance to explore the Mediterranean coastline gave Aliza life. Ben Mazza told her they would find a place to leave the horrors behind. All they had to do was dream.

Just dream.

There wasn't any dream, though. Their promised land was anything but promising, and it certainly was not guaranteed. Like everything, it had to be fought for and defended. She found herself wandering through images of her time in Palestine, pleasant and hurtful memories, until an hour before dawn. Surrounded by sleeping women, Aliza rose and dressed as quietly as possible. Without her housemates seeing, she carefully donned the belt and holster of her pistol, securing it to her thigh with a canvas strap. Making sure the folds of her desert garb covered it, she crept through the domicile and out the door into the empty street. She turned south, toward the gate of the Inner City. Once in the primary thoroughfare, she glanced over the roofs of a series of shops and low houses to the glacis above.

A group of four rough men were pushing a missile rack along the narrow walkway at the top of the wall. In several locations close by, rudimentary cranes reached over to the inside of the glacis. Pallets of ammunition lay below, waiting to be lifted. Aliza saw a pallet being moved along the walkway toward one enclosure at an external corner.

Ammunition and weapons systems on the wall. Noted.

As she walked, Aliza turned to her left and moved her eyes along the far side of the glacis to the west. At least one more weapons platform, something like a tank gun with a long, wide tube, rested farther down the wall. Try as she might, Aliza couldn't see any ammunition pallets nearby. She strained to see them and—

Walked into a brick wall. Except it wasn't a wall, but a large man with a weathered, tanned face. His dark eyes bored through her from beneath thick eyebrows and framed a wide, reddened nose. There was an odor of sweat and alcohol emanating from the scraggly beard touching his chest a few inches from Aliza's face.

"Watch where you tread, woman."

Aliza recoiled and stared up at the angry man. "So sorry."

His eyes narrowed, and he studied her face intently. Aliza gathered her garment across her chest, lowered her eyes, and attempted to scurry away like she'd seen the other women do.

A rough hand shot out and grabbed her by the sleeve. "Where are you going?"

"To the fields."

He growled. "What were you looking at?"

Aliza turned and pointed. "The *eron*. They are here every morning. Harbingers of good days."

"Harbingers?" The man stared up at the birdlike creatures.

Hearing the remains of a clipped, northern accent, Aliza sensed an opportunity. "Do you not have them where you live?"

"Of course." The man stared at her again. "In the north we do not see them as harbingers. Merely scavengers."

Aliza tried to smile. "Aren't we all, when the Sear is approaching?"

The man snorted, but his face did not break. Whatever charm she had momentarily exerted on him had passed. "You live here?"

"All my life," Aliza lied. "You came from the north?"

The man said nothing and turned away from her, back to the men arranging the missile rack on the crane. Aliza walked away quickly. She turned once and saw the man glowering after her.

Person of interest identified.

Aliza turned back to the thoroughfare and made her way to the western gate. As she walked, Aliza kept her eyes forward and on the ground. The feeling she was being watched washed over her like a wave.

You're a potential target now, Aliza. The voice was Ben Mazza's. *Now, what are you going to do about it?*

Finish my job. Find out who that man is and what he's doing here. If he's a leader, maybe follow him.

As she neared the gate, a flurry of movement along the exposed rock of the plateau's northern edge caught her eye. There were tunnels through and under the plateau's protective eave, and while she'd seen them from a distance, she hadn't explored them. Armed guards stood at every entrance and kept passersby from even looking down into them. As she watched, a group of twenty or thirty men were moving large, cloth-wrapped bundles out of the tunnel entrance and into the city itself.

What are they bringing into the city? And where did they come from?

But she could not stop and investigate without calling attention to herself. Aliza continued through the gate and moved toward the fields and the markets of the Outer City without looking back. Her mind was already set to explore the tunnels as best as she could, when she could. Whatever the men were moving into the city was either coming from spaces within the plateau itself, or had entered the tunnels through some other access point. Finding which it was, and the location of it, might be one of the most critical pieces of information she could pass to Bo, other than saying she loved him.

A man carrying a small crate dropped it in the thoroughfare near the tunnel entrance. He climbed atop it and put his hands on his hips.

"First ten people who want an extra kr'it tonight, come with me and unload our caravan." He pointed emphatically down the tunnel. "I must secure the loads before the heat rises, and I will pay handsomely."

Aliza started toward him. Murphy's guidance was to not take any excessive chances pursuing information. But given the relative emptiness of the thoroughfare in the early morning, this was an unusually low-risk opportunity. Far too many of the citizens had imbibed too much *alaat*, a sour mash alcohol, on the opening night of their festival. The noxious smelling brew appeared quite potent, and Aliza had only sipped at the beverage when one of the other women had handed her a sample at the festival.

The man atop the box looked at her. "You, sister? More kr'it for you and your family?"

That sounds like an invitation.

Aliza nodded. "Yes, with gratitude."

"You are strong, yes?" The man grinned down at her. Several of his teeth were missing. "Then you may earn more for your efforts, yes?"

And that sounds like trouble.

"I can help for a load or two before I must be at the fields for harvest," Aliza replied with a hint of strength in her voice. The pistol was heavy against her thigh, and it comforted her. Even with the heavy, hooded robe, she believed she could draw the weapon quickly if required. Yet the security of the weapon was second to the security in understanding those around her, something at which she'd always excelled.

At the word "harvest," any malicious intent in the man's face vanished, and he called to others around her with renewed energy. Imsurmik's populace was obsessed with processing food and kr'it. Soon, she'd learned, many of them would trek farther north in an attempt to escape the heat. For their journeys, they would need all the sustenance possible.

"Fine. Yes. Come with me." The man gestured behind her. Other volunteers were gathering. "All of you, yes. Follow me."

Aliza fell into the middle of the group. There were ten or twelve of them, and half were women. They passed the armed guards into the relative cool of the tunnel. Aliza adjusted her hooded garment and pulled it up against her neck and shoulders. Suppressing a shiver, she told herself it was merely the result of the temperature difference, not her rising anxiety.

She studied the low-powered lights and the ancient conduits between them. Lighting must be necessary given the length of the tunnel itself. How deep into the plateau did it go? Carved from the rock over thousands of years and braced every ten to twelve steps, the tunnel's interior walls were worn smooth enough to appear polished. In some places, the artwork of children decorated them, but the chipped paints told her it had been many years since anyone other than those in authority had walked these tunnels.

Pondering why, Aliza moved deeper into the tunnels behind Imsurmik.

Chapter Twenty-Two

Under the dangerous light of R'Bak's approaching Sear, only white clothing made sense, with "white" being relative. The common people wore thin, cheaply woven robes that might once have been considered white but had long since become a pattern of muddy browns after years of sweat and dust. Most couldn't afford extra clothing, and, even in the cooler years, washing was a luxurious waste of time and water. The custom of face painting had evolved, which had even reached the court of the F'ahdn, where nobles and hangers-on seeking their ruler's favor each had their own unique design.

In contrast to the worn garments typical in the Outer City, Yukannak's robe shone in the sunlight that came in through a high window. He remained motionless and aloof as his face was painted. As the satrap's silci to the F'ahdn of Imsurmik, he needed to project the power and authority of his master. That meant he'd been able, in advance of his visit, to commission the city's most skilled weavers to fashion his robes using their best cloth and to have cobblers make him several pairs of the peculiar local boots. Held tight by strap-over ties, their heavy soles allowed for easy travel on hard surfaces like the city streets, as well as the rocky outlying areas.

To further signify his importance, Yukannak had ordered red and blue stitching along the hems and collars of the robes and embossed scrollwork on the boots. Such extravagances showed he could afford flourishes beyond the reach of common people, as befit a man of his stature. Brand new and never worn, these richly adorned garments spoke of wealth even more than did his paint.

Inspecting his reflection in a burnished disc of steel, he turned his face from side to side to make certain the mask of intricately painted lines and geometric shapes maintained its symmetry in all respects. He wasn't sure how the fashion had evolved in Imsurmik and a few other cities, since most people of the region relied on too-thin clothing and facial coverings to ward off skin damage from the harsh suns, but he was glad it had. Facial coverings and such were considered rude by the upper class, suited only to the primitive villagers and farmers. Paint colors and designs also marked distinctions—often subtle—between the classes. The cost of some colors, such as the gold and silver so prominent on Yukannak's face, was more than most commoners earned in a year. The white on Subitorni's J'Stull guards wasn't as expensive as his colors, but it wasn't cheap, either.

"Your work here is satisfactory," he said to the mature woman standing to one side, brush in hand. He was careful not to put too much approval into his words. "Tell your master I approve."

"I have no master, lord; I am not a slave."

Yukannak stood and reached for his robe. The woman had painted her own face in a uniform brown, the least expensive color to use, which showed cracks near the temples. Despite her skill at masking, she obviously wallowed in poverty like most of the city. Cracked paint indicated a base that could flake off, leaving the skin below exposed to the killing sunlight. Yukannak approved of not allowing the woman to use better quality paint for her own face; it showed that the F'ahdn knew how to keep his people under control. It also gave Yukannak a possible wedge to drive home.

"Perhaps not yet," he said, finally responding to her statement. "But such matters are prone to fast changes for those who forget their place."

"My apologies, lord."

She bowed her head and backed away, staring at the floor, but he could tell she wasn't really chastened.

"Be careful then," he said in a more compassionate tone. Servants always knew secrets they shouldn't, and he needed as many informants as he could develop. He now doubted there were listening devices in his quarters, but he dropped his voice anyway. "I have heard the F'ahdn has the Bleeding Black and blames you. That seems unfair to me; if he did not approve of your work, he would not have hired your services. To blame you after the fact seems like something the satrap should know about, and, as you know, I am the silci in this region."

The woman hesitated. Yukannak knew she was smart enough not to believe him at face value.

"Thank you," she said eventually. "I put all of my skill into my work, lord. But I am beneath the notice of one such as you, or the satrap."

"Nonsense. What is your name?"

"Nomi."

"Well, Nomi, the satrap cares for all his people, as do I. I am here as the eyes and ears of my people and the satrap, and I only seek the truth. If the F'ahdn is blaming others for things that are not their fault…" He stopped, letting Nomi's imagination fill in the rest. "Consider me a sympathetic ear, Nomi. Come to me with anything that troubles you; can you do that?"

"I can, lord."

"Good. And if I have questions for you, will you do the same for me?"

"Questions?"

The smile he gave her was well practiced: reassuring yet with a hint of menace. "Yes, questions."

"I—of course, lord."

"Good. You may go now, Nomi."

The chambers he occupied had been cut into the plateau against which Imsurmik had been built and were well elevated from the level of the Outer City, thereby keeping the stench of open sewers away from the wealthy and powerful. As a further division, a glacis wall separated the filthy inhabitants of the Outer City—which was mostly a ramshackle slum interspersed with fields—from the tidy and well-kept streets of the Inner City. Yukannak stepped through the heavy wooden door of his quarters into a wide tunnel lit by lanterns and open shafts cleverly cut into the rock ceiling. Those led to the surface some ninety feet above and reflected sunlight into the tunnel using a series of mirrors. The mouth of the tunnel exited onto a narrow viewing platform. Looking right, he could see over the Outer City. To his front lay the Inner City, the wall, and irrigated farmland, with the river beyond them. Marshland protected the city on his far left. Stairs carved into the rock led down the right side of the platform to a back alley of the Inner City.

He emerged onto the platform and was pleased to discover that the brute he had expected—a person of some significance named Waornaak—was at least punctual. More cunning than smart, the hulking militia leader had earlier arranged a meeting to ingratiate himself with the silci. Judging that Waornaak's loyalty was something purchased, not earned, Yukannak had immediately given him a task. He suspected a trap, of course, and so set one in return. Now, after glancing about as if making sure that nobody could eavesdrop, Yukannak asked in a low voice, "How goes the collecting?"

"Some of the medicinals are in bigger quantities than we expected."

"Which ones?"

"It's not my job to keep all those names straight. I only care that the Harvesters get what they need when they need it."

"And I can assure you they appreciate it."

Squinting with his left eye, Waornaak sucked his teeth, something Yukannak found disgusting. "By 'they' don't you mean 'we?'"

He's not as stupid as I thought. Ignoring the comment, Yukannak pushed back against the man's impertinence. "The silci doesn't answer questions, he asks them. Now, what do you have for me? I spoke fine words about you to the satrap. Do not make me retract them; I would not like it."

Waornaak made a low sound like a growl but swallowed whatever he might have said. "Since I've been here, I've heard hints and rumors of a secret cache somewhere. No mention of what it is, or where it is, until late last night. An apprentice of one of the F'ahdn's Masters of Healing got into the medicinals and took too much—a lot too much. He started babbling, but within all that nonsense, there was mention of this secret stash, and it didn't sound like it was plants or medicines. More like…I don't know; just not plants. He used a word I hadn't heard before: *hyshvass*. Does that make sense to you?"

"*Hyshvass*? It is an archaic word that means 'archive.'" *A word from the older languages.* Yukannak cocked his head slightly toward the larger man. No twitch of the eye or flaring nostril betrayed his suddenly racing heart. "Are you certain that was the word?"

"I had to ask him to repeat it, so, yeah, I'm sure."

"An archive…" He snapped out of his thinking with a more intense tone. "Where is this secret cache? Did he say?"

"No."

"Find him and find out."

"That risks the F'ahdn discovering what I'm up to."

"Then I suggest you be careful. Is there anything else?"

"We might have spies in the city, too."

"Spies? What do you mean?"

"I caught a woman looking around where she shouldn't be. She had her face wrapped, so I couldn't tell what tribe she was from, but there was something about her I didn't like."

"Have you seen her since?"

"She's around."

"Be wary of her then; she might be working for the Offworlders. They are clever."

"Clever wouldn't stop an axe from splitting her head."

"No," Yukannak said, allowing himself a slight smile. "It wouldn't. But I wish to question her, so do her no harm. If she does work for the Offworlders, she can tell us much."

This time Waornaak did growl. "I won't kill her. I can't guarantee she won't be a little…used."

"*No* harm! I am the voice of the satrap when he is not present, and you will *not* hurt her in any way. Are my words understood?"

"She might—"

Raising his voice had drawn the attention of a woman walking through the alley carrying a bundle of reeds over one shoulder.

"Are my words understood?" Yukannak asked again in a harsh whisper.

"Yeah, I hear you."

"One more thing. Speak nothing of this to Subitorni."

Waornaak squinted again, this time in obvious suspicion. "Why not?"

"You can never be certain where true loyalties lie."

"Oh…" Waornaak said. He scratched his chin, thinking. "No offense meant, Silci, but he lives here, and you don't. Also, Subitorni is not the forgiving sort. What's in it for me to keep quiet about this hyshvass thing? If anybody knows about it, it's Subitorni."

"I have my reasons." Yukannak's smile grew wider, and he clapped a hand on Waornaak's hardened shoulder. "And, because you are my friend, I'm looking out for you. What if you have not heard of this archive because to hear of it means death?"

"What do you—? Oh, I see what you mean."

"It must be secret for a reason. And who would the F'ahdn rely on to execute anyone who learned of its existence?"

"Subitorni!"

"Yes, my friend. The satrap protects his friends and punishes his enemies, and so I am helping you. Are you bonded to a female?"

"I'm hetman of my village; of course I am bonded."

"And does your bond-mate share *all* of your secrets? Do you tell her everything?"

"Uh…huh. I never saw it that way before."

"I serve the satrap as silci, because only he can rule his people fairly, and it is in my people's interest that he does so. Anyone who aids him in protecting the people of R'Bak is a friend worthy of his protection, while those who oppose him deserve only destruction."

Less a growl than a double-grunt, Waornaak's response conveyed more than a paragraph's worth of response. It was a common vocalization of agreement among some of the Ashband tribes. After Waornaak clomped down the stairs into the streets of the Inner City, Yukannak signaled to a figure lingering inside the tunnel. He wore a dull robe and unadorned purple paint. He seemed far less intimidating than the hulking Waornaak, but Yukannak knew the opposite to be true.

From the instant they'd met, Yukannak had marked Zeesar as the man to befriend, the man who made things happen—things the F'ahdn did, and didn't, know about. He likely knew more about what was happening in Imsurmik than even the man he served.

"You heard?"

"I heard."

"What do you know of this hyshvass, Zeesar?" he asked.

"Nothing at all."

Among the many liars he'd met during his career, Zeesar was one of the best. Not only were his expressions and body language perfect, the inflection of his voice matched his physical stance. If his life hadn't depended on knowing a lie when he heard it, Yukannak would have believed him. But gentle correction would not send the right message. "Would you like to reconsider that answer before I take offense?"

Zeesar lifted an appraising eyebrow, an obvious admission he'd misjudged the silci. "I had thought it a myth," he finally said. "Not worth troubling over."

"Not like the entrance I came through."

Zeesar didn't try to hide that the memory made him angry. "No."

"But you *had* heard of it?"

"Rumors only, nothing to bother the silci about. Had I more information, I would have come to you with it."

"Would you? Perhaps so, although I doubt it. But I saw your reaction to that tunnel we used to enter the city. That was something new to you, a secret, and, as the F'ahdn's yuzbazzi, you didn't expect there to *be* any secrets. Yet Subitorni *did* know of the concealed entrance, and there were fresh tracks." He decided to throw out a guess to gauge Zeesar's reaction. "There was a recent operation, and you knew nothing of that, either."

Zeesar squinted and didn't try to hide his surprise. "You're well informed. Imsurmik has more spies than I thought."

"I can be your ally, Zeesar, but only if I can trust you. Remember, my trust brings with it the trust of the satrap."

"And the Harvesters?"

"That goes without saying." The lie came easy. Yukannak paused then, content to watch as Zeesar calculated where his best interests lay. After nearly a minute, the yuzbazzi nodded.

"You may rely on me, Silci."

"And you on me. From now on you are to inform me of all rumors, whether you give them credence or not. Are we agreed?"

"We are, and in return you will tell me if my name comes up?"

"Of course."

Being the satrap's eyes and ears had long since trained Yukannak to still his tongue and hide his emotions, especially relief. So instead of smiling at the militia leader he let his face go slack and moderated his tone.

"You have my support in the days to come," he said. "We shall both be glad."

"Yes," Zeesar said, "we can certainly hope so."

Chapter Twenty-Three

Eager to get moving on an actual operation, Bo had his troops ready by 0900. Astride the whinnies, they traversed the narrow end of the valley to reach the western edge of the plateau, a total U-shaped move of more than fifteen kilometers by 1300 that afternoon. The speed and sure-footedness of the alien creatures made the journey easy. Clambering up where the plateau's exposed rocks were only a couple meters tall, they were prepared to hasten eastward...but the whinnies slowed, and finally, a kilometer up the plateau, refused to go further.

Bo frowned. As a teenager on the family farm in Mississippi, he'd been out riding one day when his horse, Magic, slammed on the brakes and nearly threw him to the ground. After Bo had caught his breath, he'd seen a copperhead crossing the path. The big whinnie's reaction was frightfully similar.

"What is it, Scout?"

Scout turned his triangular-shaped head hard to the right as if to study Bo with one dark eye. Then the whinnie pointed with its snout at a tall, stalky plant with a curious assortment of purple and gold flowers roughly ten meters away. There were more in the distance, gathered in loose bunches, drawing a line across the plateau.

Bo squinted. "The plants?"

Scout didn't respond, as usual. They sat for a long moment and Bo wondered why until he heard rustling on the ground ahead of them. A six-legged, lizard-like creature scurried across the rocks near the plant, and the plant flinched. Several lower branches swung toward the advancing animal. Bo heard several small popping sounds and saw, with the last, a tiny, white projectile strike the animal on its hindquarters. The lizard thing frantically tried to run away, making it about three meters before it fell over, twitching. Less than thirty seconds later, the animal was dead.

Well, shit.

Loitering at the base of the plateau was not part of Bo's plan. The reason for the whinnies was to move quickly and avoid detection as they crossed the valley and scaled the higher terrain. Observation of the roads showed no one on them that morning, and Bo was confident in their ability to cover their tracks when they crossed the roads so no one would know they had passed. But, no matter whether the biological defenses had been planned or were naturally occurring, the patrol was not only stopped a kilometer up the flank of the plateau, but in increasing danger of detection.

Bo tugged gently on Scout's reins to the left, intending to move north and find a way around the plants. Scout refused to budge in that direction. When he moved, the whinnie turned hard against the reins to point back toward the relative cover at the base of the plateau.

"You want to go back?"

Bo heard another whinnie approach. He looked over his left shoulder and met Lieutenant—former Sergeant—Stewart's eyes. "What's the trouble, sir?"

Bo gestured toward the plants ahead of them. "Some type of defensive flora. They're all over before us and far as I can see on both sides."

"And the whinnies won't go through?"

"I get the feeling they could go through, but I don't think any of *us* would make it."

"We can't find another way around?" Stewart asked.

"I don't know," Bo replied.

Stewart nodded at the colorful plants. "You know, the intel we had on some of these plants said they were diurnal; they go dormant at night."

Bo looked at the young lieutenant. "These? You know that for sure?"

Stewart shrugged. "I don't, sir. But it may be worth checking in with headquarters."

Breaking radio silence outside of scheduled reporting times was not something Bo wanted to do, especially to ask for clarification on an alien plant.

"You think we should wait until nightfall?" He wasn't just asking Lieutenant Stewart. As soon as the words left his mouth, he realized it was fairly stupid to believe Scout or any of the whinnies knew what he was talking about.

Stewart replied, "I see two options, sir. Wait 'til nightfall and find out if we can go through. Or we risk going around, which might take days. Last I recall, we didn't have that kind of time."

The young officer was right so they turned back to the western edge of the plateau. Bo directed the patrol down into a thick grove of alien trees. They reminded him of the baobabs he'd seen in Africa, short and stocky, but they had trunks and hexagonal leaf combinations which were decidedly alien. A type of moss or lichen grew in a thick, flat carpet atop each of the thick stalks. They provided some shade, though, and if the patrol was going to wait until nightfall, shade was important. He relied on Scout and the other whinnies to graze and find a water source on their own.

"We'll try again at sundown," Bo told the patrol. "If we can't make it, we'll figure out what our options are. Rest up, drink plenty of water. When the time comes, be ready to move."

As he waited, Bo Moorefield couldn't help but think he was leaving Aliza without protection. He hoped she would understand.

Approaching Imsurmik posed difficulties greater than slipping through a swath of defensive plants. Moving at night, presuming they could get past the damned dart-firing flowers, was an advantage he intended to exploit to its fullest, even if it meant missing his report time with Aliza, since there wouldn't be any line-of-sight connection between them. She'd have to report to Sergeant Cook at the assembly area.

Bo leaned against a tree and lowered the brim of his cap over his eyes. As he drifted into an uneasy nap, he wondered what

Aliza was doing at that moment. Was she safe? Did she miss him?

Because he most surely missed her.

Aliza estimated that she and her fellow volunteers had walked through the dimly lit cavern for about fifteen minutes when daylight appeared in the distance. Given that they hadn't made any significant turns to the right or left, it seemed the passage had cut almost directly through the plateau. But from what she remembered of the intelligence briefings, that made little sense: it should have been a much longer walk. Her curiosity piqued, Aliza focused on the opening of the tunnel in the distance, hoping to get a better idea of what they were looking at and where they would emerge.

The tunnel opened on the backside of an exposed rock formation. From the other side, Aliza surmised, it would look like it was part of the plateau, when in reality the formation stuck out along a small spur, creating a V-shaped canyon on the far side. Based on his observation position and planned route of approach, she knew Bo and the others had no idea it was there. Murphy might have seen the small notch from orbital sensors, but he likely hadn't seen what it held.

Inside the vaguely triangular canyon, Aliza saw a sizable wall, at least ten meters high, to her far right. Men were assembling it from piles of loose rock and boulders. Above it, she saw the familiar point on the escarpment that she had seen and noted from the thermal pond outside Imsurmik. The rocks there were not the edge of the plateau but an eroded outcropping. She glanced quickly to the far left and saw a wide spring emerging from the rocks. The watercourse was mostly empty and the spring appeared to be flowing at half of its capacity, likely another casualty of the approaching Sear.

Near Camp Stark, there had been similar features carved by water and wind into the regional geography. This canyon resembled what Bo and the others called a box canyon, like the one she'd occupied and defended during the J'Stull Job, with the plateau twenty meters above them on both sides.

On the north side of the canyon, she saw two figures walking across the top of the rock formation. A hundred meters to her left, the two walls of the canyon merged. The mere presence of a secretly accessible box canyon met one of Colonel Murphy's critical intelligence requirements. He'd asked for the location of any cache sites, and this was certainly one under construction. Everywhere she looked, the secure compound held equipment and storage containers. Some of them looked like nothing Aliza had ever seen. Several were so coated with dust and rust it was impossible to theorize what they might have been. Based on their condition, they might have sat in the exposed yard for years, maybe even longer.

Sergeant First Class Whittaker had once commented that the storage facilities at Camp Stark were a junkyard, and Aliza finally understood what he meant. She missed the grizzled veteran and his fatherly presence, but also imagined his ghostly finger pointing toward the stores as if reminding her that Lost Soldiers' lives might depend on her discovering what was there besides a bunch of ancient junk.

In contrast, there were also rows upon rows of newer items. More storage containers were arranged in silent, orderly grids. At least a dozen vehicles with mounted weapons systems stood in a line among others which appeared to have been modified for the transportation of goods. The vehicles were arrayed with their front wheels pointed out toward the fence that sealed off the open end of the canyon. Aliza surmised there must be a gate there and that, once loaded, the trucks would drive forward and meet the major road network to the east of the plateau. From there, she envisioned them turning southwest and heading toward the sea. All of it was well designed by a well-established enemy that knew exactly what it needed to do.

The leader of her cohort of volunteers pointed them at a truck brimming with more of the canvas-wrapped parcels and ordered them to unload it. She approached the back of the cargo bed, and one of the bundled parcels was handed to her. Alongside was one of the converted transports, where another group of men were alternating between loading bushels of medicinal plants and removing long, dark boxes. Many of the plants were species she recognized from her expeditions near Camp Stark. Whatever was in the long boxes was being traded for the medicinals. Given what she knew of the relative value of the plants, Aliza couldn't imagine what was in the dark containers.

Aliza easily lifted the bundle onto her right shoulder, turned around, and walked into the tunnel, preparing to count her steps as she headed back. That way, she could calculate exactly how far the canyon was from the town itself. Bo would certainly need to know she had found something none of them had expected. With any luck, she could drop off the parcel, make a second trip, and attempt to see what else she could learn about the storage facility.

High value, indeed!

A group of men carrying more modern tools approached. Two of them carried a black and gray box, one man on each end. They set the box heavily on the ground outside the tunnel and rested.

"Where is this package? Outside the gate?"

The other man wheezed. "Yes. I think so. Sobiturni was not specific."

"Fine," the first man huffed. "We can get the components to Waornaak when he arrives today. He will know what to do with them."

Aliza picked up her pace. Before counting her steps, she smiled to herself. *This Waornaak is almost certainly someone of importance.* And Sobiturni was a name she'd heard before. He was a member of the J'Stull command in the town. And this Waornaak certainly sounded likely to travel in the circles relevant to her intelligence objectives.

Hopefully, I'll have enough time to find out who he is and just how important he might be.

Chapter Twenty-Four

Aliza emerged from the tunnel into the city. She'd make sure the math was right later, but she estimated the tunnel through the rock on the southern side of Imsurmik was roughly a half-mile long. The collection of vehicles and the other items in the cache site were a critical intelligence requirement that needed to be reported. Aliza delivered the parcel where the leader pointed.

She turned back to him and asked, "Again?"

The man grinned at her, showing several missing teeth, and nodded. He pointed back down the tunnel, and Aliza set off. She counted her steps a second time, wanting to ensure her count was right, and by the time she emerged on the far side she determined she'd been close enough. When she reached the transport, there was a long line of volunteers waiting to receive parcels. Aliza took her place in the queue and glanced around the complex as much as she deemed safe. Given Bo's position on the far side of the valley, she was certain he couldn't see this site at all so any additional information she could gather, particularly on the number and type of guards and weapons systems, was critical.

Along the top of the canyon, armed guards stood watch or walked patrols on both walls. They were high enough that an attack would be hard-pressed to get through them and down into the canyon itself. There was no way for the vehicles in Bo's complement to attack, either, without coming out of the valley and revealing themselves as they moved east on the wide road. Bo was too prudent to take that kind of chance.

Aliza smiled. *He is cautious and good.*

The line of bearers paused and didn't move for several minutes, so she stepped out of the queue and moved to her right, along the southern canyon wall. She was able to get close enough to the outer wall to see its level of fortification and the number of soldiers guarding it. Both were prohibitive. Constructed of rock, she estimated the wall was at least seven meters wide at its base and rose to a pathway at least two meters wide based solely on the number of people she saw. Several weapons were mounted atop it as well. There was little doubt it was fortified all the way across, but her position did not allow her to see any details beyond the near lip.

Aliza passed several large cylindrical tanks and tried to discern if they were for fuel or water; no luck. As she moved further around the curved edge of one tank, a tall, powerful man stepped into her path. She recognized him immediately as she'd literally run into him not more than a half hour before. He'd somehow beaten her to this side of the plateau, and, given the fury in his eyes, he'd recognized her as well.

"Waornaak," called a voice from behind the brute. His eyes did not move from her. Aliza couldn't keep up the intense glare and dropped her eyes. He wore bandoliers over both shoulders and there was a large knife strapped to his left hip.

Waornaak? I know that name!

"Get this woman out of here," Waornaak said over one shoulder without taking his eyes off hers.

Aliza swallowed and kept her face up. "I, uh…"

"Never come back here, woman," Waornaak growled. "Return to your line. This area is not for you."

"Why not?" she asked, finding her courage. Waornaak's eyes widened slightly, as if he wasn't used to being questioned. Aliza pressed her advantage. "Are we not all gathering supplies to survive the Sear? And aren't you guarding them to protect them for our city? I could help you. Maybe as a guard, even?"

Waornaak sneered. "I have no use for you. Get back in your line and do not put your eyes where they do not need to be."

"So sorry," she said. "I was looking for a…latrine."

The man's stare eased, and one side of his mouth curled under. He pointed back toward the tunnel entrance. "Down the other wall from where you came in."

"Thank you," Aliza replied and made to leave.

Turning away, she heard another man call, "Zeesar's first caravan will be here within the hour, Waornaak. We must make ready."

Zeesar. I have heard of him, as well. Another person of interest.

Appears I've hit the jackpot.

Aliza filed away the name Zeesar along with what she observed of Waornaak: that he was someone in charge, someone with a small band and obviously keen to the goings-on of the town. This Zeesar person also would need to be found sooner rather than later.

Aliza tried to look chastised as she made her way back to the line where people still waited to gather new parcels. The truck was mostly unloaded, and in front of the parcels she was delivering, Aliza saw several tubes that appeared heavy—carried by one man on each end.

Some type of missile?

The line finally moved. Aliza collected a parcel, placed it on her shoulder, and turned back toward the tunnel. Clearly, Imsurmik wanted protection as the Sear approached. But from whom? The arrangement made little sense unless the warlords had a history of squabbling over territory as resources became more scarce.

Gaining more intelligence on the cache site was going to be difficult. She considered asking some other women to follow her and see what they could discover on the far side of the tunnel. Yet Aliza realized they probably wouldn't know what they were looking at. The collection of technologies and equipment was old and varied. Maybe some of the women had seen similar things before, but most of them likely had not.

But right now, coming up with more intelligence gathering strategies was of secondary importance. What mattered was reporting what she'd seen in as much detail as possible. And that meant remaining innocuous until her call-in to Bo.

Just before nightfall darkened the plateau, Scout and the other whinnies stirred from their resting positions beneath the trees. Earlier in the day, they'd found a small water source, a spring surrounded by more of the increasingly familiar vegetation, and drank their fill. Bo's forces were also rested and ready to go. After ensuring the patrol was prepared, he crossed their perimeter and climbed aboard Scout. Almost immediately, the big whinnie started back in the direction they'd come—moving east up the plateau.

Darkness rolled over the higher ground and the valley below as Bo and the others edged up the plateau to where they'd first seen the venomous plants. There was still enough light to see the outline of the stalk-like plants as they approached. This time, Scout did not hesitate. He swept past the first closed cluster of flowers, though he kept a careful distance. Bo felt himself tense in the makeshift saddle, but there was no movement or strikes from the plants.

He reached down and patted Scout on the shoulder. "Thanks, buddy. Now we know."

But as they came abreast of the next plant, Bo saw someone had planted them in rows. No, not just rows: a staggered grid. So that anywhere you stood, you were in their needles' fields of fire.

There's definitely something up here they don't want to lose. Otherwise, they wouldn't have prepared a defensive position like this. I wonder what other surprises they have in store for us.

For two hours, they crept forward in the growing darkness. Several times the whinnies zigzagged across the terrain through the vegetation. Evidently there was more than one kind of plant that had to be avoided. While the going was slower in the darkness, they still made good time. One particular jaunt took them near the exposed escarpment on the south side of the plateau and there was just enough light from the stars in the night sky that Bo could make out familiar landmarks across the valley. They were much closer to the city than he'd imagined they would be.

As if cued by Bo's realization, Scout froze. The ripple effect went right down the line of mounts. All of the soldiers had enough experience with whinnies to know what it meant: something unexpected in the area. As they stood motionless, Bo turned to the patrol behind him and tapped his sleeve. The hand and arm signal was a silent communication to bring Lieutenant Stewart forward.

Stewart and his mount Olympia walked up two minutes later. "What is it, sir?"

Bo shrugged. "I'm thinking we may need to spread out. I can't see anything but—"

Scout shook like a wet dog drying itself. Bo brought up a hand and gave a signal—a closed fist. The formation froze again. The breeze freshened and, in the distance, he heard a murmuring sound not unlike voices. Straightening in the saddle, he let his eyes adjust. Night vision worked differently than daytime vision, being more attuned to following movement. In seconds, he saw what he'd been missing.

About a hundred meters ahead, an observation post was nestled low to the ground, with two men sitting in the darkness. One of them produced an artificial light and shone it around before turning it off. They weren't worried about noise or light discipline, most likely thinking the light would keep predators of all types at bay.

Bo turned and looked at Stewart. "Let's go north. See if we can spot any more OPs or what they're guarding."

"Could just be an entrance to the town. Maybe some underground stairs or something," Stewart suggested.

"You think so?"

"They had to get up here, sir. We know from Lieutenant Turan there are tunnels in the city, right? I bet they've got a way to get people up here that doesn't involve hiking through all those killer plants," Stewart said.

Bo thought for a moment. Stewart was more than likely right. If the enemy were simply guarding the top of the town, it made sense. "If they're not just overwatching from up here, they're protecting something below. We've got to try to see what it is."

Stewart nodded. "I'll take point, sir."

Bo let the young lieutenant move to the front of the patrol. He could use the experience, and sometimes the patrol leader didn't really need to be the point man, too. They crept north for half an hour before heading east again. Bo glanced down at his watch and realized it was coming up on midnight. Aliza would be calling in, but Sergeant Cook or one of the others at the assembly area across the valley would be the one to talk to her.

Will she worry about me? Wonder what I'm doing?

Bo decided he didn't know, and he didn't like how those kinds of questions distracted him from the mission. Aliza could wait a day. His need to focus and determine his course of action for the coming attack took precedence over everything else.

Thirty minutes later, they came upon another observation position overlooking the eastern edge of the plateau's escarpment. So: two observation posts and quite possibly more. Depending upon what was hidden back there, they might even have to be the first targets to be taken out during the attack.

Bo moved Scout up along Stewart's position. "We're not going to get any further east. Let's turn around and get back to the assembly area by morning, if we can."

"You sure, sir? I can't help thinking there's something here we're missing."

Bo nodded. "Without aerial reconnaissance, we're kinda hosed. We can see if Colonel Murphy can get us something from space, but I doubt that, too. We're on our own."

"Maybe Lieutenant Turan can get us something from the inside."

"When we talk again, I'll tell her what we found. Hopefully, she's found a few things today, too." Bo reined Scout back to the west and gestured for the patrol to fall in behind him. He prodded Scout into a trot; the whinnie didn't complain and seemed glad for the faster pace.

It was a beautiful evening for a ride. At that moment, there was nothing to do but quietly make their way back across the valley. The pieces were coming together, and they promised to take final operational shape with just one more report from Aliza…

Bo sat rubbing his hands together for a long moment. He abruptly discovered his mood had changed now that the mission was about to launch. Since his time as a second lieutenant, he'd known that he focused almost solely on one or two aspects of his life during times of stress. As he'd experienced with Sharron, that was often a detriment as it turned his struggles to express his feelings into total paralysis.

But right now, he was glad for the benefits of that focus. During, and then after, the long ride back from the top of the plateau, his mind had been purely on the impending attack. All he'd needed was the intelligence from Aliza to crystallize the various scenarios running through his head…and she'd certainly delivered.

Her account of the vast tunnel complex underneath the city, part of which stretched just over a klick to a hidden cache site on the north side of the plateau, shed new light on the overall situation.

During their week-long observation, his reconnaissance teams had seen and studied seventeen caravans that entered the outer town itself. By Bo's estimate, that put the strength of the forces inside the town at roughly two thousand—a full ten percent of the town's population—and it was growing. They had several types of heavier weapons systems, but their vehicles did not appear to have the same type of armaments or capabilities as the ones under Bo's command. From what they could tell, the Outer City also contained locations where small teams of men casually parked and secured vehicles. There were openings and possibilities. For a maneuver commander, the situation in Imsurmik made it ripe for the picking.

But that required a coherent, finalized plan. To use Murphy's baseball analogy, it was getting late in the game and the score was tied. All too soon, they would have the information they needed and could move forward. Much of that relied on Aliza's ability to remain safe inside the town and keep tabs on the persons of interest. Catching the enemy by surprise didn't appear to be a major issue. With that factor tentatively under control, the more critical aspect of mission analysis and planning came down to what the enemy might do in response to an attack.

In their first engagement, the J'Stull had reacted poorly when surprised by Bo's makeshift cavalry. They'd crossed each other's fields of fire, committed fratricide in considerable numbers, and pretty much surrendered the initiative upon contact. Undoubtedly, the J'Stull now knew there was someone out there, but because the enemy didn't understand Bo's forces or their intent, surprise was still within his grasp. However, if this batch of enemy forces were better disciplined and trained, they could hold a town the size of Imsurmik for an almost indefinite period.

However, Aliza's intelligence had given him options and opportunities he hadn't had before. While a full-frontal attack was less than optimal in this situation, the discovery of the hidden cache site was also the discovery of a weakness. A credible attack upon it might be a decisive diversion, provided what Aliza had found was valuable enough to the enemy that they would defend it in force. Given the vehicles, the guards, and the presence of heavy weapons on the wall, Bo believed they would.

Sitting atop his familiar perch looking over the valley, Bo drew in the dirt at his side with one finger, running through different scenarios in an attempt to play out what the enemy might do. The soft crunch of approaching boots caught his attention, and he looked over his shoulder.

"Just me, sir," Lieutenant Stewart replied.

"Come on up," Bo replied.

The two hadn't had a chance to talk since the long reconnaissance ride. Bo dusted his hands off on his knees as Stewart sat down beside him.

"You look pretty deep in thought, sir. Everything all right?"

At that moment, Bo was glad he was sitting in the dark. Otherwise, the young officer would've seen him flush. He'd been told many times early in his career that he wore his emotions on his sleeve. He'd gotten better at hiding them, so much so that Sharron had occasionally called him a robot. With Aliza, though, the emotional response was much more evident. Try as he might, it was hard to conceal exactly how he felt for the young woman. He knew that came across to his troopers as clear as day.

"Everything's fine," Bo replied. "Just tryin' to figure out what to do next."

"The colonel changed our mission?" Stewart asked.

"No, it's nothing like that. It's just a much bigger target than we thought. And, although we've got the intelligence we need to attack, there could be more enemy forces than we can deal with, much less chase off. Fire and maneuver only go so far."

Stewart said nothing for a couple of moments as the two of them stared across the valley at the glowing lights of the town. Finally, the young officer asked, "What did Lieutenant Turan find?"

Bo reviewed the key points of Aliza's report with Stewart. When he finished, the young man looked at him for a long moment. Bo could see the indecision on his face. "What is it?"

"Have things really changed that much? I mean from when the Ktor disappeared me to when they got you?" Stewart snorted and smiled. "I mean, I *hated* officers. Now, I am one."

Bo blinked. He'd expected to talk about the operation at hand, but Stewart clearly had other things on his mind. "What do you mean? You know the Army goes rolling along, as the song says," Bo replied.

Stewart chuckled. "I get that. I guess I'm talking about how we did business. In Vietnam, all I can recall is one clusterfuck after another. I mean, we had officers, but we hardly ever saw them. We did all kinds of stuff, and it didn't really seem like anybody had a plan. We knew a lot about the enemy and what they were doing, but most of the time it felt like we were all fighting with one hand tied behind us. The officers wouldn't lead us into combat. Here, you're expecting officers to do just that. How do you know we can?"

Bo looked at the dirt by his crossed legs. He had never counted on counseling a Vietnam veteran as part of his duties. By the time he'd commissioned, most of the Vietnam vets had long retired. He'd run into a few, but they were more an aberration than a constant in the Army he'd joined.

"I commissioned in 1987," Bo began. "At that point, we were fifteen years past what they said was the end of the Vietnam War. Its effects were still pretty real, though."

"Specialist Devolo says it was pretty rough. He heard rumors about the guys going home and getting spit on, called names and shit. Just made me think about—hell, I don't know—why keep doing what I do?"

"There's not much of an alternative here," Bo said.

Stewart smiled in the starlight. "No, there's not. But it makes me think about what would've happened when I went home. I mean, if I made it home. I know the only reason I'm here is because a bunch of sorta alien humans thought I was going to die. I don't know, sir. I just think about it."

Bo nodded. "Sometimes thinking about what might've been is one of the biggest hang-ups of being a soldier. It's hard to think about it. I was in the same boat. We were doing our jobs. You were in combat, and I was headed home. I believed it was the best thing left for me in the world. I was pretty sure my career was over. My marriage was over. I realized that I'd been watching too many people die for stupid reasons to really ever be normal again. Then I woke up here. Talk about a change of pace."

Stewart's voice was soft. "We'd just been ambushed. My whole squad was on the point of the maneuver. Charlie just nailed us. We couldn't see him, couldn't hear him. All of a sudden, they were there and that was it. We hit the ground and tried to return fire." Stewart paused. "My buddy Cotton was right next to me. I looked over as he was pulling a grenade off his vest. He got ready to throw it when it seemed like about a hundred rounds ripped right through his head and neck. His freaking helmet did nothing. His head splattered all over me. That was the last thing I thought about until everything stopped. I'm kinda glad I'm here, but I can't help thinking how it might've been if I'd made it home. But I know I wasn't going home anyway, sir."

"I get you, Johnny." Bo's use of Stewart's first name did exactly what he wanted it to. The younger man smiled and visibly relaxed. "I knew the same thing when the chopper started going down. I think I said, 'Oh, shit,' and that was it."

"Really?"

"Pretty much," Bo said. "Look, when the time comes, you'll do what you need to do. As for the Army, we learned from those mistakes in Vietnam. You didn't get to see the fruit of that labor, but now we're here and doing things the way they need to be done. Lead from the front, and everything will fall into place, Johnny."

The young lieutenant looked up in surprise and met Bo's eyes. "Thank you, sir. I really appreciate it. Now, why don't we figure out how to skin this cat instead of sitting here wondering about things we can't change?"

Bo smiled. "Sounds like a great idea, and I'm glad you asked. Part of it revolves around you taking out that cache site and diverting their attention while we attack the town."

"When? Tomorrow? Lieutenant Turan's report sure made it sound like the ball is teed up."

Bo nodded. "You're right, and I'm every bit as eager as you are, Johnny." *Much more, actually.* "But taking an extra day to prepare could be the difference between success and failure, particularly with partially trained troops like the indigs. They've never attacked a target this large or fortified. So it's best practice to give them, and all our new officers—" he grinned at Stewart, "—time to square themselves away mentally and physically. If you don't have to rush, don't—particularly when you're asking troops to do something new."

"So the day *after* tomorrow, then?"

From sullen recruit in Vietnam to hard-charging butter-bar a hundred-fifty light years from Earth—all in a few short months. Bo resisted the urge to both shake his head and smile broadly. "Yes. The day after tomorrow." Bo gave in to a small smile. "Now let's both get some sleep. We've got a busy day ahead."

Chapter Twenty-Five

At first, Aliza couldn't figure out what was bothering her. For the last two nights, sleep hadn't come easy. So, instead of lying with her eyes open in a stuffy room filled with sleeping women and children, she rose and donned her clothes. Outside the domicile, the morning air was already warm. The sky above was almost totally clear, with only a few clouds dotting the distant western horizon.

Aliza moved through the town and followed one of her many routes, all designed to provide intelligence without seeming as if she was spying on anything in particular. But the most noteworthy detail that she noticed repeatedly as morning wore toward noon was the changed mood of the populace. The festival the night before had gone well, though it had been quieter and more reserved, and it had ended earlier than normal. The crowd of revelers had also been smaller. Aliza didn't know if that was because many of the migrant farmers had decided to leave the city and press north, or if it was due to the influx of tribal militias. As the sun continued its progress across the sky, they continued to enter the city in a constant trickle of small bands, as if seeking their fortunes in beat-up, thrown-together vehicles.

The bazaar, once the central place in town for commerce and trading, now appeared to be an arms market. The different factions traded and sold weaponry next to stalls filled with produce, precious stones, and other wares. It was an odd sight, but Aliza decided it was normal when the Sear approached. As she made her way through the streets, she spoke with several people whom she knew, at least in a passing way. Many of the older inhabitants behaved as if nothing was wrong regarding the change in the town, but Aliza could tell it was different, and not necessarily for the better.

The smiles were gone. The open arms and welcoming faces of those who she'd met were closed under their thick, sun-protective paint. Tension and fear filled the air. The presence of weapons, something that had been uncommon on her arrival, wasn't the only visible change. The locals feared those gathering there. With the approach of the Sear, they expected—even welcomed—the storing of resources for both survival and defense. Yet it seemed like none of the citizens wanted it in this manic fashion. For whatever reason, they had appeared much more at ease before the soldiers arrived. Aliza couldn't help but wonder if it was a fear of the Harvesters, too.

By afternoon, she had estimated that the strength of the collected militias now stood at about two thousand five hundred, but without any clear commander or cadre. A few small bands possessed true leadership, but the others just appeared to be looking for work or hoping to be noticed. Still, there were enough of them that she feared Bo and the others would not be able to take the town, and she'd be trapped inside or have to take her chances crossing the wastes alone.

That line of thinking was nothing new. After having been a prisoner, Aliza always considered her options and tried to find places where she could retreat should the need arise. Along with her daily information collection, she started searching for those places.

It would have been easier without her tail, however.

As she returned to the bazaar, and the shadows started lengthening, Aliza realized she was being followed. Tracking her every move was a young boy, only twelve or thirteen years old. He kept to the deepest shadows but was always there. The boy reminded her of a young Ben Mazza, having the same dark hair and dimples. He'd have been cute if not for the fearful and wary look on his face. When he walked, it was all a motion of gangly arms and legs. He almost looked ungraceful and frail, yet he'd done a good job with his surveillance. Aliza didn't know how long the boy had been following her, but once she reentered the bazaar, she identified him and became certain of his intent.

As to who would want her followed, that wasn't in question. Waornaak, who she gathered was a warlord of a medium-sized element of about two hundred and fifty soldiers, had disliked her since she'd run into him. He'd probably dispatched the boy to follow her and gain intelligence. To her knowledge, she hadn't given up anything. She hadn't seen him during the previous night's festivities, and he hadn't been part of the group at the thermal pool for the harvest. Her report to Bo had been unobserved. Which was a good thing, because of how it had unsettled her.

"We're coming in soon," Bo had said. "I figure you're in the top of the ninth inning right now. I've got your relief pitcher standing by."

Aliza had closed her eyes and muttered a quick prayer. "The other team has a lot more players now. I'm worried."

Bo replied, "Try not to worry, honey. We're going to get in there and get you. I promise."

His words made her feel better, but knowing the attack was coming tomorrow or possibly the next day also put her on edge.

Aliza took her time winding through the remainder of the bazaar, taking time to visit a few of the stalls she frequented. Most of them, though, had gone. She heard conversations among the merchants. As usual, they did not hold back their opinions. Many of the families had indeed moved north. The arrival of the soldiers appeared to have heralded much more than fear and violence.

"The Harvesters are coming, and once they take what we have, they might even take us."

The overheard comment sparked Aliza's caution and speculation. Would the Kulsian Harvesters do that? Was slavery really something they practiced? Picking up innocent residents and moving them off planet to somewhere else? She believed it was possible. Hadn't their part-ancestors the Ktor done just that when they abducted her and the others from Earth? Given the Sear and how inhospitable much of the planet would become, moving people off the planet to do the dirty work someplace else wasn't that far-fetched at all.

Experience had taught her that the best way to handle such nebulous fears was to calm herself and focus on the things she still needed to do. One was to find the white-haired outsider she'd seen a couple times but had never been able to follow. The second was to locate a spot in the outer glacis that was potentially thin enough or weak enough to be breached. She would wait near that point when the battle was joined, and the cavalry came charging in.

"When you hear the guns, stop everything you're doing and move to that safe spot, Aliza," Bo had warned. "And then wait. If we're delayed enough so that you can make another report, tell me where you're going to be so we can try not to hit you."

She had laughed. "That would be nice." But even as she said the words, the mirth drained away. This was serious business. Not unlike Operation Markolet—the night of the bridges. Then, she had moved into deadly enemy fire for only the noblest of causes: freedom. Now, she had found another cause to follow. Right and wrong were not gray, shapeless causes, as her most recent memories before R'Bak had carved into her awareness. Rights must be protected, and those who saw them violated must stop the violators. She would risk her life to do both for those around her.

Just beyond the limit of the actual bazaar, Aliza looked up from a stall selling smoked kr'it and saw the man she'd dubbed "the outsider." She knew enough about the locals to recognize he did not fit in. While deeply tanned, his features were not so weathered as others only half his age, but who had endured the relentless sun and wind-driven grit of the Ashbands since birth. And, if she had seen another pair of amber-golden eyes like his among the R'Baku, she would surely have remembered them.

Her stomach twisted on itself. Here was a man who did not merely stand out from the others; he hadn't been born among them. He was a Kulsian, probably stranded here, and undoubtedly of the greatest possible interest to Colonel Murphy.

As she continued moving casually among the food vendors' stalls, she studied him. He wore the same thick paint as the locals, but his was exceptionally ornate. Reflective layers of silver and gold covered his face but were more thinly applied on his scalp. Aliza saw his hair was longer than the natives' and bright white in the afternoon light. This man was no soldier. His clothes and markings marked him as an individual of considerable importance, whose status was evident at a glance.

She reentered the bazaar in order to keep him in sight, approaching him slowly through the growing late-day crowd. As a new surge of soldiers arrived to trade their weapons and other equipment, the outsider stood haggling with the owner of a booth selling carpets. The woven fibers from the *helekaen* were exceptionally soft. Carpets like these were luxury items. In her time spent in the bazaar, she'd never actually seen a person buy one. Most came to gawk at the incredible craftsmanship and the beauty of the textiles. This afternoon, though, the outsider was clearly in negotiation to buy a carpet, though she couldn't quite make out his words. His voice was low, perhaps on purpose, but she heard enough of his dialect to confirm he was not local. He was undoubtedly a person of interest.

The bickering between the outsider and the merchant went on for a good ten minutes. At the end, the outsider raised a hand, tilted his head to one side and walked away.

"Yukannak? *Silci*, please!" the merchant called after him, almost pleading. Aliza quickly made her way toward the merchant's stall to see what the man had said. The mutterings of disaffected merchants were almost always a clue to their dealings and temperament. In this case, she didn't care. Aliza had the outsider's name and his title as an envoy of the region's satrap. A careful glance over her left shoulder verified the young, dark-haired boy was still watching her. Which gave her an idea of how to deal with him and still follow the person of interest.

While it was tempting to engage the merchant and learn more about her target, Bo and Murphy would have stressed following the outsider. Unfortunately, the boy's presence made that impossible, at least from a clandestine standpoint. Aliza started toward the stall where the boy was loitering. As her idea crystallized, she hoped the boy would not be harmed as a result of her actions. He was unlikely to be guilty of anything beyond wanting to earn some coins to keep himself—and quite possibly his family—alive.

Aliza lengthened her stride as she closed on him, working up some anger. She snatched the boy's wrist and spun him toward her.

"Give it back."

The boy's eyes came up, locked on hers, and widened. "What?"

"I saw you steal it. Taking fruit from a vendor. I am disappointed in you. Your parents will be ashamed when I tell them. Give it back."

The produce vendor, a tall burly man, came around the edge of the stall and glowered down at the boy. "You stole from me?"

Without another word, the boy spun out of Aliza's grasp and ran for the gate to the Outer City, just beyond the bazaar. Aliza watched him sprint away with quiet satisfaction. She turned back to the merchant, who squinted at her.

"He stole nothing from your stall," Aliza whispered.

"Then why accuse him?" The merchant's hands rested on his hips as his brow furrowed. He wore a leather-hilted knife but did not reach for it. "Why cause trouble? Is there not enough here now?"

She knew what he meant. Soldiers had gathered around them. Aliza could hear their murmuring to each other. She let a smile crease her face to put the man at ease. "There is enough trouble here, friend. These soldiers try to have our own watch us."

He continued to stare down at her. One corner of his mouth curled. "He spied on me? Or you?"

"Us," Aliza replied. "I won't stand for that. We must protect each other."

"We must, sister." The merchant smiled, showing a menagerie of dirty, crooked teeth. "I will watch for him."

"I don't think he'll be much trouble now," Aliza replied and turned to walk away. The crowd of soldiers parted with disappointed whispers. In the distance, Aliza spotted the outsider, and she hurried to follow him.

This Yukannak, where does he live? Who knows him? Where is he going?

Aliza tried to quiet the questions in her mind and merely observe him from a distance. He might be no one, but a feeling in her gut made her press on.

The outsider left the bazaar and made his way toward the dwellings tucked beneath the eaves of the cavern. Aliza followed him at a distance. Soon they approached a staircase cut into the stone. Aliza saw with mild astonishment that the guards who typically manned every checkpoint into the tunnels and dwellings were conspicuously absent. It was an opportunity she could not pass up. Careful to stay a good hundred feet behind the man, Aliza followed him up the stairs and among the dwellings.

If the dichotomy between the Outer City and the Inner City struck her, these dwellings almost froze her in place. While the exterior walls of the buildings were rough, the interior streets and what she could see of the surrounding dwellings displayed opulence on a scale she'd never seen before. The shaded lanes held none of the trash and detritus of the other parts of the city. Everything else on R'Bak was at least somewhat dirty, and yet these dwellings, far inside Imsurmik, were almost spotless.

There were two streets running the length of the dwellings, paralleling the inner cavern wall in a gentle arc about a half-mile in length. Intersecting streets, perpendicular to the cavern wall, were evenly spaced and framed the predominantly two-story buildings into an orderly array of rectangles. The outsider ducked around the first set of buildings, making for the inner thoroughfare. Aliza came around the same corner and watched him open the door of the second, innermost building and walk inside.

Got you.

Satisfied, Aliza turned around to retrace her steps to the staircase. At the bottom of the rough-cut stone, she saw the dark-haired boy and two older soldiers. The boy pointed excitedly at her.

Shit.

Aliza spun on her heels and made for the inner thoroughfare and, potentially, the tunnels beyond. She risked a look over her shoulder and saw the two soldiers in pursuit. The entrance to a tunnel appeared between two of the buildings on the inner wall.

Aliza ran for that dark opening.

Aliza discovered she was not in a tunnel, but at the top of a spiral stone staircase that went down into the plateau's cavern system. At the top of the stairwell, tucked into a winding crevice, was a tight maze of tilting and toppled trash bins. Instead of descending the stairs, she slipped over, around, and past them into the concealing darkness beyond. Squatting down, she pulled one of the mostly empty bins farther back to fully shield her presence. She pulled a loose lid over her, and her head rested on her knees as she waited for her pursuers to—hopefully—pass.

Only a few seconds passed before footsteps approached and raced down the stairs. The soldiers didn't bother to investigate the bins, either because the clutter looked too tight to wriggle into, or because of the noxious odors of what seemed to be the local equivalent of a composting site. Aliza smiled to herself. For her, the smell wasn't terrible. She'd smelled far worse in Dachau, after all.

In the darkness under her hood, she glanced at the luminescent hands of her watch. The time was a little after what they called 1800 hours. She took a deep breath and raised her head off her knees to listen and wait. Over the course of the next hour and a half, as the cold, stone floor chilled and seemingly prodded her "fourth point of contact" as Bo called it, only six people used the stairs. They'd come at nearly precise thirty-minute intervals and always in pairs. Patrols. Possibly searching for her. And there was no sign that they might relent.

Aliza leaned her head back down and wondered how, or even if, she could escape. Or if Bo's attack would succeed. Or if, even now, Harvester ships were approaching silently, fatefully through space. In the end, Aliza decided she could only be sure of one thing regarding her existence on R'Bak: it was better than Dachau. Infinitely better.

She listened for the patrols and hoped for the best.

Chapter Twenty-Six

Army doctrine from Bo's time described the set of tasks a leader needed to secure a defensive position. While there were no plans for his position to become defensive, since it was mostly a pre-attack assembly area, there were still things that needed to be addressed. Since arriving, Lieutenant Stewart and his indig non-commissioned officers had completed all these tasks and secured the area so that they could focus on the greater mission at hand.

The next priority was their readiness to attack and seize Imsurmik. That meant engaging and destroying the different packs of warlords and their fighters. From Aliza's latest report, the once-peaceful town had become a well-defended hub for armed caravans collecting food, medicinals, and other resources in advance of the Harvesters.

Bo's own excitement rose, and his brain, formerly addled by his inability to communicate with Aliza, had quieted into full focus upon the mission. He didn't think about reuniting with her at all. His attention was devoted to the assault, occupying the town, and limiting casualties and damage to his own force while doing so. Some part of him recognized and acknowledged that he missed Aliza, but as the plan became more concrete, refining it centered him in a way that was both welcome and exhilarating.

He'd felt a similar sensation while leading the makeshift cavalry force during their first engagement: the Battle of the East Wall Draw, but which everyone just called the J'Stull Job. Recovering Lieutenant Tapper's forces while capturing a sizable number of J'Stull vehicles left him energized and eager, despite being physically exhausted. For the first time in years—his hundred and thirty-year sleep notwithstanding—Bo felt like he was actually doing something the Army had trained him to do. Not only that, he was good at it. During his time in Somalia, stymied by both insurgents and incompetent leadership, he'd thought of himself as a failure. The change during and after the J'Stull Job had been palpable, and he'd welcomed it. He might not have a family to return to, and he might never see Earth again, but he had a worthwhile mission to perform, good—if occasionally problematic—troops, and someone to love. Once this was over, he'd make good on that last item. For now, his focus was on the task at hand.

Immediately after dinner, and with the sounds of preparation a constant mechanical clatter around them, Bo gathered the leadership to set their tasks. The first mounted movement toward the objective would begin later that afternoon in order to take advantage of nightfall to pass through the defensive flora atop the plateau. That would also give the whinnies a chance to travel without holding up the formation of vehicles he would use for the main effort. One of the oldest tricks in the combat leader's rucksack was the one-third/two-thirds rule; Bo would only take one-third of the remaining time before the operation to outline the plan, while giving Lieutenant Stewart and his subordinate section leaders the remaining two-thirds to square away their own preparations. And when that clock ran out, it would be a few hours' sleep and then time to form up and cross the LD, the line of departure.

As they gathered around, Bo took a moment and studied their faces. When he'd first been awakened by Colonel Murphy and told the situation, he'd dreaded the prospect of working with "substandard soldiers." Yet after meeting Whittaker and some of the others, he'd come away with a few hunches. Most of the Vietnam veterans were surly and immediately distrustful of officers. Bo couldn't blame them, based on what he knew of the war. For the most part, they'd realized things were very different in this future and found a measure of long dormant professionalism. Their leadership skills returned. As Lieutenant Stewart had put it, things really *had* changed since they had been taken. Beneath their slowly fading façade of indifference was a change in attitude, a willingness to recognize competent leadership, and the emergence of their own sense of duty. The younger soldiers, the ones who might not have had mentors to guide them in their original service, were harder to motivate, no matter when they'd been abducted. But Bo and the other officers found ways to bring them around. Riding whinnies had brought out the best in several of the young soldiers. They might still like to gamble and argue with one another when bored, but gradually they'd come together as a team, and Bo was proud of them.

"Okay, everybody. Let's get started. Lieutenant Stewart?"

The young lieutenant nodded and stepped into the middle of the group. On the ground, they'd scratched a diagram of the city and the plateau. Stewart used a long, thin stick and pointed at the diagram to emphasize his words.

"Here is Imsurmik and the plateau behind it. You should all know what this is since we've been staring at it for quite a while now."

There were a few chuckles in the group, but their collective attention remained on Stewart. He continued, "Okay, we know they've built a couple rows of dwellings under the shelf of the plateau. We won't worry about them until phase two if Captain Cutter's team runs into trouble, and we have to go door-to-door. There's also a tunnel system which we don't have a complete map of yet. This area here—" he pointed inside the glacis, "—is called the Inner City. It's protected by the wall—a glacis—that's about thirty feet tall, give or take. It's big and appears to be fairly strong. On the west side of the city is the main access road, which enters the city through a security gate. Here, on the east side of the city, there's a breach in the wall where a man-made canal drains into the thermal pool below. That's where they've been doing most of that harvesting we've been hearing about.

"Down the slope from the Inner City is the Outer City and all the farmland. The major difference between the Outer City and the Inner City is that one of them has planned thoroughfares and a logical arrangement to its streets, and the other does not. The Outer City is little more than a shantytown or a rice paddy village.

"From an enemy force perspective, we can estimate they've got a minimum of two thousand troops. There's no firm chain of command we are aware of. There are a handful of warlords and their own little units. We know a couple of their leaders, but there's nothing really definitive as far as their strength or their ability to work together. In that respect, we think we've got them in a position where we will have an advantage in command-and-control."

Sergeant Fahey, another Vietnam vet, raised his hand, and Stewart paused. Fahey's transition to this new reality had been particularly difficult and violent. Yet, over the course of the last several weeks, he had taken up riding and become familiar with his mount, Apollo. He'd really come around. So much so he'd been given a fire team of indigs to lead. "Could these guys have radios? Or any other communications we don't know about?"

"Great question," Stewart replied. "We don't know. We know they're not using anything UHF, at least in the bands we can pick up on our radios, but if they're using something else we're unaware of it. That's a risk we have to be willing to accept. Any other questions?"

There were none, and Stewart continued, "The weapons on the glacis appear to be rockets and maybe some larger guns. We don't know what their maximum effective range is, but we have to assume they'll have the ability to reach the road network south of the fields. That's going to be our primary avenue of approach, as the major's going to tell you in a couple of minutes.

"Lastly, when it comes to enemy forces, remember, we're going to try to grab some persons of interest or high-value targets. Lieutenant Turan has already identified some PoIs and will be working to maintain a general idea on their locations to guide us once we get in. We'll be going after their leaders as hard as we can. Someone has to know what's going on here and in orbit, too. Those are the folks we want to locate. When it comes to locating and capturing priority targets, make sure you secure them, keep 'em quiet, and, if you can't get them to Captain Cutter's strike team, get them out of the city, and we'll merge them later. Finally, make sure you're familiar with this sand table so you can orient yourself once we're on the objective."

Stewart stopped and gestured to Bo, who stood and took the pointing stick. "Great job, Lieutenant. I'll be covering friendly forces and our scheme of maneuver. I ask you to hold all questions until the end. We'll take plenty of time to go over this and have time for rehearsals."

The group settled more. A few knelt down to study the primitive diagram in the dirt. For Bo, the reminders of sandlot football were almost enough to break his concentration with pleasant yet bittersweet memories of long-dead friends.

"Here's how we're gonna get this done. We'll be moving in two different groups. Lieutenant Stewart will take the whinnies and their riders and move out this evening by sunset. They'll move in a big U like we used for the leader's recon. Be careful not to follow the same route and don't let anybody track you. They'll move during the night and take up a hasty defensive position east of the poisonous flora we found about here." Bo tapped the plateau on the sand table. "Once past them, there are a couple areas for cover and concealment so the lieutenant's team can wait out the night and into the next day as we kick off phase two.

"Along the way, Stewart's going to drop off Sergeant Fahey, Specialist Wright, and their fire team with another radio somewhere in this area here." Bo pointed toward the southwestern corner of the plateau, roughly equidistant between their current position and the observation posts that would be the primary focus of the whinnies' mounted assault. "They'll act as a listening post and relay point. Our radios only have a good range of about six klicks. We might get away with a bit more than that, but it's too risky to depend on. You guys will man the communications point and relay all the information we need back and forth until the mounted assault is complete. Be ready to rejoin Stewart and un-ass that position as soon as those observation posts get taken out."

"Yes, sir." Fahey nodded. The change in the young man from surly fighter to competent young soldier was nothing short of remarkable.

Bo pointed at the diagram. "I'll have the vehicles with me. We're going to spread out into three sections of five vehicles and try to keep a few minutes of interval between us. The idea is to look like separate caravans until the last section with the technicals moves up. Then we're going to initiate the assault.

"Alpha Section, under Lieutenant Cook and Sergeant Cleric, is going to assault the road to the gate. There are switchbacks and the road is tight, so the smaller vehicles will be under his command.

"Bravo Section will take up a position at the junction of the main road and the riverbed. This is the firing position for the mortars. If the enemy missiles can range them, they'll move to alternate positions and keep firing. Lieutenant Davis will lead them.

"Charlie Section is with me. Our goal is to hit the glacis with our heavier weapons and hold their attention. Between us and Stewart's diversion, we'll shake them up enough that Cook can punch through the gate. We'll find a weak spot on the glacis and set charges to blow a breaching hole in the wall. From there, we'll assault with all of our vehicles and secure that part of the town as an entry point for Captain Cutter's strike team. Focus first on the weapons platforms and whatever maneuver units you see. Once they're all engaged with us, the strike team will move into the town to find the PoIs. Just in case they run into trouble, we're going to have three Huey's orbiting with a quick reaction force. If Captain Cutter doesn't call for them, we'll use them to outflank any resistance and expand our control of Imsurmik. Any questions?"

Fahey raised his hand again. "What if those missiles on the wall are more capable than we think they are, sir?"

Bo grunted and let a sly grin cross his face. "Well, then this could be the shortest attack in history, Fahey. But who wants to live forever?"

Cutter knelt atop a bluff west of Imsurmik, his platoon fanned out in a defensive semi-circle as he studied the target. The day's light was beginning to fail, and the traffic crowding the road into the city from the south hurried to get inside by nightfall. Dozens of armed men accompanied the various vehicles, some powered, some pulled by animals and humans, with the fruits of their harvests piled beside personal effects. It reminded him of French refugees clogging the backroads of Normandy as they fled the fighting. Squatting beside him was Lieutenant Tanavuna, with the three squad leaders—Sergeants Riidono, Brakkel, and Scussian—just a few feet away.

"We are wasting time," Tanavuna said, low enough so the sergeants couldn't hear it. "We are here, sir; we should move into the city. Kesteluni is down there."

Cutter kept the binoculars to his eyes. "Show me where, Tanavuna, and we'll move out. Otherwise, we proceed as ordered by Major Moorefield." The younger man clenched his jaw, started to say something, then stopped. Cutter didn't so much see Tanavuna's frustration as feel and hear it. "Here," he said, passing the binoculars to the lieutenant. "Look at the road and tell me what you see."

"There are many people moving into Imsurmik. I don't need the binoculars to see that, Captain."

"No, but maybe you need them to see all the armed militia. Counting you and me, Tanavuna, we have forty-six men. They have thousands. Not even Major Moorefield has enough men or firepower for a general assault, but he does have enough to open a way for us into the city. Once inside, we hunt for the persons of interest, or 'high value targets,' we've been told to look for, not only because that's our assigned mission, but also because those are the types of people who just might know where Kesteluni is being held. The faster we find them, the faster we find her."

"It is hard, Captain. It is not our way."

It was moments like this when Cutter missed cigarettes the most. In 1944, they would have shared a Lucky Strike. There was something about a smoke that encouraged empathy and strengthened bonds. Having learned about the dangers of tobacco, he was glad he was no longer addicted…most of the time.

Cutter pushed away the memory of tobacco's smell. "You were approved for leadership because of your self-discipline and maturity, Tanavuna. I appreciate that our way of war isn't what you're used to, but we face long, long odds down there, and not all our people are going to come back. Our only hope of saving Kesteluni is if we operate as one unit, so it's more important *now* that you remember your training than if they hadn't taken her. The men will be looking to see how you react; they will do as you do. If you become angry or blind in the moment, so will they."

Cutter acted as if he expected Tanavuna to behave like a US Army officer should and took back the binoculars, focusing them in the fading light. In truth, though, he knew the success of his mission stood on a razor's edge.

After half a minute, during which Tanavuna visibly considered his response, he finally answered, this time loud enough for everyone to hear. "What are your orders, Captain?"

In the gathering darkness, Cutter gathered his squad leaders and the men of the platoon who weren't needed on lookout and now reprised Major Moorefield's plan of attack while pointing out the landmarks and waypoints. Shadows hid Imsurmik's eastern side, but all of his men knew the city's layout well enough to follow along as he spoke.

"To repeat, Major Moorefield doesn't have the assault forces to capture the city outright. His primary job is to breach selected points in the defenses and make enough trouble that the F'ahdn decides to flee to a safer place. Because the city's leadership is rigidly hierarchical, it's also brittle. So with any luck, the defense will fall apart, and Imsurmik will fall into our hands. The major's first objective is to control the main entrance and exit points from the city. Our job is to identify, find, and capture anyone who might have information on the future plans of the J'Stull or the Kulsians. Whatever they are, you can be certain they're for their benefit—and at the expense of you and all other Ashbanders that aren't their willing lackeys.

"We'll operate in three squads, the way we've trained. We can cover more ground that way, but doing so means less firepower, so avoid pitched fights if possible. First Squad will clear a path through the Outer City, entering along the main road. I'll be with them in tactical command. Lieutenant Tanavuna, using night to cover his movements, will circle to join Major Moorefield's forces on the east and enter the city according to their recommendations. Second and Third Squads will accompany him. Some of you have mentioned rumors concerning a hidden entrance somewhere north of the city. If you discover that, at the lieutenant's discretion, forces may be committed to investigate and/or block it."

Cutter paused for effect and then turned, slowly, to look at each and every man. Details faded in the night, but that didn't matter. "I know you all want to get Kesteluni back. She's your Hetman's wife, your healer, and the soul of Nuthhurfipiko. But the best way to do that is to stick to the plan. Keep your focus on the mission. And don't take foolish chances; I want to see each of your ugly faces when this is over."

Chapter Twenty-Seven

Four of the F'ahdn's guards shielded Yukannak as he strolled through the crowds coming and going through the gate. Just a step behind was the servant that the F'ahdn had also provided. Even at that late hour, the streets of the Inner City teemed with crowds, and the streets and markets were lit by braziers, torches, and lanterns. Unlike the Outer City, many of the people inside the wall wore elaborate masks made from finer paints that didn't run or crack in the heat. Heavier robes and painted skin were no guarantee against the Bleeding Black, but the healers said they helped. Whether they did or they didn't, the wealthy endured the extra discomfort with contemptuous pride since that too was considered a mark of status. The better people did it because it showed everyone else who they were, thus, even in the dark of night, they paraded through the streets displaying the full measure of their rank.

Despite the sun having been down for hours, heat radiating upward from the stone pavement collected under Yukannak's robe like the hot air in the airship that brought him to Imsurmik. As the official representative of the satrap, Yukannak affected the calm, aloof manner of a powerful man surveying his domain, untroubled by the heat, the smell, the insects, or the crowds. The reality was different.

Generations of carefully honed and selected genetics helped his body deal with the relentless heat, but even for a Kulsian, R'Bak was oppressively hot. Sweat poured off his body into the ring of cloth stitched atop his boots to absorb the liquid. Stalls set up along the wide, clean streets of the Inner City catered to those who wanted their ankle wraps changed out for fresh ones. Befitting his status, a servant boy carried extras so he didn't have to pay for having it done.

Zeesar approached from one side, matching his languid pace. As usual, the yuzbazzi was painted as if he was a common militiaman, and he carefully remained one step behind Yukannak on the right. However, nobody mistook him for anything other than what he was: the F'ahdn's highest ranking enforcer and fixer of problems. Aside from the power of his village's militia, Zeesar's reputation was that of a man who bartered for information and knew secrets he shouldn't. The powerful and elite of Imsurmik viewed him as disreputable and untrustworthy, both of which were true, but that made them fear him even more.

"Could my lord Yukannak spare this unworthy soul a moment of his time?" Zeesar asked with ritual formality.

"What words could one such as you have to interest me?" Yukannak replied in his haughtiest manner. He doubted it fooled anyone who might overhear, but some fictions had to be maintained.

"The silci is a mighty lord, and my words are meant only for him. Perhaps if we could step into that alley, I could tell him something of interest. A moment only, lord, is all I ask of you. If we can step into privacy?"

Yukannak's sigh was theatrically loud. He stopped, shook his head, and pointed to the alley in assent. He hoped that no one noticed his finger trembling at the excitement of whatever news Zeesar might have brought.

"Lead on, then."

Barely wide enough to pass through in single file, the alley lay between two solid stone buildings. Yukannak's guards automatically posted themselves at either end, while the servant boy stayed back with them.

"You have news of the archive?" Yukannak asked in a low voice so as not to be heard over the street noise of clattering carts and the calls of vendors.

"I cannot speak with you long," Zeesar said. "We are in danger, both of us. My inquiries were nearly made too late. I must leave the city before dawn, and you would be wise to do the same."

Traps within traps, Yukannak thought. Vague and dire warnings were an old trick. Zeesar might be telling the truth, or it might be a test laid by the F'ahdn to discover an ulterior motive for the silci's visit. It could also be the satrap testing his loyalty.

Feigning indifference, Yukannak waved Zeesar away. "The silci is no hetman of a squalid village. What threat could endanger the anointed envoy of my master?"

"Who are you trying to impress?" Zeesar asked. "If you'll stop ignoring me and listen, you might understand the danger we face!"

"What do you have for me?" Yukannak said.

Zeesar motioned to lower his voice. "Keep your voice down. The stone echoes our words, and there are always those eavesdropping in Imsurmik." Pointing upward with his right forefinger, he leaned forward and whispered in Yukannak's ear. "Have a guard check the roofs."

Quietly, Yukannak spoke to one of the guards, who disappeared. They stood in the shadows beyond the illuminated street for several minutes. Without warning, there was a scream over their heads. It ended abruptly, and a body rolled off a roof edge and slammed into the dusty alley. One of the guards grabbed a torch and revealed a man wearing simple robes and a face wrap, groaning as blood leaked from his head. Zeesar bent down and cut his throat in one swift motion before leading Yukannak away from the spreading pool of blood.

"We could have questioned him!"

"He would have lied."

"How can you know that?"

"Outlanders," he said, as if the word tasted bad. "Some aren't content selling their harvest or gathering plants. They see Imsurmik as a city where everything has a price, with information being its most valuable product. This man was the type you will find around any leader—no doubt the satrap, too—willing to do anything for pay. His name was Larrihoi, and his death is not worth troubling over. Whatever words he spoke would have been laced with untruths so you could not know what to believe."

"Do you speak of him, or yourself?"

Zeesar ignored the barb. "This man no doubt worked for the F'ahdn."

"Would the city's master dare spy on me?"

"Of course he would. But gathering information is the easy part. Staying alive to sell it is what is hard, as Larrihoi just found out."

"Tell me what is going on."

The edge of Zeesar's knife glimmered in the torchlight as blood dripped to the pavement. Yukannak noted how easily he handled the weapon, and how surely he'd slit the spying man's throat. Whatever his outward veneer of custom and courtesy, Zeesar was still, and always would be, the hetman in a region where lives often ended in quick, violent deaths. But just as the Kulsians would pay heavily to know of Yukannak's duplicity, the F'ahdn would no doubt value knowing that as one of his trusted aides, Zeesar was also selling information to the F'ahdn's potential enemies. *If* that was truly what Zeesar was doing. In the dark world of trading secrets, the satrap's mouthpiece didn't doubt that Zeesar had plans in place to protect against such a double-cross.

Zeesar pursed his lips. "I have been a blind fool. Without my knowing it, the J'Stull commander, Subitorni, has acted against me to become the new yuzbazzi. A woman in the F'ahdn's household, who has accepted my coins for many years, told me this story not an hour ago. He and the F'ahdn plan to defy the satrap and deal with the Harvesters directly. Bypassing the satrap will let them ingratiate themselves with the Kulsians. It seems the F'ahdn wants to become the new satrap. Subitorni would then become silci."

"Continue."

"Just after sunrise yesterday morning, men under the F'ahdn's command returned to the city carrying a mysterious person wrapped in blankets. My friend the masker heard whispers of a healer taken from a local village to cure the F'ahdn's Bleeding Black, and that it was an act carried out under the authority of the F'ahdn's yuzbazzi."

"But you did not order it?"

"No, I did not."

"Why would they not simply move against you? Why go to all of this trouble?"

"He cannot move too fast without being discovered. I am convinced he means to defy the satrap, with the intent of replacing him. The Harvesters don't care about anything except getting their plants, but even without Imsurmik, the satrap is powerful. The F'ahdn needs every man who can use a weapon to fight for him."

"But why turn against *you*? Would you not support him against the satrap?"

Zeesar hesitated. "So that you will trust me, I will answer your question honestly and directly. The day may come when I need your friendship, and it may come soon. The F'ahdn discredits me because I meant to replace *him* as ruler of Imsurmik. I have the largest militia in the area, they are loyal to me, and they are well trained and organized."

"And well led?"

Zeesar couldn't hide a brief smile. "Of course. The F'ahdn considers the villages within this region under his personal dominion and would never risk angering one without strong provocation. He would have to ensure that such an act was justified before the people. Attacking the village and kidnapping their healer discredits me."

Now it made sense to Yukannak; it had the ring of truth. He'd been caught in an ongoing power play that had nothing to do with him, except as the silci of the satrap. That was bad enough. It also meant he was in personal physical danger, and the guards blocking the alley might turn and cut him down at any moment. But, assuming they didn't, it gave him a brief window to flee Imsurmik for…somewhere else.

"If I am threatened, as it appears that I am, then you have my support. Take me with you to your village. Let us leave now."

"I cannot do that, Silci. Alone, I can slip away unseen, but with you I cannot. Instead, I suggest you find the archive and get word to your satrap. I don't know what it contains, but for the F'ahdn to keep it so secret, the contents must be very valuable.

"Perhaps you may find a way to bargain," Zeesar continued, "should that become necessary. Beware Subitorni, though. If I'm right, he is only waiting on the F'ahdn's disease to consume him. He is a dangerous and ambitious man."

"Without your help, I cannot hope to find the archive."

"Do you know of the passage through the rock to the cache area?"

"Of course. That's the main reason I am here, to oversee the collection for the Harvesters."

"And the tunnels up to the plateau?"

"Yes." Irritation crept into his tone, despite believing Zeesar was an ally.

"One of them leads west, to the entrance hidden by the trap door through which we entered the city. I believe the archive to be near there, probably down one of the branch tunnels. You might also take the main tunnel until it ends, and it will lead you to the entrance we used. But that way is always watched and guarded, and now I know why."

Yukannak's suspicions flared again. "I find it increasingly hard to believe that you were unaware such a place existed?"

"In the satrap's palace, do you know where the servants keep their brooms? It is the same in this case: I knew that area was where they worked on vehicles, nothing more. I have had other priorities."

"Perhaps you are not as clever as I first imagined. You were not aware of such a ramp being dug to the surface, and that could not have been a small project."

"No, it could not, and you are correct; the morning you arrived was my first hint that something was wrong. It is not a thing that could be built quickly or be completed without my knowing, unless someone went to much trouble to keep me from finding out. That someone would be Subitorni. But although I am the yuzbazzi, I have spent very little time in the city during the past two years. I see now that was foolish, for there are now two secrets the F'ahdn kept from me, and maybe others, too. Yet if he kept them from me, what else might he be keeping secret from you?"

"The archive."

“And perhaps other things as well. A ramp to the surface that leads nowhere, that is wide enough and high enough for powered vehicles to navigate the slope in either direction, is an impressive feat of building, but to what purpose?”

“You’ve made your point, Zeesar. It could be used to transport medicinals away from the place they are being gathered now.”

“And doing it in secret. It could also be used to transport an army. Think about it, Yukannak; the F’ahdn should be proud of such a building project, yet he said nothing to you. Why would the F’ahdn not reveal a secret entrance to you unless he planned to hide other things from you?”

“This woman you spoke of. She is reliable?”

“She is. In addition to her masking duties, she cleans the F’ahdn’s dirty robes and has done so for many years. If I didn’t believe her, I would not have brought this to your attention.”

“I may have met her. Nomi; is that her name?”

“It is, yes. The F’ahdn asked her to get something from a storage chamber. You’ve been farther down the main tunnel, where the intersecting tunnel turns east to the cache site?”

“Yes, yes. I already told you I have.”

“There are doors on both sides, beyond which are rooms for storing food, the supply of medicinals put aside for Imsurmik, emergency water barrels, and other vital supplies. I have seen these, too. As yuzbazzi, I controlled their gathering and dispersal, and I believed that I knew everything. But now I think there is much more that both Subitorni and the F’ahdn kept secret from me. Did you know there are escape tunnels cut deep underground? The fourth door in the long tunnel leads down to this escape route, as do others.”

“Get on with it, Zeesar. What does this have to do with the archive?”

“Patience, Yukannak, you must understand all to understand some.”

“You are the one who said you must hurry.”

“Several days ago, the woman saw five or six men enter the tunnel through a hidden door she had never seen before. They had someone wrapped in a blanket. Bare feet sticking out from the end appeared to be those of a woman, and she was kicking and fighting, so she still lived. They took their captive through the door to the escape tunnel, and that was the last Nomi saw of them.

"Knowing I would pay well for the knowledge of where the men had come from, she followed them through the tunnel and came at last to the road I mentioned earlier. Afraid she would be caught, she only stayed long enough to see some powered vehicles and smell the vapors indicating they'd recently been used. But as she turned to retrace her steps, she heard a strange word: hyshvass. She didn't know what it meant."

"Hyshvass? She is certain that was the word?" *A second usage of it?*

"I questioned her myself. I brought this to you before leaving Imsurmik because I gave you my word."

"You brought me this because you need allies."

Holding up a hand, Zeesar scratched his nose. "There is more. Beware of Waornaak. He is not trustworthy under ordinary circumstances, but lately he has been a friend of both camps, mine and Subitorni's, not to mention the F'ahdn's."

"He is a crude brute," Yukannak said.

"But cunning and dangerous, Silci; beware of him. You have many enemies here. Neither the satrap nor the Harvesters are overly loved by the common folk. Find the archive and perhaps it can help you, or wait for my return when I bring armed men to aid us against the F'ahdn. Stay alive if you can. Now, I must go."

Abruptly, Zeesar turned and left the alley without another word. Yukannak let him; there was nothing more to say.

Chapter Twenty-Eight

Moving through the dark atop the plateau didn't sit well with Lieutenant Johnny Stewart. With a military occupational specialty of 11C, indirect fire infantryman, he'd only had to hump a few night patrols before moving to the battalion's fire control center. Math came easy to the young soldier, and he was one of the few to really have his talents identified once in-country. Mortarmen still patrolled occasionally, though, and when he'd made sergeant, the cadre had tasked him to help train the replacements—especially in night patrolling.

Each walk through the lightless jungle had been more fearful than the last. During his earliest days as a new replacement to the unit—what the older and more experienced troops called an FNG, or fucking new guy—night patrols hadn't really bothered him. He was more concerned about how his peers regarded him and not so much about the enemy hiding in the darkness.

But by the third or fourth time he went out on patrol, Stewart was scared to death. The dark and unfamiliar rainforest was full of noises far different from anything he'd heard on the family farm outside of Chattanooga, Tennessee. Stories and gossip ran rampant through the ranks as more and more units were engaged by the Viet Cong under the cover of night.

Mortars didn't put him as far behind the line as he'd hoped, either. Patrols became necessary. Even as he progressed in rank and started leading his own fire team, Stewart had still disliked moving in the dark.

Light years from Earth and more than a hundred and some years in the future, he didn't like it any better. When he'd learned mortars were part of the Lost Soldiers' inventory, he'd volunteered for them. But Lieutenant Colonel Murphy and Major Moorefield decided he was better used with the cavalry.

He never thought to ask them why. Being on the front line unsettled him. Having to move through potentially hostile alien plants didn't do much to assuage his fears. Yet he could focus on the mission at hand by reminding himself that not only was he still alive, far away from Earth, but he was riding an alien creature…or "being," or whatever the hell it was. No matter how good the stories of his peers had been in Vietnam, none of them would have believed what he was doing now. Moreover, he realized he was good at it.

Stewart kept the patrol to the south side of the plateau. Their goal was to drop off the communications post, Sergeant Fahey and Specialist Wright, at an abandoned observation post that the J'Stull—or maybe the roving militia of the week—had once occupied. It was obvious their enemy had moved the actual observation post closer to the city itself some time before. Major Moorefield believed the local militias were complacent regarding security. His observers had seen soldiers atop the plateau but never moving from the city to those posts. Finding how the enemy did so was a critical requirement, particularly without access to aerial reconnaissance. It was crucial that Stewart drop off the communications team at the abandoned position and move forward quickly to attack and seize the two tucked-in observation posts spotted during the leader's reconnaissance.

As the patrol leader, Stewart set himself in the middle of the formation. His Alpha Team, seven whinnies and their indig riders, took the point. Soon, they would break away from the formation and travel to the far eastern observation post near the escarpment. Stewart would take Bravo Team and move on the first observation post. Stealth and caution were critical for the attack to launch on time and achieve the element of surprise.

About twenty minutes after passing the line of the departure, Alpha Team elements split away for their attack. Stewart led the others forward for another hour before arriving at the abandoned listening post. Without words or ceremony, Fahey and Wright dismounted their whinnies and set up the radio inside the rock-walled lean-to. Wright gestured to their indig support, and the six robed figures spread out into the night and laid down in hasty defensive positions. Stewart climbed down from Olympia and whispered to the others, "Don't be heroes if something goes wrong. You're here to maintain communications between us and Major Moorefield. Unless you're hit, you stay here. Got it?"

Wright's cherubic face bobbed up and down, wearing a nervous grin. Fahey merely nodded once. "We got it, sir. We'll stay in touch."

"You do that, Fahey. We'll see you guys when this is over."

Stewart climbed back atop Olympia, and they set off to the east. Forty-five minutes later, they took positions to envelop and encircle the listening post. The whinnies, and the soldiers riding them, were absolutely silent. The J'Stull soldiers, or whoever they were, weren't just bad at security; they didn't even bother with it. Three of them were asleep around the remains of a small fire. Stewart watched for several minutes, looking and listening for another guard, someone with enough discipline to actually remain awake. It became apparent there was no one on watch.

Stewart raised his right hand and pointed at the Bravo Team leader, Sergeant Morton, and then to the three sleeping soldiers. Morton's team dismounted their whinnies and crept forward. With uncanny ease, they subdued the guards. The captured soldiers said nothing; all three hung their heads in shame at being caught unaware.

Stewart stayed back and let Morton lead his forces. The young black soldier from Chicago was on top of the situation, and there was no reason to step in and change the rhythms. Morton ensured the prisoners were gagged, hands bound behind their backs, before allowing his forces to search the objective.

It wasn't long before Morton called to him in a harsh whisper. "Lieutenant? Over here."

Stewart made his way through the darkness and immediately saw what Morton's men had found. Cut into the rock, a staircase descended into the plateau itself. Most likely it connected with the tunnel complex behind the city.

"Now we know how they get up here," Stewart said. "All we gotta be worried about is how often they change the guard."

Morton grinned. “I’ve got that, sir. We’ll sit here and capture anybody who comes up through it.”

Stewart nodded. “Quietly.”

As they finished securing the objective, Stewart’s radio crackled to life. “Bravo, this is Alpha. We’ve taken down the target. No casualties. No alerts.”

Stewart breathed a sigh of relief. “Did you find any type of entrance from the plateau? A way they get up there to relieve the guards?”

“Roger, sir. There are two more towers over here with guidelines for airships. Looks like a hidden landing site. There’s also a worn trail between us and you. We’re betting it’s a straight shot used by the patrols. We found another area where the trail just ends at an unsecured trap door. These guys were amateurs.”

Stewart agreed and realized he needed to decide on a course of action. The plan originally called for the whinnies under Alpha Team to remain in place at the listening post for extra security. But unless they were missing something, the J’Stull soldiers’ lax approach to maintaining watches and failure to change their routes indicated only rudimentary security protocols. They’d relied on the plants to do their dirty work for them, expecting that no one in their right mind would patrol, let alone attack, at night.

Damn, when did we start acting like Charlie?

Stewart snorted and repressed the smile that threatened to appear on his face. If his forces were to retain the initiative, he’d need the extra combat power of Alpha Team. If the enemy reacted to the loss of their security posts and made a concerted push up from the plateau before the attack on the cache site, more whinnies and more guns were something he couldn’t pass up.

“Alpha Team, we’re going to hold this ground until phase two. Get over here, soonest.”

“Understood. Moving.”

Stewart released the transmit button on the handset for the PRC-77 radio for a couple of seconds before keying it again.

"California, this is Fastlane. Relay to Desperado Six, we are in position. All objectives green and no casualties."

Fahey's voice came back instantly. "Roger, Fastlane. Message being relayed to Desperado Six now."

Satisfied, Stewart allowed himself to relax for a moment before moving to secure the objective and build hasty defensive positions. He left armed guards to watch over the dark stairwell into the mountain. If the enemy was going to come, he expected them to come near daylight. When they did, his forces would be ready for them.

At the completion of Stewart's radio call, Bo climbed aboard his vehicle, fully crewed by indigs, and gave a hand and arm signal for a short count. Though the patrol followed strict light and noise discipline, and they moved without any artificial lights, the pre-dawn glow was enough for them to see him, and they proceeded through the battle drill without issue.

Three, two, one.

All the patrol's vehicles started at the same time. The subterfuge was necessary. One enormous, initial sound made it much more difficult to estimate the unit's actual strength.

Immediately next to Bo were two small and highly maneuverable vehicles, which comprised the forward security elements. He would place one at the road junction leading from the main road by the river to the southwest of Imsurmik, and the other would take the main road east to the road junction southeast of the town and take up a similar position so they could warn the main body of any counterattack coming from those approaches. Bo pointed to each of the vehicles' commanders and gave them the signal to move out. They crept forward and cleared the patrol base before accelerating to what was a normal speed for vehicles on R'Bak's roads.

Now the wait begins.

Bo smirked to himself; his wait would only be a few minutes. The idea was to get the two security vehicles out and on their way to their positions before moving the bulk of his force onto the road. At that time of morning, there were no travelers. They had seen no activity on the highway for more than four hours. Everyone with sense enough to sleep was doing so. Moving in darkness gave Bo and his patrol all the leeway they needed.

Five minutes after the security vehicles rolled out, Bo gave the signal for the rest of the convoy to follow him. They left the assembly area across the narrow valley from Imsurmik and pulled onto a road no wider than a logging trail. It was unimproved and rough, but passable if they took their time. Bo knew the first section of the trail crossed several exposed rocky areas and would require about ten minutes for all the vehicles to clear.

If all goes well.

Bo's plan accounted for the lower initial speed. After his vehicle climbed through the narrow rocky passage, he accelerated toward the first road junction. There, he turned north toward the main road. The distance was only a couple of miles, but Bo kept the vehicle moving at a comparative crawl. Not only were his drivers indigs like the bulk of his three-hundred-fifty-man assault force, but they had just enough training to make them dangerous. While they were capable, Bo didn't want to risk pushing them beyond their capabilities. Every vehicle in his formation was a necessary asset. They had repaired the three broken-down tactical weapons platforms from Lieutenant Tapper's raid and added them to the other eight vehicles in the assault force. Weapons of all kinds had been slung on the vehicles, and while they weren't necessarily unsafe, it was best if they kept their progress slow and methodical during the more troublesome parts of the drive. The time for crazy maneuvers and assault speeds would come soon enough, but only after most of them had offloaded their infantry and were ready for the assault.

Bo's command vehicle was about halfway between the first road junction and the major highway when he saw a broken-down vehicle to one side. Two men were standing alongside the road, staring at the unmoving piece of equipment in the pre-dawn darkness. Bo wanted to laugh at the all-too-human response; it was something he might have seen in the early morning hours back in Mississippi around hunting season. One of them, an older bald man with a long white beard visible in the dim light, flagged him down. Bo scrambled out of the top of the vehicle, ensuring he had his sidearm, and made his way to the front fender.

The old man smiled up at Bo with hopeful eyes. When he spoke, Bo recognized his dialect as one of the northern groups from the fertile lands known as the Greens. "Are you going north?"

Bo shook his head. "No, sorry. Imsurmik."

As Bo hoped, the older man's eyes widened slightly.

"You as well? I see," said the old man. "Tell the F'ahdn that Zeesar gives you his blessing."

Bo nodded and filed the information away. Every name and potential contact was in play. Still maintaining the dialect, Bo replied, "Thank you, honored one. I will. Do you need assistance?"

"No," Zeesar replied. "My friends will be along after sunrise. Blessings to you and your force."

Bo climbed back to the hatch, keeping one eye on the men. Turning his back on them would show trust, but he had none. Zeesar's friends could very well be an armed force, an entirely different proposition than the occasional tribal militia vehicle. Depending on their path, an organized convoy could target his patrol from behind. Everyone was going to have to be on guard. Their enemies were not only to their front.

Zeesar raised a hand as Bo's vehicle accelerated away. Bo returned the gesture and studied the disabled vehicle. There were parcels strapped to the rear deck which could have been anything in the darkness. Try as he might, Bo couldn't help feeling he'd missed something. His plan called for a security force to assist with securing their attack corridor, but those soldiers were not manned or equipped to hold off an attacking force such as Zeesar's might prove to be.

I need to fix this.

Under the cover of a grove of trees not unlike the baobab trees closer to the town, Bo stopped his vehicle. As he waited for the bulk of his force to catch up, he ran the plan through his head one more time.

Lieutenant Stewart was in position and ready to secure the cache site. Doing so would draw some attention there and open up the town for assault. By now, both security elements were in place and ready to take action the minute he and the remaining assault force opened fire on the objective. He had augmented the security teams, too, and Bo planned to send two more vehicles and about fifteen soldiers to each location. They'd have to move fast in order to be ready before sunrise. Once they were in place, the assault would begin.

Bo considered the adjustments to his plan. He'd done as much as he could to minimize casualties and collateral damage, but it might not be enough. He understood Murphy's intent; they needed to take the town. They needed to find Aliza's persons of interest. And, if possible, they needed to hold the town, which meant chasing, or scaring away, the various militias inside the walls before they figured out how to coherently fight as a unit. Combatants to combatants, Bo and his forces were outnumbered almost six to one. Undisciplined and untrained militia or not, Bo didn't like those odds.

As morning twilight rose to the east, Bo wondered what Aliza would be doing that morning, at least until the raid began. Once the attack kicked off, he knew she'd find a place to hide. Or, failing that, a way to fight.

Sean Davis adjusted his position atop the rusted vehicle for the hundredth time in the last hour. From where he sat, the entire valley of Imsurmik was laid out below him. For a firing position, it was perfect, except for the intense light from R'Bak's stars. Even through his dark green uniform shirt, he felt as if his skin was already drying to parchment in the growing heat. He'd grown up in east Texas long before sunscreen was a thing, but he realized a change needed to be made. Davis and the other Lost Soldiers understood the adverse effects of too much exposure. Yet old habits tended to die hard, and he'd rolled his sleeves up above his elbow before dawn. Having felt the prickling intensity of the suns' rays as the binary pair peeked over the horizon, he now pulled on the cuffs and rolled them back down as he checked his watch.

"Show time!" Davis grinned and stood atop the vehicle. He bounded down to the dusty ground, taking a quick inspection walk behind his mortar battery. "Standby all tubes; prepare to fire!"

"All tubes, prepare to fire!" his indig master gunner, Ahce, called to the five tubes spread out in the clearing. He turned to Davis. "Targets, Lieutenant?"

Davis grinned. "Stick with the plan, Ahce. TRPs 1 and 2. We fire and adjust. Simple."

"Simple," said the indig with a shake of his head and a smile that revealed a few teeth to be missing in action.

It was anything but simple, and Davis knew it. After his promotion, he'd taken over the mortar section when Staff Sergeant Key rotated into the operations staff for Forward Operating Base Masada to their rear. Key hadn't been a mortarman, though. Only a few of the Lost Soldiers were even familiar with the weapons. Old, yellowed procedural manuals crammed in their original containers proved invaluable. Fortunately, it had been enough for the Lawless, but not necessarily for their partners. Forced to learn something completely different and modifying the commands and procedures so the indigs could understand them without proper context, Davis had done the best he could. But there were still far too many opportunities for screw ups.

"Make it up as we go" ought to be our motto.

Davis smiled at Ahce and brought up his binoculars to study the gated complex on the western glacis. The angular walls would make pinpoint fires difficult, but not impossible. While there appeared to be several weapon emplacements, almost all of them were located at the junction of the acutely angled walls. Davis' mortars were targeted on them to the best of his indigs' abilities, but without a true fire direction center, his battery was shooting from the proverbial hip.

Ain't nothing new.

Davis reached for his PRC-77's handset. "Desperado Six, this is Tequila Sunrise. Standing by."

There was no reply, which Davis expected. The attack was supposed to kick off at the top of the hour, and it was two minutes prior. The main vehicle contingent would be starting their engines and preparing to move. The vehicle assault force under Major Moorefield was already rolling toward Imsurmik.

Davis grabbed the radio and knelt atop his vehicle. In the northwest, he saw dust from the main road on the valley floor. The attack was on.

Here we go.

"Tequila Sunrise," said Moorefield's static-backed voice, "this is Desperado Six. Fire TRPs 1 and 2."

"Desperado Six, Tequila Sunrise. Firing TRPs 1 and 2. Out." Davis turned to Ahce and raised his voice. "Fire mission! Fire TRPs 1 and 2!"

Chapter Twenty-Nine

Aliza startled awake, alarmed by a rattling of the trash bins closest to the tunnel. She backed away until her spine was pressed against the cold, sharp rock where the walls of the crevice came together.

The sound of voices reached her, not taut with urgency but dull with boredom and weariness. Laborers, tossing trash into the bins before departing back into the dwellings. Aliza allowed herself to breathe again but listened closely.

Nothing, except for a few creatures Aliza couldn't see as they scampered and rooted about in the rotting rubbish. At one point, something hissed like a cat in the near darkness. The noise sent a shiver up her spine as she was startled by the memory of a strange, childhood encounter with a village tomcat.

She'd fallen during a game and skinned a knee. Not wanting to let others see her tears, she ducked into a space between two of the buildings in the square, and the cat had been there. Old and ragged, with a chunk of its right ear missing, the cat always hissed at everyone and ran from any approach.

But, as Aliza had sniffled and dabbed at her bloody knee, the old cat had edged closer tentatively. Instead of a hiss, it gave a soft mewl as if consoling her. She'd frozen, unsure, and then reached out slowly. The old cat let her touch its head and ruffle its ears. Her tears stopped, but then the cat, scared by the sudden yelps of children behind Aliza, had darted away.

She flinched away from the sounds that had startled her out of her drowsy recollection. There were footfalls on the stairs moving up to the dwellings. Two excited soldiers running in her direction. Not part of the patrols she'd heard the night before. They were on an urgent errand.

"Dust clouds on the main road. Do you really think it's some kind of attack?" one with a high-pitched voice asked.

"Everything is a threat as the Sear approaches. We must fight to protect what we have taken and hold it for as long..." The deeper voice trailed off into silence as they moved beyond her hiding spot and into the dwellings.

So, it had started. Bo's vehicles were on the way. And, in all likelihood, the dwellings would be swarming with soldiers, some of whom had probably been looking for her well into the night. So she couldn't go that way.

Aliza counted to thirty and stood slowly. If not out into the town, she would have to take her chances in the tunnels. Her muscles ached, but the relief of returning to her feet and moving felt good.

Committed to her simple course of action, she descended the winding stairs as quickly as she could. Within seconds, she heard running water and realized she must be approaching the man-made canal at the eastern edge of the glacis. Far below, at what seemed to be the base of the stairs, was a pool of early morning light: an opening. Possibly, an escape route.

Aliza looked up, away from the stairs, and slowed her pace so she could figure out her next move. She heard footsteps above her, but then they ceased. Given the many apertures and small passages she'd noticed on this and her earlier trip through the tunnels, there was no way of telling how far sound was travelling, much less its actual point of origin. Resolving not to be paralyzed by every faint noise, she pressed on toward the light below her.

Her own softly padding feet were all she could hear until, with a sudden clump of boots behind her, a soldier reached down and grabbed her right arm.

Aliza spun in his grasp, reaching for the pistol holstered on her leg at the same time. She brought it up in a smooth motion, catching her assailant by surprise and landing the muzzle squarely on the soldier's nose. Aliza heard rather than felt a distinct *crack* before the young man yelped in pain and slumped back against the stairs. Behind her assailant, a second soldier froze. She aimed the pistol at his chest, and the wide-eyed young man, face painted in the red-stripes-on-white of the J'Stull—brought up his hands. He backed away, tossed down his weapon, and ran up the stairs. There were more shouts and calls, but she did not look back. She holstered the pistol, ran down the last stairs, and emerged into the eastern end of the Inner City, only a few hundred meters from the sluice and artificial waterfall through the city's walls.

Above the rising din of a city full of increasingly alarmed or active people, she heard the familiar *whump* of mortars launching.

Yes, the attack was on.

As she burst into the brightening daylight among the buildings on the inhabited side of the canal, the first explosions rocked the western side of the city. Bo and the cavalry had arrived. Numerous guns and artillery pieces opened fire outside the glacis. In seconds, the Inner City's streets were filled with chaos. People moved in all directions, clamoring for news, desperately seeking safety. Civilians rushed into their homes, crisscrossing with the soldiers who were running for the glacis walls at the same time.

Aliza heard several men screaming emphatically from the parapet overhead. A barrage of rockets leapt away from a launcher mounted on the glacis somewhere off to her right. She didn't know Bo's entire plan of attack, but he had told her what common sense was telling her now: find a safe space. With so many people running in every direction at once, she couldn't reach the spot she'd chosen. Her best bet now would either be to descend the walkway that paralleled the waterfall outside the town or to find a hiding place in the buildings built against the glacis near the eastern end of the walls.

She assumed the vehicles would come across the farmland south of the town. The western road, winding as it rose to the gate, would not be the ideal choice for a safe approach. Bo's forces would have to deal with intense fire on such a restricted approach. Whatever forces he placed there were more than likely meant to draw attention and direct fire, so he'd almost certainly bring up the heavier vehicles straight across the farmland. It was the fastest and easiest route to the objective and gave them complete coverage of the glacis. Also, coming up from below the walls might allow them to get close enough to inflict damage before the defenders could respond.

Aliza dashed across a footbridge over the canal and glanced back, seeking her pursuers. They had not followed her out of the staircase, but in scanning more widely, she discovered Waornaak staring at her from down the street toward the city square.

Shit.

In their brief eye contact, it was as if they exchanged droves of data. He was clearly a high-value target, and he believed she was a spy. Both were true. The big man started toward her, yelling to men she could not see for assistance. Aliza realized her only choice was to go under the glacis and try to hide. Heading to the waterfall and getting to the walkway would take too long. All she could do now was hide and pray Bo and the others found her before Waornaak did.

Few outside noises penetrated the space under the plateau where Imsurmik's wealthy citizens made their homes. So, when a heavy glass decanter, filled with a fermented drink popular among the locals, rattled on the nightstand beside Yukannak's bed, it took him a few seconds to hear the dull explosions that had caused it to shake. Throwing off his light sleeping cover, he opened the door of his quarters and saw, across the corridor, early morning light flooding the empty platform where he'd spoken to Waornaak and Zeesar the day before. To his right, the hallway led to the main tunnel, and he called out for the guard stationed there. Nobody answered.

Now he heard gunshots—many of them close—among the explosions outside. It was the first time he'd been near combat, but he didn't panic. On Kulsis, you couldn't always know who wanted you dead, so direct attack was actually less unnerving.

He returned to his room, belted his pistol holster around his right thigh, and slipped on the least ornate robe he possessed and a pair of worn sandals. There was no time to bother with paint, which was a good thing; fewer people in Imsurmik would recognize him without it. And while Yukannak didn't assume the attackers were hunting for him, he didn't discount the possibility either. Could open warfare have broken out between Subitorni and the F'ahdn? Or maybe somebody had discovered his interest in the archive, or his crime, or maybe they only wanted him dead because of his relationship with the satrap. Anything was possible. And, if he needed something to bargain with—if his status as silci wasn't good enough—he had nothing else. Drawing the pistol, he headed for the main tunnel; he *had* to find the archive before they did, whoever *they* were.

The dwellings of the F'ahdn and the wealthiest citizens of Imsurmik lay off a wide, central tunnel cut into the plateau. Other tunnels ran parallel to it like streets, with intersecting cross-tunnels. Being underground, such homes remained cooler than anywhere else, especially near the F'ahdn's quarters. There, several vertical shafts had been cut through the rock, down to a spring far under the plateau. Its overflow ran out through the wall then down the slope to join the river. A heat exchange system, using the current to turn a large fan, drove the cool underground air up into the passages of the privileged.

Yukannak stumbled into the tunnel, expecting someone to shoot at or grab him, or to find guards defending it. He encountered none of that. Instead, to his left, where the tunnel mouth emptied into the Inner City, men, women, and children were running for shelter, all yelling or screaming, some carrying guns. One young mother was carrying a baby in one arm as she half-dragged a toddler with her other hand. Over a rooftop, streamers of smoke from an explosion on the wall drifted skyward. The scale of the attack heartened him. If his fellow Kulsians had come for him, they would have simply asked the F'ahdn, who would happily have handed him over.

Turning right, he passed militiamen running in both directions, most looking scared, none of them paying attention to him. He pushed through the crowds; he had no plan other than to take advantage of the chaos to find the archive, although he had no idea where it was and he knew it could prove a pointless search. Nor did he know what he'd do once he found it, except for a growing suspicion that his best chance of survival might involve defecting to the Offworlders. Or at least appearing to.

A young woman ran past him, face uncovered and black hair streaming. He recognized Waornaak, who was chasing her.

Reaching out, he grabbed the big man's arm. "What is going on? Who's attacking us?"

"Offworlders," Waornaak said, stabbing a finger at the back of the fleeing woman. "She's the spy I told you about. I'm going to make her pay for this."

"What about the other thing?" With all the yells echoing down the tunnel, Yukannak didn't bother lowering his voice until he spoke the last two words. "The archive?"

Waornaak pointed into the depths of the tunnel. "I think it's that way somewhere. Now let me go." Wrenching his arm free, Waornaak lurched into a run to catch up to the woman.

Yukannak paused, uncertain. Should he follow Waornaak or seek out the archive on his own? The archive might be a bargaining chip with the Kulsians, the J'Stull, the satrap, or the Offworlders. But then again, it might not. Without knowing what the archive might be, he couldn't guess. But if the woman was a spy, then her safety—and insights—would definitely be important to the Offworlders. Without wasting another second, he took off after Waornaak, back toward the mouth of the tunnel.

Mortar rounds poured into the city's gate, though not exactly as planned. As the indig-augmented mortar platoon fired and adjusted, it took them several rounds from each tube to find their range. Once they did, they walked the rounds along the top of the glacis at its westernmost extent. Bo's first section of vehicles charged up the road toward Imsurmik like they were taking part in the Pikes Peak Hill Climb. The cloud of dust they spewed into the surrounding air rose through the Outer City, adding to the shroud of smoke covering the gate. As he'd hoped, the combined cloud tracked east with the gentle breeze and provided additional cover to their movement. Enemy forces atop the glacis were responding with increased fire into the

Outer City, but it wasn't enough to impede the vehicles. Maybe the militia were concerned about collateral damage after all?

The moment Bo decided the enemy was completely fixated on the small attacking force in the Outer City, he sent the hand and arm signal to move out. As they built speed, he directed the main assault vehicles, including the heavy technicals, onto the road where they accelerated even more rapidly. They raced east until there was nothing but farmland between them and the city's walls.

"Driver, hard left," Bo ordered.

The vehicle veered and tore into the recently harvested fields. Behind him, the other vehicles executed an almost perfect flanking maneuver, turning left at the same time. Line abreast, they ripped through the outer farmlands toward the city with their guns blazing. In less than a minute, they crossed the fields and reached the bottom of the knoll on which the city rested. Slowing, but still bringing fire onto the wall itself, the vehicles found their purchase and climbed the rock-strewn hill.

"Phase three," Bo called over the radio. "Technicals, pick a spot on the glacis and pound through it. Mortars, stand by to lift and shift fires to TRPs 3 and 4."

Target reference points allowed for swift and effective fire to be directed at specific terrain features. In this particular case, Bo was targeting the missile emplacements on the outermost points of the glacis and what appeared to be concentrations of larger cannons. In both cases, they were far enough away from the center where Aliza would shelter. Hopefully. He flinched away from that dangerous distraction and focused on fighting his vehicle up the slope.

Several small rocket impacts rocked the chassis but did only minor damage. The relative lack of effect surprised Bo, but did not slow his racing heart. Amid the explosions, he caught sight of a boulder ahead, the kind capable of high-centering a vehicle and stopping it cold. He dropped behind the makeshift cupola's protective armor. "Guide right!"

As he came back up to the cupola and worked the familiar Browning M2 .50-caliber machine gun mounted there, Bo saw the first of the technicals successfully punch a hole in the glacis to the east. He reached for the radio and paused. Several soldiers appeared on the wall with weapons that looked ominously like rocket-propelled grenade launchers.

"RPGs on the wall! Tequila Sunrise, lift and shift fire! Lift and shift fire!"

By the time the mortars engaged, Stewart and the others atop the plateau were more than ready to move; no other J'Stull soldiers or militia had arrived to relieve the observation posts. When the attack was near, he'd ordered his riders onto their mounts. While his nervous energy drove his heart rate up to prepare for their attack, Olympia and the other whinnies seemed almost bored.

"Alpha Section," Stewart called after the mortar rounds started hammering down on Imsurmik's main gate, "you're up!"

The seven whinnies bounded down the northern edge of the plateau and into the cache site. Stewart stared into the box canyon, looking for the enemy's response. The guards positioned along the top of the security wall to the east attempted to engage the whinnies as they moved but had little effect. Stewart put his fingers to his mouth and whistled sharply. The indig infantry platoon moved to the canyon's rim and fired on the security forces. In seconds, any coordinated effort by the enemy to secure the cache site fell apart. Taking casualties, the enemy soldiers abandoned their posts, most fleeing into the main tunnel, while others darted for what looked to be yet another staircase leading to God-knows-where.

Stewart found the Alpha Section leader, Sergeant Andrechyk, in the primary area of the site. His arms were held wide with his palms up as if to ask where everybody had gone. Below their feet came a sudden tremor, and a cloud of dust poured from where the wide main tunnel to the city opened into the cache site.

Oh, shit.

The enemy didn't care about the cache site. Whether they'd fully collapsed or just blocked the tunnel with explosives didn't matter. Stewart's attack would no longer have the effect Major

Moorefield was counting on. The enemy would not defend the cache site; instead, they would focus their efforts on the main attack and potentially deflect it with their collected strength.

Stewart bit his lip. There was another way in, of course: the staircase. But whether or not it went where they needed it to, and what a team might encounter along the way, were complete unknowns. On the other hand, with the tunnel presumably blocked, there were only two ways to help the main assault: go overland mounted on whinnies or go through the tunnels. And either of those ways might prove impossible; he couldn't afford to gamble all his assets on just one. Even if that meant splitting his forces.

Stewart whirled in the saddle. "Morton! Get your men down that staircase! Find a way through, if you can."

Morton immediately yelled at his men. "Dismount! Get down into that opening and find me a way to the main tunnel or the city. On the double!"

Stewart was already moving east along the canyon rim. "California, this is Fastlane. Relay to Desperado Six, we've secured the cache site without a fight. We're moving to support the attack from the east. I have troops headed down a staircase into the tunnels."

"Roger, Fastlane," Fahey replied. "The attack has slowed near the wall. You might want to hurry."

"I was afraid of that." Stewart re-attached the handset to his vest and whistled again at Alpha Section. He gestured east and gave the "follow me" hand signal. The riderless whinnies formed up around him and darted toward the escarpment to look for a way down.

Olympia bounded forward and took off after them, descending the canyon wall nose first. Stewart leaned as far back in the saddle as he could and grabbed the whinnie's reins. "Whoa! Whoa, Olympia! Whoa!"

Neither the whinnie nor her riderless companions listened; they raced down the wall as one.

"Fastlane, California. Desperado Six says to hold the site, and they'll fight their way to you."

It's a little too late for that.

Besides, Stewart couldn't reply; Olympia suddenly leapt from the canyon wall to the top of the security fencing over thirty feet below.

Specialist Vernard Morton and his section reached the bottom of the staircase without resistance. They emerged into the dwellings at the eastern end of the inner row. Despite the chaos in the city outside, the part beneath the overhang was relatively peaceful. There was another descending passageway which became yet another spiral staircase just a few meters away. Courting the shadows, Morton soundlessly directed the others toward it. He checked behind one last time and saw only one person looking their way: an older man with smeared face paint and close-cropped white hair. He had no weapons, nor did he point and call out to alert any guards in earshot. He might have been a person of interest, one of their targets, but a rattle of nearby gunfire scattered the otherwise oblivious civilians and the man disappeared among them.

Ah, fuck it.

Morton spun into the new staircase and followed his men down into the city. With the battle raging along the south and western walls, the side near the waterfall would be less defended. From there, they could flank the enemy and draw some of their fire.

It might be enough to enable the attack to succeed.

Chapter Thirty

Aliza darted between buildings, heading toward the eastern glacis. There were doors and compartments cut into the wall's thick base. She arrived at a door just as several panicked fighters burst out of it and rushed toward the central tunnels. Recoiling, she spun toward the waterfall at the extreme eastern end of the wall. There was a larger opening there with a retractable sluice gate capable of closing off the canal to retain water when the flow from the aquifer below was low. A quick glance over her shoulder did not reveal Waornaak in pursuit…or anywhere else. Hope surged in her chest as Aliza ran for the door and ducked inside.

The room was far larger than she expected. Barrels and other large water containers lined the walls. There was space enough for her to squeeze behind them, and she moved deeper into the room, against the foundations of the first point that protruded from the glacis. Along the inner wall, Aliza found several arm-length metal rods. She grabbed one and touched the M1911 pistol holstered on her right thigh, just to make sure it was still there. She ducked behind a waist-high stack of wooden poles and tried to fold herself into the darkness.

Following Waornaak at a safe distance, Yukannak had run through a small doorway that led to a descending spiral stone staircase. He heard running water below, and the rising air was noticeably cooler. When he came to a landing, he realized he was near the eastern junction of the wall and the plateau, where the man-made canal passed below it into the marshes on that side of the city. The noise of the battle told him the fighting was close.

Up ahead, Waornaak ran outside without hesitating. Yukannak followed. He didn't want to, but there seemed no other choice. If he defected to the Offworlders, it was a good idea to have one of their operatives who might speak on his behalf; there was a vast difference between "valued ally" and "useful prisoner."

They ran along the base of the wall until he glimpsed Waornaak charging toward a door the woman had just slipped through. He tore it open and leaped in. Before it swung closed, Yukannak slid quietly inside.

Barrels of water, marked as potable, lined the walls, along with boxes and empty stoneware jars. Even with the spring, the wells, and the river, it became a treasure when the Sear began. Crouching near the doorway, Waornaak didn't hear him, but he heard Waornaak laugh.

The light coming through the door flickered, and Aliza heard heavy footsteps upon the dusty stone floor.

Her hand dropped to her side, and she silently gathered the long garment up so she could grasp the butt of her pistol. Carefully, noiselessly, she worked the safety strap holding the pistol in the holster and drew it.

Waornaak laughed. "I know you are here, woman. You will answer for the trouble you've brought."

Aliza focused on remaining perfectly still. She held her breath and willed herself to become smaller and more unnoticeable. The act brought back memories of her first days in Dachau, but here there was no crowd to shrink into and no protective adults to stand behind. Likewise, there wasn't a gang of guards to cull a crowd where she might be lost. Her pursuer was one man, and he'd seen her enter the room. While it was much bigger than she imagined it would be, it was still just one room.

Footsteps crunched closer.

"Come out, woman. I don't know who you are, but you have brought trouble. Your curiosity will be your end."

Aliza flexed her fingers and re-wrapped them around the grip of the pistol in her hand. Her sweaty palms made it difficult to hold steady, but she dared not reach down and dust her palms as Sergeant First Class Whittaker had taught her. Any noise could reveal her position to Waornaak. Which was clearly what he was trying to provoke with his threats.

She crouched lower.

Yukannak felt sweat run down from his armpits as the sounds of fighting outside grew heavier. Inside the room, however, only the crunch of Waornaak's footsteps indicated the presence of another human. "Come out, woman. I don't know who you are, but you have brought trouble. Your curiosity will be your end."

It was clear now that Waornaak intended to kill her, and perhaps rape her first, the same type of cruelty Yukannak had often seen in such men. Leaning forward, he could make out Waornaak's shadowy figure. Gripping his pistol tighter, Yukannak made up his mind. If the woman *was* a spy, what better way to endear himself to the Offworlders than by killing her assailant?

"There's nowhere to hide," Waornaak growled as he searched the barrels on the far side of the room. "Sobiturni will pay me handsomely for your pretty head."

Aliza tried to picture Waornaak's location based on the sound of his voice. If she could surprise him, she might have a chance to end their conflict before it began. She closed her eyes and listened. He was close, no doubt of that. She steadied herself and wiggled her feet as silently as possible into a better position from which to spring out—

A powerful hand roughly grabbed her garment at the back of her neck and yanked her up. She sprawled painfully across the pile of logs and twisted herself from his grasp. Sensing freedom, Aliza brought the pistol up as she turned toward her assailant. There was a sickening *smack* and white-hot pain shot through her right hand and upper arm. The pistol clattered away across the stone.

Aliza screamed in both pain and surprise. But before she could move, Waornaak stepped forward and reached for her throat. She rolled and kicked to no avail. In his free hand, he brandished one of the steel rods she'd seen; she brought up the one in her own left hand as he wound up to strike. She was able to block enough of the blow so it did not smash her skull, instead causing chips to fly up from the logs to her right.

"Get off me!" she screamed.

Waornaak roared and attempted to recover and strike again. "Offworlder!"

Waornaak wasn't an agile man, and had made a lot of noise searching among the water barrels. Yukannak had risen and moved toward him, careful to make no sound. A moment later, he heard scuffling and a woman's shout. Spilling water followed a loud *crack* as somebody kicked a barrel.

The woman screamed, "Get off me!"

Waornaak yelled back, "Offworlder!"

The word electrified Yukannak's brain. She *was* an Offworlder? Here was what he'd been looking for, a chance to ingratiate himself with this powerful new force, to defect with a realistic chance of staying alive. He had to save her, if he could.

The woman shrieked again, this time in unmistakable pain, but in the semidarkness all Yukannak could see were dark, tangled figures. Waornaak was wielding some sort of weapon, which he swung downward like a club.

Aliza was suddenly aware of another sound, an unearthly shriek that she abruptly realized was coming from her own mouth. Her right arm was useless. Tears of pain blinded her, kept her from seeing Waornaak's face clearly. All she could do was kick and hit and try to block his attacks with her metal rod.

There was a shattering sound, almost like a small explosion, from the door. It was immediately followed by another sound—one she'd heard before. Aliza turned her head, and the tears drained sideways long enough for her to see Athena burst through the wall abutting the waterfall. The big whinnie's lunge carried her so far into the room that as she landed, she was already snarling and biting as the man turned to face her.

Waornaak swung his makeshift weapon again. The blow slammed into the side of Athena's head just behind her left eye. There was a *whoosh* of air from the animal's lungs as she collapsed. Waornaak dropped Aliza and stalked toward the stunned whinnie, rod rising for a killing blow.

Aliza rolled off the logs onto the floor and dove for the pistol. Her right arm screamed with pain, and she wondered if she'd have the strength to fire left-handed. As she wrapped her hand around the pistol's grip and turned to aim it at Waornaak…time slowed down.

With her left hand, she centered the sights on the back of Waornaak's head.

The pain in her right hand prevented her from stabilizing the pistol at all. She knew she could not aim well enough to hit her target. But she had to try.

When the sight was centered once more, Aliza pulled the trigger…and time returned to normal.

The bullet passed harmlessly by Waornaak's head and chewed out a piece of the wall behind him. Instead of swinging his makeshift weapon at Athena again, he turned and leaped toward Aliza.

She steadied the pistol and tried to aim for his center of mass, his chest above his heart, and pulled the trigger.

The pistol bucked out of her useless hand. Waornaak snarled and advanced, the metal rod raised for another strike. Behind Athena, through the rough gap in the wall, Aliza saw Scout making his way to the top of the falls.

He would not make it in time…

When the doorway abruptly crashed inward in a spray of wood and rocks, Yukannak had leapt sideways and slammed into a heavy crate, expecting men to rush inside, or the room to collapse. The last thing he expected was one of R'Bak's ubiquitous whinaalanis, which charged into the room, bellowing at Waornaak with bared teeth.

The animal bit at Waornaak but missed, and Waornaak struck it near the left eye with his weapon. He moved closer, raising the weapon for another blow, but a gunshot echoed through the room and caused Yukannak to flinch toward cover. When he looked up, Waornaak was standing over the woman again, a long rod held aloft in his right hand.

Yukannak raised his pistol, told himself that this was no different than practicing at the range, and believed himself just long enough to squeeze off two steady rounds.

Both rounds hit. Waornaak half-turned before his legs gave out and he fell against the logs upon which the woman had fallen.

Aliza flinched as two shots echoed, sharp and hard, in the enclosed space. Waornaak's face went from rage to shock. The metal staff slipped from his fingers and clattered to the floor. Staggering, he turned to look behind him before toppling against the log pile.

Behind him, Aliza saw the man named Yukannak with a pistol in his hands. His tanned face was smeared with the traditional paint; he was older than her and handsome. They locked eyes for a moment. Scout broke down the remainder of the wall, howling over Athena. Aliza looked away from the door to the whinnies and then stood to face the man.

Yukannak knelt over Waornaak, grabbed his bloody robe, and pulled him close.

"The archive, where is it?"

"Wha—?" Waornaak said, his eyes focusing on something Yukannak couldn't see. "Oh no, no…"

"The archive, where—?"

Waornaak never spoke again. Yukannak released him and glanced toward the woman. His eyes met hers, and they each recognized the other. He'd seen her at a merchant's stall and found her attractive. *She* was the spy?

The woman said, "Thank—"

Something smashed through the wall behind him: a second whinaalani. Without waiting for it to bite him, Yukannak darted past the beast and out the door.

"Wait! Yukannak!"

But he was gone. As if he'd never been there.

Aliza heard a low groan. Athena's eyes opened, and the big whinnie rose unsteadily to her feet. Aliza met Scout's gaze. He'd assumed a protective posture over his mate as the others outside finished climbing the wall. The big whinnie hooted at Aliza and tossed his head behind him, as if to say he had things under control here, but that she needed to get to safety.

Outside, the battle raged closer and louder than it had before. Looking around, Aliza saw the pistol lying in the dust and gingerly picked it up. Several shots echoed just outside the room. Scout snarled and stomped in place, shifting so that he was between the door and Athena. Hand shaking, Aliza brought the pistol up to cover the door.

A familiar face ducked inside and swung a rifle in her direction, then stopped. He glanced at the body on the floor and back up to her. "Lieutenant Turan? You okay, ma'am?"

"Sergeant Morton." She grinned through the pain. "Am I glad to see you."

Chapter Thirty-One

As the militia atop the glacis finally coordinated fire in his direction, Bo's vehicles returned it. At first, the militiamen froze, then they quickly resumed. Rockets streaked down at the technicals and other vehicles. Despite the intense fire rising up at them, the enemy militia continued to man their posts until the mortar shells began crashing down. The first impacts were spectacularly on target. In the chaos of explosions, dust and bodies flew widely, and the remaining troops scattered. Some tried to fall back to the nearest battlement to their east, while others fled west along the glacis. Bo heard a sharp cry from his left and saw many indigenous soldiers jumping off their vehicles, weapons in hand, making for the ragged breach that had been made by the big, dual guns of his largest, turreted AFV. The indigs pressed toward the hole in the wall even though mortar rounds continued to fall. Bo's Lost Soldiers—now officers and NCOs—held them back with frantic screams and arm motions.

Bo grabbed his radio. "Tequila Sunrise, cease fire! Cease fire!"

A few seconds later the barrage lifted, and his infantry charged in. The lead elements disappeared through the gap in the glacis, well ahead of their leaders who frantically gave chase. Bo could see his heavier vehicles in the main effort wouldn't puncture a large enough hole in the thick wall to pass through. And the odds of their climbing the rock-strewn incline wasn't that great, either. He'd overestimated the maneuverability of the assault vehicles and the thickness of the glacis. Punching a hole was possible, but not on the scale he'd hoped. A few of the scout vehicles might make it through the rough gap, but he'd have to shift them from their position at the gate. He had to trust that infantry and the remaining scout vehicles could push through the entrance and accept that the heavy vehicles might not make it up the slope as planned. If so, then entering the Inner City on foot was their best chance to maintain the initiative.

Bo motioned to the other nearby vehicle commanders to get their infantry and nonessential crew dismounted to join the attack through the breach. As they did, the vehicles kept hammering at weak spots in several other places. The enemy, though, had gathered atop the wall to the east, and they began raining down an impressive sleet of fire. It forced Bo to duck into the cupola, and he could not see what was happening. He grabbed the radio handset.

"California, this is Desperado Six. Tell Fastlane we're on our way. We've encountered heavy resistance, but we've breached the wall."

The response from Fahey came immediately. "Desperado Six, this is California. Fastlane secured the site and is en route to your position now."

Bo snapped, "He can't get through the tunnels. That's suicide."

"They're not going through the tunnels, Desperado Six. Expect to see Fastlane with Alpha Section from the east anytime now. Bravo Section has entered the city on foot. Their whinnies are moving east along the back side of the outcropping and are heading your way."

Bo didn't have time to argue. A flurry of weapons fire from outside caught his attention. The militia soldiers on the glacis above had pivoted their aim. Some appeared to be firing into the city itself.

"California, can you see the western side of town from your position?"

"Negative, Desperado Six. We can move to the edge and look."

Bo swore under his breath. "Get there now. I want you calling in fire from the mortars onto the wall. Tell me if the scout vehicles have made it through the gate. You're gonna have to guide the choppers in, Fahey. And get the mortars firing again!"

"Done it before, sir. I've got it." He heard Fahey breathing hard as he ran. "Moving now."

"Guidons, anybody have eyes on Fastlane?"

There was no reply from Fahey. Instead, there was a hiss of static, and Stewart yelped, "We're coming around the mountain in a blue hurry, sir. Something's got the whinnies riled up!"

Davis didn't wait for the command post to relay instructions. As his own *de facto* fire direction center, he consulted his hand-drawn chart and called down the unconventional fire commands to the individual gun tubes.

"Gun 4, fire TRP 3, six rounds!"

"Gun 3, fire TRP 6, six rounds!"

"Gun 5, fire TRP 8, six rounds!"

Ahce continued monitoring tubes 1 and 2 as they pounded the gate and largest shelter atop the wall at the far western side. As the tubes resumed firing one round every eight to ten seconds, he couldn't help but grin.

If it's stupid but it works, it ain't stupid.

Davis proudly noted rounds accurately falling on the top of the wall. But every round that fell inside the city made him wince. Collateral damage was inevitable, but Colonel Murphy's orders were to minimize it as much as possible. If the attack went well, they'd be sleeping within the walls tonight. Being surrounded by live and happy citizens was imperative to the mission. No one knew how long they'd have to hold Imsurmik.

"Drive the militia out but leave enough of a city we can defend," Major Moorefield had said.

The first of the tubes reached the end of their fire mission and looked to him for a new target. Davis raised his binoculars with one hand and studied the town. He held his other hand palm out to the guns, telling them to wait.

Stewart held on for dear life. As soon as Olympia landed atop the reinforced tunnel exit from the city to the cache site, she leapt to the dirt floor and made a hooting noise. The other unmounted whinnies followed her to the ground where they rendezvoused with the riders of Alpha Section and turned east.

"Lieutenant Stewart?" Andrechyk called. He rode up on a smaller, silvery whinnie named Frost. "None of our guys have come through the tunnel. Looks like the J'Stull are holding it. There's a squad of them deep inside with some kind of crew-served weapon."

"Forget them," Stewart replied. "If nobody's coming through to fight us, there's nothing here they give two shits about. We'll sort it out later. The attack's gonna stall if we don't do something."

Andrechyk nodded but said nothing. Olympia hooted, and the big whinnie, Scout, trumpeted and ran for the cache site's eastern entrance. Along with his mate, Athena, Major Moorefield's mount easily crashed through the timber and wire gate and charged east along the exposed rock. Stewart held Olympia back for a moment before she ignored him and followed the other whinnies, both mounted and unmounted. Though he'd seen firsthand how fast the whinnies could run, their speed surprised him. There hadn't been a chance for him to say anything before Olympia tore out after the others, faster than he'd ever ridden her.

The exposed rock outcropping between the city and the box canyon was roughly three-quarters of a mile long. Within a couple of minutes, the whinnies rounded the spur and darted west toward the thermal pool and the waterfall on Imsurmik's eastern side. Immediately south of the falls, where a runoff creek ran from the pool to the river south of the town, was a wide, shallow marshland. With the approaching Sear, the ground didn't appear too damp or unstable for the whinnies. As fast as they were moving, Stewart wouldn't have been surprised to see them barely tracking mud from the ground. Ahead of him, Scout and Athena charged toward the pool, hugging the wall on its northern side. The radio crackled to life as they reestablished line-of-sight and the radios could "see" one another. Major Moorefield was asking where they were.

Stewart grabbed the handset from his vest. "We're coming around the mountain in a blue hurry, sir. Something's got the whinnies riled up!"

Scout trumpeted loud enough that Stewart heard him over the battle inside the town. The unmounted whinnies broke away from Stewart and Alpha Section. He saw Athena reach the waterfall first and climb the wet rocks with relative ease. Whatever they were going after, there was no way a mounted whinnie was going to climb the sheer vertical wall. Stewart studied the terrain ahead and rallied the section on him.

"Over here. Let them go. We'll go left around the pool." He pointed at the narrow band of rock-reinforced shoreline. "Follow that and bound up to the wall. Let's see if we can find a way to the top."

He realized as soon as he said it that going up a vertical wall by the waterfall versus going up the taller but not-*quite*-so-steep glacis seemed silly. Yet given the rough structure of the wall itself, he had a feeling the whinnies could handle the climb and not lose their rider in the process.

Ahead, on the wall of the fortress itself, Stewart saw a potential path. While it appeared smooth and well-made in places, there was an area that looked like it may have once been breached. The patch was rough stonework that stood out from the rest of it by a couple of feet at the base and tapered up gently into the wall itself. It might have been a weak spot if they could have hit it with artillery, but without any guns bearing on this side of the city, it didn't matter. What it provided, Stewart thought, was claw-holds and purchase for the sure-footed whinnies.

Olympia must have seen the same thing. Without a command, she leapt onto the wall and scrambled more than halfway up in the space of a couple of heartbeats. From there, the going was tougher, but before Stewart could rein her in, she scrambled to the top of the glacis and stood spanning the two-meter-wide walkway. There were no soldiers from his vantage point all the way down to the waterfall on his right. Only a handful were visible on the first section of the wall to his left.

They saw each other at the same moment, and both sides brought up their weapons.

The *crump* of detonating mortar rounds caused Captain Cutter's fists to clench with tension. He was sitting with his back to a boulder, two hundred yards southwest of the last row of houses in Imsurmik's Outer City. Between his position and the city were farm fields, shacks, and drainage sewers. They'd been in place for hours now.

Nearly two hundred years had passed since he last heard such explosions, but he'd passed those centuries in cold sleep; to him, it seemed like last week. The blasts sounded no different than any other detonating mortar shell. He'd been in desperate need of R&R then and was even more so now. But, as the old woman he'd met sitting in the ruins of her home in St. Lô, France, had said to him in a hopeless tone, "*C'est la guerre*." If anybody knew about the fortunes of war, it was the French.

It wouldn't be long now until Cutter's platoon went into the city looking for the HVTs Colonel Murphy wanted so badly, and he felt a rising panic he'd never felt prior to going into action before. When they engaged the enemy, how the men performed was entirely dependent on how well he'd trained them, and the burden of that responsibility weighed heavily on his mind. It might be hours yet before the assault force, under Major Bo Moorefield, secured the city firmly enough for his men to enter, and it was imperative he give the impression of calm. So, facing the day's rising heat as the sun topped the horizon, Cutter closed his eyes and pretended to nap, although in reality he followed the battle's progress by the sounds.

Eventually, echoes from the last explosions faded, leaving only occasional bursts of rifle and automatic weapons fire to indicate ongoing fighting at the points of penetration. Some reports came from nearby in the Outer City, but most were muffled and distant, indicating Moorefield's men were fighting either in the tunnels that cut through the plateau, in the streets of the Inner City, or at the cache site beyond the city's eastern fringe. Two-thirds of his own men were there, under Lieutenant

Tanavuna, facing what he hoped was the safer option of clearing the tunnels and Inner City, rather than the more easily defended warren of crowded homes in the Outer City. Tanavuna had fought in plenty of battles, sure—it was part and parcel of an Ashbander's life on R'Bak—but never as part of a larger coordinated force. So much could go wrong.

Soon, he knew, the order would come for them to move into the city and begin their search for persons unknown, against enemy opposition of undetermined strength and quality, through unfamiliar streets, and likely a hostile populace. The plan hadn't changed for months, and Cutter had been privy to every detail, but now that the time had come to put planning into action, the realities of his mission seemed impossible. *What the hell was Murphy thinking? What was* I *thinking, accepting such a hopeless mission?*

With the echoes of fighting coming from the nearby Outer City, Cutter stood over the radioman who was attempting to raise Tanavuna. He didn't bother lowering his voice, and he used the platoon's tactical call signs instead of those reserved for higher headquarters. "Shadow Six to Shadow Five, do you copy?"

He'd refrained from calling every ten minutes like he'd wanted to. Experience had taught him that his men fed off his energy; if he was nervous, they'd be nervous. So, grinding his teeth, Cutter had waited out the attack in silence.

Unlike Moorefield, Cutter only had one platoon to comb an entire town. He wouldn't have to kick down the gate, but he had to comb every nook and cranny for armed men who didn't want to be found and likely had a lot of other armed men helping them stay that way.

Tanavuna's voice crackled faintly out of the speaker. "Shadow Five copy."

The radioman handed Cutter the handset. The radio protocols were from the modern US military, not the World War Two army he'd known. Cutter still hadn't gotten the hang of them, although he'd tried. It was doubtful the J'Stull had signals-intercept equipment at Imsurmik, but radio discipline was never a bad idea.

"What's your status, Shadow Five?"

"We're in position and standing by. Scouts are looking for other ways into the city. Are you in contact with the enemy? Shadow Five over."

Tanavuna's question must have been prompted by gunshots heard over the radio, as Cutter heard them, too. He found that reassuring, since it meant the rest of his platoon really wasn't that far away. "Negative, we are not yet in contact with the enemy."

Cutter wanted to remind the distraught lieutenant not to get reckless in pursuit of saving his wife, but bit his lip as he weighed the risks. The J'Stull were technologically backward compared to the Lost Soldiers, but a bullet was a bullet and dead was dead, no matter how you got killed. After a few seconds in deliberation, he decided to risk it.

"I know you're anxious, Shadow Five, but remember your training. You're entering enemy territory, so movement and fire support are critical. Don't get ahead of yourself and don't try to be a hero. If you go charging in looking for the subject target, you will only wind up getting killed. The city is swarming with militia. Most probably don't want a fight, but they won't mind shooting you if you give them an easy target."

"I understand, Shadow Six. I want Kes—the target—back, but dying won't accomplish that."

"Good man. Shadow Six out."

As a young second lieutenant going through his officer's basic course at Fort Knox, Kentucky, Bo learned from a Marine major how a combat engagement could change in a moment. A competent combat leader needed to understand the situation and decide quickly how best to seize or retain the initiative. Without question, the militia and J'Stull soldiers atop the glacis were firing into the center of town. Bo could assume they had either come apart at the seams due to a lack of leadership, or that his security element had been able to push through the western gate and get inside the city.

Movement to the right caught his eye. Atop the wall, a few soldiers were scrambling down a narrow passageway. Behind them, riding tall over the battlements, came Lieutenant Stewart on his mount, Olympia, followed by three or four mounted whinnies. Further to the east there were riderless whinnies on the wall, but they hung back, close to the waterfall. Bo was surprised he did not see Scout or Athena among them.

I can't worry about them right now.

The successful attacks had shaped the fluid situation enough that Bo recognized they had an opportunity. He leaned down into his vehicle's hatch and yelled at the crew, "Lay down suppressive fire. As soon as I'm through the gap, give me a minute or two and then keep working on the wall. If we can get one of the heavy assault vehicles up this hill and through the wall, great. Otherwise, just keep their infantry off our ass."

Bo didn't wait for a response. He reached for his M-16 and jumped out of the vehicle's cupola onto the top of the shoddy armor plating. At this particular moment, the irony of his class motto at Fort Knox—"Death before Dismount"—almost made him smile in the midst of the battle.

Bo sprinted up the slope toward the ragged gap in the outer glacis. Legs burning, he pushed hard, running through it and joining up with the infantry on the other side.

They'd been able to create quite a beachhead inside the city itself. No organized defense or hardpoints stood in their path. The militia were scattered among the deserted streets. Bo heard the *whump* of several mortars launching in rapid succession. Rounds impacted a corner of the glacis where at least one heavy rocket launcher was emplaced. There was a tremendous secondary explosion from the top of the wall that shook the ground and threw dust and dirt everywhere. Davis and his mortars were doing a great job.

Bo pressed further into the city. As he came around a building that flanked a major thoroughfare, Bo found Lieutenant Cook with two squads of indigenous infantry pressed against a wall, preparing to charge into the flank of the retreating militia.

"Lieutenant Cook, report."

Cook grinned. "My scout vehicles breached the gate without casualties. I left them inside the gate to swat down some pretty strong resistance. They're pushing the militia back. I've got the mortars taking out the weapons up top, and I've sent an indig squad to clear the top of the wall from the west. The enemy are falling back everywhere, sir. As soon as our vehicles come into view, we can swing out ahead of their militia from the side and flank 'em. If we do that, though, they'll either surrender or fall apart completely. We just have to hit them at the right point, sir."

"Outstanding," Bo replied.

Again, there was a rapid succession of mortar launches, and another corner of the upper glacis felt the brunt of multiple impacts. The whinnies on the parapet's walkway charged further west with their riders firing. They met no resistance.

From the east, Stewart rode his bounding whinnie down from the wall's midpoint. The other riders pushed their whinnies further west, driving the fleeing militia before them. However, Stewart swerved aside toward Bo. "We've got the eastern wall secured, sir. Mortars are hitting other weapon emplacements. We can see friendlies moving east up there."

We've secured the wall. Now for the militia.

"Time for phase two," Bo said. "Tell Fahey to release the cavalry."

Stewart spoke into the radio. "California, this is Fastlane. Relay to guidons, phase two initiated. Release the cavalry."

"Roger, Fastlane. Break." Fahey dropped off the frequency for five seconds. "Guidons, guidons, guidons, this is Hotel California. Initiate phase two and release the cavalry. Contact Fastlane on station."

Given their position, Bo and the others couldn't hear the response. A wave of gunfire came from the northern wall. Bo peered around the corner of the building and saw the ragtag militia. He expected them to be moving straight to the east. Instead, they appeared to be moving north toward the central part of the city and the open space of the bazaar.

"They're moving toward the tunnels. There must be another way out through them." Bo glanced up at Stewart. "I thought you guys were holding the main one from the other side."

"You needed us over here," Stewart said. "They've collapsed the central tunnel. I figured they were more concerned with fighting you off than anything in the cache site. We couldn't get through and then the whinnies got excited and took off, sir. All we could do was stay in the saddle."

From deep inside the city came the steady rattle of machine gun fire. Bo recognized it as one of the M-60 machine guns, most likely from Bravo Section.

Dammit.

"What did you find on the top of the plateau? Was there some way into the city?"

Stewart nodded. "We found a staircase, sir. The militia did not try to replace their guards."

"Who'd you leave up there?"

Stewart replied, "Morton's entire fire team, sir. But they went down into the city. I sent that through Fahey."

"I didn't catch that." Bo shook it off. "Doesn't matter. So, if they're headed into the city, that's Booker firing the 60." He quickly did the math. Morton and eight men had descended tunnel-stairs somewhere in the city and now, with just that one machine gun and their rifles, they were holding back as many as four hundred militia who were determined to escape through the tunnels.

This ain't gonna end well.

"Any ideas?"

Stewart replied, "We can't try to take the whole tunnel complex, sir. That's suicide."

Bo nodded. He saw Cook glance up at Stewart. The two newly commissioned officers traded a long look, and both smiled.

"What are you two thinking?"

"Hounds to hunters, sir," Cook replied and then glanced at Stewart. "Meet ya in the middle, Johnny." Cook turned to his squad and motioned them to move around the corner to the west. They moved so fast Bo didn't have a chance to ask where they were going. At the same time, Stewart and the other whinnies bounded to the east and turned north around a building a hundred meters away.

Bo understood in an instant what they intended to do. Pinching the escaping militia between them, they were hoping for surprise to crumble their hasty defense. If Morton and the others could hold off the outlying militia and reinforcements that might arise from any undiscovered tunnels for even two or three more minutes, Cook and Stewart could pincer them. Once they felt they were surrounded, the militia would almost surely surrender. Bo checked his weapon, moved the firing switch from safe to semi, and prepared to follow Cook's squad.

A staccato burst of weapons fire from the east got his attention. Bo stared down the narrow thoroughfare and saw a woman running hard to the south. In the space of a millisecond, he recognized the unmistakable form and face of Aliza Turan. She ducked around the corner of a building just before it exploded in a cloud of dust and debris. Aliza was now behind his line and there was no one from his forces who could help her without disengaging from their attack.

Bo was stuck. Everything he knew about leadership said he needed to stay with his team and lead them. But a vital part of that team was cut off and alone. She might be unarmed or injured. Given the intelligence she likely possessed, and if the enemy suspected she had it, they would be trying to kill or capture her. There just wasn't another choice. Besides, Stewart and Cook had the situation in hand. *All he was going to do was get in the way.*

Or so he told himself.

Bo ran east toward Aliza.

Chapter Thirty-Two

Injured and unable to return fire, Aliza frantically searched for cover. Morton and the others had called in her position and then pressed west toward the fight. Not a minute later, four rough men appeared, searching the eastern edge of town for Waornaak. When they saw her, they opened fire. As the rounds slammed into the wall behind and above her, she dove behind a stone watering trough and crawled up to the junction between it and a ramshackle building. They called for him by name and went toward the storage room where they would be sure to find him.

She'd left the water trough and ducked into an evacuated shop as the men began their search. Immediately, the whinnies roared and stomped, and she heard the gunfire add to the general cacophony. Thinking she had an opportunity to flee, she'd run from the shop toward the south, but they'd seen her. After undoubtedly seeing Waornaak's dead body and having been confronted by Athena and Scout and any other whinnies remaining behind, they'd withdrawn and taken up the pursuit.

But they haven't got me yet.

Aliza could see the wall, but there was no one atop it, neither friend nor foe. She pressed herself low against the building as more rounds tore into its mud-and-stone sides. Aliza pulled her knees to her chest and pressed her back against the rough surface. Dust rained down on her. A sharp piece of stone sliced into the skin of her forearm. Another round of weapons fire tore through the air around her and more fragments pelted her scalp. The near-continual shower of debris frightened her more and more. The memory of Operation Markolet's end, losing Ben Mazza, and the sound of enemy fire coming closer washed over her. Aliza squeezed her eyes closed. Cradling her injured arm and sobbing with pain, her mind raced to gain control of her emotions. This was not the time to give up. This was the time to fight back.

From the opposite direction of the oncoming men there was a new sound. Aliza opened her eyes and looked west, down a nearby street, and gasped. Moving her way along the next row of buildings came a lone figure. Carrying an M-16 rifle, Aliza knew it was one of the Lost Soldiers, but she couldn't see who it was through all the dust and debris. The figure moved at a run, stopped at the corner of the building, and fired several rounds at the attackers nearing Aliza. At that moment, she recognized him.

"Bo!"

He glanced her way and brought the rifle up again. She saw him squeeze the trigger quickly, firing several shots at her pursuers before lowering the rifle.

"Can you move?" he yelled from across the street, maybe twenty meters away.

Aliza shook her head. She hoped the way she was cradling her arm was enough to show him that rolling to a standing position and running would take far too much time.

"Stay down. I'm coming to you."

He fired again. There was a muffled scream from the end of the street. Bo fired another four shots quickly before lowering the rifle and dodging across to her. He had just reached the middle of the street when the men opened fire again.

A round tugged at Bo's pant leg and Aliza saw a spray of blood as the round exited his left calf. Teeth bared in pain, he managed another step at full speed and dove toward the cover of Aliza's position.

He almost made it.

Stewart led Alpha Section into the bazaar and stopped. To his right, under the stony overhang, a gaggle of militia were crowded against the rocks that surrounded the entry to the tunnel complex. Eyes wide with fear, they tossed their weapons onto the dusty soil. Whinnies pranced around and growled at the frightened men. Young and old stared in shock, whispering intently to each other while pointing at the men riding the whinaalani. He knew they probably had never seen anyone ride the lizard-like creatures, despite having used the more docile ones as beasts of burden. Given the shock in the eyes of the natives, Stewart wondered if they'd surrendered because of the attack itself or the mounted riders.

Probably a bit of both. He grinned to himself. Wait 'til they see this shit.

He grabbed the handset for his radio off his load-bearing strap. "California, this is Fastlane. The LZ is secure. Over."

"Copy, Fastlane." He heard Fahey release the transmit button and then press it again. "Gunsmoke Lead, this is Hotel California. LZ secure. Over."

The Huey's lead pilot, Sergei Karlovich, drawled in reply, "Copy, California. Flight of two gunships thirty seconds out. Over."

"Copy, thirty seconds. Weapons free. Some remaining militia on the ground," Fahey said.

"We'll mop up the stragglers. Just hold that LZ. Shadower is eight minutes behind. Gunsmoke Lead, out."

As he fell, Bo bit the inside of his cheek hard enough that warm, coppery blood filled his mouth.

"Fuck!"

The surrounding dirt practically exploded with the impacts of enemy rounds. He pushed with his good leg and dug his elbows into the ground hard enough to split the fabric. Head down, he pushed again and felt a powerful hand grab him under his left armpit. Aliza was there, on her knees, straining to drag him behind her improvised cover with her one good arm.

"*Yalla!*" she grunted and fell backward, pulling his head and shoulders behind the water trough. He scrambled around quickly.

"You okay?" He blinked dust out of his eyes and stared at her for a long second.

"I'm fine. You're the one who got shot."

"Don't remind me," Bo replied. He moved into a crouch of sorts, with his good leg underneath him. He brought up the rifle, flipped the selector switch to automatic, and raised it blindly over the trough's edge. He pulled the trigger and held it for a couple of seconds, just long enough for the last eight or nine rounds in the magazine to be fired. As the weapon stopped, the noise from the other end of the street diminished. Her pursuers were likely taking stock of the new threat.

Without looking, he fished another magazine out of his load-bearing harness while his other hand held the rifle at the junction of the upper and lower receivers. He ejected the empty magazine and slapped the new one into place. Bo yanked the charging handle back and let it go, slamming a new round into the chamber. Out of habit, he tapped the forward assist mechanism to seat the cartridge and readied himself to pop up for another burst. More rounds tore into the far side of the trough and the building above them. In the swirling dust and rain of rocky debris, he stared up at Aliza.

"I don't have a radio. The others don't know we're here, Aliza. They're gonna be coming, but we have to hold our own."

She didn't respond.

"Do you have a weapon?"

"Yes," she said. "But it's useless with my arm like this."

"What happened?"

"A man came after me, Bo. One of the high-value targets. He beat me with a metal rod."

Bo shook his head. The volume of fire from the end of the street seemed to double and then triple before it waned again. "I'm sorry we didn't get here in time. Look, I've got one more magazine, Aliza. Thirty rounds. It's not enough to stop those guys. We have to get you out of here."

She blinked. "What do you mean?"

"Can you run or not?"

"I can," she said.

"Then get ready," Bo replied. He rose up and blindly fired a quick burst over the edge of the trough. "This isn't going to hold them back for long."

"What do you want me to do?"

Bo grinned. "When I get up the next time, I want you to run. Get to the wall and move west. Stay along the wall; the fight's closer to the dwellings. There's a breach on the western side of the glacis. Get there if you can. If not, get to Lieutenant Stewart and the others."

"What about you?"

Bo shrugged. "You've got intel on these guys, right? Know someone who might fit the profile Murphy gave us?"

"There are a few, yes."

"If you die here in the street, he doesn't get that information. You can run, so you're gonna run. Got it?"

Aliza nodded. Her dark eyes were wide. As he studied her face, carving it into his memory, tears brimmed and ran down her cheeks. He reached out to catch one with his hand and inadvertently smeared dirt on her cheek.

"Why are you frowning?" she asked.

Bo raised the rifle over his head and fired another quick burst. "I can plan an attack, take a whole damned town in the process, but I can't ask the woman I love to marry me."

She laughed through her sudden tears—a surprised yelp of a sob. "You have impeccable timing, Hubert Moorefield."

He laughed. "Guess so."

"My answer is yes." She reached out with her good hand and squeezed his arm. "I love you."

"I love you, too," he squeaked out of his tightening jaw. He cleared his throat and pushed the emotion back. "Now, get ready to run, Aliza. Get Stewart and come back. I'll cover you for as long as I—"

An unearthly scream echoed along the street. Weapons fire erupted, louder and with a higher volume than before, but the surrounding air was still. Bo put the rifle to his shoulder and eased up to look over the trough, but ready to drop if seen.

Whinnies filled the far end of the street by the waterfall. Athena roared from the midst of the collected militia and soldiers, thrashing and stomping her mighty feet. Another whinnie lay on the ground, bleeding profusely and writhing in the street.

"Sonuvabitch!" Bo stood fully. "Stay here, Aliza."

His rifle up in its firing position, Bo limped into the street. As a target appeared, he fired. Again, and again. Ambling toward the engagement and trying not to hit the whinnies in and among the enemy, Bo pressed forward. His mind was calm, almost detached. A part of him recognized the threat, and even the larger picture, but he was wholly outside it, something he'd first felt in a skirmish near Mogadishu. Every nerve ending seemed to fire all at once. His eyes were clear, and the weapon felt like an extension of his central nervous system.

Track, fire. Track, fire.

The familiar sound of approaching Hueys caught his attention as the last of the militia fell to the charging whinnies. His gaze flashed back to the street. The whinnie lying there had stopped moving and its head was facing his direction. Across the distance, he felt the whinnie's eyes on him. The rifle nearly slipped from his grasp. Bo picked up his pace, hobbling more with each step.

Weapons fire from the militia ebbed to nearly nothing. Riderless whinnies screamed and fell upon the men, bounding over their fallen herd mates. Another whinnie fell in the street. Bo saw the coloration; his heart leapt into his throat.

"Scout!" Bo yelled. "Scout!"

The big whinnie rolled his head to peer down the street at Bo. He gave a low, throaty call and turned back to one of the other fallen whinnies wobbling for a moment, as if dazed. Then Scout's head and neck went limp, and he fell to the dusty ground with an audible *smack*.

"No!"

Adrenaline coursed through Bo's system as he shambled down the street on his injured leg. The militia's guns had fallen silent. Some of the ones with face paint were running hard to the west. Bo wasn't watching. He reached Scout just as he heard Aliza wail from behind him. Now she was running down the street, her good arm cradling the bad.

A whinnie's trumpet echoed through the quiet town from the west, and Bo raised his eyes. Overhead, two Hueys hovered in security positions. They were close enough to see their gunners scanning the streets for targets. One of them waved, and Bo responded. The helicopter slid slowly toward them and hovered directly above. The gunner was pointing down at the carnage around them. The pilot turned and studied the ground. Bo could see them talking on the radio. Exhaustion crashed over him as the adrenaline wore off.

Bo knelt by Scout and stroked the smooth leathery skin on the animal's head. *But* were *you just an "animal?"* Fresh tears filled his eyes, and Bo tried not to let them come. He failed. His head swirled with dizziness, and he collapsed onto the ground next to his mount.

We almost made it, Scout.

Almost.

"Hotel California, Gunsmoke Lead. Desperado Six needs assistance. He's down. I say again, Desperado Six is down. East side of town near the wall. At least one other injured with him. Over."

Fahey and the others moved toward the stairwell into the city. "Copy, Gunsmoke. Fastlane, send security and medic that way now."

"Fastlane, roger. Out."

"Gunsmoke Lead, good copy. Hueys are three minutes out. LZ status?"

"The LZ is green, Gunsmoke," Fahey replied. From the top of the plateau, he was roughly at the same altitude as the hovering helicopters. More noise came from the north, and Fahey turned to see the quick reaction force approaching at high speed. The UH-1s appeared to be about a yard off the deck as they streaked east over the plateau.

Damn, Major Lee. You not only taught them what to do, but how to do it with style.

Impressed, Fahey shook his head and laughed. After all, helicopters didn't really fly. They simply beat the air into submission.

As Lieutenant Stewart and a section of riders arrived, Aliza knelt in the dusty street by Athena's lifeless body. Words wouldn't—couldn't—manifest in her tight throat. They'd had so little time together, yet Athena was special, and not only to

Aliza. Her hand traced the angles of the whinnie's jawline and her serene face for a long moment.

She died here with her mate. They died protecting us.

Our greatest allies.

Aliza sobbed and clapped her dirty hands to her face. Tears flowed freely down her cheeks. She wiped at them with a dust-covered sleeve as Stewart dismounted and walked over to Bo where he sat with his back against Scout.

"We have the town secured, sir. Most of the militia have surrendered. We're mopping up the others now. Our guys took the tunnel."

"Casualties?"

"One of ours dead, PFC Rich. Crazy asshole took out some kind of crew-served weapon in the tunnel's entrance and turned it on the militia trying to get through. Stopped them cold, sir. Fucking incredible. We lost at least forty-seven indigs; we're gathering bodies now. Morton is going door-to-door looking for the F'ahdn. Cook has established a security perimeter around the bazaar. It's big enough for an LZ and Fahey's directing them in from the top of the plateau."

"How many wounded?" Bo asked.

Stewart looked down at Bo's bloodied lower leg. "Counting you and Aliza? Sixty-one. Most of those are minor. Let me get a medic up here, sir."

"I'm fine, Johnny," Bo replied.

Aliza looked up and saw Bo trying to laugh off his own wound, but he was pale and his clothes were almost black with sweat. She went to him and knelt at his side.

"Lay down, Bo."

"I promise I'm fine," he replied with a smile. Aliza did not reciprocate, and his bravado evaporated in an instant. "No, I'm not, huh?"

"Not at all," she replied. "You're going into shock. Help me with him, Johnny."

Stewart went to Bo's other side. They turned him and raised his legs carefully, resting them on Scout's body.

Bo's eyes were on Scout's still head; his face threatened to break. "He—they—"

"They fought for us," Aliza whispered. "You were doing the same for them, yes?"

He nodded. "I was."

"Then leave it be, Hubert."

"Stop calling me that." Bo half-smiled.

Aliza smirked. "It gets your attention."

His eyes cleared up a little. "Where are the targets? The people Murphy wants us to grab?"

"I have some names. Militia leaders mainly," Aliza said. "I'll get them to Cutter. There were others: a man named Zeesar who may be in town. And the J'Stull commander Sobiturni: he's here somewhere, too."

She was aware that her voice had trailed off, and Bo quickly asked, "What is it?"

"There's another man. He's…he's not from here. Maybe he's Ktor or Kulsian, but he's not from R'Bak, and he's not one of us. I can't explain it, but he's eluded me for several days. When this happened—" she raised her arm, "—he shot the bastard in the back. This man, this Yukannak, killed him and ran. He saved my life, Bo. We have to find him. Something tells me he's the person Murphy will want to speak with the most."

Above them, the *whup-whup* sound of the approaching Hueys filled the sky. Bo sat up, grimacing with pain. "Stewart?"

"Sir, Lieutenant Bird is on his way with the medic bag—"

Bo waved him off. "Bring me your radio. Do we have comms with Captain Cutter?"

"I don't know, sir. We can check with the CP."

Bo motioned for the radio.

"I can do it," Aliza said.

Stewart shrugged out of his rucksack and set it down beside her. He pushed the handset into Aliza's hand. "I'm going back to the men, sir. I'll leave a security element with you, and Bird will be here in a minute."

Aliza met his eyes even as she passed the handset to Bo. "Thank you, Johnny."

He touched the brim of his hat, not unlike how Bo always did. "Aliza."

She watched him mount his whinnie with ease and ride off to the west side of town. There were still sporadic flurries of weapons fire echoing through the city. Around them, people peered out of houses and buildings. The curious face of a child appeared in a window across the street. Aliza met the little girl's gaze and smiled. She'd hoped for a similar response, but there was none.

Maybe there'll be a time for joy here, someday.

"Aliza?" Bo called. "Help me up; we've got to get going."

"Where?" His color had returned somewhat but he was in no shape to move.

"The central bazaar. Part of our quick reaction force is on the way. Once the troops are on the ground, the Hueys will medevac the badly wounded. Once you've talked them in, you need to contact Cutter with the PoIs' names and probable locations. We're going to hold Imsurmik per Colonel Murphy's orders. After that, we have to secure the roads through this sector."

Her face screwed in confusion. "The roads?"

"I met your guy Zeesar this morning on the road southwest of here. Nice enough to talk to, but I'm not taking any chances. He was waiting for friends. If he's a warlord and one of the satrap's buddies, I don't want him attacking our exposed—" Bo struggled to get to his feet.

"You stay down," Aliza snapped. He laid down again as Lieutenant Bird and an indig healer sprinted their way. "Bird is almost here and until he bandages your leg, you're not going anywhere."

"Yes, ma'am." Bo snorted, and a smile appeared on his face. "I mean, 'Lieutenant Turan.' So, you still wanna marry me?"

With her good hand, she punched his upper arm. "I'll go anywhere you go, 'Hubert.' So of course, I'll marry you. We have too much to lose and too many gifts we fail to appreciate."

She watched him look past her. The riderless whinnies had gathered around them in a protective circle. Like Bo, she recognized their behavior. Her grief threatened to erupt again. They'd been through so much with these aliens. They were far more than beasts of burden, and there was so much the humans could learn from them.

Finally, Bo met her eyes and nodded. "You're right about those gifts—about everything—honey."

She smiled in return. "It's about time you came down from your fences."

Before he could respond, the radio handset squawked. "Desperado Six, this is Shadower. I have the ingress point under observation. Waiting on your instructions. Over."

She raised the handset, winked down at Bo, and depressed the send toggle. "Shadower, this is Queen of Hearts. Have location and identification of primary targets. Prepare to copy."

Chapter Thirty-Three

There was one unnerving thing about the long-awaited go-ahead message: it was issued by Lieutenant Turan, not Major Moorefield. The radio hissed and crackled under her voice. "Shadower, this is Queen of Hearts. Have location and identification of primary targets." She paused. "Desperado Six Actual confirms that you are cleared to enter. The troops there are ready to pass you through their lines, over."

"Shadow Six Actual responding. Copy all. Am prepared to copy details on PoIs and other HVTs."

Aliza shared everything she had heard, observed, and conjectured with impressive clarity and brevity.

"Roger that, we're moving up. Shadow Six Actual out."

"Good hunting!" Moorefield's voice called out from a distance. Well, Cutter sighed gratefully, at least the major was alive. For now.

He turned to look at the men behind him. First Squad was huddled in a draw, out of line of sight from the city. As the boredom of waiting wore off, the men's faces showed their barely contained rage from the attack on their homes. Somewhere within Imsurmik was their healer, Tanavuna's wife, Kesteluni. Although married to the hetman's son, who was now the hetman himself, healers had a matriarchal status in the village. She looked after *all* of them and taught others her skills. Aside from those they'd killed, the men who had kidnapped her had threatened the very existence of Nuthhurfipiko. They wanted her back.

Except, that wasn't the mission.

Cutter had seen this before, when his old platoon got caught up with a patrol of Waffen-SS from the *17th SS Panzergrenadier Division Götz von Berlichingen*, whom his men believed had gunned down four American prisoners. The German soldiers pleaded innocence but his men shot them down where they stood, releasing their anger by kicking the bodies after they were dead. For just a moment, Cutter had been distracted by the battlefield justice, long enough for an MG 42 crew to set up and fire on them from a nearby hill. By God's good fortune, nobody was hit, but his inattention could have cost his men their lives. He swore never to let that happen again.

"We move out as we practiced it," Cutter said, sidling down the draw in a crouch. "*Do not* forget our primary mission, do you understand me? We are here to identify and apprehend persons of interest who might have information about what the satrap, other J'Stull, or the Harvesters are planning. After the attack on your homes, those plans might also include wiping out the rest of you with their heavy weapons. And even if some of you escape, what chance do you have of surviving the Sear without food, water, or shelter?"

Without waiting for anyone else to speak, Platoon Sergeant Riidono half-stood, keeping his head below the lip of the draw. Although the nearest buildings were a hundred yards away, Cutter had drilled into them that you couldn't take anything for granted when your life was at stake. Cutter had always wondered how his platoon sergeants knew exactly when to jump in, and figured it was an instinct you were born with. Either you had it, or you didn't.

"All of you know he is right," he said with a tone Cutter associated with far more seasoned non-coms. "Imsurmik is a big city, and that plateau is cut through with tunnels and caverns; most of you have seen them from the inside when we traded with the F'ahdn or brought goods to the marketplace. The shevfashli could be anywhere. There are less than fifty of us and thousands of them. Your best chance of finding her is to find somebody who knows where they took her. That won't be a kr'it monger or a leather tanner; it will be somebody with fancy paint and nice robes, or maybe a J'Stull soldier trying to slip out of the city. Find them, and we might find the shevfashli."

Naanni couldn't quite let it go. One of the youngest, his eyes were brimming with tears. "What if she's…what if they did something to her?"

"Then we will hunt down and kill the men responsible," Cutter said, baring his teeth for emphasis. "You know my words are true, you saw what I did to the rapist back in your village. I will gladly kill such men wherever I find them, but first I must find them." He looked at each man, and, once he was certain he had their attention, Cutter continued, "I believe in the fighting spirit inside each and every one of you. We'll operate in three fire teams, as planned. First, we have to sweep the parts of the Outer City where HVTs might be hiding, if they were trapped there when the attack began. We'll cross the bridge and meet up with Moorefield's people and take up firing positions in those houses to the right of the road."

"The ones with the fields to their east?" asked Riidono.

"Yes. From there, we'll augment Moorefield's firepower as needed. Then we'll leapfrog forward. Fire Teams One and Two, you stay with me at that point. Fire Team Three, you follow Sergeant Riidono and occupy those first buildings on the left. They're about two hundred feet further north, and there's a blind spot where we can't give supporting fire. More of Moorefield's men are holding the road near the gate to the Inner City, but there aren't many of them and we could draw fire from any direction, so be on your toes."

Sergeant Riidono held up a hand to interrupt. "Won't that slow us down, sir, if we try to run on our toes?"

Cutter blinked. In 1944, he would have chewed out the wise guy, both for interrupting him and for making such a stupid joke. But it was two hundred years later, on a world he previously couldn't have conceived existed, and so he laughed. He couldn't help himself. All of the pent-up nervous tension came out in a few seconds of laughing so hard it hurt. Some of his men laughed with him, but most just looked confused.

"It's just a saying, Sergeant, an expression that means be alert."

"Oh. Thank you. I am sorry, Captain."

Cutter chuckled and wiped away tears. "Don't be. I haven't laughed in a long time. All right; any more questions?" Nobody spoke, and Cutter's smile fell away. "Remember what those people did to your friends and family. Go find your shevfashli, and if anybody shoots at you, kill 'em."

Like every soldier he'd ever known, Cutter dreaded the first moment of exposure to enemy fire. Old clips of Doughboys going over the top in World War One invariably included one where the first man to show his face toppled back into the trench after being stitched with machine gun fire. Given that image, it amazed him that anybody would ever be first, yet, as leader of more than a dozen combat virgins, he had no choice except to provide exactly that suicidal example. "Lead and they will follow" was what he'd been taught, and he prayed it held true with his new group.

It did.

Cutter didn't wait to see if his men followed as he climbed out of the draw. He jogged toward the bridge some forty yards distant. A broad river valley with shallow banks fifty yards across held sluggish water filling less than half that width. The worsening drought and rising heat leeched moisture from both soil and river like a parasite draining its host of blood. Built of heavy stone to withstand high and rushing water, Cutter eyed the bridge supports for cover in case he drew fire.

Despite the plan to keep the population inside the city until they could be screened by his men, Moorefield didn't have enough troops to accomplish such a goal. In twos and threes, people ran from the outlying homes toward the bridge, mostly women and children. Upon spying Cutter and his platoon, they veered to either side and crossed the river on foot. Instinct warned him to watch out.

"Sergeant, leave six men with me and take the rest forward as planned."

Although never having fought in a military unit before, Riidono had fought in plenty of life-or-death battles. Without hesitation, he named six men to join Cutter, who deployed them along both sides of the bridge, their guns trained on the fleeing citizens. It wasn't a second too soon.

There were knots of women, tightly packed, at a distance of about thirty yards. At a cry, they all fell to the ground, revealing several men with rifles trained on Cutter's group.

"Fire!" Cutter cried and squeezed the trigger of his Thompson. Holding the weapon firm, he put three rounds into a stocky man who was slow to aim, and knocked him backward. Holding the trigger down, he emptied the magazine into the other three militiamen as rounds from his platoon ripped into them. Screaming women scooped up crying children and fled in all directions, but no more shots came their way.

He turned around and spotted two militiamen running down the riverbank, too far away for his sub-machine gun. Two more lay in the mud near the river, one groaning and rolling in pain. That's when he noticed one of his own men half-hanging over the bridge, face down. Blood soaked the back of his face wraps. When his friends pulled him back onto the stone, Cutter saw a bullet hole over his right eye. Images of dead men flashed through his mind, Americans from his platoon and other units, Germans, French civilians; death was death, and it didn't care who you were. Now he'd gotten another man killed.

In that moment, though, something changed inside him. Although a volunteer for the US Army, he'd never wanted to bring death to anyone. But that seemed to be his destiny, and, if it was, then he'd kill, and if somebody shot him while he stood in the open, then so be it.

After instructing his men to join Sergeant Riidono, he descended onto the river flats and stalked toward the wounded militiaman, his boots sucking up and dropping clumps of mud. Stinging insects swarmed his face, so he pulled the covering over his nose and shaded his eyes from the glare of sunlight off the stagnant water.

The wounded man saw him coming and reached for his weapon, clawing in the pebbles and mud for a rifle too far away to reach. Blood stained the front of his robe, the red sharply brighter than the dark maroon of his face paint. Seeing he couldn't get his rifle, the man dragged himself toward the water, leaving a smear of blood on the shore.

He got within three feet of the river when Cutter stepped on the back of his right leg, near the ankle. Standing on the joint, Cutter heard bones snap and the man screamed in pain. Using the toe of his boot, Cutter rolled the man onto his back and stuck the gun barrel against his forehead.

"Don't kill him!" cried a voice from behind.

Craning his neck, Cutter spotted Riidono trotting toward him, leading three other men. Squinting against the sunlight, he waited while the sergeant inspected the dead men wearing the same paint. Moments later Riidono joined him.

"These are J'Stull," he said. "Men of the satrap."

"Do you know that because of their paint?"

Riidono nodded. The dying J'Stull—and he clearly *was* dying—held up his hands, pleading. But whether he was pleading for help or a quick death Cutter couldn't say. The man tried to speak, but coughed blood after every breath, and while Cutter spoke the local language fluently, he didn't know it well enough to make out the garbled words.

"Yes, that is their color. Do you see the two small blue dots over his left eye? That is the mark of his standing."

"Is he important?"

"In your army he would be an officer. Not a high officer, but not a common soldier, either."

"Like me." Cutter pressed harder on the gun. "Ask him where they took your healer."

"I am unsure if he knows, Lieutenant."

"You'll never know unless you ask. And make it snappy; this guy won't last much longer."

The sergeant's eyes reflected his thoughts. Riidono didn't ask what snappy meant, or why Cutter wanted him to interrogate the prisoner. After asking if the J'Stull soldier knew of an important woman brought captive to the city, the man surprised Riidono by answering yes, he had heard about it from a friend who went on the raid. "They took her somewhere into the tunnels," the sergeant translated, "but he doesn't know where."

"Is he holding out on us?"

"I believe him, if that is what you mean. He knows death is near and fears condemnation of his spirit."

"Ask him about important people who might be in the city."

Riidono did so and had to lean close to hear the response. Coughing out the words, he sprayed the sergeant's face with his blood, until his breath weakened too much for it to do more than bubble on his lips. The rise and fall of his chest slowed and finally stopped.

"It was difficult to understand him, but, if I heard correctly, there are three men of importance he knows about. One he names Waornaak, who he described as an important militia leader who is known to beat women. Another is a militia leader named Zeesar, who is also the F'ahdn's yuzbazzi. He said Zeesar skulks about the city listening to conversations for the F'ahdn, or so he believed. The last is Yukannak, the silci for the satrap, which means he speaks for the satrap. We will know him by his elaborate gold and silver paint."

"Why gold and silver?"

"They are hard to obtain and cost much."

Even after the man died, Cutter continued to stare at him. In his mind he saw the aftermath of a different battle, one in the hedgerows of France in 1944. A twisted corpse lay beside a narrow road overhung with tree branches, wearing the unique camouflage of a Waffen-SS *panzergrenadier*. A helmet nearby was marked at the left temple with a swastika, and by the SS *Sigrunen* on the right. He was little more than a boy, a teenager of sixteen or seventeen who'd never known any leader other than Hitler. Cutter wanted to hate him but couldn't.

"Captain? Did you hear me?"

"Mmm…?"

"Shouldn't we tell Lieutenant Tanavuna of these names, particularly since they match those relayed by Lieutenant Turan?"

"Eh?" Cutter shook off his reverie. "Yeah, sure, let's do so."

Chapter Thirty-Four

Winds atop the plateau filled the air with dust and bits of dried vegetation. For Tanavuna's men, it was a daily occurrence, and they knew how to deal with it. The younger men formed a semi-circle facing away from the gusts, using their bodies as shields for the older men who formed a second semi-circle. All of them had pulled up their face coverings to protect their eyes until the gusts died down.

As the fighting tapered off in the city below, Tanavuna couldn't sit still. Instead, he paced, frequently asking Major Moorefield's radio man if Captain Cutter had called. The man answered "no" every time and pointed out that a call from the platoon leader would probably come using the platoon's radios.

Kesteluni's spirit called to the young hetman; he could *feel* her nearby, and he knew that if he dashed down the stairway into the maze of tunnels dug into the plateau, his men would follow. His impulse was to do just that. Waiting as part of a coordinated effort was not how his people reacted when danger threatened. But Major Moorefield had warned, during the briefing on his part in the mission, that charging into an unknown combat environment would only get his men killed; he needed to let the assault troops open the way first. So instead, Tanavuna paced, waited, and cursed.

The smell of burnt gunpowder on the breeze, combined with the sounds of battle echoing through the stairs leading down into the rock of the plateau, did nothing to alleviate Tanavuna's worry. If anything, it made it worse. He had decided to lead his men into the tunnels anyway, orders be damned, when Captain Cutter finally called.

"Desperado Six's team has done all they can, Shadow Five," Cutter said. Tanavuna heard tension in his voice. "They've secured all known exits from the city and pushed forward as far as practical. Opposition is disorganized and temporarily suppressed. Desperado Six is sending a runner to lead you to our forward positions.

"He will show you the entrances from the plateau that command believes lead to the Inner City. In addition to the breach in the wall, there are a few other potential entry points. Use them or not; it's up to you. Not all are secured, and we can't say what's waiting on the other side. Have you devised a plan of entry?"

Tanavuna hesitated. Six months of intensive training in the Offworlders' way of war had been enough to instill more than basic small unit tactics, but there was still so much to learn. He didn't dare admit he only knew one way to go about his mission: go with all of your men and overwhelm the enemy. Except that wouldn't really work in a system of tunnels and passages against an unknown number of enemies. Only then did his desire to rescue Kesteluni dampen enough for him to realize what was expected of him.

Even though Cutter wasn't physically there to witness his nervousness, Tanavuna licked his lips before answering. "I had thought to charge through the tunnel, but the enemy would expect us to do that." He waved away the tiny insects buzzing near his eyes. "So, I will do as I do when hunting for meat. I will send Sergeant Brakkel down with Second Squad to move through the main tunnel from the place of plants and keep the J'Stull focused on what they expect to see. Third Squad can enter through one of the secured points along the wall that allows us to move to the parts of the Inner City that are built closest to the wall of the plateau. From there, I hope to come upon the rear of any enemies holding the tunnel. I will go with Third Squad. That will let us search more area for Kesteluni and the persons of interest."

"If the enemy is running away, don't stop him."

"I understand, Shadow Six."

Cutter started to say something else, but then waited through a burst of gunfire before resuming. "I have intelligence for you on the HVTs, but remember that the lives of two dozen men are in your hands. They are willing to die for you, and some probably will; don't waste them."

"I would never do that. They are my friends, my family."

"No, Shadow Five, not anymore, they're not. Now they're your soldiers, the men you lead into battle knowing they won't all come back. Trust your training."

Tanavuna nodded. "Yes, sir."

Cutter passed along everything he'd learned about the PoIs and other possible HVTs and said he'd continue to move north through the Outer City with First Squad. They would spread out in a mutually supporting skirmish line, at best speed, theoretically capturing any persons of interest or pushing them toward the Inner City where Tanavuna's men could capture them, or they'd be forced to surrender to Moorefield's forces.

"And you agree to my plan of action, sir?"

"You're the man on the spot, Shadow Five, and I trust your judgement. Do what you think is best."

"Thank you, sir."

"The only men you owe thanks are those following you into battle, Shadow Five. Shadow Six out."

Major Moorefield's guide found Tanavuna atop the plateau overlooking the cache site, along with a handful of men deployed there as an observation point. He directed Sergeant Brakkel and Second Squad to the stairs leading down into the triangular draw filled with medicinals and other materiel, and from there to the tunnel which led into Imsurmik and the homes of the wealthy. The guide was an Ashbander but his habits and the way he wore his robes suggested he was from a larger village. The appraising glances he directed at the men from Nuthhurfipiko weren't entirely friendly. Conflict between villages over scarce resources was common, and grudges might last for generations.

Tanavuna turned to get his own men moving when he overheard one of Moorefield's men speaking with another.

"What did you just say?" Tanavuna asked, whirling to face the man.

"Sir, I—"

"What did you say?"

"I said we found tire tracks north of the city, and it was strange because they stopped without going anywhere."

"Show me!"

Sergeant Brakkel was already descending the stairwell cut into the plateau, with Second Squad right behind him. Sergeant Scussian was about to follow the guide down to the breached wall. On hearing Tanavuna's command, he stopped and turned back.

"Lieutenant, doesn't Major Moorefield expect you to join him in the Inner City right away?"

Tanavuna squinted, thinking. Scussian was right; those were his mission orders from Major Moorefield, but he needed to pursue any clue as to Kesteluni's whereabouts. Maybe those tire tracks were nothing. It wasn't much to go on, after all, and changing the mission plan based on hope and instinct went against all of his training. Yet he also knew that he was going to do exactly that. He also had an excuse—a thin one, it was true—but an excuse all the same.

"We were ordered to find alternative exits that might be used by PoIs to escape, and I was given discretion in doing that. Find Major Moorefield and tell him I'm taking three men with me." He pointed out two of the older men, Ammaii and Kuun, plus Kuun's younger brother, Unaa. "Take the rest of Third Squad and reinforce Second Squad. Brief Captain Cutter on the situation but wait until I've been gone for ten minutes. Until you link up with Major Moorefield, you're in tactical command. If these tire tracks amount to nothing, I'll join you soon."

Scussian's expression showed that he wanted to argue, but he didn't; Tanavuna had a reputation for fairness and patience…unless you argued with him. The sergeant nodded.

"Take me to this place with the tracks," Tanavuna said to Moorefield's man. "And be fast; time is not our friend."

"I've got a small truck, Lieutenant, but I should ask Major Moorefield first…"

"I will accept the responsibility." The muzzle of his M14 shifted slightly in the man's direction. "Now show me this place!"

Standing in the powered vehicle, Tanavuna gripped a rail as it bumped across the plateau. He and his men scanned for any sign of wheel tracks. By that point, Sergeant Brakkel had to be well into the tunnel and moving toward Imsurmik underground. Part of Tanavuna still thought it was a mission he should have been leading instead of putting it off on his two sergeants. Either of them could have investigated the mysterious tire tracks...*should* have investigated them, not the only officer on the spot.

Yet wheel tracks to nowhere had to be explored; those were his orders. He had said nothing about the feeling that it would lead him to Kesteluni because, despite his agreement to carry out the primary mission first, he couldn't bring himself to pass up a chance to find her. It was selfish, reckless, and dangerous, but—in the moment—he didn't care.

"We will get her back," Ammaii said. Even with his face wrapped against the blistering sunlight, the deep-cut lines in the man's forehead showed his age. He'd been a close friend of Tanavuna's father. "I've known Kesteluni since she was a baby, and I'll die before I let these scavengers have her."

Kuun, never a talkative sort, nodded in agreement, as did Unaa and Tanavuna; more words weren't necessary.

"There," said Moorefield's man, pointing ahead. As soon as the vehicle stopped, Tanavuna jumped out. Trotting near the tracks, he motioned for the others to stay back. He walked back and forth parallel to the ruts in the dirt but always a few yards away from them. Then he waved his men forward.

"Many have passed here on foot, and their tracks end where the wheel tracks do. They came from the airship towers—" he pointed behind them, "—and several days have passed since these prints were made. There must be a way underground. Look for some type of door."

Kuun found it within a minute and signaled them over. Ropes ran under the dirt and were affixed to a scrub tree as camouflage. Brown leaves clung to its dead branches, but under the punishing suns it was only one among thousands. Seconds later, they had the door's seams outlined clearly in the dirt, but from thirty feet away, it was invisible.

Tanavuna followed the tracks leading to the trap door ten paces to the west, from the direction of Nuthhurfipiko. Shading his eyes, he could make out the trail for more than a mile.

"They brought Kesteluni this way," he said with conviction that brooked no argument. "We will find her through this door."

Moorefield's man ran back to the vehicle to inform the major of their discovery and to get further orders. Tanavuna already had the orders he needed, though: investigate any additional ways into the city. For a brief flash, he wondered if the order had originated with Murphy or Cutter, and if it was Cutter, whether the captain had foreseen the situation confronting him. His mind shifted back to action.

"How do we get in?" asked Ammaii. "We have no explosives powerful enough to blast it open."

"No, we do not." One thing Cutter had emphasized throughout his leadership training was that logic and calmness always prevailed in stressful situations. Leaders who gave in to emotion invariably failed in their missions. Tanavuna had always been quick to anger and fast to act, but he realized in that moment that Cutter was right; he needed to stay calm and think. Sure enough, it worked; he called back to Moorefield's man. "Do you have any rope?"

"No, sir!"

"A heavy staff or rod?"

The man paused, rummaged in the short cargo bed, and trotted back holding a metal shaft an inch in diameter and three feet long. One end was beveled and the other had snapped off cleanly into a flat end.

"Will this do, Lieutenant? It's a broken strut. But, sir, Major Moorefield says to secure the exit and wait for reinforcements before making entry."

"Did he say how long before they get here?"

"No, sir. But I would guess a half hour, maybe more."

"Acknowledged."

"Sir, he sounded—"

"I heard you!" Tanavuna exclaimed. Then he repeated one of Cutter's favorite lessons, "But guesses are not the basis for sound decisions."

The irony didn't go unnoticed that he had guessed the tire tracks might lead to Kesteluni, and then reversed the axiom for his own advantage. But the moment for worrying about such contradictions had passed.

Driven by the intensity of his instinct that Kesteluni was near, Tanavuna stalked to the door with an air that dared anyone to try and stop him. He knelt and probed the dirt with his fingers. He found the seam and felt the wooden slats, gauging their thickness at roughly two inches. As he'd assumed, it was much too heavy for a few men to lift. He inserted the beveled end of the broken strut into the seam, dug where the door met the frame, and gouged out a notch for leverage. Once done, he pried it open with the help of Ammaii, Kuun, and Unaa—enough to slide the butt of his M14 into the gap to keep it from closing.

Dropping to his belly, Tanavuna peered through the crack into the darkness. The narrow shaft of sunlight gave just enough illumination to show a ramp of stone slanting downward. Getting to his knees, Tanavuna called for Moorefield's man and the vehicle driver to join them. Reluctantly, they did.

Between them they rolled a small boulder into place beside the trap door. All five men then strained to lift the massive wooden platform, sweat pouring down their faces and turning the dirt on their hands into mud. When it was just over a foot above its frame, Tanavuna and Unaa shoved the boulder into place to prop it open.

They all leaned away and bent over, hands on knees, gulping the hot air. Despite his urgency, Tanavuna gave them a long moment to recover. Then, grabbing his rifle, he lay down next to the low opening.

"Tell the major we're going inside," he said to Moorefield's man. Sliding sideways, he disappeared into the shadows.

Chapter Thirty-Five

Yukannak stumbled out of the shattered doorway, barely avoiding the whinaalani's swishing tail. Bracing against the wall with his right hand, he ran toward the tunnels, glancing over his shoulder in case the beast followed.

He twisted his head toward the gunfire coming from behind the buildings to his left, so he didn't notice a man who appeared from the direction of the waterfall, raised a rifle, and fired. The bullet tugged at the collar of his robe. Only then did he realize the nearness of death in almost every direction.

Yukannak ducked left down an alley, hoping there were no more soldiers waiting for him at the other end. A second bullet zipped through the space he'd just vacated. The narrow passage opened onto a plaza, where he paused to get his bearings. Screaming people were running for doorways as militia men fired at unseen targets. A young woman fell as a bullet struck her in the back. She rolled and came to a stop at Yukannak's feet; the spreading puddle of blood leaked between the cracks in the paving stones. Lifeless eyes stared up into his.

Bullets ripped into the wall beside his head. For the briefest instant, he froze, then he flinched away from the spray of sharp slivers. At his back was the same rifleman, still trying to kill him. Out of options, Yukannak sprinted across the plaza toward the relative safety of the tunnels.

The hardest part for Cutter was letting First Squad do its job. He wanted to go first, to take the biggest risk himself so they would stay safe. Having already lost a man brought memories of France into his mind's eye, and he would rather substitute his own death for one of theirs. But he was the platoon commander, and taking all that risk personally was not only bad leadership, it was selfish. So, he held back as the point man moved deeper into the streets of the Outer City.

They advanced with two fire teams forward and Cutter leading four men as a reserve. Scattered fires, smashed vendors' carts, and empty shell casings were clear evidence of the fighting. Patches of dark blood didn't bother him or his own men, though. He'd seen plenty of gore in Normandy, and living on R'Bak meant dealing with violent death on a daily basis—usually from animals, but not always—and the indigs didn't give it a second thought.

Throughout the Outer City, clusters of adobe-and-stone shanties, some with roofs of wood or animal hide, huddled around communal wells. Bodies littered the narrow passages that served as streets, which reminded Cutter of St. Lô, France, after the savage fighting in July, 1944. Most were very young or very old, trampled in the panicked rush for safety when the shooting started. A few showed gunshot wounds, and the front of a dead fruit hawker's robe showed powder burns; the close-range kill was evidence that some of the militia were already using the chaos to plunder.

The Outer City had a pattern; the densest parts were centered on community wells, with the cleared plazas around them serving as gathering spots for gossip, trade, romance, and general socializing. Positioned in houses along the way—if the ramshackle structures could be called houses—Moorefield's men held the road itself as a path through enemy territory. Beyond them, however, Cutter and his men were on their own.

With only fifteen men, including him, it would take days to conduct a thorough house-to-house search, and experience showed there was nothing more dangerous in urban fighting than entering a house without using explosives to clear the entry. If you couldn't toss a grenade through the window or go in shooting, you ran the risk of the enemy cutting you down in the doorway. He'd lost more than one man that way in France.

They were almost halfway to the gate that led to the Inner City when automatic weapons opened up along a narrow street that was clogged with garbage and debris. Ahead, the men of First Squad moved toward a two-story building with a half-collapsed roof, returning fire while moving in stages from cover to cover. Cutter and his four men covered the doorways that might conceal enemies, following the advancing men in case an enemy waited for them to pass so he could shoot them in the back. It was standard procedure, drilled into his platoon over and over again on the hot fields during their training, and it paid off almost immediately. A man in a dirty robe wearing the mustard yellow paint of a commoner leaped out of a doorway, raised his rifle to aim between Sergeant Riidono's shoulder blades…and then jerked as Cutter poured a burst of .45 rounds into his torso. Tumbling back, the weapon fell at his feet, and the man slid down the house's exterior wall and slumped over. Screams came from inside the house.

A second, smaller figure rushed out, picked up the dropped rifle, and began firing in Cutter's general direction. He knew right away it was a child, and tried to tell his men not to shoot, but, in the confusion of the firefight, they couldn't hear him. Blossoms of red appeared on his little chest as the heavy bullets hammered him back into the dark from which he had emerged—just as a third person tried to exit. Much larger, this person tripped over the toppling body and fell face down in the street.

"Blue paint, blue paint!" yelled the man next to Cutter, pointing. On impulse, Cutter ran forward, his Thompson trained on the man wearing blue paint. Gunfire from a nearby building struck the stones behind him, ricocheting with angry whines. The figure in the doorway got to his knees as, continuing forward, Cutter lowered his shoulder and hit him under the chin, like he'd done to the tackling dummy back in high school. Driving him back, Cutter glimpsed a full beard and drove the man into the floor. Cutter swiped the butt of his rifle across the man's cheek, then swiveled it down to cover a knot of people huddling in the shadows. Dust swirled in shafts of sunlight pouring through holes in the roof, and he saw several children cowering against their mother.

"You've killed two of my children!" she said with a half shriek, half sob. "Leave me the rest, master; leave me the rest!"

Panting, Cutter swallowed and licked his lips. He'd come close to firing first and identifying his target afterward, which was never a bad idea in enemy territory. At least, that's what he'd told his men in France, where innocent victims were part of the price for liberation. Now he wasn't so sure.

Cutter couldn't think about how close he'd come to killing the woman and her children, not now and probably not ever. Instead, he grabbed the stunned man with the blue mask and dragged him to the doorway, where one of Cutter's men stood guard as he'd been trained.

"Hitler's Buzzsaw is knocked out," the man said, sounding much like a GI in 1944, his M14 never wavering from the terrified family inside the hovel. After Cutter had described the German MG 42 machine gun around the campfire one night, his platoon referred to every automatic weapon as Hitler's Buzzsaw.

"They're harmless," Cutter said, nodding backward at the mother and children.

"I mean no offense, sir, but these are my people. None of them are harmless."

"Who is this guy?" Cutter said, shoving the quaking man with the blue mask forward. "The blue means he's a militia leader, right?"

Sergeant Riidono had come back to rejoin them and heard the question. His reply held a palpable level of contempt. "It means his village supports the F'ahdn, and he will report on people who speak out against him."

"I get it," Cutter said. He pulled the man close. The blue paint obscured the lines and creases that were emotional giveaways, but no amount of paint could hide the terror in the man's brown eyes. Through clenched teeth, Cutter substituted English words for those he hadn't yet learned in the local language. "We called scumbags like this 'snitches,' and I hate snitches. The Nazis had 'em all over the place." His men all nodded, more at the vehemence of his voice than truly understanding his words. "And just like the cowards back on Earth, this bastard sends his children out to fight in his place. If

I could kill you where you stand, mister, I'd do it and enjoy every second of it."

"I'll do it for you sir," said Riidono, with an intensity uncharacteristic for the usually laconic non-com.

"His people are your enemies?"

Riidono nodded, never taking his eyes off their captive.

"No, sergeant, like it or not, this piece of shit is the reason we're here. Assign two men to get him to the rear, and hand him over to Moorefield's rear security element as a prisoner and possible HVT. Then double-time it back. We're pressing on."

"Yes, sir!" Riidono said.

"Sergeant, you are to hand over a fully *intact* prisoner."

Riidono's glee deflated into a slump-shouldered scowl.

"Yes, sir."

Tanavuna squeezed through the opening between the trap door and the dusty ground of the plateau. Once inside, the stone beneath his fingertips felt rough and pitted, not smooth. It fell away at a sharp but not severe downward angle into the dimness. At the foot of the ramp, there was a sort of landing, but the illumination wasn't bright enough for him to make out details. Between him and there lay deep shadow.

Kuun came next and clicked on his flashlight. Tanavuna immediately reached out to block the beam.

"Don't alert them we've found their secret entrance," he whispered.

Kuun clicked it off as Ammaii and Unaa joined them. The slope forced them to lean backward as they moved down. That threw off their balance enough so they couldn't keep their rifles trained ahead; if someone spotted them and started shooting, it would get bad in a hurry.

Creeping down, Tanavuna's main concern was keeping silent. With solid rock walls on either side, even their breathing sounded loud, and he imagined gunmen taking aim at them from the foot of the ramp. Instinct told him to run to the bottom as fast as he could, and six months earlier that's what he would have done…and it would likely have gotten them all killed.

Approaching the bottom, they heard voices from somewhere out of sight. The chamber at the bottom of the ramp came into focus: a large area cut from the solid stone. Twenty feet above the floor, Tanavuna and his men descended past the level of the chamber roof and the walls to either side ended. Lighting was a combination of lanterns, torches, and what appeared to be sunlight cunningly directed into the chamber from above.

Pausing, Tanavuna motioned his men to crouch as he studied the area. No sounds of battle penetrated so deep underground, which allowed him to trace the voices to their source. Various vehicles parked around the chamber confused him at first, but soon he spied one upon which two men were working. If they knew a fight was happening in the city, they didn't show it.

Numerous tunnels led off in different directions, some big enough for vehicles, some not. Orienting his team's position as best he could, Tanavuna judged the far left tunnel to the east was the large one that reportedly led to the cache of medicinals as well as the houses of the wealthy. He'd never actually been inside the tunnel, but he had seen its mouth from the Inner City several times. Four tunnels directly ahead ran to the south, toward the Inner City. The one far to his right, however, headed west, and he knew of nothing in that direction.

Using hand signals, he motioned for his men to follow and take out the mechanics working on the vehicles. They made it to the chamber floor without being heard.

Tanavuna froze. From his left he heard new voices, growing louder. They ducked behind a large vehicle missing two wheels and crouched down to wait for whoever was coming.

Chapter Thirty-Six

Sweat dripped from Yukannak's chin onto the mosaic floor of the house where he'd taken refuge. Early in his brief stay in Imsurmik, Zeesar had introduced him to the merchant who lived there, but with his face uncovered and unpainted, and wearing a plain robe, the man not only refused to believe he was the silci, but also shunned him and ran into the depths of his home. The higher social classes of Imsurmik not only wore cloth or masks as protection from sunlight, they also considered an uncovered face a grave social mistake.

Yukannak didn't care about that now; the only thing on his mind was getting into the main tunnel and finding the archive. There was no way to know whether the Offworlders were raiding the town or conquering it, but it didn't really matter; the archive would be a valuable bargaining chip. For all he knew, the Offworlders would kill a Kulsian or emissary of the satrap on sight. Even if they left, he still faced possible discovery by the Kulsians—with its potentially fatal consequences—or being caught up in the power struggle between the F'ahdn and the satrap. But if the Offworlders stayed, turning over such an asset would prove his seriousness about defecting. Whatever was in the archive had to have a special value, otherwise why hide it?

Fighting around the waterfall, gate, and wall had died down but not ended. Gunshots still rang out from both the Outer and Inner Cities. Without his identifying paint, he might alternately be thought too insignificant to shoot, an Offworlder to be killed on sight, or a target for anyone trigger-happy enough to shoot the first target to come along. Judging it better not to seem hostile, he returned his pistol to its holster. Closed shutters obscured the events outside the house, so all he could do was listen and wait for silence.

His patience didn't last long, however. His pulse pounding in his ears, Yukannak decided he couldn't wait any longer, and he threw the door open, turned right, and sprinted toward the tunnel mouth one hundred feet away. A knot of men rummaging through an overturned vendor's cart saw him and opened fire for no reason. Kicking his knees higher and fueled by adrenaline, he ran faster than he'd run his entire life. Whether the men intended to kill him or were shooting to chase him away, it backfired. As Yukannak disappeared behind a house, behind him he heard the staccato sound of a submachine gun, followed by explosions and screams.

Between the last house on the street and the tunnel mouth lay fifty feet of open ground. To the right of the tunnel was the viewing platform where he'd first learned of the archive…but people running through a combat zone tended to attract attention, and he did.

A voice from the direction of the waterfall called out, "Stop! You there, stop running."

Instinct told him soldiers would be better shots than militiamen, and he managed to dodge left an instant before he heard the *crack* of a gun. He went right, followed by another left, and then he was into the tunnel. His burning lungs begged for oxygen but he didn't slow down until he passed two of Subitorni's J'Stull guards. Normally, an unadorned man would not be allowed into the tunnel without a challenge, since it was the realm of the powerful and wealthy. With Offworlders assaulting the city, though, one man with no standing and no weapon represented no threat.

Few people were abroad now. The wealthy had shut their doors, and the militia and J'Stull soldiers were caught up defending the city. The few people he saw weren't walking, and desperation drove him to shout about the hyshvass as they ran past. Nobody responded. He kept moving forward.

Echoing gunfire caused him to turn back to the tunnel mouth, now several hundred yards behind him. Several figures ran past, dark against the blinding light, but the gunfire didn't come from them. Then he heard it again and realized it was coming from further inside the plateau, near the cross-tunnel leading to the cache site. That could only mean the Offworlders were attacking from the site itself, and that they'd already seized the medicinals.

Logically, the archive was highly likely to be somewhere near the entrance they'd brought him through: secret entrance, secret archive. If it wasn't there, it could be anywhere, and he didn't know the city well enough for a blind search. Now, though, if the Offworlders fought through to the main tunnel before he could get past it, he'd be taken prisoner with nothing to trade. They might even ransom him back to the satrap or the Kulsians.

Nearby voices rose above the sounds of battle. He looked up and saw a knot of figures near the tunnel. Winded, he paused. A series of muzzle flashes suddenly lit the faces and uniforms of Subitorni's J'Stull forces, followed by the hollow echoes of their reports. Single shots followed: the distinctive sound of a pistol to make sure the victims were dead. Subitorni and his men ran into the passage leading to the underground parking area, the same place Yukannak was headed.

Yukannak redoubled his effort and ran after Subitorni. There was enough light to see the bodies were those of an entire family: four children, a mother, and the heavy-set father. All wore well-made garments and shoes, but none wore paint; the attack had come too early for masks to have been applied for the day. That made it easy for Yukannak to see the black patch on the man's left cheek, the telltale disfigurement of the Bleeding Black.

The dead man was the F'ahdn.

He fought the impulse to turn down the tunnel toward the cache site and surrender to the Offworlders. With bullets filling the passageway in both directions, simply running past the opening was dangerous enough. Instead, he put his head down and ran so fast that he stumbled, hoping no bullets would find him.

Cutter called for a short rest, and his squad deployed around a small plaza centered on a well. Under Sergeant Riidono's eye, they formed a perimeter defense. After half an hour of moving through the Outer City, Cutter had stopped worrying whether Riidono could handle being a combat sergeant. Some men were natural non-coms, and he was one of them.

Like the rest of the Outer City, shattered pottery crunched underfoot in the plaza, particularly near the well itself. Discarded clothing and bodies—already bloating in the heat—lay scattered in irregular heaps. The unmistakable reek of a nearby sewer hung heavy in the air, and Cutter pitied the people who smelled that every day of their lives.

The angle of the sun had shifted enough that a small patch of shade was created by the buildings near the square's northern side. Cutter knelt there, trying to avoid gulping the hot air, not only because it hurt to breathe too deeply, but also to keep his men from seeing the extent of the mental strain with which he was already dealing. Draining the last drops from his canteen, Cutter nodded at the well.

"Think the water's potable?" he asked the radioman.

"Sir?"

"Is it safe to drink?"

"I'll find out."

"No—"

The young man, Suukamanu, was the second youngest in the whole platoon. He set his radio aside and sprang toward the well. Everybody else was under cover. They'd cleared the area, but Cutter's brain rejected that reassurance. Instead, it offered images from a tiny French village where a German sniper hit two of his men long after they thought the village secure. Unable to stop Suukamanu, he brought his Thompson up to the ready position and scanned their surroundings.

He sensed movement in the periphery of his left eye. The corpse of a shriveled old woman, her throat sliced open so deeply it had nearly decapitated her, inched upward. Cutter squinted against the glare and caught a brief glint of sunlight off dark metal. Some part of his brain identified it as a rifle barrel even before the thought was fully formed. He swung the Thompson around but the hidden gunman fired at the same instant he did.

Suukamanu staggered under the impact of the big slug, and his legs locked in place for almost two seconds before he collapsed like a sack.

Cutter's initial three-round burst ripped into the body of the old woman the gunman was using for cover, and at least one penetrated enough to hit him. The man rolled over, howling. Cutter pushed to his feet and covered the twenty feet between them in four strides. Behind a dirty face wrap, the man's eyes met Cutter's as he tried to bring his rifle to bear. Cutter kicked it away, then slammed the toe of his boot into the shooter's jaw, and put a final burst into his chest. Shooting him in the throat would have been more satisfying, but a ricochet off the stone plaza flooring was not something he could risk; any over-penetrating bullets had no place to go but straight back into the body.

Oddly, as the life drained out of the man's eyes, the vicious satisfaction Cutter had felt when killing the Waffen-SS wasn't there. The man may not have been a supporter of the F'ahdn at all; he might simply have been defending his home. Even if he *had* served the F'ahdn and satrap, it was likely the only life he'd ever known. On R'Bak, those autocrats represented order in his life, and Cutter was the invader. Sure, the Lost Soldiers were trying to help these people throw off the yoke of servitude to those who stripped them of their greatest wealth, the planet's medicinals, but how could the dead man have known that?

"Suukamanu's dead," Sergeant Riidono said. "He didn't feel it."

Cutter stood over the gunman's body, feeling the sun burning the back of his hands and didn't answer right away. If he knew how to do anything well, it was to kill, but keeping men alive was a different story. "Spread the word: new procedure. From here on, check every body—man, woman, or child—to make sure they're dead."

"And if they're not?"

"If they're unarmed, tell 'em to get lost."

"What if they've got a gun?"

"Kill 'em."

"Sir?"

Whatever his motivation, the gunman who killed Suukamanu had been the enemy, and living enemies could only be given two choices, surrender or death. Any trace of compassion vanished from Cutter's mind, so the determined scowl he gave Riidono underscored the absolute certainty in his voice. "This is close quarters urban combat, Sergeant. Hesitation gets men killed. I've lost two men today; I don't intend to lose any more. We can't guess *why* people might conceal a weapon; we can only operate on the assumption they mean to use it against us. Don't let 'em."

Riidono swallowed hard. Cutter's platoon had never seen his true ruthless side, the genuine version that only emerged during combat. "I understand, Captain. I'll spread the word."

Chapter Thirty-Seven

After they double-checked all the bodies within their perimeter, First Squad refilled their canteens from the well. The surrounding wall was made of rough, waist-high stones, fitted with the usual overhead crank-and-bucket to bring water to the surface. Leaning over to see how deep the water might be, Cutter noticed rusty iron rings set into the stone: probably to simplify descending to retrieve dropped items, particularly pollutants. What surprised him was the circular lattice grill about twenty feet down, with a central opening for the bucket to pass through. Perhaps it was to catch things like dead animals—or incautious children—that fell down the shaft.

"Militia headed this way!" called a sentry from a narrow alley on the plaza's western side.

"I need a number!" replied Sergeant Riidono before Cutter could ask the same question.

"Ten or more, and they heard me. They're fifty feet from my position."

"Same here," yelled another sentry, this one located a hundred feet down a wide street to the south. "At least a dozen armed men. One is wearing red paint, and the others have a red mark down their noses."

"Red paint?" Cutter asked Riidono. "Another tribe?"

"Yes, sir. Just like blue paint: it means a militia leader favored by the F'ahdn. They get special privileges and a share in the harvest in return for their loyalty and support. People know to leave them alone. To use your words, the one with the red paint is another high value target."

Cutter had seconds to consider the tactical situation. Earlier, they had discussed the possibility of sending men onto the roofs, both for a firing advantage and to keep the enemy from doing the same thing. The problem was their unfamiliarity with the buildings they were moving through. On Earth, Cutter would have called the Outer City a slum, and the houses shanties or shacks, even though they were partly made from stone. Only a few had a second story, and many had collapsed walls from a lack of quality mortar. The roofs were in even worse shape and couldn't be trusted to support a man's weight.

"Is that militia from Imsurmik?" Cutter asked.

"No, sir. The F'ahdn doesn't like having too many armed men in the Inner City that are not his own. That's why this militia is restricted to the Outer City and why there aren't that many J'Stull; the F'ahdn fears a revolt. He trusts no one and sees enemies everywhere."

"Good. That means they don't know the ground any better than we do," Cutter said. "Or which roofs might hold a man's weight. That makes it a two-dimensional fight."

"I don't—"

Cutter held up a hand. "The main assault will come from there," he said, pointing to a broad street running north toward the wall of the Inner City. "We've already got fire teams in place against incursions from the south and west. Deploy the third fire team to block that north road, and use the other three men there, at the eastern exit, to cover our retreat."

"Are you sure, Captain?" Riidono peered over his shoulder at the empty road to the north. A shot came from the western attack group.

"Moorefield's men hold the road along the wall, and that gives the enemy too little room to assemble for an attack. Moorefield's men would see them and engage. That's why they're trying to drive us north, probably into an ambush they've set between us and the wall. When we don't bite, they'll move on the plaza. Hold your positions as long as possible, then retreat in stages to the east."

"What about you, sir?"

Cutter changed the magazine and charged the Thompson. "I'll be in the well."

Behind him, Yukannak heard the sounds of battle approaching the intersection of the cache tunnel and the main one. Zeesar had told him the entrance to the archive might be in the cache tunnel, but exploring that option had now been overtaken by events. He had no choice but to follow his own instincts about where it might be.

Ahead, he heard the growl of an engine starting. Although the light was bright enough to read by, at a distance of three hundred yards he could barely make out Subitorni and his men piling into a large vehicle and then heading into the tunnel to the north. During his arrival, Yukannak hadn't noted how far he had traveled down the tunnel before reaching his quarters. It hadn't been relevant then. Now, tired and on foot, it was very relevant. It was a long, long way.

A stitch in his side grew with each breath. How far could the passage possibly go? The original passage might have been carved by natural forces, but widening and squaring such an immense space must have taken thousands of people and many years. Here and there, narrow side tunnels branched off, and he reckoned they all led to the network of tunnels rumored to run throughout the region, perhaps even to the rumored escape passage. None was large enough for a vehicle, though. Yukannak had a growing suspicion that Subitorni not only knew where and what the archive was, but, with the F'ahdn dead, he was planning to take it for himself and escape through the secret entrance. That realization leant new speed to Yukannak's steps.

Eventually, the tunnel turned sharply to the left. About two hundred yards ahead, he saw the glow from the large room he remembered, the one with the vehicles in it, and he slowed. Subitorni might turn out to be an ally, or he might simply kill the silci on sight. The worst case was if the Kulsians had discovered his crime and sent out a capture order. There was just no way to know, so it was better for him to hide, listen, and wait.

Tanavuna, Ammaii, Unaa, and Kuun lay on the cool stone floor, watching from under one of the powered vehicles Captain Cutter called a "truck" as a similar one rumbled past and stopped near a pair of large double doors set into the western wall. Nine men climbed out of the truck's bed, and it surprised Tanavuna to see they wore not the red, blue, green, or purple paint of the four major militias who served the F'ahdn, but instead had the white paint of the J'Stull guards. He was further surprised when Kuun elbowed him and pointed to Subitorni, the local J'Stull commander. That changed everything.

Why was the J'Stull commander down here when the city was under attack? He should have been leading the defense against Major Moorefield's assault teams. Was the F'ahdn down there, receiving treatment…perhaps from Kesteluni? No answer made sense except that they were protecting the city's leader.

Subitorni's presence made Tanavuna's decision to investigate the entrance look like a shrewd tactical move instead of disregarding orders. Other than the F'ahdn himself or the Kulsian rumored to be in the city, the J'Stull commander was the very definition of a PoI. And for him personally, the raid on Nuthhurfipiko had all the marks of a J'Stull operation, including the use of trucks. That meant Subitorni had not only approved it, he had likely also planned it, participated in it, and was directly responsible for the murder of his father and all the others. For that, Subitorni deserved death. Instant, terrible death. But Tanavuna could not obey that reflex; in addition to remaining focused on his mission objective, if anybody knew where Kesteluni was being held, it would be Subitorni.

Once the last of the J'Stull passed through the open doors, Tanavuna and his men advanced until they were twenty feet from the two men talking in the truck's bed. Based on their lack of face paint and the smears of dirt and lubricants on their skin and clothing, they rarely went to the surface. He made out snatches of their conversation but became alert when one spoke about the beautiful black-haired healer; that could only be his wife. With rifles shouldered and aimed at the two mechanics, he, Kuun, and Ammaii walked forward in a skirmish line, ready to shoot.

Across the room from Yukannak, Subitorni's vehicle had backed up to a wide doorway in the western wall before its engine was shut off. The J'Stull commander was surrounded by his men, giving them orders Yukannak couldn't hear. He'd even pulled the mechanics over, making it clear he needed their muscle to load something. Two men climbed into the vehicle's open bed while the rest disappeared through the doorway.

With their backs to him, Yukannak intended to slip past the ramp and hide behind the vehicles parked against the wall on his left, most of which were in various stages of repair. Crouching in the shadows, he rose to run for cover but detected movement to his right. He stopped and crouched.

Four men dressed like tribal militia flitted between the carts and vehicles on the far side of the ramp, moving toward the door through which Subitorni had disappeared. Yukannak shrank further back into the shadows.

Chapter Thirty-Eight

The two mechanics glanced up at Tanavuna and his men, at first with eyebrows raised in a gesture of unspoken question, then in narrowed squints at the rifles aimed their way.

"Speak one word, and you're both dead," Tanavuna said. "You have a choice, either point out rope and a cloth to bind you with, or I'll have to cut your throats." Both mechanics raised their hands and climbed down. Minutes later they were tied and sitting in a corner.

Tanavuna stood before the double doors, and a quick peek inside showed stairs going down, with no way of knowing how deep they went. All he could think about was Kesteluni at the mercy of the J'Stull, so rather than wait for someone to return he took half a step into the darkness with his rifle pointed ahead.

Kuun's hand stopped him. "We can't afford to lose you," the man whispered, without explaining if he was referring to his role as lieutenant or hetman. Not waiting for Tanavuna to respond, Kuun led the way down, his brother close behind.

The tribals caught the two men in the vehicle bed by surprise, motioned them to a corner, and tied and gagged them. After checking the mechanics' bonds, the militiamen followed Subitorni into the darkness.

Yukannak ran for the far side of the now-empty cavern. High above, at the head of the ramp, a slit of sunlight showed how the invaders had gotten in, probably after finding the trap door from the wheel tracks. One thing the Kulsians and J'Stull knew about the Offworlders was that they were professionals, not amateurs like the forces allied with the satrap. Hiding a secret entrance was a brilliant idea, but showing its exact location by leaving wheel tracks was utter stupidity.

He reached a vehicle near the darkened rectangle of the doorway. Leaning with his back to the front tire, Yukannak tried to slow his breathing so he could hear anything coming from inside.

Tanavuna and his men remained close to the wall, courting the few shadows they could find. Lanterns set at intervals along the walls shed wan light on the steps, with illumination at the bottom coming from rooms or passages to either side. The stairs were rough-hewn and wide enough for firm footing but with worn indents that could trip the unwary. A tumble might well prove fatal, even without the J'Stull waiting below. Tanavuna had taken eight steps down when Kuun sped downward to the small landing at the bottom and wheeled right, M14 leveled at his waist. Unaa took a hasty step to follow, but Tanavuna grabbed the back of his robe.

"Who are you?" somebody yelled. Kuun sent a stream of fire in that direction. Tanavuna now understood why he was holding the weapon tucked against his hip; firing an M14 at full automatic from the shoulder made it impossible to keep on target, no matter how good you were. The 7.62mm rounds packed a heavy punch, but the tradeoff was a strong recoil that threw off aim, particularly at anything more than a steady, semi-automatic rate of fire. Captain Cutter had repeatedly emphasized that the only time it made sense to use full-automatic was to spray a small area where it was hard to miss, or to drive the enemy to ground.

"Let me go!" Unaa yelled, but Tanavuna held on. Return fire ripped into Kuun before they had a chance to move. Racing to his aid would have brought them directly into that storm of bullets.

Bleeding from a dozen hits, Kuun somehow remained standing and kept firing. When his first magazine ran dry, he took three seconds to swap out magazines and, staggering, started firing again. Brass casings clinked on the floor. The gunshots echoed like thunder in the stairwell, and the air stank of burnt gunpowder. Return fire from inside the room blended into a cacophony that made it impossible to tell one shot from the next. Kuun's body jerked both from holding the gun and being ripped apart by bullets. Blood sprayed the walls and turned the front of his robe crimson.

When the second magazine was empty, the dying man waved the others back up the stairwell. He met the eyes of his sobbing brother and waved again. Incredibly, even as more bullets hit him, Kuun clicked a third magazine into place and held the trigger down. When the last bullet left the chamber, he finally slumped sideways.

Tanavuna was only halfway from the bottom when Subitorni stepped into view, pistol extended toward the dying tribesman. He shot Kuun once in the head. Tanavuna raised his rifle but a second J'Stull came up behind Subitorni, saw them, and started shooting.

Tanavuna dragged Unaa back up the stairs, bullets zipping off the walls with at least one hitting a step and ricocheting back down the stairwell. A loud grunt indicated it struck J'Stull flesh, and no more shots followed them out. By a miracle, they got back to the top without injury.

Tanavuna pressed himself against the left side of the opening, while Unaa and Ammaii did the same on the right. They aimed their rifles through the doorway and fired several rounds in case the J'Stull tried to follow them up.

"You should have let me kill them!" Unaa said, between heaves that were half gasps and half sobs. "I could have—"

Tanavuna cut him off. "He is beyond our help now. We will honor him later. Now we must find a way to get back down there."

"They must have to come back this way to leave," Ammaii said.

Tanavuna was about to risk a glance below when a voice caught his attention.

"There may be another way out."

"Who said that? Where are you?"

"I am behind the vehicle to your right. I am armed, so please do not try to attack me. I am not your enemy, but I *will* defend myself."

"If you are not our enemy, why are you hidden?"

"Forgive me, but merely because *I* know that I'm not your enemy, does not mean that you will agree."

Tanavuna held his rifle steady but had to admit the man's words made sense.

"What did you mean there could be another way out?" Ammaii said. "Are there more tunnels below?"

"There are tunnels throughout this plateau and this region. Some are naturally made, some are not. The water which runs through the wall around the Inner City is said to come from a spring that flows beneath us, and I do know there are other tunnels down there. They might connect to passages leading out of the city."

"I cannot make a plan based on mights and maybes," Tanavuna said.

"I know not why you are here," the voice said. "But we may have common cause."

Tanavuna had heard enough to notice the stranger's accent was distinct from natives of the region. Amaii started to say something, but the young hetman waved him to silence. "Perhaps we do have some common interests. Tell us your name."

"I am Yukannak."

Of all the names Tanavuna expected to hear, that was the most surprising. "The silci for the satrap?"

"He is me, and I am him." He spoke the words in a different dialect, one that somehow added weight to them. "But I am more than that; I am Kulsian."

"That is…why should I believe you?"

"Why should you not?"

That stopped Tanavuna cold. *Why shouldn't he?* The bizarre nature of the encounter lent credence to it being the truth…unless it was a trap. But if that were so, why alert them to his presence? Yukannak, if that's really who he was, could have just shot them.

"And what do we have to offer the silci?" Tanavuna said, trying to stretch out the conversation for time to think.

"Sanctuary."

"Sanctuary," Yukannak said. He knew better than to drag out the parley.

"How can I give you sanctuary? There are only three of us."

"You are with the Offworlders. I wish to join them."

"You're a defector?"

Relying upon the clarity of insight that had kept him alive for so many years—years when others died because they couldn't maintain the delicate balance of lies required for survival in Kulsian power-politics—Yukannak knew that whatever he said to these three now could be rationalized later. "Yes, I am a defector."

"Come out, then, but make no sudden moves; I will not hesitate to kill you."

Yukannak emerged with his hands raised, and he kept a close watch on their faces. Their suspicious expressions confused him until he remembered that he wore no paint and only a simple, unadorned robe intended for use in his private quarters. Nor were his boots of the quality expected from the satrap's silci. "Do not judge me by my appearance; I was asleep when your attack began."

"You look like a beggar, not a friend of the satrap. Tell me something to convince me you are who you say you are."

"The F'ahdn is dead."

"That might or might not be true; I have no way of knowing." The gun barrel inched sideways to point at Yukannak's chest. He instinctively sensed that the time for keeping his options open had come to a close. He had to choose now or risk being shot.

"The man below is Subitorni, commander of the J'Stull contingent in Imsurmik. He killed the F'ahdn, with the intention of replacing him."

"Get over here," the obvious leader of the three men said. Once against the wall, Yukannak was instructed to sit with his legs crossed and hands behind his head. "I know who Subitorni is. It sounds to me like Subitorni would be our ally."

The speaker was immediately to his left, blocking his view of the other man on the far side of the door, but Yukannak didn't need to see him to know that when he started to speak and was cut off by his leader, there were lies in that statement.

"Then kill me now," Yukannak said, playing the gambit he knew would be necessary at some point. He hoped his voice was steady. "If you know that, you must also know about the hyshvass…and the rest of it."

The leader didn't try to conceal his surprise. In the tangled world of the Kulsians, where nothing was ever as it seemed, such an honest reaction would have been viewed with suspicion. But such practiced duplicity had no place among the militias of the Greens and the Ashbands, where trust was considered the most valuable currency.

"What is this hyshvass?" the militia leader asked.

One of the other men leaned into the doorway and squeezed off two rounds. The leader looked at him over his shoulder and lifted an eyebrow in an unspoken question.

"Just in case," the man answered.

"It is a very old word for an archive. I only heard of it recently," Yukannak said. "The person who spoke of it is dead now, but he had no more knowledge than the term and that it was located somewhere down in these tunnels. Since then, I have thought much of what it could be, and, in truth, I came here looking for it. Your attack on the city was my chance to roam without being seen."

"If you're silci for the satrap, why didn't you ask the F'ahdn?"

"The F'ahdn has kept this secret from the satrap for a reason. If I asked about it—"

"He'd have cut your pretty throat."

"Or worse. Do you have a name?"

"I am Lieutenant Tanavuna, hetman of Nuthhurfipiko."

"Why do *you* seek this archive?"

"I seek my wife, not this archive. My village was attacked by the J'Stull, and she was taken. I believe Subitorni has her or knows where she is being kept. What does this word mean?"

"It is not a common word in your language, but in mine, which is closer to the original Ktoran, it means a protected or special collection of objects. Most often books or other records."

"Records of what?"

"I do not know. That is what I came here to discover. So, the Offworlders attacked Imsurmik to get your wife back?"

Tanavuna inhaled three times before answering. "No. My mission is to capture persons of interest in Imsurmik."

"And have you found any?"

"I just did."

Sounds of movement came out of the stairwell. Tanavuna nodded at Ammaii, but Unaa jumped toward the entrance first, determined to avenge his brother. The older man caught him with one hand and threw him back, then he and Tanavuna pivoted; each fired two rounds into the darkness. Cursing rewarded their effort, but that didn't get Tanavuna any closer to the bottom, or to Kesteluni. Rushing down the stairs would likely get them all killed. What they needed were explosives, and Major Moorefield could probably supply them. But the same explosions that would surely kill the J'Stull might also kill Kesteluni, assuming she was down there.

Nor was it a standoff. If Tanavuna's sense of direction hadn't failed him, the tunnels opening into the chamber from the south led toward the Outer City, and the man who claimed to be the silci said there were more, farther below. There might be another way to reach the foot of the stairs using a different tunnel, but Unaa, Ammaii, and he were too small and vulnerable a team to leave the stairs and roam in search of possible tunnels on the chance they might find one that brought them to the complex below. If Subitorni probed the staircase again, he'd find it undefended. He'd slip away with Kesteluni, and Tanavuna would never know it. Cutter might have encountered something similar during his first war, but he wasn't there to offer words of experience to Tanavuna.

Then there was the matter of what to do with Yukannak. The handheld radio hadn't worked since they'd gone underground. According to the mission instructions, he should leave the chamber and deliver the silci to Cutter or Moorefield immediately. But that would mean abandoning any chance of rescuing his wife, if Kesteluni was down those stairs. And that was unacceptable. So that left only one alternative.

He turned sharply to face Unaa. "You shall escort this man to the nearest friendly unit. There you will turn him over to the ranking soldier and report the existence of the entrance and all the tunnels we have passed through in coming here."

"No!" the younger man yelled, his neck veins distending. "I am not going! I mean to kill those who killed Kuun!"

Tanavuna's patience only went so far when someone challenged his authority. As the hetman's son, he had learned from an early age the difference between empathy and weakness. Had the doorway not stood between them, with a J'Stull possibly standing at the bottom with a rifle aimed on the opening, he would have thrown Unaa against the wall. As it was, he let the anger loose in his voice.

"What you are *going* to do is obey your hetman and superior officer! Because of your youth and the death of Kuun, I will overlook your insubordination, but I will not do so again. You *will* obey my orders, otherwise I will consider it a personal challenge. Is that what you wish?"

A personal challenge to the hetman was not simply a private matter; it was a statement of the challenger's intent to replace the hetman, and it meant a fight to the death.

Unaa bowed his head, sullen. "No."

"Good. This matter is over and forgotten." Tanavuna turned to the stranger. "Listen carefully, Yukannak. I must get word to my commander about this unknown passage and the J'Stull who are trying to escape, but we cannot hold this staircase with less than two. You will go with Unaa. As you can see, he would like to shoot anyone who is allied with those who killed his brother. Should you attempt to escape, he will be under orders to shoot you. He will shoot to kill. Do you understand?"

"Yes," the silci answered. "I will not betray you."

Tanavuna ignored him. “More of our men should be in the tunnel coming from the cache site. Unaa, once you have delivered this man safely, find one of the sergeants and tell him to come right away with his whole squad. Then find Captain Cutter. It is likely he is still in the Outer City or at least near the wall.”

“Cutter. That is a strange name,” Yukannak said.

“That is not your concern. Unaa, brief the captain on our situation and tell him he must move to block any tunnels on the southern wall of the plateau that exit to the Outer City. Those may be escape routes.”

Unaa turned away, but Tanavuna could hear the scowl in his voice when he said, “Yes, sir.”

“Good. Go now.”

Unaa circled behind the closest truck to avoid showing himself in the doorway, then they took off, moving quickly. The muzzle of Unaa’s M14 never left Yukannak’s back.

“Now,” Tanavuna said, turning to Ammaii, “let’s figure out how to get down there.”

Ammaii nodded thoughtfully. “I believe I have an idea.”

Chapter Thirty-Nine

Ammaii backed along the wall to get a running start and was past the doorway in two steps. No bullets came for him. He stalked toward the two mechanics they had bound. He stopped beside a pile of small barrels stacked against one wall. He touched a smudge near a plug on one of them and rubbed the oily compound between his fingers to smell it. He wiped the residue on his robe, approached the mechanics, and crouched to remove the cloth stuffed into the mouth of the nearest one. Tanavuna watched as best he could, while listening for anyone coming up the stairs.

"Is that the fuel for your vehicles?" Ammaii said in a voice loud enough for Tanavuna to hear.

The older mechanic had gray in his eyebrows and deep lines in his forehead, but the one he'd spoken to was little more than a boy, probably an apprentice. In answer to the question, he shook his head, eyes wide with fear.

"Is it used by the J'Stull to make things burn?"

"Y-yes."

"Have you a fire-making kit?"

"Over there," the boy said, pointing with his head. "In that chest."

The older man glowered at him as Ammaii replaced the boy's gag and retrieved the ignition kit, a long cloth, and one of the barrels. On his way back to the doorway, he grinned at them.

"What is this?" Tanavuna said.

Ammaii worked as he spoke, rolling the cloth into a long, thin cord. "Do you remember when I was fifteen and the J'Stull captured some of us, thinking we were marauders?"

"Of course, I went with Father to look for you."

"I was still a prisoner of the J'Stull when they found the camp of the real marauders. They'd taken refuge in a rocky place that was proof against gunfire. Not even explosives could get them out. So the J'Stull brought out two small barrels exactly like this one, with the same markings."

Kneeling beside the barrel, Ammaii used the butt of his knife to knock out the plug. Then, coiling the cloth, he pushed it halfway into the liquid within the barrel. "They inserted a cloth, lit it like a fuse, and rolled the barrel into the rocks. It burst into a huge ball of flame and dripped through cracks but burned out fast. Afterward, the marauders looked like grilled meat.

"Once the cloth is burning, I will go halfway down the stairs, and throw the barrel to the bottom, where it will burst into flame. As it falls, I will run back out, and when the flames have died down enough, we will run back down, kill any J'Stull still alive, and rescue the shevfashli."

"Captain Cutter told me of something like this, but much smaller. What did he call it? A motov tail, I think."

"It is simple but effective, and by using it we *will* rescue the shevfashli."

Tanavuna laid his hand on Ammaii's shoulder. "You've known Kesteluni all your life, my friend. She was Kesteluni to you long before she was the shevfashli."

"All the more reason to save her, then."

"It is far too dangerous for me to allow it, for you and for her. If she is really down there, the flames could consume her."

"You are not thinking straight, Tanavuna. They are not aware that Kesteluni is your wife, so they will not hold her safety as a threat against you. Indeed—and I am sad to say it—if the F'ahdn is truly dead, and Subitorni is in revolt, then he has no reason to have kept her alive this long." He held up his hand, stopping Tanavuna's retort. "But if she *does* yet live, he must have a reason, and so it only makes sense that he would keep her safe, away from our bullets. And so, this fire as well. And if that does not convince you, then maybe this will: I see no other choice."

"This is far too dangerous. Let us instead throw the container together, and then go down as the flames begin to die down."

Ammaii opened his mouth to argue further but stopped when a voice echoed up from below.

"You, at the top of the stairs, this is Subitorni of the J'Stull. I have no reason to harm you, but we are coming up. If you continue to shoot, I will kill you. I have fifty men at the ready."

"We have more than enough bullets for your men, commander."

"Do I know you?"

"No, but you soon will."

"Let us pass. This is my last warning."

Striking a spark from the kit, Ammaii lit the cloth and hefted the barrel. "And here is *our* final word!" he said, moving through the doorway onto the stairs.

"No!" Tanavuna yelled. He tried to grab Ammaii but was a moment too late.

Although Ammaii had planned to rush down the steps, he appeared to slip on one of the step's slick surfaces, and he slowed. The flame had only gone halfway down the cloth when shots struck the barrel, spilling fuel all over Ammaii's robe. A draft from below carried fumes to Tanavuna's nose seconds before the burning cloth ignited the barrel's spilled contents.

Ammaii had a brief moment where he could have dropped the barrel and stripped off his burning clothes. Maybe it would have exploded at his feet, maybe it would have rolled to the bottom first. But he didn't drop the barrel, not yet. Transfixed with horror, Tanavuna watched as the living flame that was his friend Ammaii hurried down the steps, absorbing shot after shot until he finally leapt forward at the bottom.

The fuel exploded with a *whoosh* that propelled a furious geyser of flame halfway up the stairwell.

For a moment, time froze for Tanavuna. There was only the fire, the screams, and the acrid smell of the burning liquid. But, within seconds, the flames subsided enough for him to charge after Ammaii, the M14 recoiling into his shoulder as he fired round after round down the stairs. Frenzied howls reverberated off the stone, and he recognized them as his own. Sparks in the darkness marked ricochets, and he stopped firing.

The wrap on his face helped against the smoke and fumes. With all the fuel consumed, only flickers remained, dancing atop the bodies piled at the landing, now blackened as their robes burned. One of them was Ammaii. There wasn't time or need to check for signs of life; his friend was dead, just like his father and Kuun and all the rest. Nor could he grieve or wonder why they had to die—why any of the violence had been necessary—not in that moment, at least. He still had to find his wife.

As the smoke started to clear, he spied a tunnel to his left. It ran directly south and was wide enough for two men to walk abreast. With no light that way, he couldn't see far, but he assumed it led to other branches, levels, and probably back to the surface. On the right was another doorway which led into a square, lantern-lit room with three more openings, all leading in different directions. More J'Stull corpses lay twisted on the floor, their burned limbs drawn up, their fingers bent like claws. The silence of the dead blanketed the area and seemed to muffle his quick, gasped breaths.

He tried to concentrate on what to do next. Enemies could be concealed just beyond any of the doorways but so could Kesteluni. He backed into the corner on his left, putting a wall behind him, but also moving away from his escape route back up the stairs. Expecting a sudden attack out of the dark, he heard, or thought he heard, a whimper through the left doorway, only a few feet from where he stood.

Driven by the thought of his wife suffering at the hands of the J'Stull commander, Tanavuna moved into the passage with the M14 held at his waist, finger beside the trigger but not on it; he would rather die than risk shooting his beloved by accident. Instead of a room, though, he came to a short flight of stairs leading down. Beyond the last riser, a wan light poured from a room. Careful to make no sound, Tanavuna crept to the bottom and gaped at what he saw.

A vast rectangular chamber stretched away for at least one hundred feet. He estimated the walls to either side were at least thirty feet away. Hewn from the living rock, support columns ran in three parallel rows down the room's length. The room was lit by tall candles in metal holders, and the area stank of tallow. Beyond the light of the candles, deep shadows obscured details. None of that was what stunned him, however.

Every inch of wall space was covered with shelves crammed with binders of paper and parchment, scrolls, stone tablets, pots of various sizes, and dried plant stalks. Thousands and thousands of items spilled onto the floor. Picking up a page near his right foot, Tanavuna felt the rough texture of animal skin and frowned at the characters, diagrams, and illustrations that crowded to all four edges of the smooth side.

Being the hetman's son, he'd been taught to read, but most of the words were foreign to him. Nevertheless, he could make out enough to determine that it was about the effects of some medicinal plant. Nearby, stacks of square stone tablets harkened back to an earlier time, with barely legible letters chipped into them, probably by a hammer and chisel.

A sniffle in the distance made him drop into a crouch, his rifle aimed down the center of the room. He saw a faint light some fifty or sixty feet away. Against its glow, he could make out a partial silhouette. As he crept closer and panned the gun in a semi-circle, Tanavuna watched as the gradual increase in light imparted more detail to the dark outline, ultimately revealing it to be the face of an old woman, her skin bleached nearly white as only long years out of the sun could do. A bony hand held a writing stick, which she dipped in water and scratched upon an ink block before writing on a long roll of parchment. She was shrunken, like he'd seen the sun do to mummified corpses, and she hadn't noticed him yet.

She sat at a table inside a cage with heavy iron bars. A hole in a corner of the floor must have been the privy. The only other furniture was a crude wooden bed with a blanket. Ominously, two identical but empty cages were positioned on either side of it, one of which had a blanket on the floor and its table and chair overturned.

"Hello?" he called out.

The old woman looked up, squinted, and went back to writing.

He came closer. "Who are you, grandmother?"

"What? Who's there? I don't recognize the voice."

"My name is Tanavuna. What is yours?"

"My what?"

"Your name."

"Oh…my name. I had a name once, yes, you're right I did. Let me see…Paaku-something."

Tanavuna stood without realizing it, more shocked than he had been at the sight of the room.

"Paakunami? Is that your name?"

"Hmmm…yes; yes, that was it. Paakunami. Good, that's good, I'm glad to remember that."

"But…you disappeared thirty-five years ago from a village east of the city. We have all heard the story; all of us in the region. You were thought to have been taken by a predator while out gathering medicines."

"Was I? Thirty-five years, you say? Well, no matter, I am here now." Putting her nose an inch from the parchment, she went back to working.

"Was there a young woman here last night?" he asked, voice rising in urgency, "Tall, with black hair and brown eyes?" Now that the shock of finding the room and the old healer was wearing off, his sense of urgency returned, stronger than ever. Tanavuna thought he could *smell* his wife's scent.

Paakunami peered at him, annoyed. "What woman?"

"She would have been in there," he said, pointing to the cage beside her.

"Oh…her. Woke me up with her screaming when Subitorni came for her."

"When?" In the urgency of the moment, he raised the M14 as a threat, but the hag showed no fear. He doubted she could see it.

"I don't know; was I supposed to remember that?"

Realizing he'd gotten all he could from the woman, Tanavuna whirled and ran back up the stairs…just in time to hear the faint echo of a woman's voice from the hallway beyond the staircase leading to the upper chamber.

"Help me!"

It was Kesteluni.

Chapter Forty

Yukannak's footsteps rang through the empty tunnel. At Unaa's prodding, he tried to force himself to run, but a lifetime of relative ease had not prepared him for so much physical exertion in one day. Nevertheless, the determination that had kept him alive when so many others died served him well now. Unaa had a mad look in his eyes, and Yukannak didn't doubt the young tribesman would welcome having a reason to kill him. So, even when a tight spasm of pain began knotting his side like contracting metal, he kept moving toward the main tunnel. Once there, they turned south toward the Inner City.

He stumbled as they approached the cross-tunnel leading to the cache set aside for the Harvesters. The aftermath of battle littered the passage. Two men lay dead in each other's grip, having been shot mid-grapple. Unaa's face tightened when he recognized a man from his village. He had his thumbs in the eyes of a militiaman wearing yellow and green paint. That man's corpse still gripped the knife buried in his enemy's stomach. Bloody drag marks led to bodies piled against the wall where they had been moved out of the way. Men who'd been living minutes earlier were now nothing more than meat.

But the fighting wasn't over. Yukannak dropped to the floor as bullets whined off the wall near his head. Was somebody targeting *him*?

No, not at him, but at figures crouching in the shadows ahead. Yukannak glimpsed the situation in the light of muzzle flashes. Deployed on either side of the tunnel, maybe a dozen men armed with the same kind of rifle that Unaa carried were firing toward the Inner City. They were either Offworlders or allied with them. Near the tunnel mouth, a clutch of the satrap's militia fired back. Unaa stood and called out to the nearest group, waving his rifle overhead...and then toppled backward under a hail of rifle fire. The impetuous youth never took another breath.

Unaa's death cry alerted his apparent comrades to their presence, but when they turned around, all they saw was Yukannak lying on his belly beside one of their own lying dead in a pool of blood. The safest reaction in such a combat situation was to shoot first and ask questions later, which they did. Bullets sparked off the stone floor and whined as they shot at him. He hid behind Unaa's body—if the young man hadn't already been dead he surely was now—as round after round struck his corpse.

"Stop! I'm a friend!"

More shots.

"I have a message from—"

A ripple of gunfire drowned out his words. The invaders weren't in a mood to listen, and Yukannak had to do something fast or die. There was nothing he wanted to do less than what he planned to do next.

He leapt to his feet and yelled, "Don't shoot, I'm your friend." He ran toward the militiamen at the mouth of the tunnel, waving his arms, with both sides shooting at him and each other.

Yukannak screamed, "Don't shoot, don't shoot! I am the silci!"

Cutter's shoulder ached from hanging inside the well longer than expected. He couldn't help be proud as he'd watched his men deploy according to his orders. He'd trained them well, yet he had no illusions about their holding their position against a determined assault. Imsurmik was jammed with amateur militias who'd spent their lives only fighting each other. Unless they'd tangled with the J'Stull, which certainly wouldn't have gone well for the tribesmen. And Cutter's Cutters were better than the J'Stull, because he'd trained them as if they'd had to fight the enemies he'd fought in the past: some of the toughest, meanest, least scrupulous soldiers in Earth's history. But this time, he feared the militia would press the attack home with their numerical advantage, driven by a force they feared more than any enemies before them—the leader who was behind them.

Yet, in Cutter's experience, the best attacks were made right away, before the enemy had a chance to prepare their defenses. Maybe the apparent reluctance of the militia to launch an assault meant that First Squad might not have to defend the plaza after all.

As if timed to demonstrate the ingenuous optimism of that thought, the enemy rushed the Cutters' positions from both the south and west, supported by a brief sputter of covering fire. Cutter hung from the iron rungs within the well, a dangerous *ruse de guerre*, since one brief glance downward by a passing enemy would discover him in his hidey-hole. If they didn't see him, though, he could hit them when they didn't expect it and disrupt their whole attack. It was a high-risk, high-reward ploy that captains were supposed to assign to others, but he couldn't do that, not this time around. If he died, well, he'd already done that once, so what the hell?

By sheer bad luck, the angle of the sun was now hitting the side of the well where he was clinging to the ladder. When he'd first climbed inside, the heated iron blistered his palms, which made holding onto the ladder even more problematic. Eventually the metal under his hands cooled, but he couldn't move them because the iron around his hands remained scorching hot. And, even though the backs of his hands burned like somebody had focused a magnifying glass on them, all he could do was endure and hang on.

The well distorted the sounds of battle above. From the proximity of shots and screams, it sounded like his men took quite a toll on the attackers and held the line for several minutes. Then he heard Sergeant Riidono yelling for retreat and, as First Squad withdrew from the plaza, calling out, "We are pulling back, Captain, I'll shout 'now' when the enemy is in position."

Good man, Cutter thought. *He's company sergeant material.*

Gunfire swept over the plaza. Voices came from around the well. Hanging by one hand, Cutter braced the Thompson's stock in the crook of his arm and pointed the barrel skyward. If somebody discovered and started firing down at him, well, he wasn't going to die alone. Now that he thought about it, his ruse no longer seemed like such a great plan.

Nobody peeked over the side, though, and the voices grew fainter, passing on.

Riidono shouted, "Now!"

Trusting the sergeant with his life, Cutter stepped up one rung, balanced, leveled the Thompson, and opened fire at the backs of a score of local militia.

Everything about the Thompson, from its weight to the hammering recoil into his shoulder, was like play-wrestling with an old and trusted friend. At a range of thirty feet, the .45 caliber rounds ripped into the backs of the tightly packed enemy. Panicking, those who weren't hit fled in all directions. Right on cue, just as the gun clicked on an empty chamber, his own troops counterattacked and poured back into the plaza, providing him with the cover he needed to climb out of the well.

Heaps of new bodies clogged the area, some still twitching. A quick head count showed only twelve of his men firing at the red militiamen, including Riidono. There was no time to think about that as he regained his footing on the stones. Swapping the empty magazine for a full one, he scanned in all directions and understood the danger of their position. They'd hurt the enemy badly, but the enemy would soon regroup—faster than he'd imagined, as it turned out.

"They are attacking!" someone cried. A quick glance showed enemy troops coming down all three streets at once.

"Pull 'em back, Sergeant," he ordered, pointing to the eastern alley. "Get 'em back to the main road."

Riidono barked orders as Cutter fell back, climbing over corpses to find a good firing position. He crouched behind a smashed wagon and steadied the Thompson on a cargo-bed's rail. He remembered doing the same at a farmhouse near Mortain, chickens squawking as German rounds ate into their coop, holding off a whole platoon long enough for four of his soldiers to run to the safety of the farmhouse. Now he'd do it again.

Once the last of his men ran past, he waited three seconds for the enemy to enter the plaza. They all wore the dull mustard paint of Imsurmik's poorer classes, except with the red stripe from the bridge of the nose down to its tip. Instead of spraying bullets like he'd done the first time, Cutter fired three-round-bursts to pin them down. He changed magazines again and glanced behind him. He saw two of his men thirty feet down the street, kneeling with rifles up to cover his retreat, with two more thirty feet behind *them*. In full combat mode, thought became action, and he ran from behind the wagon, slowing to step over the dead body of an old man clutching a small animal under one arm, also dead.

When he was only halfway to the first of his men, they opened fire, but he didn't look back. He put his head down and ran. He felt the ache of pounding on the unforgiving stone in his knees and feet, although that beat a bullet in the back. Only when he was past the second two-man team did he duck around a corner, sucking in the hot air and gagging on the fetid reek of an open sewer across the road. Half a minute later, Sergeant Riidono and two men ran back from the east, gesturing in the direction where Moorefield's men held the main road.

"We cannot get through that way, Captain. The enemy is forcing women and children to hold hands and block the road while they stand behind and shoot at us. We cannot fire back without hitting the innocents."

"Human shields," Cutter said. A genuine hate began to build in his gut, as it had in France. "Damn…" First Squad had already killed a lot of men, but there could be hundreds more, and while the enemy tactics were crude, they didn't seem to shy away from combat or the threat of dying.

He surveyed his surroundings again, looking for an option he'd overlooked. Even if he had been ruthless enough to gun down the human shields, it would slow them down enough for the red militiamen coming from the west to take them in the rear. The narrow southern street was impassable because part of a house blocked it like a landslide. That only left the north, and

Cutter's intuition told him that way had been left clear for an ambush, as he'd suspected earlier. Nor could he expect help from Moorefield's thinly stretched men at the road; they were under strict orders not to leave their posts, no matter what they heard in the tightly packed warren of Outer City.

"We're trapped, aren't we, sir?" Riidono asked.

Cutter was about to answer "yes," when he saw the answer. "No, Sergeant, we're not trapped. But they might be."

Chapter Forty-One

The street leading north had tightly packed buildings on the western side, opposite a large open sewer pit. A long, wide oval, its surface was not recognizable as water or anything else liquid. Discarded debris clogged the pit, and opportunistic vegetation grew among the clumps of garbage that, over the years, had solidified and composted into something fertile enough to allow plants to flourish.

As he crouched low in that putrid slime, Cutter counted the heads of the twelve surviving members of First Squad protruding from the muck like so much flotsam, their weapons resting on small islands of decayed garbage. The light color of their robes had stood out like a beacon against the mostly dark brown of the open sewer, so the first thing he and his men had done upon wading into the thick slime was to dunk their heads. As nauseating as the experience was, it rendered them invisible to those on the street a mere forty feet away.

They'd heard the red militiamen coming and taken cover under the raw sewage. The people of Imsurmik, having been near it most of their lives, had gotten used to the sight and smell of it, as well as the vermin and insects it attracted. The militiamen who weren't from Imsurmik, and those with enough wealth or influence to live away from the sewers, considered being near them a disgusting circumstance to be avoided, as they would persons of the very lowest class. Nobody, however—not even the people forced to live beside them—would dream of voluntarily immersing themselves in the horrific sludge.

Which is why Cutter and his men did it. They'd trained for it, yes, but he'd never expected to actually have to do it in combat.

Red militiamen filtered into the area, wondering where their quarry could have gone. There weren't as many as Cutter feared, maybe three dozen. After banging on a few nearby doors or rough analogs of them, and listening as the people cowering inside denied harboring outsiders, the man with the red face ordered several of the homes searched. Cutter watched as it happened.

Now, breathing through his nose and fighting the urge to vomit as sewage dripped into his eyes, he waited for the right moment to spring his ambush.

Slowly, so as not to attract attention with fast movements, Cutter rose. First Squad followed, hunched behind what cover they had, and picked up their weapons, careful not to get them dirtier than they already were. The enemy didn't notice. Cutter's robe hung like lead weights on his shoulders, having soaked up the rancid liquid until saturated, but its brown color was the perfect camouflage. When the militia leader only had five men around him, Cutter aimed the Thompson at the one furthest to the left and fired.

Being trapped and outnumbered outweighed any risk of accidentally hitting the militia commander, but Cutter had trained his platoon well. All five targets twitched and fell under a fusillade of bullets while their leader covered his head and crouched against the wall. Slipping out of his robe so it didn't slow him down, Cutter splashed forward in his underwear, the wet sewage blocking the burning UV rays like body paint.

Within seconds, he'd deployed men to cover the road to the north and south, and two men to maintain a watch eastward across the sewer. Cutter grabbed the cowering leader's robe and pulled him to his feet, putting his lips within inches of the other's red-painted face. The dilation of the man's nostrils told Cutter that his reek nauseated the militia leader. *Good.*

"I don't have time for bullshit," he said, using the English word. His men smiled, having heard it so often they knew its meaning, even if the idea of a bull was foreign to them. "Do you want to live, or should I kill you where you stand?"

The man, tubbier than most citizens of Imsurmik, made an attempt to resist. "Do you know who I am?" he said.

"Yeah, another dead guy in the street, unless you do exactly what I tell you. Now answer my question."

"I do not want to die."

"Good answer. Here's what's going to happen." Cutter barely had time to give instructions before the rest of the red militiamen rounded both corners at a dead run. Rifles came up on both sides, but the militia leader called for his men to stop. He was pushed forward with the barrel of Cutter's Thompson under his chin, and he ordered his men to back off and let them pass. Cutter and his squad withdrew east, back toward the main road, guns ready and pointing in all directions

But the militiamen didn't seem eager for any more fighting. As Cutter suspected, once their leader was in custody, they had a good excuse to go back to their lodgings...and stay alive. None even hesitated; as one, they turned around and melted back into the ghetto.

Experience taught Cutter to take nothing for granted in a free fire zone, so they kept their guard up until Moorefield's men spotted them at the intersection with the main road. By then, the brutal sunshine had evaporated all the moisture from the sewage clinging to First Squad's bodies, leaving only a cracked and flaking shell. The stench remained, however, and, while handing over the militia leader, Moorefield's men waved Cutter and his squad back.

"There's a well over there...sir," one of them said, his head half-turned in disgust. Cutter insisted that his unit clean its weapons first, and then allowed the men to take turns standing watch while the others used buckets of water to get off as much of the now-dried muck as possible.

Rinsing off was no substitute for immersion in the river, but they removed enough to once again be tolerable to other human beings. Cutter returned to the main road to discuss getting new robes and was mid-sentence when several of Moorefield's men leveled their rifles at someone running toward them. The man was wearing a simple robe smeared with blood on the left leg, left shoulder, and several places along his side, but he didn't seem badly injured. He wore no paint or face covering, and his skin was not much darker than his white hair. He was ordered to halt, and he did so, bending over, hands on knees, breathing hard.

"I seek a Captain Cutter," he said between gasps.

"Who are you?" Moorefield's guard asked. "Why should we trust you?"

Cutter waved the trooper back, too tired to worry about any tricks. If the newcomer tried something, Moorefield's men would cut him to ribbons. "I'm Cutter. What's it to you?"

The man's eyes shifted, and for the briefest instant Cutter saw doubt there, which wasn't surprising. A stinking, semi-naked man didn't exactly present an image of authority. But the newcomer only hesitated for a moment.

"Lieutenant Tanavuna needs your help. He said there may be tunnel exits to the Outer City against the plateau wall, but for you to bring reinforcements to the main tunnel."

"Is that where he is?"

"No," the newcomer said, shaking his head. "He discovered another exit, and beyond that an archive of some kind, but the J'Stull have it blocked. He said to hurry."

"Can you show me?"

"I can try, but as you see, I am wounded."

"Sir, you can't trust this man," Riidono said. "He's leading you into a trap. Look at him, he's a nobody; I've known Tanavuna all of my life, and he would never send such a man to find you."

"I have to agree," said one of Moorefield's men.

"Tanavuna sent a young man with me, named Unaa. He was killed in the tunnel leading into the plateau from the Inner City."

"You see?" Riidono said, stepping toward the man.

Cutter stopped him with an outstretched hand. "Then how did he know the lieutenant's name, Sergeant? And he'd have to be suicidal to deliver himself to us if he planned betrayal. No, either the enemy has captured Lieutenant Tanavuna, or this man is telling the truth. My gut tells me he's not lying." Holding the Thompson in the crook of his right arm, he turned to face the newcomer. "But be aware, if you *are* lying, you'll be dead before I am."

Oddly, Cutter saw fear in the man's eyes. Based on his overall demeanor, he hadn't expected the threat to have an impact. "What's your name?" he asked.

"I am Yukannak, Captain Cutter."

"You are not an Ashbander," Riidono interjected, with a tone that showed he still had doubts. In the moment, they had all forgotten Moorefield's briefing.

"I am not. Nor from anywhere else on R'Bak."

"You're the Kulsian," Cutter said, not bothering to hide his excitement.

"Yes, Captain. I wish to defect."

Chapter Forty-Two

Tanavuna's mind replayed the faint cry over and over again in his mind, until no doubt remained that it had been Kesteluni who'd cried for help. He'd considered responding, but that would only alert Subitorni that he was being followed. Because he had no doubt it *was* Subitorni who'd taken her. The question he couldn't answer was *why*.

Although the lighting was dim, once his eyes adjusted, occasional skylights in the tunnel allowed Tanavuna to move without fear of stumbling. So far, there had been no pits or traps of any sort. Given the nature of the tunnels, as underground refuges for the worst days of the Sear and unseen escape routes during crises such as this one, the lack of safeguards was no surprise.

However, despite the need to hurry after Subitorni, an inner instinct warned him not to step blindly into a tunnel intersection. It left him conflicted when he came to each one. He would be exposed for ten feet, and even if he were not killed outright, being hit in the leg or foot would allow Subitorni to escape with Kesteluni.

So, he stopped, closed his eyes, and listened.

He heard no voices, but, in the otherwise absolute silence at the third intersection, there came the faint, unmistakable sounds of someone breathing. So, it *was* an ambush, and even if he got past without being shot, there was nothing to stop whoever was waiting around the corner to chase him from behind.

Just then, footsteps came from the direction of the stairs. More than one man, and they were coming his way. Tanavuna turned around, knelt, and took aim. The dim blob of a figure materialized in his sights, becoming sharper as it neared.

Scussian! With three men following behind! Yukannak had kept his word. The sergeant and his men joined him and knelt close. Remembering their training, no one spoke. Tanavuna outlined the tactical situation with hand gestures. Scussian's men nodded their understanding. The sergeant put up two fingers and pointed at Tanavuna, asking *where are the other two?* He mouthed their names: Kuun and Ammaii. Tanavuna cast his eyes down, the custom in his village when referring to the dead.

Scussian was never one to hide his feelings, and Tanavuna saw the anger that came over him. He and Kuun had been close friends; he wanted a chance for vengeance. Tanavuna backed up, slung his M14 over his shoulder, got a running start, and crossed the intersection. At the same time, Scussian ordered suppressing fire, which caught the J'Stull off guard; their shots missed Tanavuna. Shooting continued as Tanavuna ran down the tunnel.

He still could not puzzle out the full meaning of the room with the legendary healer, the stone tablets, and all the dried and preserved healing plants. Kesteluni's original capture made sense if she had been intended to treat the F'ahdn. But he didn't understand why Subitorni was making off with her now: she would only slow him down. So he had to have a reason to keep her alive…but for how long? If he was threatened, would he kill her before fleeing? There was no way to know.

The tunnel twisted back on itself three times and branched off repeatedly. Tanavuna realized that if he stopped at every one to consider his choices, it wouldn't matter if he chose well, Subitorni would be too far ahead to catch. He took only a few seconds to make up his mind, and he gambled on the hope that he was making for an escape tunnel that emerged beyond the city itself. As best he could tell, they had been going generally southeast, so he did the same.

He passed more intersections and several shafts of sunlight, but despite the mostly-level rock underfoot, the overall direction was tending downward, which would be consistent with an escape route that passed well beneath the city and its upper tunnels.

For a man used to the heat on R'Bak's surface, the cool air in the tunnel allowed him to move faster and longer than he usually could. With no way to gauge distance, Tanavuna only knew he'd run a long way.

His doubt grew as he went on with no sign of either Subitorni or Kesteluni. If he'd chosen wrong, he might never see his wife again. But, as the tunnel began to angle sharply upward, he heard the faint sound of water. The stones became slick with condensation and the air heavy with moisture. He had slowed to find niches in which to plant his foot, when a man's voice rang from beyond the lip at the top of the ascending slope.

"Stop that, you bitch!"

"I'm not going with you!" a woman yelled back.

It is Kesteluni! Tanavuna realized, in the same instant that Subitorni yelped in pain. A meaty slap followed.

Tanavuna did not remember slinging his rifle, because his brain had ceased to be guided by rational thought. He scrambled upward, tearing his fingernails as he fought for purchase on the wet rocks. Once at the top, another skylight reflected off water droplets like sunlight off a river. With his eyes adjusted to the underground darkness, a corona of red sparkles filled his vision. He turned away from the sudden brightness—and the stock of his rifle hit the wall with a loud *thunk.*

Through his semi-blindness, Tanavuna saw, no more than forty feet down the passage, Kesteluni lying on her back and kicking at Subitorni. The lower half of his body seemed hidden, but, the noise made by the rifle hitting the wall brought his eyes up, riveted on his pursuer. Kesteluni tilted her head back and for the briefest instant her eyes locked with her husband's.

"Tanavuna!" she cried, reaching out to him.

Tanavuna unslung his rifle and took aim, but that gave Subitorni time to draw a pistol and fire twice. The first shot missed, but the second ripped through the outside of Tanavuna's left arm.

Pain shot into his shoulder and down to his hand. Blood soaked his robe. He fell backward, and the M14 skewed sideways. He dared not shoot for fear of hitting his wife.

Subitorni took his time to aim his third shot, but as he squeezed the trigger, Kesteluni kicked him in the jaw. Now off balance, he toppled backward and fired; the bullet ricocheted off the tunnel ceiling.

Tanavuna ignored the pain in his arm and, with his eyesight still impaired, pushed himself up and staggered to where his wife lay. Subitorni had vanished. Tanavuna knelt beside Kesteluni and, closing his eyes, hugged her. He whispered how much he loved her, how sorry he was that he hadn't been home to keep her safe, and how happy he was to find her again. He wept and felt hot tears on his cheek. Rocking back and forth, he kissed her.

But she didn't kiss him back. His vision cleared, and he saw her unblinking gaze fixed on something beyond the sight of living men. The liquid on his cheek wasn't her tears. It came from the red stain ringing a bullet hole in her forehead, just below the part in her thick black hair. Subitorni's last shot at Tanavuna had been a wild miss…but still, it had struck home.

The faint light from the skylight shimmered on dark water running near at hand. Based on its speed and angle, Tanavuna knew it had to flow down toward the river east of Imsurmik. Rage gave way to despair as some part of his grief-clouded mind realized that Subitorni had escaped…for now. Then the clouds of misery gathered into a black storm and drowned his ability to think at all.

Hours later, Riidono found Tanavuna still holding his dead wife, emotionally spent. He was halfway back to the surface when his anger began to build again. When he finally met with Captain Cutter in the day's fading light, he knew what he wanted to say.

"Permission to go after the man who murdered my wife, sir."

"Not alone, Lieutenant."

"Sir, I—"

"We're all going."

Cutter's Cutters had performed their mission so well that, with Colonel Murphy's permission, Major Moorefield issued supplies for them to go after the escaped J'Stull commander. The escape tunnel emptied into the river east of Imsurmik, and they searched fifteen miles downriver with no trace of Subitorni. The frustration that he had escaped burned not only in Tanavuna's heart, but in his men's as well. When the search was called off, several openly wept. When they no longer had any tears left to shed, they sat together as each man planned how they would exact their personal revenge on Subitorni, if he was caught someday.

In keeping with her beliefs, Kesteluni was buried in a fertile place near the river, covered in the simplest of shrouds. Healers from other villages came to pay their respects, putting medicinal plants on her grave so that her body might nourish them. Even Paakunami, the old woman held captive by the F'ahdn for more than thirty years, attended the ceremony. At the suggestion of Cutter's surviving soldiers, and the families of the nine men lost in the fighting, their dead were buried nearby. With the river receding under the increasing heat, the oldest locals explained that the Sear would likely mummify the bodies until the rains returned, at which point their remains would also feed the plants. Cutter found it comforting.

At nightfall after Kesteluni's burial, Cutter found Tanavuna standing on the bluff overlooking the river. Leaning forward against a waist-high boulder, the indig officer had a panoramic view of the valley below. In the middle of the river stood a line of rocks that, during rainy periods, became white-water rapids. Now only sluggish streams flowed around them.

Tanavuna hadn't reacted to Cutter's approach, so the Lost Soldier stood back and didn't say anything for a while. Tanavuna's eyes roamed the skies in search of something he'd never find, as Cutter knew all too well. He had seen and done the same thing, for the same reasons, a long, long time ago, on a planet far, far away.

"You won't find it out there," he said finally, coming to stand beside Tanavuna. There was no reason to further define "it;" they both knew what he meant. "You won't find it anywhere, because it doesn't exist. Every man I've ever known who survived combat wanted to know the reason for the death and destruction they'd lived through. On my world, we called it survivor's guilt. The answer to why you and I lived—and why Kesteluni, Kuun, Ammaii, and all the rest died—is that there *is* no answer. At least, not one we can understand."

"I don't know what to do next, Captain."

"Call me TD when we're alone."

"What does this TD mean?"

Cutter smiled. "Some would say it's from a sport my people play. Or play*ed*, maybe. I can't say if they still do or not. But that's not actually where it comes from. My full name is Tyree Denning Cutter, so T and D are the initials of my first and middle names in my native language."

"Why do you need three names?"

"I don't know. It's just what my people did."

"What should I do now, TD? Without Kesteluni, my life has no meaning."

"Life always has meaning, my friend. Nobody ever knows how to deal with death, particularly senseless death. But you don't have the time to dwell on that, Tanavuna. You are hetman of Nuthhurfipiko. You must try to make your people whole again, rebuild your own life, and protect your village. But you shall not have to do it alone: you and your men are our brothers now, and Colonel Murphy will not forget you."

Raking his lower teeth over his upper lip, Tanavuna blinked to stop from crying. "I know you are trying to help, but I have no life to rebuild." Lines in the corners of his eyes deepened as his face folded into grief.

It was the opening Cutter needed to prod the young man into joining the leadership cadre Colonel Murphy was building for the growing indig army. He only needed to speak a few well-chosen words to convince Tanavuna. The lieutenant trusted him and would likely take whatever advice he gave.

Which is why Cutter couldn't do it. "Rebuilding is all there is, Tanavuna. It's all you can do."

"No, friend TD, it is not. There *is* another way, another choice." The lines that grief had cut into Tanavuna's lightly weathered skin were suddenly stretched smooth as the hetman's expression changed from sadness to something harder. Anger made the cords of his neck jump into high relief. "I can do as you have done. Did you not fight in your first war to free the…Fench?"

"French."

"Yes, French. Were they your people?"

"No. I am American."

"Yet you and your men fought anyway. I want to fight those who attack my people, and all the other people of R'Bak. We cannot do anything about the Searing, but you have shown us that the forces of the satrap and the J'Stull may be defeated. The F'ahdn of Imsurmik is dead, but the satrap is not, and, while he lives, my people are in danger. All the people of this world are in danger."

"What you're asking will change your life, Tanavuna, so you must be clear about what you want. You must say it. I will not put words in your mouth."

"Then let there be no mistake: I want to become one of you."

Surrounded by a wall of cut-stone blocks, the large village of Seeak occupied the crest of a hill. It overlooked semi-arid plains that were slightly too far south to escape the ravages of the Sear. A deeply rutted road led down the slope, paralleled by a spring-fed stream, both of which ran toward the distant river. The dried stalks of harvested plants filled the fields on both sides of the road, but only churned dirt lined the creek, leaving it barren of plant life.

Tanavuna stood in the cupola of the leading armored personnel carrier, arms folded to project an authority he didn't feel. Jolts from the rutted roadbed made footing unsteady, but the brutal sunlight turned the APC's hull into something akin to a blacksmith's work-in-progress. Touching it left fingertips scorched, so Tanavuna used pressure from his legs to maintain an upright stance.

He avoided staring at the mutilated stream because he knew at first glance what it meant. On previous visits to Seeak, usually leading a trading mission on behalf of his father, Tanavuna had admired the lush medicinals that grew in the wet, rich soil near the stream. Now those priceless plants had not been simply harvested, they had been dug up by the roots. It was an irredeemable loss to the people of Seeak.

Captain Cutter followed in the second APC and Major Moorefield in the third, standing stiffly. That was unusual because, as a commander whose experience was in just such armored fighting vehicles, he usually was very relaxed and loose-jointed when riding them, one hand on the rim of the hatch. But beneath the level of its deck, Tanavuna knew that the major's leg was both bandaged and braced. The Sarmatchani healers attached to his headquarters band—they called it a "company"—had added their ancient arts to the science of the Lost Soldier's medics and had finally pronounced the victorious officer fit for travel.

Which was fortunate since Major Moorefield had been determined to come along for this journey, even before Colonel Murphy suggested it. The major understood that his presence would add a great deal of credibility to what was, in actuality, not just a visit, but a critical recruiting mission. So far only four men of Cutter's Cutters had signed on for long-term duty in the Free Bands of the Hamain. Despite their confidence in Cutter and Tanavuna, it was a major commitment and many had families to care for back home. Consequently, Cutter's Cutters had agreed to tour nearby settlements to talk about their part in the Battle for Imsurmik, but it was no secret that recruiting success in places like Seeak would have a strong bearing on their own final decision whether or not to stay with the Bands.

To that end, Moorefield brought four of his own Lost Soldiers who flanked the column riding whinnies. Nobody on R'Bak had ever seen a whinnie tolerate a human rider before the Offworlders showed up, and Tanavuna assured the major that having them on hand would impress the people of Seeak more than anything else.

Half a mile down slope from the town's main gate, a delegation awaited the convoy. A dozen figures surrounded a bent figure in a clean robe. They all lifted gloved right hands in greeting. Reading expressions in the shadows cast by their hoods wasn't possible, but their uplifted faces and waving hands told Tanavuna they'd already heard about what happened at Imsurmik.

One of the APC's crew passed up a rolled animal skin covering with three holes along one edge. Slipping the holes over three prongs inside the cupola to hold it in place, Tanavuna unraveled the covering down the vehicle's side so he didn't blister his skin climbing down. Jumping the last two feet to the roadbed, puffs of dust hung in the still, hot air. Joined by Cutter and Moorefield, Tanavuna led the group forward to meet the waiting leaders from Seeak. Despite their raised hands, they showed no other signs of being glad to receive the newcomers.

"Are you sure they are glad to see us?" Major Moorefield asked. "I've seen more enthusiastic statues."

Tanavuna nodded. Not yet used to the sarcasm of the Offworlders, he took the comment literally.

"They do us a great honor, major. They show their welcome by meeting us outside the gate. The hetman will now lead us into the walls, both to show the people that we are friends and to chase away any danger in our path."

"So it bodes well for our mission?"

"Yes sir, it does. I believe many men of Seeak will join us."

"Well, hell then," Cutter said, "what are we waiting for?"

PART THREE

Chapter Forty-Three

Mara Lee tilted her head from side to side, rolling her shoulders to try and relax the muscles there. Lately, she'd been spending too much time working at a desk and not enough working out in *Spin One's* surprisingly well-equipped gyms. The tension in her body was a dead giveaway.

"Mara!"

She turned at the sound of Aliza's delighted voice and smiled as the other woman walked down the corridor toward her, spreading her arms wide as she did so. Mara leaned into the hug, giving her friend a squeeze before letting go and stepping to the side so that they could speak without obstructing the other traffic moving toward the refectory in their section of the habitat.

"I didn't expect to see you here," Aliza said. "You've been taking your meals in your office."

"I had to get out," Mara confessed. "I took this last afternoon cycle off and spent the time with Dio and Zenya. Nalyiriz offered to put them to bed, so I decided to see if I could remember how to hang out and relax with friends."

"Ooh! I can help," Aliza said with a smile. She hooked her arm through Mara's and tossed her loose dark hair back over her shoulder as she resumed walking.

Falling into step beside her, Mara breathed, "Good. Because all I really remember is that there should be wine of some kind."

Aliza laughed. "Definitely. I'm not sure the SpinDogs have much in the way of fine vintages, but I'm certain we can come up with something." As they continued down the corridor, Mara began to pick out a few strummed notes underlying the general murmur of conversation echoing back from the refectory.

"What is that?" she asked, tilting her head to the side. "Is it a…guitar?"

"Yes!" Aliza said, excitement threading through her tone. "You have picked a good night to remember fun, Mara. Bobby has been bringing his guitar down for the last few nights, and tonight he and I have something special planned."

"Oh? Is that why it feels like you're vibrating next to me?" she asked, smiling to soften the dry tone of her question.

Aliza laughed and nodded. "I am nervous. Excited, too, but nervous. It has been a long time since I performed for anyone."

"You sing? I mean, I've heard you singing to yourself now and then when you're cleaning or whatever, but I had no idea you actually performed."

"Never professionally." Aliza shrugged slightly, in that self-deprecating manner so common to those of the Lawless born before Mara's own era. "But I have always loved to sing. In Dachau, sometimes, I would sing for the others. It was a tiny bit of joy: our little rebellion of hope, in a way."

"Yeah," Mara said softly. As usual, her mind reeled ever so slightly at how casually Aliza spoke of her experiences. Like every American kid in the nineteen eighties, Mara had read about the horrors of the Holocaust. But Aliza had lived it.

Tough chick.

Mara squeezed her friend's arm once more, and Aliza flashed her a lovely smile before the two of them filed in through the refectory doors and made their way through the growing crowd.

"Whoa," Mara said. "This place is *packed!* Is every Lawless ever thawed in here?"

"Word's been getting out," Aliza said, and this time Mara could hear the nerves running through her friend's voice. "Bobby's really quite good."

"Aliza," Mara said, turning and reaching up to touch her friend's face. "Listen to me. I've never heard you sing, but I guarantee that anyone who can bring hope to the darkness of Dachau can absolutely *slay* this room. You've faced down much worse than these knuckleheads, girl. You've got this."

Aliza let out a little laugh and shook her head. "Thank you," she said. "I think. I don't know what a 'knucklehead' is, but I believe I take your meaning."

Mara snorted. "American slang. Don't worry about it. My point is, you're going to be great, because you already are. Have confidence!"

"Confidence," Aliza said. "Right…" she trailed off, looking over Mara's shoulder. Mara turned to follow her gaze, and an unbidden smile bent her lips. Bo Moorefield was sitting at a table with Johnny Stewart and a few other members of his cavalry unit. Even from that distance, Mara could see Bo's eyes locked on Aliza with the intense focus of a man deeply in love.

"Go sing your song," Mara said, nudging Aliza forward. "Sing it for him." *Him.* One simple pronoun called up Ozendi's face, his touch, his smile. The smile that their daughter had inherited.

Grief slammed into Mara, threatening to close her throat. She swallowed hard and kept her smile in place by sheer force of will.

"Thank you," Aliza said, refocusing her eyes on her friend's face. Her tone softened, and she hugged Mara slowly, gently, carefully. "You'll love again," she whispered. "When the time is right. When you're ready."

"I know," Mara whispered back. "And I won't waste time telling him when I do. But now it's your turn. Don't waste any more time, Aliza. Go sing to your man." She straightened up and let go, still smiling, even though her eyes were wet.

Aliza nodded and turned to walk toward the dessert line. Bobby sat next to it with his white-blond head bent over his guitar. His was the only table not packed, as if people wanted to give him plenty of room to play.

"Mara!" another voice called, and Mara turned to see Kevin Bowden waving her over. He pointed to an unoccupied seat at his table. She smiled, nodded, and began to thread her way through the crowd to sit beside him.

Bobby stood up as Mara took her seat, and he strummed a little louder. "Hello everyone!"

The dull roar of conversation died down and heads and chairs swiveled in his direction.

He answered with another chord and a wide, face-splitting grin. "Thank you all for coming! I guess word got out that tonight was gonna be something pretty special," he said, playing an intricate cascade of notes all the while. "I think I know all of you, but just in case, my name's Bobby, and I'm the Lawless' resident music fan."

"Nerd!" someone yelled, and laughter rippled through the room.

"Yeah, probably," Bobby said, his fingers continuing to dance over the strings. "But it passes the time and more importantly, music is something that brings us all together. Right after I was thawed out, I went on a mission planetside and Captain—now Major—Lee let me hook up my eight-track to play the Stones while we worked on her bird. Then she used the music to help inspire her team to kick some serious raider ass, and that got me thinking: what else can music do? I'm a Vietnam guy, but now I've played my music for Brits from a generation before, for Merrill's Marauders, for the SpinDogs. Hell, I've played it for Russkies from the 1980s and for Charlie—excuse, me: *Mister* Charles—his own damn self!"

He inclined his head toward a nearby table where several ex-Viet Cong and NVA were sitting in a cluster. One of the men let out a little cheer and raised his glass in Bobby's direction. Bobby played a flourish on his guitar in return. Mara laughed along with most of the others in the room.

Bobby let his fingers ramble over the strings again. "'Cause here's the thing about music; it's universal, right? Doesn't matter whether we're long-dead soldiers from forgotten wars a million miles away or aliens lurking in science-fiction space habitats. Music speaks to all of us."

"*You* are the alien, Bobby!" one of Mara's former student pilots called out, exaggerating his SpinDog accent to make his point. The room rippled with laughter again.

"Yeah," Bobby said, still playing. "That's me. Nerd and Alien. Lost Soul. Forgotten Soldier. Human Being. Music lover. Just like all of us here. So tonight, Aliza and I have got a song we've been working on, and we'd like to share it with you." His melody shifted slightly, and a shock of recognition jolted through Mara.

"I know this song!" she whispered to Kevin. "This is Jo Stafford's 'You Belong To Me!'"

"I'm not familiar," Kevin murmured back. "Is it a country song?"

"It's old," Mara said. "From the Fifties. Big band torch song. It's a woman telling her lover not to forget about her while he's off on his adventures. My Mom loved this song!" Privately, Mara wondered if this was the song that Aliza was really going to sing tonight. Sure, the song was beautiful and romantic, but most of the Lawless had left someone behind, and she wasn't sure a song reminding them of that was particularly healthy.

The lights in the room dimmed, pulling Mara from her thoughts. She looked around briefly, impressed that Bobby had managed to pull that off given the SpinDogs' routine unwillingness to let anyone fiddle with *any* of the settings in their habitats.

"I wonder how many favors the kid's gonna owe the SpinDogs for that," Kevin murmured next to her. Mara snorted softly and nodded agreement, but refocused her attention on Bobby as Aliza stepped up next to him. He played another measure of the song, and the romantic longing inherent in the music swept through Mara as her mind filled in the lyrics her mother had loved.

But when Aliza opened her mouth, her deep, rich contralto delivered something different and totally new:

See the breakers on R'Bak Isle
Fly a chopper with a lost exile
Keep me close my darling all the while
In your memory.

See the Marketplace in Imsurmik
Walk the desert with a native's stick
Just remember when you get homesick,
I'm your memory.

Cross the stars inside a sleeve of ice
Fight to build and win your paradise,
Find new love and darling don't think twice
About your memory.

I...learned to love, without you.
Don't you be lonesome too, and blue.

Across the night and centuries away
In the coming heat of Searing days
In your heart I know I'll always stay
In love and memory.

As Aliza delivered the new lyrics in a voice that was equal parts velvet and ache, faces rose up in Mara's mind: her son; Kai, her ex-husband; Cam; Ozendi…she felt the love she still carried for each of them like a precious wound in her soul. Like a new tattoo, a thing of beauty and pain all at once. She blinked back the tears that threatened to fill her eyes and looked around as Aliza crooned, and caught sight of Nalyiriz in the doorway, holding Diozera's little hand and cradling baby Zenya in her arms. Mara waved her over, and the SpinDog healer smiled and began weaving her way through the crowd.

"I'm sorry," Nalyiriz whispered as she crouched nearby. "But the baby woke up and wanted you. And of course, that woke Dio."

"Who then also wanted me," Mara whispered back with a smile. She held out her arms, and Diozera clambered up into her lap and put her little head on her mother's shoulder.

"Exactly," Nalyiriz said. "Is that Aliza?"

"Yes. Gorgeous song, isn't it?"

"Yes." Nalyiriz's eyes scanned the crowd, stopping rather suddenly when Aliza sang about finding new love. To Mara's surprise, the SpinDog woman's cheeks flushed just a tiny bit, and she lifted her chin as if in unspoken challenge.

Without trying to be too obvious about it, Mara slowly turned to see who held Nalyiriz's attention. She shifted her body slightly, angling just to the left…

And froze as she recognized the profile of Rodger Murphy as he turned back to face the show.

Mara's brain seemed to lock up. *What?* Both *of them?* She looked over at Nalyiriz, her eyebrows raised in inquiry. Her friend and sister-of-the-heart simply smiled and shrugged and bent to kiss Zenya on the top of her downy head. Mara smiled back and cuddled Diozera close.

Not my business, Mara thought as the music continued to wash over her. *Even if…well. Not my business.*

Aliza held the last note, letting it die away slowly. Bobby's playing faded too, and the entire refectory sat in silence for a moment before erupting into ferocious applause. Diozera clapped too, but Zenya sent up a thin wail of distress.

"I will take the baby back," Nalyiriz said and started to stand.

"No," Mara said, reaching out a hand. "I'll take them both back to my room for the night. You stay and talk to…whomever."

"Mara—"

"Don't wait, my sister. If losing Ozendi taught me anything, it was that."

Nalyiriz said nothing, only nodded. As Mara coaxed Diozera to stand on her own feet, she leaned forward, kissed the other woman on the cheek, and then took the blanket-wrapped bundle of sleepy infant gently into her arms. She turned to smile a "goodnight" at Kevin, who waved back with a half-saluting type motion. Up front, Bobby started to play again, and this time, it sounded like one of Janis Joplin's hits.

As she stood, Mara met Aliza's eyes over the crowd. She let go of Diozera's hand long enough to kiss her fingertips in Aliza's direction. *Beautiful*, she mouthed over the heads of the crowd in the refectory. Aliza inclined her head in thanks and closed her eyes…before opening them at the same instant she broke into the opening lyrics of "Take Another Little Piece of My Heart."

"Come on, little loves," Mara said to her daughters as she shepherded them out of the noise and back toward the quiet of her room. "Let's go lie down, and Mommy will teach you the words to this song."

Chapter Forty-Four

On a windswept hilltop deep in the high desert that humans called the Hamain, six whinaalani gathered into a circle, heads bowed and aimed inward. At their center—like a hub fixed at the middle of six living spokes—was a pair of leathery eggs. Thin cracks already seamed one and the other was shaking slightly. When the first hair-thin fault appeared on the second egg, the oldest whinaalani present raised its head and breathed out the almost odorless effusion that summoned the many, many memories of the others into present thought.

As the two eggs began to tremble, more cracks appeared. As if responding to that as a sign, the six whinaalani bent their necks low, closed their eyes, and leaned their heads forward until they all touched in an unbroken circle. The rhythm of their respiration became increasingly consonant. As it achieved perfect synchrony, they exhaled in unison, filling the air around the opening eggs. And so, they ensured that the newtlings first breaths were steeped in the Musk of Times Past, which was both the repository of all things important, and the exudate that joined them to the heart and soul of all whinaalani.

As the cracks in the shells widened, the heavy scent of the ancient particles also awakened a pulse of expanded perception through the six adults performing the ritual. Their entwined senses suddenly blossomed into a shared memory of the earliest times of their species. Of the awareness of their existence as thinking creatures. Of the dawn of their collective consciousness.

In the blink of one nictating eyelid, the past was as real—and as immediate—as the present. The world was every bit as new for the gathered adults as it was for the two newtlings just wriggling out of their eggs. The ritual circle of six was made one as they basked in reliving their first thoughts and the new, bright days of sharing the world with the First Ones, who were rarely seen but always careful and attentive, much as a mother devoted to guarding her clutch of eggs. But there was also a measure of observation underlying their solicitousness, as if the First Ones were watching for the emergence of traits and tendencies that might prove significant.

They did no less with the other species that were present. Most of the other creatures remained indifferent to the whinaalani, yet some had been moderately friendly, such as the bipeds they now knew as humans. But the reactions of other species was ultimately of little consequence. The endless cycle of sunrises and sunsets framed an existence in which safety and simplicity was unexceptioned, want of water or food was unknown, and fear remained as unfathomable and distant as the stars that burned in the night skies.

But those bright days ended in a sudden fury of flame and darkness that announced the arrival of the Tormentors, who swept that existence away and with it, the timeless peace that had filled the earliest years—or was it millennia?—of whinaalani sapience.

The Tormentors were not at all like the First Ones. Instead, they resembled humans, both externally and internally. But their smell was completely different—and disturbing. And it seemed to get stronger the more terrible and violent their actions became.

The First Ones had become such infrequent participants in the world over which they presided that the whinaalani could not tell if the Tormentors had slain or violently expelled them, or they had left some years or centuries earlier. The structures they had extruded from the very stuff of the world were the first targets, struck by fire that reduced them to dust and vapor. The tiny shining stars that distinguished themselves from the others by the speed and regularity with which they rushed across the night sky brightened and fell, leaving trails that started as white, became yellow, and finished in sudden orange flares.

Before long the Tormentors controlled every part of the world upon which the sun ever shone, and had forcefully bred with all the humans they could find. In the space of a few of that species' brief generations, the Tormentors' smell and ways had spread so widely among them that they were no longer the same creatures with whom the whinaalani had walked upon the world and sat beneath the stars. And so the once-easy fellowship with that strange and rather hideous two-legged species came to an end.

But it was not simply a parting of ways. These mixed-smell humans had forgotten who the whinaalani were. They forgot that the whinaalani had memories and thoughts. Friction soon arose between them, although at first it was no more or less so than what might occur between any two species.

But the Tormentors, who were careful to keep their breed pure within their own communities, did not forget. They sought the whinaalani, attempting to either enslave or exterminate them. Because they knew what the whinaalani were. And because the whinaalani were aware that the Tormentors possessed that knowledge.

The whinaalani were never able to discern how either species came to have such surety about the other, but it was as certain and unmistakable as the prickling in the air just before a lightning storm. Perhaps the Tormentors smelled something as disturbing in the whinaalani as the whinaalani smelled in them. But this much was plain: their mutual knowledge pointed to the only point they had in common. They were mutually exclusive species.

However, although the whinaalani were not timid, they were also not combative by nature; the few conflicts that arose were preemptively quelled by their collective sense of affinity. But even if they'd had the same avidity for destruction and bloodshed as the Tormentors, they did not fashion implements from the stuff of the world and so, to meet the invaders in battle would simply hasten their own extinction.

The whinaalani perceived that their only hope of survival lay in avoiding all those places visited by the Tormentors. But even that was not enough. Any community with mixed-smell inhabitants were simply the extended eyes and ears of their Tormentors themselves. So the whinaalanis had little choice but to estrange themselves from all of the troubled and troubling bipeds by relocating to places that they deemed especially forbidding and remote.

Ultimately, there was only one part of the world which sufficed; the great wastes where neither the humans nor Tormentors dared to go for fear of the heat. It was even a hardship for the whinaalani, but over the course of untold numbers of hatchings, they eventually became one with those harsh climes. However, during the terrible Time of Two Suns, even they still had to travel with care as they hunted and ranged across the burning sands and rocks.

Generations passed, mounting one upon the other upon the dozens, with no counting or reckoning, except in the senses of the diminishing number of whinaalani whose honor and burden it was to keep all memories and pass them on. At some point, the Tormentors left just as they had come: quickly and without warning. But the whinaalani, now one with the sand and the rock, did not return to the green lands from which they had fled. Those places were now teeming with humans and they were forever estranged from that species.

Until, a year—or an eyeblink—ago, a few of the original humans returned from beyond the sky. But they were not *exactly* the same as that long-gone breed. It was as if the original humans had not only been cleansed of the smell of the Tormentors, but were miraculously natural and simplified—as if even the careful influence of the First Ones had been erased. And while these new humans from beyond the sky had no knowledge of the whinaalani, there was also nothing in them which resisted the old fellow-feeling that had existed between the two species.

Indeed, it seemed that these humans were the antithesis of the Tormentors. So if the Tormentors ever returned, it would be through fellowship with these new humans that they could and would be defeated. Not merely because of the rekindled affinity and alliance between their species, but because their different abilities were not merely complementary but powerfully synergistic. Together, they would become a whole that would prove far greater than the sum of its parts.

The eggs split wide. The whinaalani that the humans had labeled Frost and Olympia leaned down and gently exhaled the new particles that would complete the Musk of Memory ritual: the lived experience of whinaalani who had recently passed.

As the two silver newtlings lifted their heads up from the shards of their eggs, they caught and inhaled that thinly-scented exhalation—and with it, the chemically-encoded essence and memories of two expressions of the collective consciousness:

The whinaalani that the humans had labelled Scout and Athena.

Chapter Forty-Five

Murphy realized that standing outside the door for another thirty seconds was not going to make his next encounter any easier. He pushed the privacy button, and waited.

After about five seconds, he heard an unfamiliar voice from the overhead speaker. "You are Colonel Murphy." It was a male voice.

Could my timing really be this *bad?* "Yes, it's Colonel Murphy," he said, marveling at his own eloquence.

"I shall alert Nalyiriz." The circuit broke.

Despite having been on *Spin One* for almost 360 local days—or therefore, about three quarters of an Earth-year—he still felt like an utter outsider. No matter how much he paid attention to, and tried to study the nuances of, SpinDog society, the differences of its manners and expectations still routinely surprised him. Gladly, nothing had actually shocked him for some time now. However, on rare occasions, he could still find himself quite bewildered.

This was one such occasion. Was the male voice coming from within Nalyiriz's private quarters a relative, a colleague, a suitor? Hell, did SpinDog women even *have* suitors? Clearly, the Guild-mothers had considerable influence over genetic pairings, and it was possible that—

The moment the doors slid open, he realized that he now had even more reason to be confused.

Nalyiriz's private quarters were anything but private. What he saw through the entry was more reminiscent of what he thought of as a quad from his college days, but one that was organized around the habitat equivalent of a courtyard. The sound of trickling water was strong around the plants, not all of which seemed to be there for hydroponic purposes. And of the doors that ringed the walkway around the central greenery, there were as many open as there were closed.

It was the same kind of momentary disorientation he'd experienced when he'd first entered the non-military, non-front-facing section of the Otlethes Family's secure compound. He'd expected something like a blended mall and residential area, the kind that had been becoming more prevalent back in the States when the Ktor fished him out of the Indian Ocean. However, shops and commerce, such as he understood it, were not evident at all. There was a kind of bourse in a large open plaza where that kind of business took place, but it was clearly conducted only by the lowest class of individuals in each family: the most distaff branches of the primary "geneline." These same people seemed to have equally peripheral and basic housing arrangements; none of the ones he'd asked knew anything about the residential zones occupied by the core or "high-blooded" members of the Otlethes Family, other than its general location. And the more Murphy saw of them, the more SpinDog "Families" seemed more akin to far-flung clans with extreme stratification, mostly based on where one was connected to the ancestral tree.

One of the doors on the far side of the courtyard slid open to reveal Nalyiriz already walking toward him. "Colonel Murphy," she said, her voice more surprised than he'd ever heard it before, "had you given me a warning, I would have made sure that you were received in a proper fashion."

Murphy had no idea what a proper fashion might be, but was pretty sure that a parade of elephants was out of the question. He just smiled. "I don't need to be received. I was just dropping by to say hello and ask a favor."

She frowned at the phrase, "dropping by to say hello" as if this was a very strange concept indeed. "I am honored that you would think of me as a person of whom you would ask a favor. Please, come into my quarters." However, instead of leading him to the doorway from which she had emerged, Nalyiriz gestured toward a different one that opened as they approached, revealing what Murphy conceived of as a very shrewdly designed studio apartment. But far more impressive than the cleverness of its arrangement was its highly efficient use of space, which left very little in the way of open areas. This presented a difficulty he had not anticipated.

She noticed his reaction. "Did you expect to find somebody else here?"

"No, I was just noticing the floorplan."

"Yes." She nodded. "I am very fortunate to have so much room to myself."

Murphy managed not to show his surprise that she could construe his comment as a celebration of spaciousness. It also meant that the Lost Soldiers had been given far better accommodations than they had assumed. Clearly, what they had all considered cramped was typical of the conditions in which well-placed family members spent their whole lives.

"So what is this favor that I might do for you?" she asked him.

"Well," he said, hoping that his smile looked congenial rather than painfully shy, "the last time I had the privilege of being with you at a celebration, you may recall that I drew you onto the dance floor so that we could leave and find the Dornaani data buoy in deep space."

She frowned. "Yes. My memory is not so flawed that I would forget that."

He shook his head. "No, no; that's not what I mean. I wasn't thinking that you'd forgotten it. But I wanted to remind you of it. You see, the favor I would like to ask actually relates to that night."

Her frown was no longer merely quizzical, but charged with both apprehension and anticipation. "I am now thoroughly mystified, Colonel. Please, what is this favor?"

"Well as it turns out, the Lost Soldiers will be celebrating a marriage soon."

"This is your ceremony for bringing together prospective mates, is it not?"

He managed not to flinch at the term "mates." "Yes, that's correct. And it is traditional that at these weddings there's dancing." He smiled. "But you see, I'm a little out of practice at dancing. More than a little, if the truth be told."

"I see," she said. "So, you wish me to teach you *our* dances?" She sounded flattered but confused all at the same time.

"No, we have our own traditional dances, but they are done with a partner."

"Many of ours are as well," she said.

"Yes, but I've seen those dances. They are what we would call line dances or social dances. Even though each person may have a partner, they are usually dancing apart or across from each other."

"Yes?" Her tone indicated that she was encouraging him to go on and was also hopelessly lost.

Well, I knew this wouldn't be easy..."Our dances involve two people being in contact and coordinating their motions in time to the music."

Nalyiriz's eyebrows climbed. "We have such dances, but they are very rare and are mostly ceremonial."

Murphy nodded and accepted that this just wasn't going to work out; the concept was either far too alien for her to wrap her head around, or she was cannily trying to deflect him. *Well, it was a good try,* he thought. "I'm sorry; I didn't understand that there would be so little overlap between our traditions of dancing," he said. "I'm sorry to have disturbed you for no—"

"Perhaps if you showed me," she interrupted.

Her eyes seemed very wide at that moment. And Murphy had noticed that Nalyiriz only interrupted people if she had something truly important to interject. He was, however, unsure if she had ever stood quite that close to him before. He looked around. "I am not sure it would work in this room. It generally requires a little more space."

"Are these very vigorous dances?" she asked.

"Not really," he said. "But there can be a kind of, a kind of...well, a sweep to them."

"Well," she said, "why don't we try and see if it works? Do they have special music?"

"In fact, they do. A great variety of music."

"Must we master it all?"

"We couldn't." He laughed.

"Why?"

"Because there are thousands, probably tens of thousands, of songs we could choose from."

"You have so many songs?" she asked wonderingly.

"Well, sure. Don't you?"

She shook her head sharply. "No."

"Don't your people write songs?" he asked.

"Sometimes, but it is not held in high regard among us. I think that is a shame, though."

"Why?" he asked, a spark of hope rekindling someplace high in his chest.

She frowned slightly. "I have seen that songs can be somewhat like the ties of a family. Those who sing with each other seem to create a bond that often lasts after the song is over."

He nodded, wondering and somewhat horrified at the idea of what it must be like to grow up in the austere society of the SpinDogs, to say nothing of the even more severe Ktoran culture that had given rise to it. "Well," Murphy said, "we'll need a song that doesn't have a very quick tempo, because the faster a song, generally the more room you need to dance."

She nodded, her eyes never leaving his. "That sounds prudent," she said.

He managed not to smile at her characterizing his dance suggestions as "prudent." "I think so, too. We'll start with one that's a little old fashioned, but shouldn't require a lot of space. It has a rhythm that's very easy to follow."

He took a SpinDog data chip out of his blouse pocket and gave it to her. She inserted it in the all-purpose communications and computing center that seemed to be ubiquitous in private and public SpinDog spaces. She stood aside so he could see the list that blinked into existence on the screen. "Which is the song you spoke of?"

He scanned the long compendium of songs he had compiled—and had refamiliarized himself with—for this very occasion. He rested the tip of his index finger on the dullest and the safest one, but it seemed to stare back at him reproachfully.

What the hell, he thought and went for broke. He chose the title above it. "This one."

She moved the cursor and clicked on the one he'd indicated.

Long, languorous notes rolled out of the speaker, words riding atop them like moonlight on gentle waves. Murphy put out his hand. She stared at it, uncertain. "So," he said, "we start with you putting your right hand over my left hand."

"And our other hands?"

"Well, typically, you put yours on my shoulder, and I put mine on your waist."

She promptly put her hand on his shoulder. "And now you put your hand on my waist?"

"Uh, yes, that's correct." He did so. "Now we move to the music."

...don't know if it's cloudy or bright...

She started to move, even before he did.

"Um...well," he smiled. "The way this starts is that I lead you."

"You lead me?" she said, surprised. "That sounds military."

He laughed. *Leave it to a SpinDog to think that way.* "No, it's not. Just follow me and try to match your steps to mine."

"I shall," she said.

He began very slowly.

...I only have eyes for you...

"This is very strange," she said. She smiled. "I like it."

"I'm glad." He smiled back. And noticed that, every time he looked into the singular violet of her eyes, the color seemed to change slightly.

She kept staring at him. "But there is one thing I still do not know."

"And what is that?" he asked, remembering to breathe.

"When do *I* lead?"

"That," he said with a broad smile that clearly puzzled her, "is a very interesting question."

Chapter Forty-Six

Aliza Turan clutched her arms tight around her chest and shivered. Adjusting to life in space had been surprisingly easy for the most part, except for two things. First, she dearly missed R'Bak. She didn't miss the constantly swirling dust in the winds of the Hamain, but the feeling and freedom of being outside was something she couldn't simply set aside. The reminder of being sealed inside an airtight can nagged at her so much she needed a distraction.

Since Colonel Murphy had commissioned her as an officer, most of her waking hours had been working hours. While her tasks certainly kept her very busy, what little down time she had she spent with Bo, or, when their schedules didn't allow it, she wandered *Spin One*, staring at the data screens and out the few portholes and observation panels. But only her hours with Bo kept her mind off the other thing she so missed about sun-baked R'Bak: warmth. In the habitat there was always a hint of coldness in the air, in the fixtures, in the very hull itself.

For the last several days, she'd been unable to shake that sensation. Colonel Murphy's presence on the spin lent itself to meetings and planning sessions they'd never had time for on R'Bak. Aliza understood the necessity, but she'd hoped to have more than a few hours to interact with Colonel Murphy, as well as the others. There were so many unanswered questions in her mind. While she understood the mission, and the necessity to remain in the Scatters, the possibility of returning home to Earth called to her. She knew others in the Lawless were asking the same question to each other. *Why can't we go home?* They all knew the answer to that question, as well as the answer to what was usually the second question: is Earth still home?

It wasn't, really, because while they could eventually return across the space which separated them from it, there was no way to traverse the gulf of time that now yawned between them and everything they had ever known. As the resignation to their situation settled in, and everyone struggled with their own emotions, they were also coming to realize the truth waiting at the end of all their regrets and worries: all they really had left was each other. And that would have to be enough.

Clutching a bulb of hot tea in both hands in a desperate attempt to warm them, Aliza took a deep breath and held it for a moment before turning away from the darkness of space to see newly promoted Sergeant First Class Morton approaching. The look on his face terrified her.

"What is it, Morton?"

"Ma'am?" Morton shook his head and blinked several times. Eyes wide, he looked up at her. "There's been an accident in the supply room. You need to come with me."

"An accident?" Her heart skipped involuntarily, but she knew Bo was nowhere near the supply room. "What's happened?"

"I don't know, ma'am. There was…there was some kind of spill." Morton shrugged. He ran a hand over his short, curly hair. "We're cleaning it up now, but…ma'am?"

Aliza's brow knitted even as dread built in her stomach. There weren't many personal items locked away in the storage room. She only had one bundle there and…

"What is it, Morton?"

The young man's dark eyes glistened. "I'm so sorry, ma'am. The extra material we saved for your wedding dress, ma'am. The ones the Indigs gave you? It's all been spoiled."

"Last time around the table—any alibis?" Colonel Murphy's expectant gaze went from face to face. They'd just concluded their third day of conferences to establish unit-wide standard operating procedures. While not necessarily mind-numbing in its intent and conduct, three days of meetings was far too many for Bo Moorefield. Alibis, in a military sense, were last chance efforts to engage a target.

"Going once. Going twice," Murphy said with the hint of a smile on his face. His eyes came to rest on Bo's face. "Meeting adjourned. Good work, everyone. One more day, and I think we're set for a while. Get some chow and some rest. Major Moorefield? I need you to hang back for a few minutes."

Well, shit. The Old Man using rank is never a good sign.

"Good luck," Kevin Bowden said under his breath, slapping Bo on the shoulder. The aviator had become one of his best friends amongst the Lawless.

"Yeah, thanks, man," Bo chuckled.

Murphy's action wasn't unprecedented. All week long, at the end of every day, he'd kept one officer behind for a private discussion. The model was familiar. While there was no "big Army" looking over their shoulders and no requirements for evaluation reports or administrative counseling, Bo figured Murphy had finally found the time and the command footing to be able to delineate his expectations. Over the course of his Army career, Bo had both given and received counseling many, many times. Yet, during his time with the United Nations in Somalia, he'd never sat down with his immediate commander to discuss anything other than how to avoid failures. Colonel Murphy had no interest in anything other than how the Lawless could survive their mission with the most personnel and equipment retained. Bo respected the approach, even if they'd argued about the need to leave people behind on R'Bak.

"All the gains we've made matter, sir," he'd argued.

Murphy shook his head. "We have a mission, Bo. This isn't Somalia and winning hearts and minds is part of a longer game. For now, we've done what we can on R'Bak, and we got the PoIs we needed to move on to the next phase. Yes, the indigs need as much help as we can give them, but their real enemy isn't on that planet and you know it. You—everyone—did outstanding work down there, but right now we have other things to do. Up here."

As the room cleared, Bo realized Murphy was staring at him. Cutter was the last man out the door and as soon as it was shut, Murphy grinned.

"Good work on the SOP. Makes a difference when we are all on the same page, huh?"

Bo nodded and smiled even as he realized there was bite behind Murphy's words. "You're right, sir. Our mission is critical."

"It's not just about achieving the mission, Bo. It's about helping our people." Murphy grinned. "You were ROTC, right? You remember the Cadet Creed?"

"Not all of it," Bo confessed, but found himself nodding at Murphy's insinuation. "Just the important part. Mission first and people always."

"Precisely." Murphy leaned back in the chair. "I've been doing these meetings as counseling sessions. Since you're one of the folks from my time, you understand that. I think we've had enough conversations over the last couple of weeks to know what I need from you. Continue doing what you did on the surface, Bo. That's what I need."

"I'm trying to do that, sir."

"You've done well, Bo. I mean that, but there is one area of your performance I'm worried about."

Bo blinked. "What do you mean, sir?"

"You and Aliza." Murphy's grin widened. "You asked me about marrying her weeks ago. I said yes. So, what's the problem?"

"The…problem?" Bo asked. "There's no problem, sir. We just wanted to wait for a better time. Some time or place where we can—"

Murphy's smile faded. "No. There's never going to be a better time, Bo. We may not have a better place, either."

"But I'm pretty sure this isn't what Aliza wants. I mean, she wants an approved wedding with a rabbi present. I want to honor her wishes."

Murphy nodded and ran a hand through his hair. "Which is exactly what she said yesterday."

"Then why push to do this right here? Right now?"

Murphy smiled. "Because there is no right time or place, and, if you continue to wait, you both could wind up regretting that mistake. I don't want that to happen."

"You don't want what to happen?"

"A good commander thinks about what's good for their people, Bo. We don't get many guaranteed tomorrows in this business. You know that and, yes, I have a personal interest in this."

Bo squinted. "What is your interest, sir?"

"Aside from never thinking something like this would happen on this mission? There's a whole life we left behind and a shit-ton of things we wish we'd had the opportunity to do. You know that better than anyone. I, for one, wanted to be able to give a bride away. My sister, maybe, or, who knows, even a daughter—one day. Doesn't matter, now. I'm here. You and Aliza are here. Dandridge is ready and prepared to marry you both tomorrow. I've appointed him Chaplain."

"It won't be legal," Bo stammered. "Aliza wanted an interfaith Jewish wedding, or at least an approved one. We don't have a rabbi, sir."

Murphy raised his palms to Bo and shook his hands. "Look, officially we're all dead, right? While we don't have any official authorities, not to mention a real chaplain or rabbi, who's to say we can't perform a wedding ceremony in any way we're able to now? Am I in command of this operation or not?"

"You are, sir."

"And I have the authority, at least for the time being, to recognize and declare your marriage official. Bowden is technically in command of our shuttle and that fits the defined prerogatives of a skipper under maritime law. Dandridge had an actual license from Earth prior to his leaving for Vietnam. How he came about it doesn't matter. What does matter is this: should we all survive this mission and somehow find a way back to Earth or some other human society, I'll arrange for the official wedding you want. But you'll still have to pay for it. Deal?"

Bo reeled as if slapped. "But Aliza wants a cake and a whole bunch of things we didn't think we could—"

"You didn't think we could do that?" Murphy stood, and Bo did the same. "After all we've done so far, what makes you think we can't pull this off?"

Unable to do anything else, Bo laughed and shrugged. "Okay, sir. You win."

"Good," Murphy replied. He pulled up his arm and exaggeratedly stared at his watch. "Right now, it's 1500 ship's time. At 1500 tomorrow, in the main hangar space, you're marrying Aliza Turan. I'd suggest you get ready."

There was a knock at the door. Captain Cutter stepped in and locked eyes with Murphy. "Sir? We have a problem."

In any list of the noisiest places in a typical unit headquarters, a supply room would never merit inclusion. However, one typically didn't equate a supply room with the absolute silence of a funeral parlor, either. Aliza followed Sergeant Morton into the room and several sets of eyes turned to her. In the center of the group, Bowden stood frowning. At his feet were six parcels, all wrapped in hides, which meant they'd been brought up from the surface of R'Bak. Two of them were priceless medicinals—*londauid* and *ogh-ul*. Both were flowering plants with impressive, and ultimately necessary, therapeutic properties. *Londauid* possessed regenerative capabilities for extremities and was extremely rare. *Ogh-ul* was a preservative especially useful for wounds on extremities. Based on what Murphy and the others had seen in Somalia, having a cache of those medicinals was necessary. Even with two spoiled cases, what remained was enough for operations.

The other four parcels were personal effects. One of them was hers and she could see a good-sized hole that had gapped wide in the hide wrapping. Nearby, a massive drum of purplish fluid had toppled over and had been breached by the fall. The resulting leak had of course found the hole in the hide casing and the noxious liquid had entered and rapidly spread through the materials in that parcel.

Aliza's breath caught in her throat. Inside that parcel had been ten yards of a beautiful white fabric: a wedding gift from one of the merchants in Imsurmik's central bazaar. She'd intended to use it as the train for the dress she'd had made before leaving the planet, but their mission had ended before she'd been able to arrange a proper fitting to design the train itself. Believing they'd return to the planet, she'd simply packed the parcel away in the supply room for storage. The dress was fine, but the train was ruined.

Several of the soldiers murmured apologies. One of them, Sergeant Fahey, stood with his hands in his pockets shaking his head. "Lieutenant Turan. We're sorry. A few of our indig soldiers were playing grab-ass and they broke open a barrel of hydraulic fluid. They'll be on extra duty for a month, you have my word on it. Fuckin' imbeciles."

Aliza met his eyes and released the breath in her chest. "It's okay, Sergeant Fahey. Things…happen. It was just some fabric. I'll be able to get more whenever we head back down to R'Bak. After all, it is replaceable."

Fahey looked away. So did several of the other soldiers. Kevin Bowden's initial frown grew more distinct as he surveyed the situation. As the others became quiet, he stepped toward her.

"What is it? Kevin?"

"Aliza," Bowden said, "it is fabric, and it is replaceable, but there's another problem."

She blinked. "What? What is the problem? It was fabric for the train of a wedding dress, it is replaceable, and we aren't getting married anytime soon. I don't see what everyone's so upset about."

Bowden shook his head and then laughed softly. "Well, the problem is that right about now, Colonel Murphy is telling Bo what I'm supposed to be telling you as we make our way to the vacc suit repair shop to have the train made, and your dress finalized."

"*What* are you supposed to be telling me?" Aliza felt her temperature rising. "Why are you all making such a big deal out of this? Did I say that right? Big deal?"

"Yeah," Bowden nodded. "You told Colonel Murphy you wanted to wait to get married, right? For a fully official civil ceremony?"

"That's right."

Bowden raised a hand to his smile and rubbed his chin. "Well, since I've been appointed the captain of the shuttle

Murphy leased from the SpinDogs, and with the adjustments made to maritime law in the 2050s, I apparently have the authority to approve the performance of a civil union with Chaplain Dandridge presiding."

"That's great…I think. But what—" The words died on her tongue. "You mean right now."

"Technically, in twenty-four hours, yes. Colonel Murphy's orders, at least for us, are to provide what we can to do your marriage justice. There's a cake in the mess hall oven right now. I have a crew with Major Lee decorating the hangar." Bowden pointed. "I was supposed to meet you here to pick up this material and get you fitted for your dress and train."

The supply room doors opened, and Aliza saw Bo following Colonel Murphy and Captain Cutter.

Murphy's face flushed when he saw the mess of hides and the ruined items on the floor. He glanced at Aliza, his face twisted in a menacing frown—at the universe in general, not her—before he turned to Bowden. "Kevin? What the hell happened?"

Bowden stepped over to Murphy and Cutter and gave his report. Aliza felt, rather than saw, Bo move to her side.

"Oh, honey. Your dress?"

Aliza shook her head. "No, the dress is fine. It's the train. The really light, gorgeous fabric we were given. As a gift. In gratitude." Tears formed in her eyes, and she felt an unexpected sob rising in her throat. "It's ruined. And Murphy wants us to get married? Tomorrow? How can we get married without it, Bo?"

He smiled and gently brushed an errant tear away with his thumb. "People get married in all kinds of clothes these days, honey."

"But I wanted…"

She couldn't finish the sentence. From the moment of the arrest that led to her incarceration at Dachau, Aliza had given up on almost everything. But now, with a second chance at life, things she'd believed trivial suddenly had great importance. Having a wedding ranked among the things she now most wanted to experience and savor. Given the reaction of the others—Bo included—they felt it, too. While preparations for operations had continued apace, and the Lawless evolved away from what they'd been into whatever they were going to become, they had nonetheless increasingly embraced little, portable things from their old life. Just weeks before, Murphy declared one day Thanksgiving and together the unit broke bread at the same time—even those who weren't on *Spin One*—and celebrated accordingly.

So the soldiers in the supply room weren't terrified that she was angry with them. They were mortified—and personally hurt—at the mere idea that they had spoiled something wonderful, some cherished reminder and remainder of what had once been "normal" on *their* Earth.

Murphy hadn't been keen on the marriage idea, originally. Yet, as he walked over to her and Bo, he pointed at them with a hint of a smile on his face. "First things first. You, Major Moorefield, cannot be here. You are remanded to quarters. Sergeant Morton?"

"What?" Bo erupted. "Quarters?"

"That's right." Murphy tried not to grin and failed. "Quarters, Bo. There are traditions which need to be upheld. Follow Sergeant Morton. Don't make him put you in restraints."

"Sir?" Morton's eyes were as wide as dinner plates. As realization dawned that the instructions were partially in jest, Morton chuckled and breathed a sigh of relief.

"Take Major Moorefield to his quarters. He'll stay there until summoned for the ceremony." Murphy grinned at Bo. "Isn't that right?"

Bo laughed, glanced at Aliza. "Can't see the bride before the wedding, honey. See you later. Let's go, Morton."

Bo kissed her quickly, squeezing her hand before leaving the supply room. Aliza watched him go before turning back to the smiling face of Colonel Murphy, who asked, "Now, where were we?"

Aliza shrugged. "I was reacting to losing the fabric I'd saved for finishing off my dress, sir."

"About that," Murphy turned and pointed to Cutter.

Cutter nodded. "We have a backup plan, Aliza. And just enough time to get it done." Cutter smiled. "Do you trust us?"

Chapter Forty-Seven

"There she is." Mara Lee smiled as Aliza entered the small vacc suit repair shop. "We're just about ready for you, Aliza. Let me have your dress."

Aliza squinted at the young woman who'd become a fast and close friend since their return to space. She handed over the parcel containing her dress. "'Just about ready?' What are you talking about?"

Lee grinned mischievously. "Colonel Murphy's been planning this event for the last couple of weeks. We were set up to start working with your R'Bak fabric, but Cutter let us know there was a solution in almost the same breath he told us there was a problem."

"A solution?" Aliza laughed in sudden confusion. "Everyone seems to know what's going on but Bo and me."

"Yep." Lee turned to a table and spun around holding a cloth tape measure, a pencil, and a small notebook. "That was the plan. We need to verify your measurements and make sure the dress is in good shape. We're going to create the train and anything else we need from scratch. Cutter? You got that package?"

Cutter smiled and raised up the oblong, khaki container. Atop it was a large, silver D-ring. "One reserve parachute. It was packed in 1943 but the pack looks good. I'm betting the silk is in good shape. I don't know what the Ktor put this stuff in, but it even preserved K-rats." He frowned. "Not as though that was a *good* thing."

Lee took the package, placed it on the table, and pulled the D-ring. The pack opened, revealing the snow-white parachute underneath. Hands flying, she pulled and straightened it while handing some to Aliza and Cutter. "Help me spread this out."

Aliza studied the silk parachute for holes and discolorations even as she realized the plan. This was to become her train. "It's beautiful."

"Was quite the thing in World War Two for paratroopers to keep their reserve chutes to take home for wedding gowns," Cutter said. "I'm not sure where the Ktor found this stash, but they really got some brand-new stuff. I doubt this one ever saw an actual field rigger. Looks like it's straight from the factory. There's no logbook, though."

The billowing white silk soon filled the room. Aliza could no longer see Mara Lee because of it. She heard her friend's voice, though, and it made her smile. "I don't see a thing wrong with this one, Cutter. That means we should be able to get you into a dress with a train, Aliza."

Sudden tears blurred her vision. "I...don't know what to say."

The billowing cloth was pulled down and the young woman smiled at her with affection that seemed to envelop and hug her from across the room. "All you have to do is hold still, let us get some measurements, and then go relax for the evening. We'll handle the rest. I have a few folks who really want to sew you a dress."

"I don't think I can refuse." Aliza laughed. "The colonel sent Bo to his quarters under guard."

Lee laughed and nodded. "All part of the plan. We didn't want him messing up anything here or elsewhere."

"Elsewhere?"

"You think this is all about a dress?" Lee asked. She cocked her head to one side and then shook it. "This is something for all of us, honey. We're not going to let you fall. You can't get married without a dress, a beautiful ceremony, and a reception. The nearest DJ, though, is a few light years away."

Her brow furrowed. There were so many terms and sayings among the Lawless that she didn't know. Their collective lexicon seemed to continually change and grow into a swirling maelstrom of language and idioms intermixed with acronyms which never failed to trip her up. Like this one.

"What's a DJ?" she asked.

On the way to his quarters, Bo couldn't help but shake his head in disbelief. Colonel Murphy's plan obviously touched more than the officers and the Lawless themselves. Like his Thanksgiving celebration, it was something they all dearly needed to remind them they were not only still human, but valued humans. If they could come together with each other to support a special event like a marriage ceremony, they would come together on the field of battle. Since they'd collectively done the latter on multiple occasions, the special events and activities were more necessary, now. Bo had to admit it was a brilliant and inspired piece of leadership—something he'd had to do without during the last few years of his previous life.

At the central passageway, he turned forward and toward his quarters. After a second or two, he realized Morton's footsteps weren't echoing his own.

"Uh, sir?"

Bo turned and looked over his left shoulder. "What? My quarters are down this way."

Morton shook his head. "Lieutenants Stewart, Cook, and Davis asked me to bring you over to Lieutenants' Row."

Bo chuckled. "They're really still calling it that?"

Morton grinned in return. "As long as the Old Man lets them, I suppose."

On *Spin One*, the spaces for both officers and enlisted were intermixed as required. Most of the lower enlisted shared spaces with three to five others. The officers were given more space. Bo had a room to himself, at least officially, for a few more hours. The lieutenants, all very recently sergeants or lower, had found a way to group together. Colonel Murphy's guidance had been to spread everyone out, but Lieutenant Cook and the others devised a way to accomplish everything Murphy wanted and still put themselves in a group of rooms toward the aft end of the section the SpinDogs had set aside for the Lawless.

Bo shrugged. "Okay, then, Lieutenant's Row it is."

Lieutenant Cook was waiting for them in the passageway, leaning against a bulkhead. He pushed away as Bo approached. He didn't salute given that they were inside. Instead, Cook nodded and stuck out his hand, which Bo shook.

"Congratulations, sir," Cook said. "Should be a fun day tomorrow."

"Seems everyone knows about it but Aliza and me," Bo replied.

"Secrets are pretty hard to keep. I mean, I don't think anything ever spreads faster than rumors," Cook said. "Anyway, we brought you down here to check something. C'mon in."

They stepped into the four-man stateroom. Stewart and Davis both stood when Bo entered. Morton disappeared the way sergeants tend to do when officers congregate. Bo didn't blame him at all.

"Where's Lieutenant Cleric?" Bo asked.

"In the hangar. He's in charge of the decorations. Well, him and Major Lee," Stewart replied. "But I think the major was…um, busy with something else for a bit."

"Gotcha," Bo replied. Their subterfuge was amusing, if also a bit grating…but Bo let that part go. He glanced at Davis. "So, what's going on?"

Davis grinned. "Well, we got to thinking, sir. When the colonel asked us all to participate in this little ceremony thing, we figured there were two things we could do to keep tradition. You know?"

Bo nodded—and then shook his head. "This isn't a bachelor party, is it? Cleric isn't going to come out dressed like a stripper or anything, right?"

Cook stepped in. "Oh, God, no! No, sir. Nothing like that at all. But we did get permission to buy you a drink. Colonel Murphy said it was okay."

"And what are we drinking? *Alaat*? Or something worse?"

Stewart reached into a cabinet on the wall and pulled out a bottle of Jack Daniels Tennessee whiskey. "Colonel Murphy found all kinds of crazy shit in the Ktor stockpile, sir. Including a couple of bottles of this and some other stuff he keeps locked up."

With good reason, no doubt.

"We kinda knew about it, though," Davis said. "You know how things go, sir."

"I do," Bo replied. He'd known about the whiskey, some expensive and rare French wines, and a few other libations in the stash. Murphy hadn't revealed how exactly much, but there was enough to keep it locked up to use only for appropriate celebrations. "You have glasses, right?"

Cook grabbed four shot glasses from the cabinet. "Worked to get these fabricated just right with the 'Dogs. Took a few tries, but they'll do the trick."

Stewart poured the same amount in each of the glasses before putting the bottle down and turning back to Bo. "But the real reason we wanted you to come down here before the wedding is something way different."

Davis reached again into the cabinet and pulled out a topless can of C-rations. He carefully and almost reverently held it close to his chest. He looked up at Bo. "It ain't much, sir, but all of us lieutenants wanted to give you and Miss—I mean, Lieutenant Turan—a gift. When word got around you'd asked her to marry you, we started talking with some of the indig merchants—"

"What Davis is trying to say, sir, is we got something for y'all," Stewart drawled.

Bo reached for the can, which Davis passed his way. Bo peered down inside and snorted before rolling the can upside down and pouring the contents into his hand.

"I'll be damned, guys," Bo said. He blinked away a sudden flood of tears and emotion.

"They're some kind of bushing from one of the Hueys," Cook said. "Major Lee said it would be a close enough fit and we could re-size them with the tools up here if we needed to. We estimated from your gloves and all."

Bo gently grasped the twin rings between his fingers. Each was a simple band of plated gold. They were different in size, even if Bo thought the larger one was too big for his hands. The light in the small cabin glinted off them beautifully.

Bo couldn't help but smile at each of the Lost Soldiers. "Thank you, guys," Bo said. "I love them, and I know Aliza will, too."

Davis collected the four shot glasses and passed three to Cook, Stewart, and Bo. He glanced at Stewart who cleared his throat. "No, sir. Thank you. From all of us. You made us believe we were soldiers again. Gave us a mission and a purpose none of us knew from Vietnam. We couldn't be happier for you and Aliza."

"Thank you, Johnny." Bo clinked his glass against Stewart's. He repeated the gesture with Cook and Davis both before raising his glass slightly. "Too bad we don't have enough chairs to properly mount, but that doesn't matter. In the honored tradition of the cavalry, gentlemen. If you ain't Cav…"

"You ain't shit!" they finished before tossing back their shots as one.

Aliza woke early with her nerves on fire. Concern over the dress and the events of the previous day filled her mind, but everyone around her had seemed so…relaxed. And happy. To take a cue from them seemed the best approach and had worked well enough the day before. When it was time to get dressed, her resolve crumbled and anxiety tore at her as she slipped into the dress, Mara standing by with a mirror. Aliza turned, glanced at it…and stopped moving.

There are no words.

Aliza stood staring at her reflection in the small mirror. Mara Lee's smile hadn't stopped growing since Aliza tugged on the dress and tears flowed down both their cheeks. Neither of the women made any attempt to brush them away.

Aliza's mind was abruptly awhirl with images and recollections of her mother and father, wondering how they would have reacted were they still alive. In that instant of memory, she missed them dearly and hated what fate had done to all of them. Her sisters would have been the ones holding the mirror and adjusting the beautiful purple flowers in her hair.

Her brothers would be the ones camped outside the rigger shop covering smiles as they waited patiently.

"You're beautiful," Mara Lee said through her constant smile. Her breath hitched with a happy sob. "Oh, Aliza, it's perfect."

The dress was simple and gorgeous. Strapless and perfectly tight around her torso, the lower portion flared into a wide, ruffled skirt. There was no doubting the source of the material by the rounded edge of each ruffle. Aliza smoothed the skirt and relished the feel of the cool silk under her hands. If there was any better representation of both her love for Bo and their new lives together, she wouldn't have believed it. The dress was perfect.

"I'm stunned," Aliza managed to squeak out. There were several women in the Lawless from a variety of backgrounds. She'd not known any of them to be seamstresses. "It's—How did you do it?"

Lee laughed. "Turns out the SpinDogs are pretty handy with needle and thread. They didn't like it, at first. One of them said, 'Terran, I cannot have understood you correctly. You want us to do what?'"

"You didn't?" Aliza laughed.

"We did." Lee grinned. "Add the right amount of female supervision and quality control and *voilà!*"

She laughed and cried at the same time. Aliza stepped forward and opened her arms to embrace Mara Lee. The two women held each other for a moment. As their emotions quelled, Aliza heard Mara's voice in her ears.

"It's almost time, Aliza."

"I know," Aliza said. "I have a favor to ask."

They released each other and stood close, face-to-face. "Sure."

"Be my maid of honor?"

Mara grinned and nodded vigorously, her own emotions swelling visibly. The two clutched each other again until their fresh tears and happy sobs ended. A knock came from the door.

"Ladies?" Colonel Murphy's voice inquired. "It's almost time."

Lee stepped around her and opened the door. Murphy's eyes tracked immediately to Aliza, and he grinned. Bright-eyed and blinking sharply, Murphy shook his head. "Damn, Bruce. You all do good work."

"Damned right," Lee replied. "Excuse me, sir? I'm the maid of honor, and I need to make sure things are ready."

"Don't let me stand in your way," Murphy said and left with a nod and a smile.

They paused at the door to the hangar, just out of view. Aliza could hear a muted thrum of voices from the vast, high-ceilinged bay. There was laughter and banter, and it made her smile. Of all the cavernous spaces aboard *Spin One*, this hangar was their home. Aliza realized there was no finer place for their ceremony. Her friends and her family had taken care of everything. How they did it so quickly was a testament to the bonds they'd built, and it filled Aliza with gratitude. She paused and took a deep breath, steadying her emotions. Colonel Murphy appeared at her side.

"Everything's ready, Aliza," he said, smiling down at her. "Now, are *you* ready?"

She nodded and licked her lips in sudden anxiety. "I am, sir."

"Congratulations." He clasped both of her hands in his before closing his eyes for a moment. "I'm honored to walk you down the aisle. Thank you for asking me."

A lone guitar strummed to life. The first strains of the "Wedding March" played, and the crowd inside the hangar grew quiet. The only sound was the guitar. Aliza's heart hammered in her chest. She smiled, and Murphy returned it.

"If you'll permit me? A kiss on the cheek for luck?" She nodded, and Murphy leaned down and kissed her on the cheek.

"Thank you, sir. For everything."

"You're welcome, Aliza." He offered her the crook of his left arm. "Shall we?"

Aliza took his arm, and they stepped forward, turned into the hangar, and paused. She gasped. "*Gott im Himmel*!"

Murphy chuckled and whispered down to her, "Yes. They're all here, Aliza. Everyone we could spare."

She didn't know how he'd done it, but almost all of the Lost Soldiers and even a few of their indig counterparts stood facing them. All of them were smiling. Bobby Stevens, the white-blond-haired Huey crew chief everyone called Steve-o, provided the music. A toothy grin stretched suddenly across his face when he saw her.

Down the aisle, she saw Bo standing with Kevin Bowden. Across from them stood Mara Lee. She clutched a small bouquet of purple flowers like the ones in Aliza's hair. Between them stood the bespectacled former clerk-typist who'd become, out of necessity, their chaplain. Doug Dandridge nodded at them, and they stepped forward fully through the hangar door and paused. There were smiles and happy gasps from the crowd as her train filled out behind her like an air sprite moving through a sea of clouds. The native fabric of her dress, styled into a 1940s contemporary style, blended seamlessly with the parachute silk. Her dress would almost certainly set a standard for any of the Lawless who chose to follow suit. Likely a few of the SpinDogs and the indigs would be taking notes, too.

Aliza glanced at Dandridge. "Is he really a chaplain?" she whispered out of the side of her mouth.

Murphy chuckled. "Store-bought license from Tallahassee, Florida. He thought it would get him out of combat in Vietnam. Close enough for our purposes. And his maternal grandmother was Jewish."

"We never do things normally, do we?"

"I wouldn't have it any other way," Murphy laughed. "Here we go."

As they walked, she caught Bo smiling at her, and her anxiety fell away. She locked eyes with so many of her friends and fellow soldiers. She smiled at all of them. To some, she mouthed a silent 'thank you.' To others, the ones she hadn't seen in weeks, there were shared whispers of hellos and good wishes. Before she realized it, she and Murphy were standing in front of the chaplain, and the music faded. Lee took her place to Aliza's left as Bo stepped beside Murphy and took her hand.

"Dearly beloved," Chaplain Dandridge said. "We are gathered here today to join two of our own in matrimony. We celebrate and lift up the love and trust of Major Bo Moorefield and *Captain* Aliza Turan. Who gives this woman to be married to this man?"

Murphy drew in a breath to answer. Out of the corner of her eye, Aliza saw Mara Lee do the same—

And in one voice, over a hundred strong, the Lawless called out:

"We do!"

Chapter Forty-Eight

Murphy wandered back into the ops center with a rare feeling of well-being. At least for now, all the Lost Soldiers who had been finally and truly lost on R'Bak seemed to be smiling down in approval upon him. Even his own medical worries seemed very far away. Although not so far that another shot of an intriguing libation from the Greens couldn't help keep it back just a little bit farther, a little bit longer.

He poured out a measure of the light straw-colored liquid which had the texture of water but the smell of that unusual French brandy that was made from apples.

What was it called again? Oh yes, calvados. He'd had it once on a dare while waiting in Charles de Gaulle Airport. He'd been rotating into Germany before rotating into the Mog and hadn't been very impressed with the aperitif at the time.

But at the time, there was a whole world of different alcoholic beverages to choose from, one more interesting than the next. On R'Bak, there were very few that actually tasted anything vaguely like what he remembered from home, and he cherished those that did.

He swirled the kinda-calvados around the glass so he could smell it a little bit more, sat down, sighed, and did something he never did, except for when he was alone: he put his feet up on the desk.

Which was when he noted that Pistol Pete Makarov was in the other corner of the room, leaning away from his computer screen and running his hand back slowly through his thinning hair. Murphy decided that it was better command image to go with just leaving his feet where they were rather than obeying his reflex: to scramble them off the table with all possible speed. Hell, if he did that he might lose his sense of balance.

And given his current condition, that wasn't something he wanted to do any more than necessary. There were going to be enough slips and spills and drops in his future, anyhow, and he needed to preserve the appearance of normal function as long as he could.

Atypically, Makarov did not stand to attention. He didn't even look over but kept staring at the screen, nodding absently to acknowledge the presence of his commander. That was more worrying than Makarov's customary response to a crisis: to come jumping around the corner of his desk, urgently clutching sheets of data, his face a harbinger that the world was about to end—which of course it never was. But since he was evidently too distracted to become his usual excitable self, Murphy began to wonder if this was, in fact, what Pistol Pete actually looked like when the Apocalypse drew nigh. "Captain Makarov?" he asked.

Makarov started, jumped to his feet. "Sir!" he exclaimed. "I was just—"

"At ease, Pete. But I'm guessing you have something you need to tell me."

Pistol Pete frowned, rubbed his chin. "Well sir, I have *two* things to tell you."

Murphy smirked. "Let me guess. It's the old choice between good news and bad news."

Makarov nodded tightly. "*Da*," he muttered.

A laconic Makarov worried Murphy a lot more than an excitable Makarov. "Well, unless you're trying to kill me with suspense, give me the good news first. Maybe it'll fortify me against the bad news." He raised his glass in Makarov's direction and nodded for his staff officer to begin.

Despite being told to stand at ease, Pistol Pete did what he almost always did: he fell into a formal at-ease position with his hands folded behind his back. Murphy doubted the Russian could have stood any straighter, even if he'd had a broomstick jammed way up north of his navel.

"Sir, we have just received the first debrief of subject Yukannak of Kulsis."

"And?"

"And he is a most interesting fellow, sir. It seems he is from what would be considered the lower middle class. Actually, the lower middle class of a rather insignificant nation."

Murphy wasn't even aware that he'd pulled his feet off the table and was now sitting ramrod straight. "So there are actual autonomous nations on Kulsis, despite all the Overlord references."

"There are indeed distinct nations," Makarov nodded. "Not such as we would think of them, though. They are—or at least, originally *were*—defined mostly by linked families and genelines. And there are a set of unique hierarchical structures and caveats which seem to determine priority and decision-making, both within and between the different political entities. This is because these nations are all in some way descended from each other, usually along lines of supposed inheritance from the different Exodates that arrived here, with the recent ones holding more power than the earlier ones. As it turns out, our new friend Yukannak is from a minor nation that traces its origins to a small family that diminished significantly since arriving with the First Exodate."

"Let me guess. He hasn't exactly been well treated in the status- and family-conscious culture of Kulsis, has he?"

Makarov's smile was wintry. "No sir, he has not. He is at the very least happy to provide us with detailed information on the political and military conditions there. His willingness to become an accomplice—or more significantly, a double agent—is less clear at this point."

Murphy nodded. "He's probably trying to size up which team to side with in order to ensure his own long-term survival."

"Yes, sir. Although I'm not entirely sure that the only survival he is concerned with is his own."

Murphy nodded sharply. "Explain."

"If Yukannak has any loyalty to something beside himself—and there is still considerable doubt on that point—it would be to others who, like him, have been passed over, pushed down, or pushed aside by the greater powers. If he perceives that our long term aim is to effect a reshuffling, or at least paralysis, of the power structure on Kulsis, he might become more amenable to closer cooperation."

"Amenable, yes," Murphy agreed, "but for his own purposes and in the furtherance of his own ends. I doubt that would include allowing the SpinDogs and us to prevail as a permanently autonomous entity."

"Perhaps not, sir. But he certainly seems willing to consider that as a short-term concession to achieve a greater goal. And by that time—"

Murphy nodded. "—and by that time, we could be beyond the point where anyone can reverse what he'll help us achieve: the ability to stand against Kulsis."

Makarov nodded. "This was my thinking, sir."

"Well, we will need to be careful as we assess just how cooperative he might become. But while we're doing that, we can't afford to be careless or incautious regarding what we share with him. The Overlords sent him here to put the wheels into motion for the Harvesters—and not as a one of the reavers. He was one of the overseers: capable of planning, restraint, and above all, manipulation."

Makarov nodded. "Just the sort of role that a capable fellow from a lesser family in a lesser country might be given, since he would not be allowed to ascend to a similar position among the surveyors or Harvesters."

"Which means that we've got a tricky job ahead of us," Murphy said with a nod and a frown. "We've got to bring him on board as a fellow traveler, but without revealing any information that he would be able to trade for a better situation on Kulsis. I'm guessing that if he does have any fellow-feeling for others who've been pushed down the way he has, that sympathy only extends so far. If he can piece together enough information to assemble a useful tactical picture of our capabilities and limitations for the Overlords, he'd betray us in a blink.

"So when we're dealing with this Yukannak, the information has got to flow only one way. That means remembering, at every second, that we can't ask anything without potentially providing *him* with intel. He will try to reverse-engineer every question into a hypothesis about what it reveals about *us*."

Makarov nodded. "The KGB operatives I worked with had a saying: an incautious interrogator reveals more secrets than he learns."

"Exactly." Murphy reached out for the calvados-scented R'Bak potion, took a decent belt of it. "And now I am fortified for the bad news. Lay on, MacDuff."

"Sir?"

"Never mind. I read a few plays by Shakespeare."

"Ah, Macbeth. But sir, I have not been from my mother's womb untimely ripped."

Murphy smiled. "Just tell me the bad news, Pete."

"Well sir, I wouldn't exactly call the news bad, but it might be concerning."

"You're killing me here, Mack. What's going on?"

Makarov nodded deferentially. "If the colonel would be so good as to come study the display."

Murphy resisted the urge to down what remained of his R'Bakuun pseudo-calvados and joined Makarov in front of the large computer screen. It was dominated by a highly stylized diagram of the 55 Tauri binary system. All the icons and guidons and vector indicators he expected to see in the Shex system were precisely where he expected them to be and were largely unchanged. However, there were a number of new red arrowhead guidons in the Jrar System. Several of them were elongated.

Murphy nodded at the new symbols. "Are those what I think they are?"

Makarov took a moment to answer. "Sir, if by that you mean, 'are those new active signatures?' then yes, sir. They are all under thrust and have just entered the outer detection range of the Dornaani satellites in our system."

Which, given that the distance was still over ten AU, was not just impressive but bloody goddamn amazing. Murphy jutted his chin at the enemy bogeys. "Since they've just moved into the sensor envelope, I'm assuming that they have already been under thrust for some time."

"That is correct, sir. The output is consistent with what we've seen before. It's a fairly primitive version of what the Terrans use: heavy particle thrusters. Most likely, the plasma is heated in, and focused by, a magnetic bottle."

Murphy took a quick guess at the number of new guidons. "That doesn't look like enough to be the Harvester fleet."

"You are correct, sir; it is not. On the other hand, there are more signatures than are associated with surveyor flotillas."

Murphy nodded. "Which is what we projected. They were sure to send a bigger force when they lost contact with their reavers." He leaned back. "No, Pete, this is neither bad news nor good news. It's just our wake-up call to start getting ready for them."

"We can't fight them, sir."

Murphy felt a slight twinge of guilt that he hadn't read Makarov in on the next set of plans…but only a *slight* twinge. "I don't mean to fight this bunch, Pete. I mean to have them give us what we need in order to fight the Harvesters that will come after them."

Makarov looked sideways at him, disbelieving. "Sir, surely you do not expect the surveyors to be in any way cooperative?"

"No Mac, I don't." Murphy smiled. "And frankly, that's the part I'm going to enjoy the most."

"Shall I call a meeting of the command staff, sir?"

Murphy frowned. "How long until the surveyors get here? Two to three months?"

"At least, sir."

Murphy shook his head. "Then, no." He raised his glass in the general direction of the Lost Soldiers' billets. "First things first."

"What 'first things' are those, sir?"

"A honeymoon, a bunch of hang-overs, and a few days of R&R with nothing to worry about."

"Except you, sir."

Murphy shook his head. "I've had my R&R today, Pete. Now, it's time to get back to work."

"Where shall we start, sir?"

"*You* start by heading out that door and living a little bit, Pete. No arguments. Get out of here."

Murphy watched the Russian leave, then turned back to the screen, staring at the Kulsian guidons that had aimed themselves at R'Bak. At the Lost Soldiers. At the only family and friends he had left in the entire universe.

He glared at the blood-red bogeys. "We're waiting for you."

He felt his glare turn into a savage sneer.

"So c'mon and get some, mother-fuckers."

ABOUT THE AUTHOR

Dr. Charles E. Gannon's Caine Riordan hard sf novels (Baen Books) have all been national best-sellers and include four finalists for the Nebula, two for the Dragon Award, and a Compton Crook winner. In 2020, the "Caineverse" expanded into an exclusive imprint, Beyond Terra Press, under the aegis of Chris Kennedy Publishing. It has already brought the essential side series *Murphy's Lawless* to readers, has a second "season" in process, and is also reissuing the anthology *Lost Signals of the Terran Republic*.

Gannon's epic fantasy series, *The Vortex of Worlds*, debuts in 2021. He collaborates w/Eric Flint in the NYT/WSJ bestselling Ring of Fire series, has written two solo novels in John Ringo's Black Tide Rising world, and co-authored three volumes in the Starfire series. He's also worked in the Honorverse, Man-Kzin, and War World universes. His other writing credits include lots of short fiction, table-top roleplaying games (Traveller, 2300 AD, Twilight: 2000, Dark Conspiracy) and years of work as a scriptwriter/producer in NYC.

As a Distinguished Professor of English, Gannon received five Fulbrights. His book *Rumors of War & Infernal Machines* won the 2006 ALA Choice Award for Outstanding Book. He is a frequent subject matter expert for national media venues (NPR, Discovery, etc.) and for various intelligence and defense agencies. He resides in Annapolis, Maryland, with his wife and four living children.

The Caine Riordan Universe

The Caine Riordan series and Terran Republic universe deliver gritty yet doggedly optimistic hard scifi in a world that is a believable and embattled successor to our own. For those who are not familiar with the series' hallmark blend of exploration, alien encounters, intrigue, and action, you can find them all right here:

The **Caine Riordan** series
(Baen Books)

Fire with Fire
Trial by Fire
Raising Caine
Caine's Mutiny
Marque of Caine
Endangered Species (forthcoming)
Protected Species (forthcoming)
Triage (forthcoming, with Eric Flint)

The **Murphy's Lawless** series

Shakes
Obligations
Man-Eater
Promises
Pearl
Waveoff

The **Watch the Skies** series

Sundown
Desperado
Shadows

Other works in the **Terran Republic** universe

Lost Signals (Re-release January 29, 2021)

Since that list includes a winner of the Compton Crook Award, four Nebula finalists, and two Dragon finalists, they're not hard to find. Just go wherever books are sold. Want to learn more about the Caine Riordan series? Easy. Contact any of the publishers, or you can reach out to me at contact@charlesegannon.com.

Want to see more of what's going on in the Terran Republic universe? Check out http://www.charlesegannon.com for exclusive written and visual content.

And if you decide you don't want to miss a single new release or announcement, then go to http://charlesegannon.com/wp/sign-up/ to join the all-inclusive mailing list for sneak peeks, special offers, and features you won't see anywhere else.

And most important of all…welcome aboard; we're glad you're here!

The following is an
Excerpt from Book One of the Revelations Cycle:

Cartwright's Cavaliers

Mark Wandrey

Available Now from Seventh Seal Press

eBook, Paperback, and Audio Book

Excerpt from "Cartwright's Cavaliers:"

The last two operational tanks were trapped on their chosen path. Faced with destroyed vehicles front and back, they cut sideways to the edge of the dry river bed they'd been moving along and found several large boulders to maneuver around that allowed them to present a hull-down defensive position. Their troopers rallied on that position. It was starting to look like they'd dig in when Phoenix 1 screamed over and strafed them with dual streams of railgun rounds. A split second later, Phoenix 2 followed on a parallel path. Jim was just cheering the air attack when he saw it. The sixth damned tank, and it was a heavy.

"I got that last tank," Jim said over the command net.

"Observe and stand by," Murdock said.

"We'll have these in hand shortly," Buddha agreed, his transmission interspersed with the thudding of his CASPer firing its magnet accelerator. "We can be there in a few minutes."

Jim examined his battlespace. The tank was massive. It had to be one of the fusion-powered beasts he'd read about. Which meant shields and energy weapons. It was heading down the same gap the APC had taken, so it was heading toward Second Squad, and fast.

"Shit," he said.

"Jim," Hargrave said, "we're in position. What are you doing?"

"Leading," Jim said as he jumped out from the rock wall.

* * * * *

* * * * *

The following is an
Excerpt from Book One of the Salvage Title Trilogy:

Salvage Title

Kevin Steverson

Available Now from Theogony Books

eBook, Paperback, and Audio Book

Excerpt from "Salvage Title:"

The first thing Clip did was get power to the door and the access panel. Two of his power cells did the trick once he had them wired to the container. He then pulled out his slate and connected it. It lit up, and his fingers flew across it. It took him a few minutes to establish a link, then he programmed it to search for the combination to the access panel.

"Is it from a human ship?" Harmon asked, curious.

"I don't think so, but it doesn't matter; ones and zeros are still ones and zeros when it comes to computers. It's universal. I mean, there are some things you have to know to get other races' computers to run right, but it's not that hard," Clip said.

Harmon shook his head. *Riiigghht,* he thought. He knew better. Clip's intelligence test results were completely off the charts. Clip opted to go to work at Rinto's right after secondary school because there was nothing for him to learn at the colleges and universities on either Tretra or Joth. He could have received academic scholarships for advanced degrees on a number of nearby systems. He could have even gone all the way to Earth and attended the University of Georgia if he wanted. The problem was getting there. The schools would have provided free tuition if he could just have paid to get there.

Secondary school had been rough on Clip. He was a small guy that made excellent grades without trying. It would have been worse if Harmon hadn't let everyone know that Clip was his brother. They lived in the same foster center, so it was mostly true. The first day of school, Harmon had laid down the law—if you messed with Clip, you messed up.

At the age of fourteen, he beat three seniors senseless for attempting to put Clip in a trash container. One of them was a Yalteen, a member of a race of large humanoids from two systems over. It wasn't a fair fight—they should have brought more people with them. Harmon hated bullies.

After the suspension ended, the school's Warball coach came to see him. He started that season as a freshman and worked on using it to earn a scholarship to the academy. By the time he graduated, he was six feet two inches with two hundred and twenty pounds of muscle. He got the scholarship and a shot at going into space. It was the longest time he'd ever spent away from his foster brother, but he couldn't turn it down.

Clip stayed on Joth and went to work for Rinto. He figured it was a job that would get him access to all kinds of technical stuff, servos, motors, and maybe even some alien computers. The first week he was there, he tweaked the equipment and increased the plant's recycled steel production by 12 percent. Rinto was eternally grateful, as it put him solidly into the profit column instead of toeing the line between profit and loss. When Harmon came back to the planet after the academy, Rinto hired him on the spot on Clip's recommendation. After he saw Harmon operate the grappler and got to know him, he was glad he did.

A steady beeping brought Harmon back to the present. Clip's program had succeeded in unlocking the container. "Right on!" Clip exclaimed. He was always using expressions hundreds or more years out of style. "Let's see what we have; I hope this one isn't empty, too." Last month they'd come across a smaller vault, but it had been empty.

Harmon stepped up and wedged his hands into the small opening the door had made when it disengaged the locks. There wasn't enough power in the small cells Clip used to open it any further. He put his weight into it, and the door opened enough for them to get inside. Before they went in, Harmon placed a piece of pipe in the doorway so it couldn't close and lock on them, baking them alive before anyone realized they were missing.

Daylight shone in through the doorway, and they both froze in place; the weapons vault was full.

* * * * *

* * * * *

Made in United States
Orlando, FL
07 March 2022

15480472R00248